continued . . .

Once Upon a Winter's Night

"Exuberant . . . never less than graceful . . . a solid, well-rounded fantasy that readers will enjoy as much on a summer beach as on a winter's night." —*Publishers Weekly*

"Engaging." —*Locus*

"Intelligently told, romantic . . . and filled with the qualities of the best of the traditional fairy stories." —*Chronicle*

Once Upon a Summer Day

"An interesting twist. . . . McKiernan's writing is evocative, and much of the novel's enjoyment comes from sinking into the story. He paints vivid landscapes and provides lots of good action sequences. The book is valuable as much for the journey as for the destination." —*The Davis Enterprise*

"Romantics, rejoice! McKiernan's retelling of Sleeping Beauty is the way it should have been done the first time around. . . . The lines between good and evil are clear, and romance and chivalry and true love are alive and flourishing. McKiernan's magic invites readers to dive completely into the story, as children do, and conjures the same overwhelming wonder that children experience." —*Booklist* (starred review)

"McKiernan takes the tale in some unexpected directions. He also offers an engaging, clever, and resourceful hero in Borel, as well as entertaining sidekicks in Flic, Buzzer, and Chelle herself. Recommended." —*SFRevu*

Once Upon an Autumn Eve

"McKiernan's latest entry in his four-part fairy-tale cycle goes beyond the reworking of the classic fairy tale 'The Glass Mountain' to depict a world of magic and enchantment." —*Library Journal*

"Using a fairy tale as its basis, McKiernan creates all-new heroes and heroines, placing them in a fantastical setting and giving them tribulations that would overwhelm the Brothers Grimm. . . . Readers who enjoy a well-told tale, full of enchantment and high adventure, will discover wonders and marvels to beguile their time." —*SFRevu*

"No one beats McKiernan at the traditionally styled adult fairy tale, with something for everyone . . . quite simply enchanting." —*Booklist*

Once Upon a Spring Morn

"Entertaining. . . . The relentless, fantastical action will satisfy series fans." —*Publishers Weekly*

"Dennis L. McKiernan is a wonderful world builder who reminds readers of the magic that can be found in fairy tales . . . an enchanting tale that will have readers spellbound." —*Midwest Book Review*

"An inspired reenvisioning of two classic tales of love and adventure." —*Library Journal*

"McKiernan seamlessly sews together two fairy tales and adds unique twists and enhancements in his fourth volume of a world of Faery that ought to have been." —*Booklist*

Once Upon a Dreadful Time

"A magical and beautiful fairy tale." —Alternative Worlds

"Exhibits the author's unflinching charm and obvious mastery of his art." —*Library Journal*

"Solid. . . . Series fans should be satisfied." —*Publishers Weekly*

"Features the author's takes on a diverse group of fairy tales—complete with riddles, challenges, trickery, and a surprise ending." —*Library Journal*

"[Dennis McKiernan] is one of the few writers who can hold my interest. . . . [*Once Upon a Dreadful Time* has] some clever tricks with time and magic that were more than usually amusing." —Critical Mass

"A satisfying conclusion to an imaginative world." —Monsters and Critics

By Dennis L. McKiernan

Caverns of Socrates

THE FAERY SERIES

Once Upon a Winter's Night
Once Upon a Summer Day
Once Upon an Autumn Eve
Once Upon a Spring Morn
Once Upon a Dreadful Time

THE MITHGAR SERIES

The Dragonstone
Voyage of the Fox Rider
HÈL'S CRUCIBLE
Book 1: *Into the Forge*
Book 2: *Into the Fire*
Dragondoom
Stolen Crown
The Iron Tower
The Silver Call
Tales of Mithgar (a story collection)
The Vulgmaster (the graphic novel)
The Eye of the Hunter
Silver Wolf, Black Falcon
City of Jade
Red Slippers: More Tales of Mithgar (a story collection)

DENNIS L. McKIERNAN

STOLEN CROWN

A NOVEL OF MITHGAR

A ROC BOOK

ROC
Published by the Penguin Group
Penguin Group (USA) LLC, 375 Hudson Street,
New York, New York 10014

USA | Canada | UK | Ireland | Australia | New Zealand | India | South Africa | China
penguin.com
A Penguin Random House Company

Published by Roc, an imprint of New American Library, a division of Penguin
Group (USA) LLC. Previously published in a Roc hardcover edition.

First Roc Mass Market Printing, March 2015

ISBN 978-0-451-41989-7

Printed in the United States of America
10 9 8 7 6 5 4 3 2 1

To the memories of those who came before
And the promise of those who come after

Acknowledgments

To Martha Lee McKiernan for her enduring support, careful reading, patience, and love. Additionally, much appreciation and gratitude goes to the Tanque Wordies—John and Frances, in this case—for their encouragement throughout the writing of *Stolen Crown*.

I also thank Jim Grams, who, using one of my maps plus my written and oral descriptions, made a more detailed rendering (map) of Caer Pendwyr, a modified version of which I use herein.

Too, I am very grateful to my firstborn son, Daniel, for redrawing the maps of two legendary places: Stonehill and Arden Vale.

To three friends in Oregon—Thom, Ian, and (the) Brian—for their support of my works on their podcast: The Sideways Tower.

I also would like to acknowledge General and President Ulysses S. Grant, from whom I borrowed part of his quote on the simplicity of war.

Lastly, to those who, through snail mail, e-mail, message boards, at conventions, and via other means, urged me to write this story, some parts of which were mentioned in passing by various characters in other Mithgarian tales.

Foreword

After being vexed, harassed, threatened (not really, but, what the heck, it's my foreword), and chivvied into writing this tale, I found that I was really enjoying getting into the story. It was, however, a tale that I was certain would be no longer than a short story, perhaps a novelette at most.

Wow, was I wrong.

You see, although I knew the relatively simple story I had envisioned was really quite straightforward, what I hadn't considered was how the doings of those who became involved in the tale complicated *everything*. So, the story wasn't really about what one central character did, but instead was about the involvements of all of those people caught up in the events surrounding him. And that's the nub of it: *most* stories are about how conflicting interests swirl about the characters caught in the grip of events, and what they do in response. Some drive the story, some merely respond to whatever might come, others are quite passive and their conduct one way or another has no lasting effect.

The trick is to make the actions of the principal characters drive the story down expected as well as unexpected paths.

I hope I've done so herein.

—Dennis L. McKiernan
Tucson, 2011

Notes

In many instances I have used various foreign-language words and phrases—some completely made up—to denote that people in different countries speak their own tongues. In the main I have not provided a translation, yet the context alone should provide the meanings.

DelfLord is but a single word, though an uppercase L nestles therein. And I really do mean to use the word "waggon," spelled with two g's.

Research shows the long-rides described herein are at the far edge of both horse and rider abilities, and, though improbable, are possible. (Come on, guys, both riders and horses are heroes.)

In this Era of Mithgarian history, depending on the quality of the chandler, there were between ninety and one hundred candlemarks in a full day (from sunup to sunup), hence the duration of each candlemark was approximately fifteen minutes. It wasn't till the beginning of the sixth Era that High King Ryon changed the definition of the candlemark so that it was approximately one hour in length.

The maps used come from several different sources: some have the coastlines correct, but the interiors of various countries are lacking in fine detail; others have good interior detail, but the coastlines are sketchy. It all seems to depend upon whether the cartographer was a seafarer or instead an overland explorer.

Finally, always in Mithgar, a league equals three miles.

Lady Fortune favors the bold.

—JORDIAN ADAGE

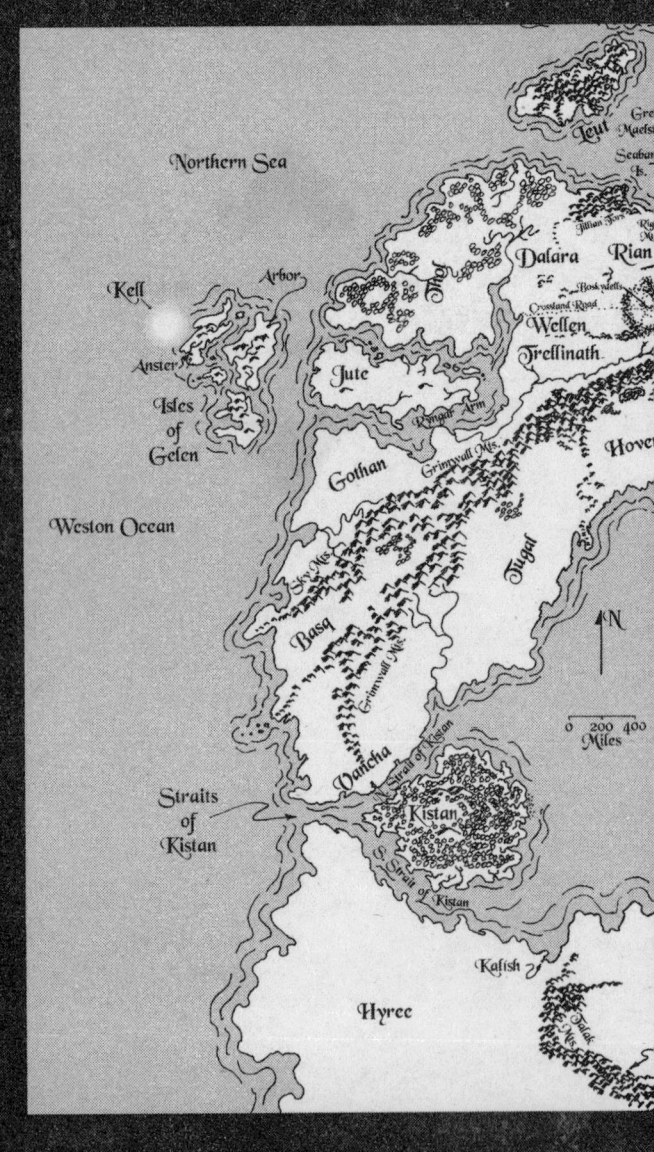

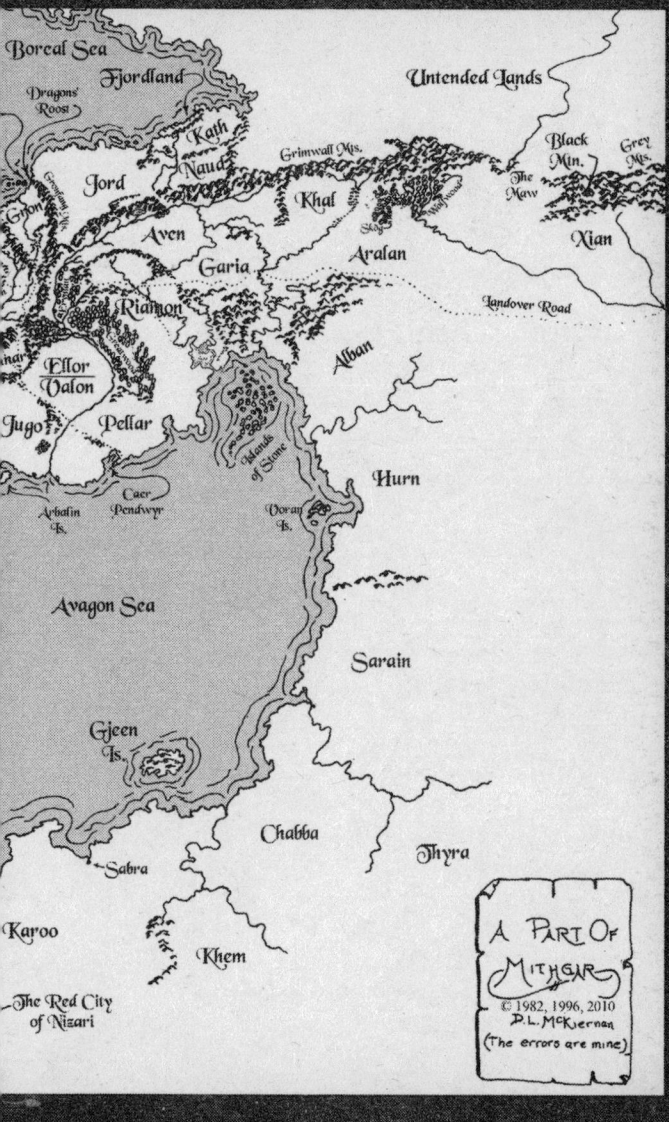

Borcal Sea

Fjordland

Untended Lands

Dragons' Roost

Kath Nard

Grimwall Mts.

Black Mtn.

Grey Mts.

The Maw

Skog

Jord

Khal

Xian

Aven

Garia

Aralan

Riamon

Landover Road

Ellor Valon

Alban

Jugo

Pellar

Islands of Stone

Hurn

Arbalin Is.

Caer Pendwyr

Voran Is.

Avagon Sea

Sarain

Gjeen Is.

Chabba

Thyra

Sabra

Karoo

Khem

The Red City of Nizari

A Part Of Mithgar

© 1982, 1996, 2010
D.L. McKiernan
(The errors are mine)

Downfall

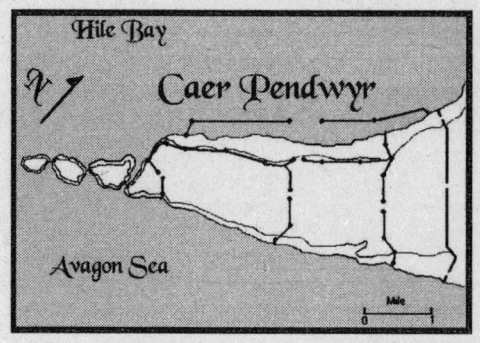

"**F**aster, Jamie, faster! I can hear them at the main door."

"I'm going as fast as I can, Ramo. This blasted lead has turned to steel."

The distant dull thump of the battering ram against the great bronze portal thudded through the deep stone in counterpoint to the steel-on-steel ping of Jamie's hammer against the chisel as it peeled metal from the seam.

"You think they got away?" asked Ramo.

Not pausing in his task, Jamie replied, "We can only hope."

Behind the two, a lad—a court page—wept but said naught as he held one of the two lanterns on high.

Ramo held the other lantern for Jamie to see the lead-sealed joint. "Lor! Lor! I can no believe it, the Queen bein' dead and the King hisself not long to live, him with the arrow lodged in his gut."

"He might"—*Ping!*—"already"—*Ping!*—"be gone," said Jamie, while far above the ram crashed against the door.

With a clatter, Jamie dropped his hammer and chisel. "There! I think we got it! Help me with this."

Ramo set the lantern down and, grunting, he and Jamie shoved against the heavy granite cover.

The page behind stepped forward and held his own lantern aloft for them to see by.

And with stone grinding against stone, the lid gave way, and they pivoted it aside.

"There he is," said Ramo.

Jamie reached in and lifted the bundle out. He turned and gave it to the youth. "Now, fly, lad, fly, else all is lost."

Lantern in hand, bundle in arm, the youngster darted away and up the twisting stairs.

"Back to work," said Jamie, and he and Ramo shoved the heavy stone lid into place. Then Jamie retrieved his hammer, while Ramo took up a mallet of his own.

Even as they began their task, the boy raced up the stony flight, his breath coming in gasps. Zigging this way and zagging that, among the many confusing turns and levels he sped, the bundle faintly clattering as he ran. At last the boy burst onto the main floor of the castle and dashed toward the throne room. Behind him servants slammed the doors shut.

And still the great ram—*Boom!* ... *Boom!*—smashed against the main bronze portal, demanding entry.

As the page scurried into the Chamber of State and passed among the few survivors of the King's guard, he broke out in tears anew, for the slain Queen lay upon a mass of wood set for a great pyre, and the King, sword yet in hand, sagged against the bier on which rested the oiled timber. The monarch was pierced through by an arrow up to its feathers, the long shaft entering just below his rib cage and angling down to thrust out from his back. Streaming blood steadily flowed along the outjutting length to fall from the wicked steel point.

Boom!—the bronze door juddered and mortar dust fell.

"Quickly," whispered the King, gesturing upward toward the Queen in her deathly repose.

The lad set his lantern to the floor and scrambled up and gently lay the bundle in the arms of the slain Lady, and then he jumped back down.

"My lord, I don't think I can—" began the boy, but the King interrupted him and said, "I will do it. Light the torch."

Boom! ... *Boom!*

The page took up the stave from the pedestal and set the oil-wrap-cloth ablaze, and then handed the fiery brand to the sovereign.

"Now run, boy, run!" commanded the King.

But the lad fell to his knees in grief.

Boom! ...

... And a block of lintel stone crashed down.

The King hobbled about the bier, thrusting the flame into the pyre.

The blaze hungrily leapt upward, the tinder-dry, resinous wood eagerly clutching the fire unto itself.

Boom! One of the mighty hinges gave way.

Shouts of victory sounded.

Boom! The other hinge gave way, and . . .

. . . with a thunderous *Blang!* the door fell inward and onto the stone of the throne chamber.

Arrows flew, and the first to die was the boy.

Next were slain the remnants of the King's guard.

The King raised his gore-slathered sword to meet the onrushing foe, but before they reached him the King fell dead, as the through-piercing arrow took its final toll.

Yawling bloodthirsty cries, the Garian soldiers hurtled within and raced throughout the castle, and none of the servants survived.

Moments later, the new High King of Mithgar strode into the fiery chamber, where the dethroned King lay dead and his slain Queen and her bundle burned.

While far down in the catacombs within the tall spire of Caer Pendwyr, Jamie and Ramo tapped the lead back in place to seal the sarcophagus once more.

And even farther below in the night, a small boat put out to sea, its own cargo precious beyond compare.

Ocean and Seas

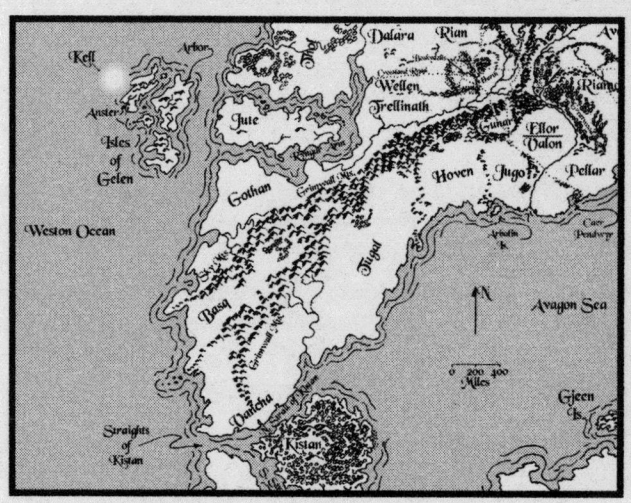

The High King's realm is bordered by water on three sides: to the south lie the warm, indigo waters of the deep blue Avagon Sea. From the Islands of Stone in the northeast to the tangle of the Isle of Kistan in the southwest it spans. Rich farming and grazing lands lie upon the Avagon's northern coast, and wealthy but desert lands upon its southern shores.

This wide sea debouches through the rover-infested, perilous Straits of Kistan, beyond which lies the vast Weston Ocean. The Weston itself is hazardous, too, but not because of pirates. The ocean has a measure of rovers as well as storms, but they are not the primary danger; rather the immensity of this vastness requires navigators of considerable skill, and so most of the commerce hugs the shores.

The High King's realm is bordered on the west not only by this great water, but also by the storm-driven Northern Sea, whose cold and violent black waters are perilous enough to discourage all but the most daring or desperate.

The Boreal Sea lies on the north of the High King's lands, and its waters are frigid beyond imagining. It is from these waters that the Fjordlanders come in their Dragonships to raid and plunder their enemies of old. But among the principal dangers of the Boreal are the Great Maelstrom there at the end of the Gronfang Mountains and the Krakens living therein, as well as the Dragons who roost above this deadly vortex.

These four waters that embrace the High King's domain on three sides are perilous ... but each for a different reason. Yet the High King has his residence along the shores of one....

... And in that residence ...

*　*　*

HIGH ABOVE, on the tall stone spire atop which sat Caer Pendwyr, the new High King and his Garian soldiers celebrated the demise of the old. At the behest of their sire, the revelers cut off the former King's head and mounted it on a pike outjutting from the battlements, so that it looked down at its arrow-pierced headless corpse dangling by grume-slathered ropes just above the gate, with its elbows splayed outward as of a broken scarecrow waiting for the dawn when the ravens would come for their due.

And in the high-vaulted Chamber of State the victorious soldiers cavorted about the smoldering remains of the funeral pyre containing the ashes of Queen and child. The new High King himself lolled upon the seized throne and drank bloodred wine and smiled at the antics of his men. He was filled with glorious power and exultant satisfaction, for he was certain the former King's misbegotten bloodline had been extinguished entirely, thus avenging an old and festering injustice at last.

But far below and as silent as a midnight shadow, the small craft with its precious cargo glided southeasterly out upon the starlit waters of the deep blue Avagon Sea, the ocean now gone ebon in the moonless night, but for the glitter from above. With her dark sails set to make the most of the breeze, southeasterly she fled, and at the hands of her master she deftly slipped past the Albaner carrack on patrol.

The ship sailed a sea-league or so before turning west-southwesterly, and in the spangled night a whispering zephyr filled her silken sails to gently carry her across the calm waters. And she was another seven sea leagues along this course ere the waning moon, naught but a thin crescent, rose in the east.

Soon the sun would follow.

As the silvery glimmer of dawn light delicately painted the oncoming morning skies, the boat was some eight leagues away, well beyond the lax attention of carousing Albaner lookouts abaft. And even were they to spot her, most likely it was naught but a small fishing craft out for the early catch.

Vanidar Silverleaf at the tiller gazed at the last visible gleamings above and bade the stars farewell, even though, as it is with all Elves, he knew where they stood no matter the mark of day or season. Given his immortal breed, Silverleaf appeared to be no more than a lean-limbed youth, though his actual age could have been one millennium or ten or more. He had golden hair cropped at the shoulder and tied back with a simple leather headband, as was the fashion among many of Elvenkind. Under his dark cloak he was clad in grey-green and wore a golden belt that held a long-knife. His feet were shod in soft leather and he stood perhaps five foot nine or ten. At his side lay a silver-handled horn-limbed bow and a quiver of arrows fletched green. And as he sat in the dawning, he made a small change to the tiller, and adjusted the sheets to make the most of the quickening wind, now blowing out from the land of Pellar to strike the starboard beam.

As the day drew upon the world and the sun illuminated the clear waters of the sea, "I deem it safe now to come above," he called.

From the tiny cabin below a female answered, a tremor in her gentle voice. "Soon, Lord Vanidar. I am feeding Reyer, now."

Silverleaf nodded to himself, and, tying the tiller, he took up a lantern and replaced the glass with a bracket, then he lit the flame beneath. He set a small copper teapot upon the tiny improvised stove and added fresh water. Soon he infused the steaming liquid with a few generous pinches of tea and set it aside to steep.

Up and out from the small quarters below, a slender, young, dark-haired woman clad in men's garments emerged. Her face was drawn and gaunt—from fear and grief and lack of sleep—and her dark blue eyes were shot with red from weeping.

Saying naught a word, Silverleaf handed her a cup of the warm tisane.

Gratefully, she took it, clutching it in both hands. After a sip, she said, "They're both sleeping: Reyer and my own Alric."

"We are going to have to give Reyer a different name, Lady Gretta."

The Jordian woman looked into Silverleaf's pale grey gaze. "My Lord Vanidar, why would we—? Oh. I see."

"Just so, my lady," said Silverleaf.

"Where are we taking him, Lord Vanidar?"

"By order of the High King, to Kell."

"The westernmost isle of Gelen? The one not on any map?"

"Aye. It seems shipmasters and their navigators are reluctant to put it on any map, for it was a time hidden by a remote ring of mist, though once on the isle, no mist wafted in the distance upon the sea, either near or far. Whether it be Mage- or god-made, one might think that strange, neh? And fearing to displease Magekind or mayhap Garlon, god of the sea, ocean pilots and captains did not record its position, and they still hew to that tradition, even though only natural mists now and then hide the isle. Aye, even to this day no map marks its place, yet all sailors of any worth ken where the island lies, so its location is not a great secret, yet once it was and to some still is. Regardless, strange or not, superstitions be damned, 'tis to Kell we go."

"Then we should call him something that fits the Kellian tongue."

Silverleaf nodded. "We should."

"I don't know any Kellian names," said Gretta.

Silverleaf burst out in laughter. "Neither do I."

They stopped twice in small seaside villages along the way to pick up supplies and fresh water and to gain respite from the small craft, but always they sailed onward, heading for Arbalin Isle. Altogether a fortnight passed ere in a driving rain they rode the braw breeze and a flowing dusk tide into safe harbor to take anchorage at Port Arbalin.

Sheltering the pair of two-year-olds from the downpour, Silverleaf led Gretta to a modest inn—the Gull—and that night they slept soundly for the first time in days. The next morn, Silverleaf went to the harbormaster and arranged for passage to Kell. "With warship escorts through the

Straits of Kistan, mind you, to ward off the Rovers lurking there."

Upon his return to the Gull, bearing needed provender and goods he tapped upon Lady Gretta's door. As they unloaded the wares, he said, "I stopped at the Red Slipper and had a drink with an old friend, and I now have a Kellian name for Reyer."

"What is it?" asked Gretta, stowing the commodities while keeping an eye upon the two wee lads—Reyer fairhaired, Alric dark-. Both children, free at last from tight ship's quarters, happily toddled about the chamber to now and again stop and examine something, all the while babbling away in a language they both seemed to understand.

"Rígán. We will call him Rígán, a fitting name."

"Has it a meaning?"

"Aye. Little King."

"Won't that be telling?"

Silverleaf shook his head. "Aravan says many a Kellian lad is named Rígán."

THREE MONTHS LATER, as he had been instructed by the now dead High King, Silverleaf bearing Rígán, and Gretta holding Alric, rode from a small seaside village on the western shores of Kell and to a cattle-and-pig farm carved out of the forest in the green-clad rolling hills beyond. They met with a widower named Conal—forty or so—who had been a captain in the King's Guard some ten years past.

When Silverleaf rode away the next day—with Gretta's mount on a lead following after—he left Gretta and Rígán and Alric behind in the loyal care of a soldier, a farmer, a drover, a King's man.

Moreover, that the forest surround also harbored Dylvana was of no small import in the plan.

Boskydells

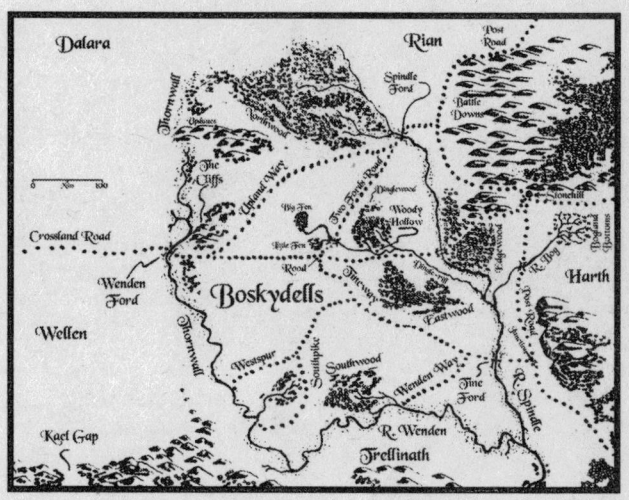

In a world of many things of wonder, perhaps the most exceptional is a place called the Boskydells. It is a land of fens, forests, and fields west of the Spindle River and north and east of the arc of the Wenden, and south of the Dalara Plains. It is a Warrowland, a place that is well protected in times of strife by a massive and towering barrier of thorns—Spindlethorns—growing in the river valleys around the Land. This formidable maze of living stilettos forms an effective shield surrounding the Boskydells, turning aside all but the most determined. There are a few roads within long thorn tunnels passing through the barrier, and during times of crisis, inside these tunnels Warrow archers stand guard behind movable barricades made of the Spindlethorn, to keep ruffians and other unsavory characters outside while permitting ingress to those with legitimate business. In generally peaceful times, however, these ways are left unguarded, and any who want to enter may do so.

As to the Warrows themselves, they are a small folk, for the most part the adults standing somewhere between three and three foot eight, though there are stories of some grown Warrows being two inches shorter to four inches taller than this general range. Their ears are pointed, and their bright, jewellike eyes have a tilt to them, with irises of amber like gold, the deep blue of sapphire, or pale emerald green.

Warrow home and village life is one of pastoral calm, but do not let this rustic lifestyle fool you, for, with their bows and arrows and slings and stones and stealth and guile, in times of strife Warrows are perhaps the most deadly warriors on the face of Mithgar.

But for the most part they are quite peaceful, and the eld buccen tend to gather at pubs and taverns and inns throughout the Bosky and talk of the times and ruminate over any news that might have come that day or that week or that month or events that might have happened, or surely did so, in the distant past. . . .

. . . And in one of those small inns . . .

"Did you hear, Gran, that the High King's dead and a new High King now sits on the throne?"

Granlon Brownburr shucked out of his slicker and hung it on a peg by the door. Naught but a distant drumming to those two flights below, the rain hammered down on the roof of the One-Eyed Crow, the only inn in Woody Hollow. Granlon bent over and swiftly brushed his hair with his fingers, knocking the excess water to the floor. As he made his way from the foyer toward the bar, he turned his emeraldine gaze upon his questioner. "How could I not hear it, Dabe? I mean, it's all over the Bosky and beyond."

With his own jewellike amber gaze reflecting disappointment, Dabe's face fell a bit, his morsel of news not news at all. "Wull, I just thought, you being up in the Jillians and all, tradin' Downdell leaf and such, that you might have missed it."

"Oh, no. No chance of that. I mean, a Garian herald came to the Tors and announced that King Valen was dead and that someone named Arkov was the new High King."

"Is that his name? Arkov? We didn't know."

"Yar, was king of Garia. Now is High King."

As if making some kind of resolute stand, Dabe pulled himself to his full three foot four and looked Granlon dead in the eye. "They overthrew him—Valen, I mean—and that just don't seem right, if you ask me."

Granlon sighed and nodded. "I hear what you're saying, Dabe, and you're right that it's just not right."

Other patrons in the small inn looked at one another in agreement, and the common room seemed filled with tangible unrest. Granlon took a deep breath and slowly let it out, and then he stepped to the bar and ordered a stiff brandy.

"On the house, Gran," said Will, proprietor of the 'Crow. "How about some warm soup? Arla's best."

"I'd like that. And might she have some of those oatmeal and raisin cookies for after?"

"When has she not ever had them, Gran?"

Gran gave Will a wry smile and took his brandy to a table by the fire, Dabe following after.

The inn had its usual gathering of Warrows, some, like Gran, showing evidence of the storm, many of whom were also drawn to the hearth.

"How did them Jillianers take the news?" asked Dabe.

"They shrugged it off," said Granlon. "They've been in rebellion for as long as any care to tell. Not that it's a bother to any of the High Kings." Granlon smiled. "I mean, back in the day, old King Renner sent a troop up there to collect taxes and such, and they couldn't find nary a soul. The Jillianers simply took to the tors—sheep, cattle, and all—and hid out till the troop gave up and went away."

Granlon burst out in laughter and all others joined in, for though the Boskydellers had heard the story many a time, still they took pleasure in it.

"I wonder what we'd do if this so-called new High King decides to send soldiers to the Bosky to take what we've worked hard to earn?" asked Norv, the local barber, and at three foot seven he was the tallest buccan in the crowd. "Would we rebel like the Jillianers? Rally the Thornwalkers and slam the Thornring shut?"

"Not ever going to happen," said Will, bearing a steaming bowl of Arla's split pea soup to Granlon, along with a half loaf of fresh-baked bread. "The High King, whoever he might be and no matter his reign, is ever in the debt of the Bosky. I mean, Tipperton saw to that, during the Great War."

A murmur of affirmation muttered through the patrons, and some removed their caps at mention of Tipperton Thistledown's given name.

"It isn't right, you know," said Caden, owner of the granary and mill on the north bank of the Dinglerill.

"What isn't right?" asked Dabe. "Taxes? The Jillian rebels? What?"

"The overthrow of the High King," said Caden. "I mean, now there's a usurper on the throne."

A general murmur of agreement muttered throughout the common room.

"Still, it's not like we're going to march on Caer Pendwyr, now is it?" said Granlon.

"And who's to say we won't?" retorted Caden, his sapphire-blue eyes glinting with rebellion.

"Without something or someone to deal with the King's cavalry, we wouldn't stand a chance out in the open," said Norv.

"What about them at Challerain Keep?" asked Dabe, turning to Granlon.

Granlon paused in his slurping and dipping of bread. "On my way back, I heard whispers that the ones at the 'Keep won't have anything to do with this Arkov."

"Yar, but with Valen and his queen and only heir all dead, it's not like we have a choice in the matter," said Norv.

"Well, let me ask you this," said Will. "With a usurper on the throne of the High King, what are we going to do if the Gjeenian penny shows up at our borders?"

But for the drumming of rain and the crackle of fire, Will's question brought complete silence to the common room.

But then Arla appeared bearing a spatula and a full baking tin hot from the oven. "Cookie, anyone?"

Challerain Keep

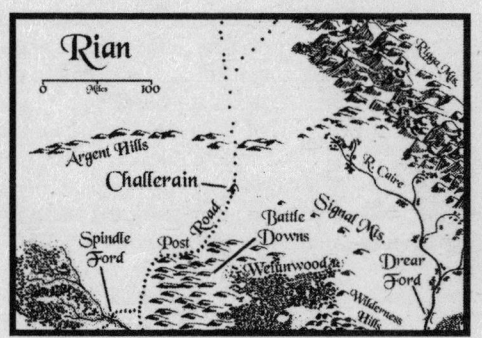

Long ago, in very ancient times, there had been no city of Challerain; it was merely the name given to a craggy mount standing tall amid a close ring of low foothills upon the rolling grassland prairies of Rian. Then there came the stirrings of War, and a watch was set upon Mont Challerain: various kinds of beacon fires would be lit as signals to warn of approaching armies, or to signal muster call, or to celebrate victory, or to send messages to distant realms via the chain of signal fires down the ancient range of tall hills called the Signal Mountains and south from there over the Dellin Downs into Harth and the lands beyond. War did come, and many of those signal towers were destroyed, but not the one atop Mont Challerain.

After the War, this far northern outpost became a fortress: Challerain Keep. And with the establishment of a fort, a village sprang up at the foot of Mont Challerain. Yet it would have remained but a small hamlet, except the High King, himself, came north to the fortress to train at arms; and he established his summer court there, where he could overlook the approaches to the Rigga Mountains, and beyond, to Gron.

Year after year the King returned, and at last a great castle was raised, incorporating the fort within its grounds. It was then that the village grew into a town, and the town into a city. The city prospered, and it, too, was called Challerain Keep. Thus it had been for thousands of years. . . .

. . . And on that mountain within that keep and inside that castle in a council chamber . . .

LORD RADEN OF RIAN, a bear of a man, jumped to his feet, toppling his chair to the floor. "I say we stand against this Arkov, usurper that he is."

Lord Cavin, King Valen's appointed Steward, looked out

over the sitting Northern Council. Many nodded in agreement, while others were more cautious in their demeanor.

"You mean, muster and march?" gasped corpulent Mayor Hein, his eyes wide with shock.

An uneasy shifting rustled through the Council membership.

"Perhaps not muster and march," said Aarnson of Thol, dark-haired and dark-eyed in spite of his nationality, "but instead we resist paying any taxes and tariffs and tolls he might see fit to levy against us for upkeep of the kingdom."

The thought of retaining funds in their coffers brought nods from many.

"Like the rebels in the Jillian Tors, eh?" said Axton, the slender, sharp-featured viscount from neighboring Wellen.

Steward Cavin, a grey-haired man in his late middle age, frowned and said, "Raden, you realize you are advocating insurrection, rebellion, sedition, and treason, do you not?"

Raden slammed a fist to the table. " 'Tis no more than what Arkov himself did. If anyone should be held for treason, it is that . . . that *Garian* who now sits on a stolen throne."

A murmur of agreement muttered about the table.

"If we do this," said Axton, stroking his narrow chin, "then Arkov is likely to muster and march upon us."

Once again Mayor Hein quailed, and he clutched his chain of office as if to keep it from flying away.

"Pfaugh," scoffed Raden. "Let him. To march upon Challerain Keep will cost him more than he can bear." Raden swept his arms wide in a gesture taking in the whole of Mont Challerain. "We live in the strongest fortress in Mithgar. Nothing, no one, will ever conquer this place."

Lord Cavin shook his head. "I would have said that about Caer Pendwyr, but look what happened there."

"How did Arkov manage to break that bastion?" asked young Lord Leland of Trellinath, the southernmost realm seated on the Northern Council.

"Treachery, I say," said Aarnson of Thol.

"How know you this?" asked Cavin.

For long moments it seemed as if Aarnson would not

reply. But finally he said, "My, um, sources at the Caer tell me that the Garians came by sea, and, instead of peaceful cargo, the ships carried an army. It seems that by the time anyone knew that fact, a small force in the King's Guard had treacherously swiveled the swing bridge outward, which let the Garian Army onto the spire just in time for another Garian squad to open the outer gates. And then, well . . ."

"By Hèl!" shouted Raden in fury, his face as red as his wild beard. He kicked his overturned chair aside and began storming up and down the chamber. "Treachery indeed."

"They came in Albaner ships," said Aarnson.

"Albaners?" demanded Raden.

Aarnson nodded and added, "And it is said that there were men from Sarain and Hurn and Chabba in Arkov's force."

An uproar filled the chamber, Raden cursing loudest of all. "Sarainian Fists of Rakka? Chabbanian Askars? Did they learn naught from the War of the Ban?"

Viscount Axton said, "If Arkov has made pacts with our enemies of old—worshippers of Gyphon, that is—then 'tis Arkov who is the traitor here. If for naught else, he deserves to be put to the gallows."

Oaths of agreement burned the air, and Cavin let the uproar run its course. Finally, he said, "Is there aught else you can tell us, Lord Aarnson?"

"Just that Queen Mairen was caught out in the courtyard and was immediately slain. King Valen and loyal King's Guards mounted a sally and managed to retrieve her body, but in the effort the High King himself was sorely wounded— pierced through by an arrow. It took a while, but finally the great bronze doors fell to the Garian battering ram, and then all were slaughtered therein."

"If all were slaughtered, Aarnson," said Viscount Axton, "just how did your sources escape?"

"They slipped out as the Garians rushed in," said the Tholian Lord.

"And no one else managed to flee?" asked Mayor Hein, dabbing an embroidered kerchief at his sweating face.

"It seems that Vanidar Silverleaf was at the Caer," said Aarnson, "but no one knows where he went."

"Good thing they didn't kill him," said Cavin, "else Arkov would have to answer to the Lian."

Quietness fell upon the Council, even Raden stood stock-still. Finally Steward Cavin said, "Here's what I propose we do: in essence, nothing for the nonce—"

"What!" demanded Raden from the far end of the chamber. "Are you just going to let this usurper—?"

Cavin thrust out a palm to halt Raden's tirade. "Hear me out, Lord Raden. Hear me out."

Grinding his teeth and fuming, Raden stomped to his downed chair and jerked it upright and resumed his place at the table.

Cavin turned to Aarnson and asked, "What say your agents about Prince Reyer?"

Aarnson stroked his dark goatee. "They sent word that the child's body was in his mother's arms on the funeral pyre. It was a secondhand report from one of the Garians."

"That confirms the announcement the herald made," said Mayor Hein, his double chins wobbling as he bobbed his head.

"Even so," said Cavin, "I wonder just how the boy died. Was there a report of sickness? Did the Garians somehow kill him? Was there a traitor within the castle chambers who smothered him, poisoned him, throttled him, slit his throat? How did he die?"

Aarnson shrugged.

Cavin took a deep breath and slowly let it out, after which he said, "Then this I propose: you each return to your monarchs and see if we can reach unity in our actions against Arkov. In the meanwhile, we look for a suitable heir to the High King's throne."

Raden slapped a beefy hand to the table. "Suitable heir? Valen had no other children. Reyer was his one and only."

"Agreed," said Cavin. "Yet, list, for this I know: some hundred or so years agone, Eddin, who was the then High King and naught but a youth, died in the great fire in Luren—"

"That would be one hundred and nineteen years back," said Lord Leland. "Eighteen sixty-six of this, the Third Era."

When the others looked at him, Leland shrugged and added, "Part of the history of Trellinath. That High King, too, died without an heir."

"Just so," said Lord Cavin. "And that was the last time ere now that a search was conducted for a suitable heir."

"What has this to do with aught?" demanded Lord Raden.

"Just this," said Cavin. "When King Eddin died in the fire without issue, three families were claimants to the throne: Arkov's line, Valen's line, and Ulrik's line."

"Ulrik of Jord?" asked Hein, yet clutching his chain of office.

"Indeed," said Cavin.

The mayor looked about the table. "Well, it seems to me that Ulrik would be the rightful—?"

"Not necessarily," said Cavin.

"Get on with it," snapped Raden.

Cavin nodded and said, "Back then, among those three lines, by sworn oath they each agreed that whoever was first to bear a male child, that child would assume the throne. And it so happened that within a year and even as the skies ran red with aethyrial lights in the north, three queens went into childbirth labor: Lessa of Riamon, Keth of Jord, and Trekka of Garia. And they each bore a male who would be in contention for the High King's throne. The Seers said Trekka went into labor first, and Lessa last. But Lessa had an easier time of it and bore a living child before the other two. Yet there was some dispute, for the Seers' visions were somewhat distorted by the aethyrial fires blazing in the skies above, especially in Jord, northernmost of the three kingdoms. Still, the Seers generally agreed that Lessa's child came before Trekka's and hers before Keth's, though that last is the most uncertain.

"Jordian King Haldor and his Queen Keth immediately gave up all claims to the throne. But Riamon's King Rand and Queen Lessa's claim to the throne for their son was hotly disputed by Garia's King Borik and Queen Trekka.

Riamon and Garia fought many a skirmish over the right of succession. Finally, Riamon completely defeated Garia—Rand actually killing Borik the Oathbreaker—and the Riamonian boy, Devon, took the throne when he came of age."

"Nice history lesson," growled Raden.

"At least it might explain Arkov's reasons for usurping the throne," said Viscount Axton.

"By Hèl, it does at that," declared Baron Fein of Harth, a steel-haired man in his middle years.

"They say revenge is a dish best served cold," said Aarnson, a sardonic smile on his face. "And this was a very, very cold dish."

"He's still a bloody usurper," gritted Raden.

"But given the history of the dispute, why isn't Ulrik the clear and rightful one to take Arkov's place?" asked Mayor Hein.

"Because, Mayor," said Aarnson, "there's been a lot of begetting between what happened back when Luren burned to the ground and now."

"Oh," said Hein. "I see. You are saying that if we follow Valen's line back to then—back a hundred and nineteen years—we might find someone more directly in line for the throne."

Aarnson nodded without comment.

"So, Lord Cavin, what do we do about it?" asked Viscount Axton.

"Send for a Seer," said Cavin, "for only a Seer can untangle these interwoven threads of inheritance."

"Don't you think the Seers might be reluctant to interfere with the doings of us lowly Humans?" asked Baron Fein, a tinge of resentment in his voice.

"Perhaps, yet we need to try," said Lord Cavin, knowing that in the past Magekind had refused to take a hand in clearing Drearwood of its dreadful inhabitants; the excuse of the spell-casters was that they needed <rest> to recover from the <fire> spent in the Great War of the Ban. And so, Harth and the Wilderlands were still beset by the creatures of that haunted wood, lying just across their eastern borders in the largely abandoned land of Rhone, and many Harthians and Wilderlanders, Baron Fein among them, bore a grudge against Mages of all stripe.

"Well and good," said Axton, "but, Lord Cavin, what do you suggest we do till then?"

Cavin looked about the table, finally settling his gaze upon the viscount. "What I said before, Lord Axton: each of you must return to your kingdoms and speak with your monarchs and seek unity in this course we take, for we will certainly need to act as one, with mutual defense as well as a combined army, should Arkov decide to attack.

"Too, not only should we strive for unity among the nations of the Northern Council, we should also seek out nations of like mind. Hence, we should send emissaries to other realms and see if they will join us." Cavin turned to Aarnson. "My lord, will you send someone to the Isles of Gelen to feel them out?"

Aarnson nodded, for Gelen was a trading partner with Thol.

"I'll make queries of the mad king in Jute," said Viscount Axton of Wellen, "though whether I can make him see the right of our cause, I cannot say."

"And I will deal with Gothon and Basq," volunteered young Leland. "Trellinath has good relations with both."

"What about Jord?" asked Raden. "And for that matter, Fjordland."

"And Kath and Naud, too," said Baron Fein.

"Vancha as well," added Leland.

"Also the Lian," said Axton.

"I believe the Elves will not get involved—neither the Lian nor the Dylvana, nor the Dwarves, for that matter," said Cavin. "But for a few individuals of their Kind, they tend to leave Human matters to Humans."

"Bah!" snorted Raden.

"There is this as well," said Aarnson. "We will need agents in the court of Arkov, for, once we are formed, should he decide to march upon us we will need warning to muster and resist."

Heads nodded in agreement, and Cavin said, "We should all act upon that; insert agents into the court, I mean; 'tis meet that we discover whether these rumors of Arkov making pacts with our enemies of old are true."

"Worshippers of Gyphon," muttered Raden.

Baron Fein said, "Likewise we need to recruit commoners in the town and on the docks."

"Aye," said Cavin.

Long into the night did the Council discuss their plans, but finally fatigue claimed an end to the meeting. At last, just before declaring adjournment, Lord Cavin said, "When we have secured a mutual agreement among the northern nations, and until the right of inheritance is decided, we will declare ourselves a government in exile, our seat here at the northern throne."

"Then Mithgar will be split in twain," said Axton, "most likely leading to civil war."

"Not if we settle the right of inheritance and it falls upon someone other than Arkov," said Baron Fein. "Then all the nations will rise up and overthrow the usurper and his allies."

"Hah! You think so?" said Aarnson. "Me, I think most nations will let others do their battles."

"Wh-what about Arkov?" asked Mayor Hein, a catch in his voice. "I mean, what if he comes to claim the High King's summer residence? What if we spurn him? What if he sends an army here, what will we do?"

"Fight him," declared Raden, glaring at the mayor. "Unlike at Caer Pendwyr, there are no traitors here."

Aarnson leaned back in his chair and cocked a skeptical dark eyebrow at the quivering mayor. The others turned to the Tholian lord as he burst out in cynical laughter.

Grimwall

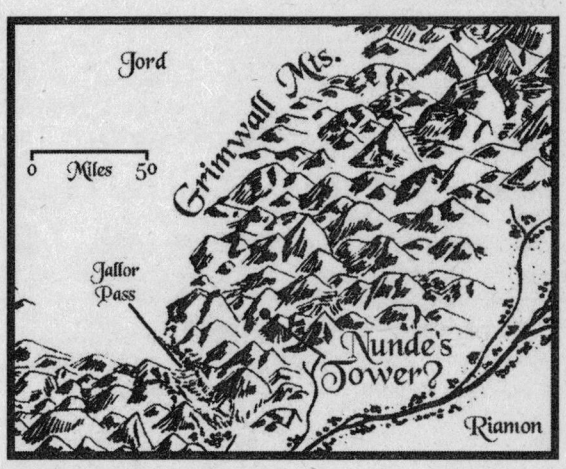

Like a great backbone rearing up from the land, the Grimwall Mountains stretch across the High King's domain, dividing his realm in half. This forbidding range starts far southwest in the land of Vancha, and it marches northerly to turn northeasterly to continue its lengthy run. Along the way, a spur breaks off and runs southwesterly to Portho, to divide Vancha from Basq. But the Grimwalls continue onward, where another spur known as the Sky Mountains splits off to the west to turn south. Farther along, another spur—the Gûnarring—breaks away to curve around the realm of Gûnar before rejoining the primary chain. Still farther, the Grimwall turns northerly to run for many leagues, and just at the point where it veers again to run northeast once more, two spurs—the Rigga Mountains and the Gronfang Mountains—split off northerly like a great claw yawning wide to clutch the dark land of Gron in its grasp before reaching the frigid waters of the Boreal Sea. But the mighty chain of the Great Grimwall continues on, to finally come to an end at the wide open plain between Far Xian to the south and the Untended Lands to the north. Several passes breach this mighty chain, some known to many, others not: Ralo Pass and Gûnar Gap and the cols known as Crestan and Grûwen and Jallor and Kaagor, to name a few.

Dwarvenholts are delved under the roots of these peaks: Skyloft in the Sky Mountains; Blackstone in the Riggas; Kraggen-cor and Kachar in the Grimwalls.

Yet the Grimwall itself is a sinister range, said to be the haunts of Trolls and Rûcks and Hlôks and other spawn of evil. . . .

. . . And in one of these grim lairs hidden in the remote fastness nigh Jallor Pass . . .

*   *   *

In a tall tower hidden deep among the crags and crests and massifs of the Grimwalls, that long and ill-omened mountain chain slashing across much of Mithgar, a being of dark Magekind sat in his dire sanctum and read again the words deciphered from the coded scroll, and he chortled in rare glee. Few and far between were his bouts of laughter, for he was filled with rage, and seldom did good humor come his way. His bitterness was seated in dire events two millennia agone, for nearly two thousand years had passed in all since the end of the so-called Great War of the Ban. That was when Modru had gone down in defeat there at Hèl's Crucible, and had fled to the Barrens far north to await the coming of—what?—Nunde did not know. And Adon had sundered the ways between the Planes and had visited a terrible retribution on all of Dark Magekind and their minions. Adon's reckoning had fallen hard on Gyphon's allies, for the Sundering preventing the arcane passage of Foul Folk from Neddra into the High- and Middle-Worlds. And the Ban, the terrible Ban, prevented Foul Folk and Dark Magekind from the light of day, hampering their efforts to control this world. Were they to ever be found by the rays of the sun, they would suffer the Withering Death, crumbling to dust in mere heartbeats. But Gyphon had sworn to return and conquer, and Nunde awaited that glorious day when he would be set free from this banishment from sunlight; then he would take his rightful place among Gyphon's rulers of all creation. Ordinarily, Nunde would be seething with hatred over the victory of the High King's Alliance and the downfall of Gyphon's plans, but even more so over the Ban and the Sundering. Yet none of these things occupied his mind, for this night word had come that Caer Pendwyr was in disarray: the High King had been overthrown, and a new High King occupied the throne. Unquestionably, this would split the realms in twain, and surely Nunde could take advantage of the turmoil. But first he had to verify for himself whether the events he had been informed of had actually taken place.

"Radok, to me!" he shouted.

"I hear, Master," called Radok from a distant chamber.

Bearing a lantern, down black hallways he hurried to the side of the Necromancer. A look of anticipation filled the pale, white face of the tall, thin, bald, and beardless apprentice—for he had heard his master's laughter.

"We have an opportunity," declared Nunde, his dark eyes gloating as he ran his long, bony fingers through his waist-length hair, tossing it back and over a shoulder to hang nearly to his hips.

"An opportunity, Master?"

"Yes," hissed Nunde, a wide grin flashing across his narrow face with its hooklike aquiline nose. "The High King is dead at the hands of a usurper. Ha! Long live the new High King. But I must verify the events my agent has reported."

"How will you do so, Master?"

"Bones, you fool. Bones. Fetch me the bones of the deposed High King and I will raise him and ask."

"And I will assist you?" A hint of expectancy quivered across the ascetic features of Radok.

"Yes—yes, you will assist me. But first we need the bones. And if not the entire corpse, then at least his skull."

Tamping down his exultation, Radok asked, "And then what, Lord Nunde?"

"After which I will raise him"—the Necromancer negligently gestured with a black-nailed hand as if conveying a foregone conclusion—"and I will use whatever I discover to sow dissent among those fools . . . and if not actually bring them to war, then at least lead them to the brink, where I can tip them over."

With his apprentice bearing the lantern and bustling at his side, Nunde strode out from the chamber and down a dark-granite hallway to a corpse-littered laboratory. Neither Nunde nor Radok paused to admire the flayed bodies on the many tables in various stages of decomposition and dismemberment. Those were merely the leftovers of their dark and arcane arts. Nunde stepped past these mutilations to a large desk made of an esoteric grey wood. He sat, pulled a small slip of thin parchment out from a drawer, and began to write tiny letters with a razor-sharp quill, his words in code, while Radok hovered nearby. *Ah*, thought Radok, *orders*.

Finally, Nunde spoke a <word> as he sketched a minus-cule rune at the end, and the mark faintly glowed and then faded. Nunde then rolled the tissue and slid it into a small tube. He passed the cylinder across to Radok and hissed, "Send this to our agent in Caer Pendwyr."

As Radok headed toward the tower, he opened the tube and pulled out the delicate slip and read the contents, and then he rolled it and put it back. Up the spiral stairs to the tower he went, hurrying, for dawn would soon come, and Radok would not have the light fall upon him. At the top he reached the rookery, and called a black bird unto him. Quickly he slipped the tube into the leg-holster and made certain that it was secure. Then he whispered a word to the dark fowl, and set it free into the air as even then dawn began paling the east.

Sissing in fear, Radok spun on his heel and fled into the blackness below. Yet in spite of his dread, Radok eagerly looked forward to the arrival of the former High King's bones.

He and Nunde would then raise the dead, to the detriment of those they despised.

Kell

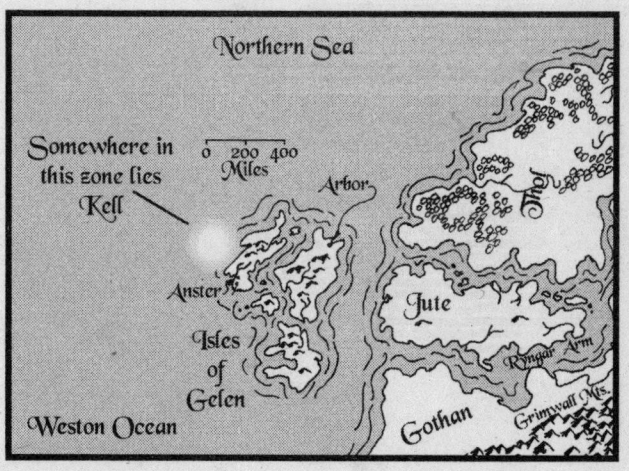

Islands dot the seas of Mithgar, as well as its rivers and lakes, some in clusters, some alone, some no longer alive. South of the High King's realms lies the Avagon Sea: in its waters far to the east the Islands of Stone abide, the channels within forming a veritable labyrinth providing refuge for smugglers and freebooters and fugitives; nearly all the way across to the Avagon's southern shore sits the Isle of Gjeen, whose penny—a small and plain dull gray disk with a hole in it—is said to be the most worthless coin in all the realms, yet this base-metal specie bears a significance too worthy to ignore; along the northern shore lies Arbalin Isle, the abode of a banking empire and a central trading port, transshipping cargo from all over the world; and at the western extent of the Avagon lurks the Isle of Kistan, large and overgrown and the base of rovers terrorizing the shipping lanes.

Far to the northern extent of the King's domain lies the Boreal Sea, containing the island of Leut at its western extent, a cold and forbidding place, inhabited by fishermen only in the chill of summer. Also in the Boreal lie the uninhabited Seabane Isles, made up of crests of the Gronfangs, where they run on into the frigid sea and under to drown; between the Seabanes and the Realm of Gron lies the Great Maelstrom, a dreadful vortex.

In the Weston Ocean there once were islands known as Rwn and Atala. When Rwn disappeared beneath the waves, it marked the end of the First Era. On that isle sat the College of Mages in Kairn, the City of Bells; it is said that on the waters above where it once resided, when the ocean is glassy calm, one can hear bells ringing far below from deep in the sea. The island of Atala drowned during the Great War of the Ban, when its fire mountain, Karak, exploded, set off, say some, by Gyphon Himself, or by his agent, Modru. Atala held the great weapon-shops of Duellin, the weapon-shops of Elvenkind; these marvelous arms are made there no more, for all is sunk below the waves.

On the eastern edge of the Weston Ocean lies Jute, a nation of Dragonship raiders, with a mad king who sits on a black throne. Jute lies between Gothon and Thol, and, strictly speaking, though Jute is an island, it is made so by the broad and deep surrounding waters of the Ryngar Arm of the Weston, where rivers flow to meet the ocean, salt to the west, fresh to the east, and brackish in between.

Between Jute and the memories of Atala and Rwn lies the nation of Gelen, principally made up of four large isles, the westernmost of which is Kell, a green land of forests and fields, often beset by storms. The Gelenders, and especially those who live on Kell, still have oral histories of the times great waves swept over their isles—when Rwn was destroyed by the Black Mage, Durlok, and then again when Atala fell, perhaps to the dark god, Gyphon, perhaps to the wizard, Modru.

To two of these island nations—Gelen and Jute—as well as those continental, emissaries from the Northern Council slowly made their journeys by horseback and coach and some by boat to distant nations, and as a dark agent in Caer Pendwyr waited for the right time to steal a corpse, or at least its skull, time passed and time more, until altogether another year elapsed.

But elsewhere, two toddlers grew on a farm surrounded by a primeval woodland on the unmarked island of Kell. And often visitors came—some were bards, for Kell is known for its silver-tongued poets and singers and storytellers and a language to rival that of Sylva, of Elven; others were traders, come to buy cattle or pigs, or merchants with something to sell; yet others were tinkers and cobblers, plying their mending skills in their gaily decorated waggons, on their journeys across this emerald domain.

But the most frequent guests of the stead were a folk reclusive and yet learned and skilled and crafty, and they spent time with the children, speaking in their own melodious tongue and teaching the children many things of wonder. . . .

And on this day, they brought another visitor, one quite rare in these times . . .

"A SEERESS? Lady Driu, you are a Mage? What are you doing here?" Leaning on the rail fence, Conal ran a hand through his burr-cut brown hair, a tinge of gray at his temples.

"Silverleaf sent me," said the slender, dark-haired female, now unsaddling her dun horse. She was of middling height and looked to be no more than thirty or so. Her eyes were brown with a sprinkle of green flecks. A meager scatter of freckles splashed across her nose and onto her cheeks.

"But I thought all Mages were gone down with Rwn," said Cuán, a youth and one of Conal's drovers, "or were killed in the Great War."

A fleeting look of distress swept across the face of the Seeress, quickly replaced by a semblance of calm.

"Not all," Driu replied, handing the saddle to a lad standing by, one of Conal's swineherds, a boy of thirteen or so. "Many are in Black Mountain, <resting>, while others, such as I, yet stride the world."

As the Seeress turned to unlade the packhorse, Conal said, "My lads will take care of that, Lady Driu." He looked at the boy and said, "Run along, Breccan. Care for the horses and bring the lady's goods into the house."

"Which stalls, Tiarna?"

"Put the mount in next to Uasal Donn's stall, and the gelding across the way."

As Breccan led the mare and the pack animal toward the stables, Driu called after him, "First give them water and a ration of oats and rub them down and curry them, if you will. Then you can bring my goods to the house."

Without looking back, Breccan raised a hand in acknowledgment and continued onward.

Seeress Driu turned to Conal. "Your horse is Lady Brown?"

"You know of her? Of Uasal Donn?" asked Conal.

Driu smiled. "It's all the talk in Killain—whether Lady Brown will win again in the Kell Ride."

"Oi, she should win all right," said Cuán. "Durgan will be astride."

Conal shook his head and frowned. "I don't know. She's up against Iarann Rob, and that grey can run."

"Aye, that's what the talk was all about," said Driu. "Iron Bobbie and Lady Brown in the same race." She paused and then asked, "Durgan is your son?"

"Aye, and a fine rider he is," said Conal, grinning and pointing toward a distant lad of perhaps ten or eleven who was switching pigs across a field toward an oak grove. "He has dreams of owning a colt of Lady Brown and Iron Bobbie. I told him if he wins, we'll see." Conal turned again to Driu, and his smile faded somewhat. "But enough about racing horses, Lady Driu, instead tell me why that rascal Silverleaf sent you to me."

Driu glanced across at the circle of Dylvana sitting on the grass and laughing and entertaining two toddlers, while Gretta sat off to the side and smiled. "I'd rather we speak of this in private, Tiarna Conal."

"Pah!" snorted Conal. "No lord am I, no matter what Breccan said. I'm just a plain soldier who once served King Valen."

"That's not the way Silverleaf tells it," said Driu.

Conal laughed as he climbed over the rail fence. "Did I not say he was a rascal? But, no matter, if it's privacy we need, then privacy we'll have." He turned to Cuán and said, "Get out of there and run ahead and tell cook to put a kettle on and to set out some of those scones. Then get back here and make ready for the calving; we've several who are ready to let fall their burdens, one I am worried about."

As the youth scrambled across the fence and ran toward the house, Conal offered his arm to Lady Driu. "Shall we?"

Driu laughed and linked her arm with his, and they strolled toward the manor, while off on the grass the Elves spoke and sang in their fluid speech, the captivating words rolling off their tongues and into the attentive ears of two children.

*   *   *

"DANGER? RÍGÁN IS IN DANGER?"

"Aye," said Driu. "Rígán, Reyer, by any name, peril will come for him."

They sat upon the verandah overlooking the sward, tea and scones at hand.

"Arkov?"

"Most likely he is the one behind it," said Driu. "But as to just who will present the immediate danger ..." She shrugged.

"But you are a Seeress," said Conal. "Don't you know just who it will be?"

"Someone or something is blocking me," said Driu.

"Blocking you?"

Driu nodded. "I cannot see the possibility, or rather I should say the many possibilities."

"Who would do so, and how?"

"Another Mage, and by use of the Art."

"Another Mage, eh?"

Again Driu nodded. "Most likely a black one—a follower of Gyphon."

"When?"

Driu frowned at Conal's question, but then she said, "Ah. I see. As to the when, the most probable time lies some years from now, as the boy enters his teens. Until then, I know they will be searching. We must remain on alert."

"But not for a number of years, right?"

Driu shook her head. "Not so. You see, there are many branches leading from now to next. Each decision, each choice made by us and others could lead to salvation or disaster or joy or sorrow or to something completely humdrum."

"So, you don't know when, right?"

Driu sighed and said, "Right. Yet each day I will cast runes and see what that day might bring. But nothing is carved in stone, so we must be ever on alert."

"You plan to stay, Lady?"

"I do. For I will veil this location from those who would use the Art to search."

"Veil, eh?" said Conal, a faint smile on his lips at the feminine choice of words. "Like the Black Mage veils Arkov's plans from us?"

Driu smiled and nodded and took a sip of tea.

As she set the cup down, Conal replenished his and hers. Then he looked at Driu and said, "With these storm clouds on the horizon, I will continue training my men in the art of spear and sword and bow and arrow and long-knife and dagger and shield. We will be ready when they come."

"You are instructing your men in the ways of battle?"

"Aye. Raiders from Jute come in their Dragonships and plunder and pillage. They have never ventured this far inland, but if they do, we will stand and fight."

"Ah," said Driu. " 'Tis best to be prepared for that which might never come than to be unprepared for that which does."

"Just so," said Conal.

"Armsmaster," said Driu, giving Conal the title he had had when he served Valen, "you must also fiercely train Reyer, um, Rígán and Alric when they come of the age to do so."

"I will begin ere then, Lady. All must be ready when peril arrives, be it raiders or assassins."

"You will not put them at risk, though."

"Nay. If they are yet unprepared, and perhaps even if they are, I will make certain to have an escape planned for Rígán and Alric."

"Thank you," said Driu. She glanced across at the circle of Elves. "Heed, the Dylvana will be on ward as well."

"Good," said Conal. "Then, no matter what peril comes, we have a fighting chance."

Caer Pendwyr

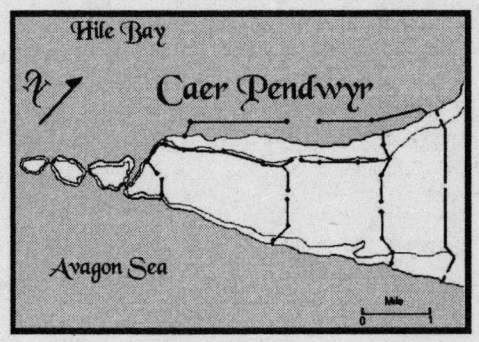

Hile Bay

Caer Pendwyr

Avagon Sea

Mile
0

Back before the counting of Eras, Awain, who was king of Pellar, through the force of arms, conquered several nations and united them in trade and self-defense. He declared himself the High King over those nations and began measuring the years, 1E1 being the first year of the first Era of the first High King's reign. In that year he established his throne in a brand new city in Pellar, nigh the mouth of the Argon. Some sixty years later, in a trade dispute, an army from the nation of Chabba invaded and burned that city of Gleeds to the ground. At that time, Rolun, grandson of Awain, was the High King, and he and his army slaughtered the Chabbains to the last man ... even though some had surrendered. Knowing that ever after, the Chabbains would seek revenge, Rolun decided that he would not rebuild burnt Gleeds, or at least not place his capital there. Instead, he selected a site more easily defended—the three high stone spires sitting in the Avagon at the very end of the Pendwyr Headland in Pellar.

The first spire, the largest of the three, would house his fortress-castle and be connected to and protected from the mainland by a swing bridge.

The second spire was to be attached to the first by a rope-and-board bridge; this spire would contain housing for his closest advisors.

The third and final spire would contain the King and Queen's residence, along with the servants' quarters. Access to it would be by another rope-and-board bridge.

The buildings on the headland nearest to the spires would contain quarters for the standing army as well as house various government agencies.

Beyond these buildings, high battlements of stone would be built as the first line of defense.

And all construction would be of stone and tile so that, unlike Gleeds, the buildings would not burn.

As for a supply of water, rain is frequent upon the headland, and clever catchments and cisterns were to be made for the runoff from the tile roofs. And as it is with any city, food would be grown in the fertile plains beyond.

As the work on the capital commenced, various masons and merchants arrived, and soon a city grew beyond the defensive wall, rising a stone-and-tile-roofed building at a time as merchants and craftsmen settled on the headland to be near the fortress. As the city grew, additional bulwarks were erected for defense.

Below the city, and along the southeastern shore of Hile Bay, men constructed docks, and a switchback road crawled up the headland to reach the plateau above. Ocean trade commenced.

The port and the city and the castle all took on the name Caer Pendwyr, though the official name for the town was simply Pendwyr.

But no matter the defensive measures taken, they mean little when traitors negate them, as was the case when Arkov overthrew King Valen. . . .

. . . And in that city, behind those walls, within the castle itself, in the third year of Arkov's reign . . .

"MY LORD KING ARKOV," said Counselor Baloff, "I have here the list of honors." The tall, thin, stringy-haired advisor handed the list to Arkov.

Quickly, the King skimmed down the list, marking off some, adding others, changing the titles and lands of some. He paused over the name Viliev Stoke, who had been the one to open the gate into the courtyard during the invasion. Arkov shook his head. "No, no, Baloff, this will not do. Not a viscountcy for Stoke. Instead give him a barony in the Skarpals and send him away."

"My lord?"

Arkov sighed. "Baloff, as did the others, he betrayed Valen, and, like they, he is not to be trusted, for what's to keep him from betraying me? His loyalty lies with the highest bidder."

"You could just kill him," said Baloff.

"No," said Arkov. "I would slay neither Stoke nor any who betrayed Valen. Were I to do so, then should we need someone else betray their liege, they would hesitate. Instead, I would merely have Stoke out of the way, as we did with the others. Old Baron Drechin's estate is abandoned. Give it to Viliev Stoke. I'll not have him in my court."

"As you will, my King."

Arkov paused and asked, "What of these local uprisings?"

Baloff said, "Whenever they occur, your loyal troops ride out from the garrisons and put a quick end to them. They are diminishing and are of no moment, my lord."

Arkov nodded and returned to the list—commenting here, changing it there, adding and deleting names and ranks and titles. Just as he handed it back to Baloff, a page came scurrying in and quickly knelt before the throne, holding his tongue until given leave.

"Well, what is it, boy?" asked Baloff.

"My Lord King Arkov, Lord Baloff, someone has taken Valen's corpse from above the gate."

"What!" demanded Arkov. "Taken the corpse?"

The boy quailed and mumbled, "Yes, my lord. Skull and all. 'Twas done sometime in the night, the ward says. They made no notice of it until just now."

"Damned rebels up north!" cursed Arkov. "They mean to make a martyr of Valen and entomb his bones at a revered site. I'll have their hides for this."

"Indeed, my lord," said Baloff.

Yet seething, Arkov said, "Find who actually took the remains. We'll make an example of him. And from our agents at Challerain Keep discover where those rebels plan to entomb Valen. We'll burn the remains and scatter the ashes and put short work to that scheme."

"Aye, my lord."

But for Arkov's fuming, silence fell, and Baloff glanced at the page. "Dismissed, boy."

As the lad ran away, Arkov gained control of his breathing. Finally, he asked, "How go the negotiations?"

Baloff looked to make certain the page had gone and had closed the chamber door after. Then he softly said, "Alban, Hurn, and Sarain are with us, but Chabba still demands more."

"Damn dark bastards," said Arkov. "What do they want now?"

"No tolls on the trade routes imposed, they say, by Rolun. That and the right to hallow and prohibit all but Chabbain from the grounds where their army was slain in 1E60 nigh the site of Leeds." Baloff then shook his head and said, "They have long-held grudges and long-held memories, these men of Chabba, especially when it concerns their dead ancestors."

"I will not reduce the tolls. And we must never give them the ground, yet tell them they can visit freely."

"My lord? Chabbains on our soil after we put down the insurgents?"

"Ah, Baloff, heed me: because much of my army is tied down quelling these uprisings in Riamon and Aven, we will need our southern allies when we decide to march against the so-called Northern Alliance. Afterward we can always rescind any treaties with the Southers when we are stronger," said Arkov, smiling.

"As you will, my King, but still I hesitate to include Chabba."

"Worry not about Chabba," said Arkov. "Instead concentrate on dealing with Challerain. They are who I will conquer, and if I must make a temporary alliance with enemies of old, I shall do so."

"As you wish, King Arkov."

"Speaking of enemies of old, Baloff, what of Khal?"

"My lord, Khal and Aralan declare their neutrality. Jugo and Hoven, especially Hoven, passively resist us, but are not in open rebellion as are Aven and Riamon."

"Well, none of them has a claim on the throne, so I would expect no better of them. It's that traitor Cavin, Valen's lackey, who's behind this resistance as well as the local unrest. He would have the throne for himself. And we must be ready for his invasion."

"My lord, our agents in Challerain do not think the rebels are anywhere near mustering and marching. They are squabbling among themselves. Many believe, as say you, Cavin is out to grab whatever he can."

Arkov clapped his hands. "Hah! Did I not tell you this?"

"Yes, my lord, yes indeed."

Arkov suddenly sobered. "What of Jord? Does Ulrik have any designs in this?"

"Not as far as we can tell, my lord."

"Better for them if not," said Arkov, clenching a fist.

"My lord," said Baloff, "Jord gave up all claim even as Riamon, in its collusion with corrupt Seers, stole the throne from Garia."

"Even so, they might revisit the issue," said Arkov.

"Well, my lord, by bird my agents report the traitor Cavin has recently sent an emissary to Black Mountain."

"Black Mountain? What for?"

"A Seer."

"But Black Mountain is closed, they say," said Arkov. He pondered a moment and then said, "This is a ruse, I think. Some plot of Cavin's to trump up a pretender."

"Aye. And what would you have me do?"

"Make certain that the so-called emissary does not return to Challerain with aught: no Seer, no pretend Seer . . . naught whatsoever. Send a company with remounts. Tell them to make haste, and failure is not acceptable."

"As you will, my lord. But how will we—?"

"To journey from Challerain to Black Mountain, Lord Baloff, an agent will travel much of the way through Garia."

Baloff nodded. "Ah, yes . . . on Landover Road. And then, my lord?"

Arkov grinned. "At the crossing between Garia and Riamon, that's where I would have my company of assassins lie in wait to waylay the envoy and his party and kill them all."

Jord

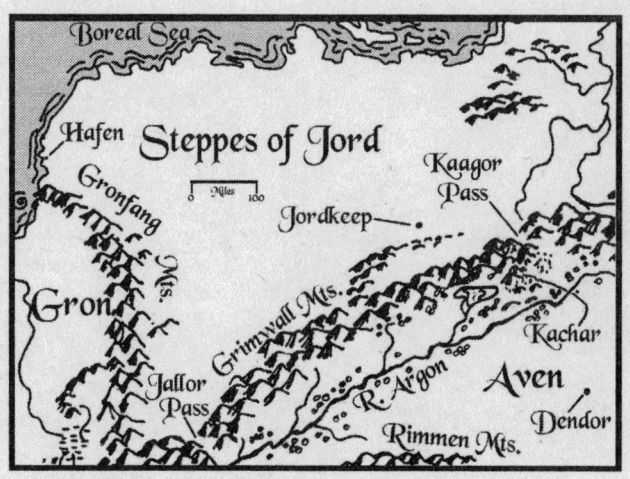

Bounded on the north by the Boreal Sea, on the east by the Judra River, on the south by the Grimwall Mountains, and on the west by the Gronfangs, lies a great steppe of low rolling hills. Frigid with ice and snow in the cold dark days of winter but blessed with endless green grass in the long bright days of summer, it is the land of Jord, a nation of horsemen, tall and fair, much like their kinsmen the Fjordlanders. For centuries upon centuries the realm of Naud has disputed Jord's claim of its eastern border, and many a skirmish has been fought over the wide wedge of land between the Judra and Grey rivers. At times Naud is joined in this clash by Kath, longtime allies against Jord. But nearly four hundred years have passed since the Naudron's last probe into the town of Arnsburg, when once again and soundly had the intruders been defeated by the warriors of Jord.

Proud are these descendants of Strong Harl, the mighty king who had founded the nation of Jord long past. In his honor they named themselves the Harlingar—the Blood of Harl. He had come to this land with his Vanadurin—his Warriors of the Pledge—who were formidable horse-borne fighters. And they included Warrior Maidens among them, skilled in battle as well, with a long tradition of fighting beside their men. Yet after the Great War of the Ban, the Warrior Maidens were disbanded, for the nation had suffered greatly, and the then Jordian King Raynor deemed women were too precious to risk in battle—at least until the nation recovered from their losses on the wide-flung battlefields of that war. Some sixteen hundred years later, the one exception to this lack of Warrior Maidens was Elyn of Jord, about whom many a bard's tale is spun and sung.

Long have the Jordians been in this land, where they

raise the finest steeds in all of Mithgar, highly prized in realms far beyond the reach of the West.

But always have the Harlingar—the Vanadurin, the Warriors of the Pledge—been allied with the High Kings in times of trouble, ever since there had been such monarchs. Yet never before had a High King's throne been usurped, as had happened three years past....

...And so, in Jord...

ULRIK, A TALL MAN with shaggy blond hair and beard, shook his head. "No, Lord Bader, I am not interested in the throne of the High King. The four Reichs of Jord is my domain."

They sat in wicker chairs under a tent-roofed gazebo out on the grassy plains. In the near distance, riders drove a large band of free-running horses, their rough shag coats of winter gone, replaced by sleek browns and tans and blacks and greys. Overhead three families of swift kestrels from several nearby upjutting crags soared, following the drive but paying no heed to the horses, but only to the panicked voles running through the grass, disturbed as they were by the moving herd.

"If not you, King Ulrik, then what of your brother?" said Bader. The emissary turned to the slender dark-haired man on the right. "What say you, Lord Valder?"

Lounging with his feet upon a wicker footstool, Valder barked a short laugh, amusement in his pale blue eyes. "Take on those woes? Not I." He abruptly sat up and swept his arms wide, encompassing the whole of Jord. "I would live here in our kingdom of grass, where I can raise the finest horses in the world. Hence, Pellar—especially Caer Pendwyr—has naught for me."

"But, my lords," said Bader, a short stocky man of Wellen, "we have as of yet not found an heir within the lineage of Devon, firstborn of King Rand and Queen Lessa of Riamon. Devon took the throne, when, as you are well aware, your own ancestral lineage might truly be the one that should have ruled instead."

Ulrik took a sip of his wine and then made a dismissive gesture, saying, "You are speaking of Wedan, firstborn of

King Haldor and Queen Keth. Bah. Jord gave up any claim to that throne long past, for which I am in agreement with Valder. Give me grass and horses, and I am content."

Bader sighed and looked into his goblet and said naught for long moments. At last he spoke: "My lords, should it come to war, will you side with the Northern Alliance or with the usurper instead?"

Ulrik looked at his brother, and then turned to the emissary. "Did you know that once long past Garia supported the spurious claim of the Naudrons for the land between the Judra and the Grey?"

Bader frowned, clearly wondering what this might have to do with answering his question.

Valder said, "That land is part of the East Reich."

"Ah," said Bader, hope glimmering in his eyes.

"Long are our memories," added Valder.

"I see," said Bader.

"But as to your question," said Ulrik, "long are our traditions, too."

Bader's voice fell. "Oh," he said, hope waning.

Ulrik continued. "Ever have we allied ourselves with the rightful High King, but in this case we remain neutral. As much as tradition and old friendships deem, I would not and will not come to the aid of a vile usurper, especially one from Garia."

They sat for long moments, speaking not, but then Bader said, "You spoke of Jord's alliance with rightful High Kings. Heed: we have sent to Black Mountain for a Seer. Perhaps even now one is in Challerain Keep. Should he find a rightful heir, then would you come to our cause?"

King Ulrik swirled the wine in his goblet. "As I said, Lord Bader—"

"Hai! But look at him run!" shouted Valder, leaping to his feet.

A large grey had broken free from the herd and fled across the wold, a group of mares running after. Riders pursued and fillies ran, but the grey outdistanced them all.

"By damn, Ulrik," cried Valder, "I do want that steed."

Back on the fringes of the main herd and above, kestrels cried and stooped upon the scatter of running prey.

Rood

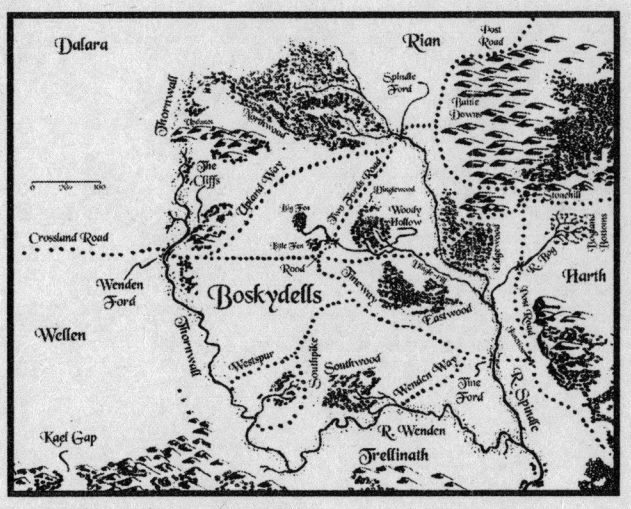

The Boskydells is so named for it is made up of seven districts called "Dells": Northdell, Eastdell, Southdell, Westdell, Centerdell, Updell in the northwest corner, and Downdell in the southeast. Roughly in the center of the Bosky lies the town of Rood, where the most serious of "official" business of the Dells is conducted. The great east-west Crossland Road runs through Rood and beyond. And from Rood the Two Fords Road fares northeast, aiming for faraway Challerain Keep, while to the southeast the Tineway heads toward distant Caer Pendwyr. And the Red Coach runs along these routes, with Rood being a main transfer point. Perhaps the town got its name because a rood is a cross and this is where roads cross. A cross is also an instrument of death, and some say that when the Warrows came, a gallows stood at this place, specifically where two paths crossed, and everyone knows that a crossroads is where the ghost of a hanged man would be trapped. Yet none had ever seen a ghost haunting the town, and so most dismissed the story of the gallows as merely being an old damman's tale. Still that might be how Rood got its name. Regardless, Rood is where the Thornwalker headquarters sit, and since the Thornwalkers are charged with the protection of the Bosky, that's where the debate had carried on for the past three years and would perhaps carry on for another three years or very much more. . . .

. . . And in those Thornwalker headquarters . . .

"I TELL YOU, Bradely, if the penny comes, we should ignore it."

"What, and lose our honor, Jem?"

"Who says it's honorable to support a usurper?"

Mayor Bradely sighed and said, "Tipperton Thistledown

made a pledge long past; are we just going to disregard that?"

"Yar, there's that," replied Jem. "Tipperton's vow. No doubt about it."

Bradely frowned and said, "Me, I think the pledge was for all times, no matter who sits on the throne."

"That can't be right," said Windlow, local captain of the Thornwalkers. "I mean, if Tipperton were here, what would he say?"

"Well, Tipperton ain't here, so we'll never know," said Jem.

"But if he were—"

"He ain't."

"Jem's right, Windlow," said the mayor, "and there isn't any use speculating on what someone who isn't here might or might not say."

Windlow rubbed his jaw. "I'll tell you what: let's send someone to the Caer and ask this—what's his name? Arkov? Aye, Arkov—ask this King Arkov what he will do if we send the penny to him. See what his answer is. Be guided by what he responds."

Alton Periwinkle spoke for the first time. "Who's the best one to go?"

"Not you, Perry. You're just as like to spit him with an arrow as to look him in the eye," said Windlow.

"Oh-oh. I know, I know, send me, send me. I've always wanted to see what Caer Pendwyr looks like, and the Argon, too, and the Red Hills, and I've never seen an Elf or a Dwarf or—"

Now Windlow turned a gimlet eye toward Digby Thimbleweed. "Oh, my scatterbrained lad, you are just as apt to go haring off after butterflies along the way as you are to get to Pendwyr. Why, you're likely to end up a thousand leagues elsewhere because you thought it would be interesting to talk to a Dragon or some such."

"Would not."

"Would too."

"Well, I've never seen a Dragon either."

"I say we send Arl," said Mayor Bradely. "He's the most

experienced buccan we've got. I mean, he runs the Red Willow, and talks to Big Folk all the time. Lords and ladies and commoners alike."

"Good idea," said Jem. "Send Arl."

"I'll run fetch him. See if he's willing."

"He'll need bodyguards. Perry and me," said Digby.

"Diggs, I—"

"Ooo, and I've always wanted to ride the Red Coach."

"Look, the Digger is right," said Perry. "Arl will need bodyguards, and I'm best with a bow, and Dig has enough crazy ideas to get us out of whatever fix we might find ourselves in."

"Crazy, Perry? My ideas aren't crazy. Instead, I'm, I'm, well, I'm . . ."

"Creative."

"Yar, Jem, that's it. I'm creative."

MONTHS PASSED, and months more, and the Red Coaches ran to and fro, but finally Arl and Perry and Digby returned to the Bosky.

"Well . . . ?"

"I don't care if he does send the penny, I won't serve him, ever."

Mayor Bradley frowned. "Why not, Perry? Arl, what happened?"

"It took weeks and weeks just to get an audience," said Arl.

"He didn't even know what the Gjeenian penny meant," said Perry.

"Even after we told him, he just laughed," added Digby.

"He refused to come to our aid," said Arl.

"Worst of all, he made us kneel," growled Perry.

Taken aback, Captain Windlow said, "Damnation! Made you kneel?"

"Called us pipsqueaks, too," said Digby, glancing at Perry. "Right?"

"Diggs, I would have shot him then and there," said Perry, "but they made us leave our weapons at the gate."

The mayor shook his head. "Let me get this straight, Arl:

in spite of High King Blaine's edict, Arkov made you kneel?"

"Yar. They forced us to our knees, like we were vassals or some such."

"Well, that settles it then."

The Maw

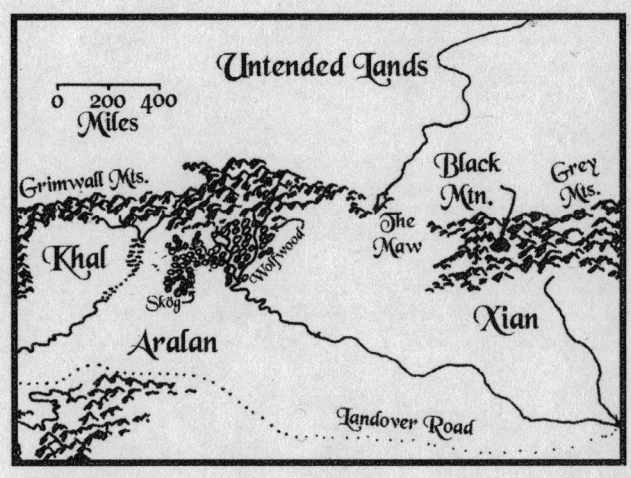

At the far eastern extent of the Grimwalls lies a broad and perilous plain; it stretches some two hundred miles across ere it fetches up against the western reach of the Grey Mountains. In winter, savage winds rage out from the north, out from the Untended Lands—the Barrens—and thunder over the wide expanse to visit violence upon the lands of Aralan and Xian in the south. Sometimes blinding snow is born on this fury; other times the wrath scours clean the terrain; and at yet other times the air is dead still, as if lying in wait for some ill-fated being to test his fortune by trying to cross over or through. In summer there is little relief, for warm westerlies from the Avagon Ocean collide with the frigid ones from the Boreal Sea and furious rainstorms flail this passage, trapped as they are in between the Grimwalls and the Greys, where the air on occasions is twisted into roaring funnels that can destroy a dwelling or a caravan in but a blink of an eye. Dwellers within or near this hazardous gape take extensive measures to protect themselves from its ragings, and travelers who frequently come nigh or traverse this dangerous course know its menace as well.

They call it the Maw, and strangers are warned.

But if one is on his way from west to east to visit the Wizards in Black Mountain in the Greys, there is no choice but to brave this crossing, for from the west the only route inward lies at the edge of the plain. . . .

. . . And on a summer eve in a wild storm, with the air shrieking arage and hail hammering from above . . .

"Captain ewan!" cried Sergeant Kandor, shouting to be heard above the howl. "We've got to find shelter, else the horses are dead, to say naught of the men."

Lightning flared and thunder crashed, and Ewan shouted back, "I know, Sergeant."

Again lightning jagged down with a deafening *Crack!* followed by a bone-rattling, juddering *Boom!*

"Ahead, a vale!" called Corporal Deyer, pointing at a shoulder of foothills, the unseen bulks of the Greys just beyond.

"It could be perilous, Captain," cried Kandor.

"Yes, Sergeant, I know, but we have little choice."

Following Deyer, the squad rode toward the lee side of the hill, though with the furious swirl of the air, which was lee and which windward made the pick somewhat moot.

THEY HAD BEEN ON the journey for nearly six months and the remaining twenty-eight men and fifty-seven horses were weary from traveling. Yet, their goal—the Wizardholt known as Black Mountain—still lay a fortnight further away. It had taken two years of diplomatic squabbling for the Northern Alliance to form, two years of wasted time, or so Captain Ewan thought. And in that interval, no Seer had been found within the so-called rebel realms. And so, to meet with a Seer, Ewan and his company were given the task of escorting an envoy to Black Mountain, where Wizards were known to dwell.

They had started in the last week of winter, riding south from Challerain Keep and down through the realm of Harth, and then eastward through Lianion along the Crossland Road. Up through the frigid heights of Crestan Pass they had fared, with its ice and snow yet heavy-laden, even though it was then early spring. Nine men and seventeen horses had been lost to an avalanche at those perilous heights, and one of those men swept over the edge to their deaths was young Lord Dinfry, the emissary they were to escort to the Mages and back.

Captain Ewan had sent one man back to tell of Dinfry's death, and then he and the remaining men had pushed on, knowing that to turn hindward would simply be to lose even more time. Another two men—unable to carry on— had stopped at the Baeron outpost on the way down; frostbite had taken their feet. Along the Landover Road in Riamon, three more had fallen victim to ague, and turned north for the healers in Dael. But the remaining men and horses continued onward, as the days and weeks and months flowed by.

And on the last day of crossing the wide plain lying between the Grimwalls and the Greys, that's when the storm had fallen upon them in fury, and, trapped in the open, they struggled through the thrashing downpour of frigid water—sporadically interleaved with torrents of battering hail—until at last they reached the foothills of the Greys and took refuge within....

"Not much shelter, Captain," called Corporal Deyer above the icy downpour now plummeting upon them.

They had ridden to a small stand of silver-birch, where the trees did cut the wind, though the overhanging branches provided scant relief from the bitter cascade and intermittent fusillades of hail.

"Off the mounts," ordered Ewan. "Blankets to dry the horses, and give them shelter from the cold."

"What about the men, Captain?" asked Sergeant Kandor.

"They'll have to make do with their rain cloaks," replied the captain. "The horses are vital; the men less so."

Even as Ewan tended to his own mount along with his tethered packhorse, by lightning flash he scanned the surround. *Not high enough upon the slopes, yet there is no shelter that way. As Kandor said, it could be perilous. I'll go lower down into the vale and see what I can see.*

As soon as his horses were cared for, in spite of the wind and rain, the captain managed to light a lantern, and then he called for Deyer.

"Sir?"

Ewan smiled. "You look like a bedraggled rat, Corporal."

With his beard adrip and his hair plastered down around his face, Deyer laughed and said, "As do you, Captain."

"No doubt," replied Ewan. "Are your horses well set?"

"Yes, sir."

"Then you are with me."

Down toward the bottom of the shallow vale they picked their way among the pale birch boles.

As they reached a small overflowing streambed, Ewan stopped and held the lantern on high. "Any evidence of past flood-scouring?"

Deyer knelt above the embankment and ran his hand across the wet loam. "Too hard to tell, sir."

"Then we can only—"

A distant rumbling interrupted Captain Ewan's words. Both men looked up. There had been no accompanying lightning flash, but the rumbling grew.

"Run!" cried Deyer, and he turned and bolted upslope, with Ewan on his heels and shouting warning to those above.

But before many could react, a towering wall of water slammed into the encampment.

Trees bent in the deluge, some to snap in twain while others were wrenched up and out from the soil to go tumbling along with rocks and dirt and men and horses and supplies. Animals screamed along with troopers, their shrieks and cries lost in the thunder of hurtling water.

Ewan was caught in the torrent and rolled under to smash against the ground, only to be hurled up and tossed high, and then to be rolled under again, the raging water plunging along the corridor of the vale, carrying all along in its mad rush.

Churning, tumbling, Ewan could only now and again get a breath, and even then he would be slammed to the bottom and the air knocked from his lungs.

But then the whole of the deluge swept out from the vale and into the broad plain, where it fled south and west and east to diminish in depth and force.

But the dell behind yet roared with the outpour as trees and rocks and horses and men were vomited forth from its roiling maw.

Shivering uncontrollably, Ewan managed to limp through the knee-deep flow to a small knoll.

Finding a Seer will be the death of us all.

*   *   *

SOMETIME DURING THE NIGHT, the storm abated and fell to a drizzle, finally to die. Dawn came, and shivering men and a handful of distressed horses managed to find one another.

All told, the survivors were seventeen men—Captain Ewan and Corporal Deyer among them: all had bruises, and five had broken bones—a collarbone, a wrist, an arm, and two with bones broken in lower legs.

As he tended the injured, Ewan commanded Deyer to take the least hurt and ride the recovered mounts to find the other horses.

He then told the remainder to salvage whatever supplies they could and to see about building a fire, though as to this latter, with everything drenched, well . . .

The vale itself continued to flow with the outpour running down from the Grey Mountains, and now and then, floating out along with uprooted trees and broken branches and debris, a corpse would issue forth on the drift: a trooper, a horse, or an animal native to this land.

Altogether, eleven men had died, some by drowning, others by being bludgeoned to death. Of the horses, some of them, too, had perished, some were never found, and some had to be put down because of their injuries.

In all, a sevenday passed before the fit and unfit managed to recover enough to bury their dead and head eastward again, Black Mountain yet their goal.

They left their wounded among the villagers of a small mountain holt named Doku, and, resupplied and with a two-day rest, they pressed on toward the Wizards' retreat.

TWELVE MEN ALTOGETHER—twelve survivors—dismounted and led their horses across a sheltered smooth stretch of stone of a wide foregate court embraced by a broad recess. At Captain Ewan's orders, with their hands on the hilts of their weapons, they spread out as they went. Stepping through shadow, they came to a pair of great iron gates, and runes and another strange script were carved or cast thereon. What they might impart, neither Ewan nor none of his men could say.

"I think these are Dwarven words," said Corporal Deyer. "I've seen their like on realmstones."

"But this is not a Dwarvenholt," said one of the troopers.

"I'll wager they made this though," said Deyer.

"And the other script . . . ?" asked the trooper.

"Magetongue, mayhap," said Deyer. "I mean, they do live here, or so I have been told."

"They had better live here," said Captain Ewan, "for all it has cost us."

He then drew his long-knife and reversed it to use the pommel to hammer for entrance.

His effort brought forth a small thunk.

"Thick," he said.

A side postern in what had seemed to be solid stone opened and an armored figure stepped out and beckoned to them.

It was a Dwarf.

AFTER HALF A DAY and another of rest and recovery, and after being fed a number of meals to quench hunger and slake thirst, finally Ewan was summoned to a chamber.

"I know why you've come, Captain," said the yellow-robed Mage, a female who looked to be in her dotage. Her hair was white and her sallow skin was age-spotted. With faded brown eyes she studied the warrior, and she smiled, accentuating the wrinkles of her old face.

"Then you know our need, Sage Arilla," said Ewan.

Arilla sighed and nodded. "I do. Yet, heed, we are not yet recovered from the Great War, and none of us has the <fire> to spend. Instead, we must <rest> and regain our vigor, our youth. The war took much out of us."

Ewan frowned. "But that was—what?—two thousand years past?"

"Indeed. Even so, we have not yet recouped much of that which we lost."

"Is there naught you can do to help us?"

"You will need to find someone who yet has the <essence> to spend."

"We have searched and found no one," said Ewan. "Our last hope is—"

"Shush," said Arilla. "I have not the <fire> to squander for a search through time to discover that which you seek, but I do have enough to aid you in finding a Seer, one who can take on the quest."

Ewan sighed but said, "As you will, Lady Mage."

"Come," said Arilla, and she stood.

Ewan offered her his arm, for he had seen how she had hobbled into the chamber to speak with him. And together they slowly moved into another room, Dwarven-carved from the solid black stone. Gingerly she took a chair before a modest alabaster table upon which sat a small cedar box, and she bade the captain to sit in a chair opposite. She unclasped the lid of the aromatic wooden case just large enough to hold a silken-wrapped deck of cards. She spread out the fabric—blue with a spangle of stars—and she carefully shuffled the cards. Finally, she said to Ewan, "Captain, think of that which you seek, and cut the deck in twain and place the half to your left."

Even as he did so, Arilla muttered a word arcane.

Then she stacked the deck right to left.

She dealt out just five cards, making a cross: one in the center, one above, one below, one left, and one right.

Then she looked at the spread and laughed and said, "Go, the one you seek will find you instead."

"But, I don't underst—"

"Captain, just go."

And when the captain had gone, Arilla looked at the cards: in the center, the Mage, upright, aiding. To the left, the Ace of Swords, inverted, opposing. To the right, the Ruined Tower, inverted, disaster. Below lay the Naïf, upright, aiding. And above, the Knight of Swords, also upright, aiding. Arilla sighed. *The Tower, opposing, as is the Ace of Swords; how sad.* She tapped the Mage in the center. *My old friend is back, and he will help them survive.*

She penned a quick note on a tissue-thin strip, and then rang a small bell.

A Dwarf appeared.

She handed him the note and said, "Send this by the grey falcon."

"As you wish, Lady Mage."

CAPTAIN EWAN AND HIS eleven men stopped in Doku for rest and respite and to see how bones were healing. Of the five men who had remained there, the lad with the collarbone fracture had mended enough to ride with them, but the other breaks had more knitting to do. And so, Ewan told those four troopers to ride when they could, and he added more silvers to the coffers of the village elder to keep the men and their horses well nourished until all had healed.

The villagers were pleased to comply, for, with the village elder translating, the soldiers entertained them with tales of their ventures and told of a world beyond the mountains. The horses, though, did frighten them. Until these men had come, they'd had only ponies in their stables, and these big beasts were like and yet unlike their smaller cousins. That is, if the horses ran amok, why, they could destroy the entire hamlet. Still, as they had been directed by the captain, they had been leading the beasts out on tethers behind the ponies to have a run so that they would maintain themselves.

The village elder tried to dissuade the captain from riding out with the youth who'd had a collarbone break; after all, if they went that way, there would be thirteen riding—surely a bad omen, for it could not be divided by two or three or any number.

But the captain and his men paid no heed, and rode westward the very next day.

THEY REACHED THE GRAVESIDES of the men who had perished in the flood, and they paused long enough to hold a ceremony. And then, to escape a repeat of the disaster, they dashed west-southwestward across the wide plain between the end of the Grey Mountains and the beginning of the Grimwalls, taking only four days to get far enough away to be out from the worst of the Maw. But the weather held, and their journey was without incident.

They continued west-southwestward, heading for the Landover Road, and as summer continued to wane, they forded the Wolf River—named so, for it flowed out from the Wolfwood, some hundred miles to the north.

On they fared, through Aralan, to finally intercept the Crossland Road just north of the Bodorian Range in Alban.

It was there that the now-sergeant Deyer said, "Captain, I keep having this feeling that someone or something is watching us, but I haven't seen aught as of yet."

"Keep a sharp eye out, then, Deyer."

"Yes, sir."

"And tell the men to do likewise."

"Aye, Captain."

As they rode a bit farther, Deyer said, "I'm glad you believe me, Captain."

"Sergeant, many a time my life has been saved by someone who 'sensed' rather than 'saw.' So I am not one to question your, um, awareness of an unseen thing. Now, alert the men."

On they traveled, day after day, and autumn was upon them as they entered the eastern edge of Garia.

Through this land they made their way, and, as they had been doing when opportunity afforded, they stopped in villages along the trek to rest and eat and replenish their supplies, including grain for their horses.

But in particular in Garia, Captain Ewan cautioned the men each day to remember their tale that they were mercenaries for hire, and not citizens of the Northern Alliance. And on they rode for the marge between this land and Riamon.

As they approached the slot in the Rimmen Mountains marking the border, a young scout pointed forward and upward above two close-set hills. "Kites, sir."

"I see them, Avril," said Ewan, gazing at the circling dark birds.

"Something dead?"

"Aye, but on both sides of the road. Sergeant Deyer, scouts out to see what has them so stirred."

"Yes, sir." Deyer sent two men to the right and two to the

left. "Caution, lads," he said, though he was no older than they.

"GARIAN SOLDIERS," said Ewan, looking down at the rent garb of the slaughtered men.

"What could have done this?" asked Avril. "I mean, they look as if they were set upon by wild beasts."

Deyer came riding upslope. As he reached the encampment, he dismounted and glanced at the massacre and said, "It's the same on the other side, Captain."

"It looks as if they were trying to flee," said Ewan, "but were brought down even as they ran."

"Captain," called one of the men, kneeling in the dirt, "I think you need to see this."

Ewan moved to the man's side and knelt beside the trooper. "What kind of a dog would make a track this big?"

"Not a dog, Lann; a Vulg, mayhap," said Ewan.

"Oh, Adon. Vulgs? They did this?"

"Pony-sized, Wolflike, but creatures of the Spawn instead," said Deyer, now standing at hand. "Black as night, they are, and banned from the light of day by Adon." Deyer took a deep breath and let it out, then said, "Captain, do you think it's Vulgs I've been sensing? Vulgs watching us?"

Ewan shook his head. "If so, then why aren't we lying slain a hundred leagues arear?"

Ewan stood and stepped back to the heart of the carnage. He paused and his gaze swept 'round the encampment, taking in its set and supplies and weaponry. As Sergeant Deyer stepped to his side, Ewan said, "Well disguised and long term. Bows and crossbows. And in the trees down nigh the turn in the road I see a low barrier; it, too, veiled."

"'Tis the same opposite, Captain, though offset. I'm thinking that this is an excellent place for an ambush."

"My thoughts as well," said Ewan.

"Brigands, thieves, robbers?" asked Lann, getting to his feet. "If so, then mayhap some animals did us a favor."

"They wear the uniforms of Garia," said Ewan.

"They could be robbers, still," said Deyer.

"Or assassins," said Lann.

*   *   *

IT WAS MIDWINTER WHEN they reached the toll takers at the base of the road leading up to Crestan Pass, and they discovered the two men who had lost their feet to frostbite had both succumbed to the rot. They debated whether to wait until spring to cross over, but since the Baeron had cleared the way of snow and ice, Ewan decided to push on instead, even though the slopes above threatened avalanche. The captain and his men tied muffling cloth upon the horses' hooves, and in near silence they slowly rode up and across and down, stopping now and again to give the horses respite . . . or to lead them afoot. And along the way they found another large paw print, as of that of a Vulg.

THEY REACHED CHALLERAIN KEEP in midspring, and still, in spite of Arilla's reading, they had not met a Seer.

They rode through the gates and up the winding road, passing under fortified wall after wall.

The council was in session, and Ewan was admitted immediately.

Lord Cavin looked up from the table and said, "Well?"

"My Lord Steward, I am sorry to report the Mages were of no aid."

"I wouldn't say that," said someone, in a voice as from afar, and suddenly at Ewan's side there appeared a man. Nay! Not a man, but perhaps an Elf instead! Seemingly from thin air he appeared: first he wasn't, then he was.

"Waugh!" men cried and leapt to their feet and swords and knives flashed out from scabbards even as Mayor Hein blundered up from his chair and bolted toward a far door, only to find it locked.

Captain Ewan reached out to take hold of the intruder, but his hand passed through the form.

"Hold!" shouted Cavin, and he smiled at the stranger, neither man nor Elf but Mage instead.

Man height he was, six foot or so, and his eyes held the hint of a tilt. His ears were pointed, and his hair hung down beyond his shoulders, a dark silvery sheen to it; in spite of his hair, he looked to be no more than thirty. He was dressed in soft grey leathers, black belt with silver buckle clasped at his waist. His feet were shod with black boots, supple and soft upon the land. His eyes were as piercing as those of an eagle, their color perhaps grey, though it was difficult to tell in the light of the chamber.

"Welcome, Lord Dalavar," said Cavin, "or do you prefer Wolfmage?"

Darda Coill

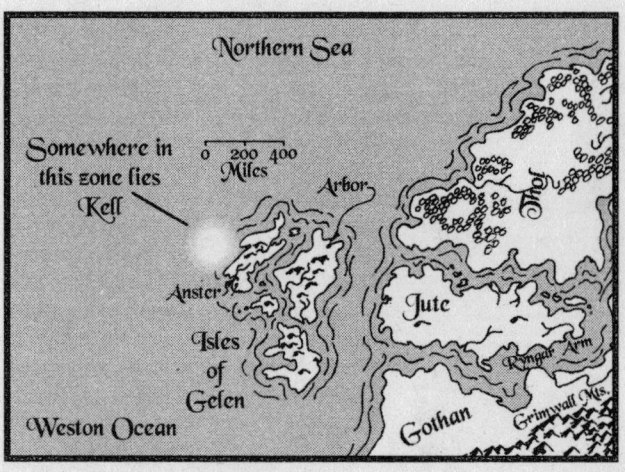

Northern Sea

Somewhere in
this zone lies
Kell

0 200 400
Miles

Arbor

Thol

Anster

Jute

Isles
of
Gelen

Ryngar Arm

Gothan

Grimwall Mts.

Weston Ocean

On the island of Kell there is a vast shaggy wood, mossy and riddled with streamlets and glades, its trees huge-girthed and old—oaks, maples, birch, ash, and white pine for the most part, along with a scatter of rowan. Rooted in rich soil and nurtured by frequent rains and warming sunlight, the ancient forest is populated by a race of lithe woodland Elves known as the Dylvana. Unlike their taller kindred, the Lian Elves, the adult Dylvana typically stand somewhere between four foot six and five foot in height. It is said that when Adon created the Lian, His daughter, Elwydd, followed with the Dylvana, the goddess making them smaller and more elusive than their kindred, after which She went on to make the Dwarves. Regardless as to whether this tale is truth or myth, the Dylvana worship Elwydd, and the ones who dwell on the isle of Kell call this ancient wood Darda Coill, which in the Elven tongue of Sylva means Forest Fair, or perhaps Forest Beautiful, in honor of their lovely creator. Elves have lived within this woodland on Kell for uncounted years . . . but when Humans arrived there was a struggle over possession of the forest, a struggle in which the Dylvana prevailed. After defeating mankind, for the most part the Dylvana forbad the men from encroaching upon Darda Coill. One result of this warfare is that the Human Kellians believe the woodland is somehow enchanted, and they adopted the name "coill" into their own language, though to them "coill" meant "forest," rather than its true meaning of "fair." Another result, however, is that though in general man does not intrude upon this darda, still the Dylvana did let some Humans—those who had sided with the Elves—to live within the bounds, under the condition that they raise cattle and other livestock, or grow grain and vegetables and additional staples. They were allowed to clear-cut trees to make these farms and to construct the buildings needed for storage and to shelter both man and animal, and to partition the fields with fences, though otherwise logging was forbidden, but for wood for fires, though here, mostly dead wood is harvested. Those cleared plots of land are highly valued, and are passed down through generations. . . .

. . . And on one of those prized farms within that ancient wood . . .

"LOOK AT THEM RUN. Like fawns they are, young roebucks." Conal laughed, his arm about Gretta as they watched Alric and Rígán—switches in hand—chase after piglets across the grassy field, yet glistening from the rain.

Gretta leaned her head into Conal's shoulder. "Has it truly been four years since we came?"

"Aye, my love. It has, though it seems just yester I first laid my eyes upon your splendid loveliness."

Gretta smiled but said naught.

They watched long moments more, secure in the comfort of one another. "Whoops," said Conal as Rígán took a tumble.

Gretta drew in a sharp breath and started to go, but Conal did not release her. "Watch," he said.

Alric stopped and ran back and helped Rígán to his feet, and they took up the chase again.

"Like brothers, they are, helping one another," said Conal. Then he laughed and added, "Though with my own brothers, I think they would have pushed me back into the mud."

In that moment, from behind, "Da!" came a cry from the stables.

Conal turned. Durgan ran out from the barn. "Da, she's down. Uasal Donn is down. I think it's time, I do." Then Durgan wheeled about and bolted back into the stables.

"Driu was right," said Conal, releasing his wife of two years. "Her runes foretold this would be the day."

"I'll bring tea," said Gretta. "You tend Brown Lady. I'll be there anon."

As Conal rushed toward the stables, Gretta called for Alric and Rígán to come. After all, Alric was a Jordian, a Harlingar, a Vanadurin, a child of horsemen, and what better time than now to learn of his heritage by witnessing the birth of a steed? Especially this foal, offspring of the two fastest horses on Kell—Brown Lady and Iron Bobbie. And although Rígán had not the same blood as Alric, still he would learn as well.

As the two lads came running, Gretta turned toward the interior of the house. Someday she would tell Conal just who Alric's father was, and then she would tell the boys. After all, if Rígán were to become High King, he also would need to know.

She entered the kitchen and said to Catlin the cook—an older woman of perhaps sixty or so—"We'll need tea. Brown Lady is ready to foal."

Smiling at the news, Catlin stirred up the fire and filled the kettle and swung it on irons above the blaze, and then fetched the tea service.

Huffing and puffing, the two boys came tumbling in like awkward young dogs not quite out of their puppyhood. But when they saw the teapot and cups, both of their faces fell.

Gretta laughed and said, "No, no, we are not going to have more lessons in court etiquette, though they will come, for you both have the need. Instead, Uasal Donn is about to give birth to Iarann Rob's child. And I want you to watch and learn."

"Oh, oh," cried Alric, "Lady Brown and Iron Bobbie. This is better than studying old, um, old pro— . . . um . . . pro—"

"Protocol," piped up six-year-old Rígán, adding, "Protocol and etiquette," shaping the words carefully.

"Birthing a horse is better than numbers and writing?" asked Gretta.

"Yes!" shouted Rígán and Alric together.

"Better than what the Elves teach?"

Rígán and Alric both looked at one another, seeking an answer but finding only doubt, for though they both loved most of what the Dylvana taught, neither had ever seen a horse give birth, though they had watched piglets and calves and puppies being born. And they did enjoy what the Elves called "beginner lessons"—sneaking through woods, making safe fire, fletching arrows, shaping bows, and the like; why, they even had their own bows and arrows fitted to their statures and draws, and they were becoming proficient in their use. Those things they were learning along with becoming more and more fluent in Sylva, for the Elves spoke to them only in that tongue. And though only six summers old, they were not only conversant in Sylva, but also in three other languages: in Pellarian, known as Common; in Jordian, Gretta's natural tongue, and she taught them both for she would have Alric know his native speech, and Rígán would be better off for it; and in Kellian, for that was Conal's innate vernacular, as well as that of most of his farmhands, and they naturally spoke it during work. Often the boys used an argot of intermingled words from the four tongues, and seemed not at all confused by their linguistic gymnastics, though at times the adults about them were. Additionally, the Elves and Gretta were teaching them to read and write, and to count and to become facile in numbers. Regardless, be it woodcraft or language or reading or numbers, it seemed that anything at all was better than learning court etiquette and protocol, including seeing a horse give birth.

Gretta, laughing, watched as Catlin took the kettle from the irons and poured the steaming water into the teapot and added leaves. "As soon as the brew is ready," said Gretta, "we'll go and watch Brown Lady bear her first offspring."

"Is it a boy?" asked Rígán.

"A colt, you mean," said Gretta.

Alric turned to Rígán and said, "Boys are colts and girls are fillies and new horses are called foals. Everyone knows that."

"I didn't know," said Rígán.

Gretta smiled and said, "Well, now you do. Yet as to whether it's a colt or filly, I cannot say, though Driu knows. But she said she'd rather it be a surprise for us."

"I'll wager it's a filly," said Catlin as she slipped a cozy onto the teapot.

Gretta took up the service and said, "Thank you, Catlin," and then said, "Come, my boys. To the stables we go."

To THE DELIGHT OF both Rígán and Alric, Brown Lady gave birth to a grey, perhaps a shade lighter than the color of its sire. As those things sometimes go, the labor was quick, in spite of this being Brown Lady's first foal. Durgan alone tended the delivery, while the others merely watched, for Conal had turned that responsibility over to his son; after all, Durgan had ridden Brown Lady to two victories over Iron Bobbie, though in each case it was by a nose.

And this foal was to be Durgan's own.

Conal said, "Well, boyo, 'tis a colt. What name would you give him?"

"Cruach," said Durgan. He turned to the boys, but he spoke to all: "In Kellian it means 'Steel.' I name him Steel, after Iron Bobbie. And with the blood of both Uasal Donn and Iarann Rob, Steel should be better than iron."

Even as Durgan named the colt, Catlin came rushing into the stables. "Oh, Tiarna Conal, something is wrong with Seeress Driu. She's sitting at the table something hardlike and gritting her teeth and mumblin' strange words."

"Oh, my," said Gretta, and she turned and rushed out and away, Catlin on her heels.

"Care for the colt," called Conal to his son. "The lads, too." He turned to Rígán and Alric. "You boys stay here under Durgan's eye." Then Conal hurried out after the two women. Rígán and Alric watched him go, anxiety in their gazes, upset because the adults seemed to be.

Conal burst into the kitchen. Driu sat at the table with her eyes closed and her fists clenched to white knuckles. And she muttered arcane phrases, sweat pouring off her brow. Her bag of runes lay before her, three stones of which had been withdrawn: one faceup, its mark clear; two facedown, their runes hidden.

Gretta looked at Conal in trepidation, while Catlin wrung her own hands in dread.

"What is it? What's the matter?" asked Conal.

Gretta simply shook her head, and Catlin whimpered, "Tiarna, I don't know."

Conal sat down and whispered to Driu, "What passes?"

Driu opened her eyes and managed to say, the words jerking out from her mouth, "Someone...something *dreadful*...searching for Reyer—Rígán. It's all I can do to shield him. All I can...all I..."

But then Driu's eyes rolled up until naught was showing but whites, and Conal caught her as she fell sideways in a swoon.

Seer

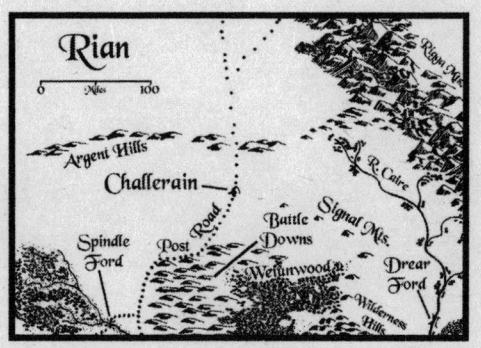

The paths are many among Magekind, among those who can see the aethyr. 'Tis the manipulation of that ephemeral substance itself that permits the casting of <spells>. As has been said by various Sages, such castings are like unto an avalanche, where the Mage merely tosses a single pebble that starts the subsequent slide. Only in this case, the first pebble is of the aethyr, and the slide itself is predetermined by the shape of the pebble pitched. Some pebbles lead to flaming bolts of fire, while others cause images to form. Some heal, while others harm. Some pebbles control animals, and some foster or wither plants. In fact, the kinds of pebbles are nearly beyond count, and can lead to all manner of castings.

Most Mages have an inborn bent for certain classes of <spells>, while other classes simply seem beyond their ken. And so, "schools" of Magekind are aimed at given aptitudes. Some schools deal with the five elements, while others deal with the mind and thought and ideas, and yet other schools deal with the living: plants and animals and fish and birds and such . . . oh, and small crawly things, as well as entities too tiny to see with the naked eye. Some schools deal with the unseen, the invisible, the hidden, and perhaps even souls. And then there are the schools shunned by most, schools that deal in specters and demons and darkness and other such dreads.

Yet in all these schools, it is the manipulation of the aethyr—the shaping of pebbles—that permits the castings.

And among Magekind, there are those rare few whose shaping abilities cross between schools, permitting castings in more than one area. In some, the ability is limited to part of one school and part of another. In others, the limits are widened, and the broader the ability, the greater the Mage.

One such Mage is Modru.

Yet for nearly the past two thousand years, Modru has been hiding away in the frozen Barrens, waiting, it seems, for ... for *something* yet to come....

... But in Challerain Keep ...

" 'TIS AN ILLUSION," gasped Captain Ewan, drawing away from the form.

"He's not here?" quavered Mayor Hein, his back against the locked door where he had scrambled in an effort to flee.

"Nay, I am not," said the image of Dalavar, his words yet seeming to come from afar, "though I am near."

"How do we know it's him?" said Hein, cowering down. And as the others glanced his way, the mayor added, "I mean, it could be anyone—any Mage—even Modru or some other terrible one, sent by High King Arkov."

"Usurper Arkov is not High King!" snapped Lord Cavin. "He is a traitor, and an ally of enemies of old, with Fists of Rakka and worshippers of Gyphon in his court. He even allows Chabbains to occupy the soil of Pellar. So tell me not that Arkov is High King; call him Betrayer instead."

A murmur of agreement swept around the table, and Hein held up his hands as if in surrender.

Lord Cavin turned back to the image of Dalavar. "If not here, Wolfmage, then where?"

"I am atop a foothill, waiting for you to alert the ward that I am coming, and that I am not alone."

"Alert the ward?"

"I would not have someone try to feather one of my companions."

Enlightenment filled Cavin's face. "Your 'Wolves."

"Wolves?" quavered Hein.

"Not ordinary Wolves, but Draega," said Cavin, "creatures of Adonar. Those are Dalavar's 'Wolves."

"The Draega are not *mine*, Lord Cavin; I own them not; they travel with me by choice."

"Ah," said Captain Ewan. "The paw prints. Silver Wolves. You and your band shadowed me and my squad. You are the one who ambushed the ambushers."

The image smiled and turned up a hand in acknowledgment.

"I will alert the guard," said Ewan, and he spun on his heel to leave the chamber.

"Wait, Captain," said Dalavar. "I would have you personally escort the pack to the castle."

"Ah, yes," said Captain Ewan. "As they safely escorted me and my squad, so shall I escort them. Where will I find these 'Wolves?"

"Just ride to the first gate and out a ways, and they will come to you."

Ewan nodded, and Dalavar's image vanished.

As Captain Ewan hurried from the chamber, in a babble of voices the council members regained their seats, all but the mayor, who remained by the far door.

ON A FRESH HORSE, away from the rugged grey citadel proper, fared Captain Ewan. And as he rode he glanced down some nine hundred feet or so at the low rolling foothills and the prairie beyond. The rough flanks of the mont itself shouldered up broadly out of those plains and hills. And he crossed the gentle slopes and wide grounds at the top and through the twisting passage within the uppermost massive defensive wall beringing the mountain entire.

And down he went.

Past the wall embracing the Kingsgrounds, on which the castle sat, began the city proper: tier upon tier of buildings of stone, brick, and wood, of many shapes and sizes and colors, all ajumble in terraced rings descending down the slopes. Running among the homes, shops, storehouses, stables, and other structures were three more massive defensive walls, stepped evenly down the side of Mont Challerain, the bottommost one nearly at the level of the plain. And as were all the walls, this first and longest bulwark circled completely 'round the lone mountain.

Only a few permanent structures lay outside the first wall.

Down through all and beyond rode the captain, to at last

reach the open, and there beside the Post Road waited seven Silver Wolves; some were flopped upon the ground, some were sitting, and one, a bit darker than the others, stood alone on ward. Large as ponies they were, with amber eyes and red tongues lolling over sharp white teeth. Their coarse top coat of overlaying fur sheened silvery white, and softer white fur lay 'neath. Their legs below their powerful haunches were long and slender, but their chests were deep, all as if built for running without rest.

At the captain's approach, those who had been sitting or lying at ease stood.

Somewhat awed and a bit on edge at the sight of these huge 'Wolves, Ewan reined to a stop, yet his horse seemed not at all skittish, as if the steed sensed these savage creatures were not a threat, and Ewan relaxed a bit.

He looked about for Dalavar, but saw him not.

"Where is your, um, companion?" he asked, though he expected no answer.

The darker 'Wolf trotted to the byway and past the captain and on toward the craggy tor, then stopped and looked back over its shoulder.

The remaining six Draega stepped to the road and waited.

Ewan yet scanned the terrain for sign of Dalavar.

A deep *Whuff* caught his attention, and he looked at the large 'Wolf standing at the fore of the six. Then Ewan turned and gazed at the darker one. It looked back at him and trotted a bit farther toward the mount. Then it stopped once again and looked hindward at the captain.

"Oh, all right," said Ewan, and he wheeled his horse and started back the way he had come. And the 'Wolves swiftly took station about the horse: two to the fore, two on each flank, and one bringing up the rear. And this is the way they entered the town of Challerain Keep.

Among the sparse buildings outside the first defensive wall they went, to come to the high barrier. Its portcullis was up, and fur- and fleece-clad, iron-helmed soldiers in red-and-gold tabards stood atop the barbican and they all leaned forward to see these creatures of legend, ringing 'round the captain, pass into the corridor under.

Through the zigzagging cobblestone passage within the thick granite they went, passing below machicolations high above through which hot oil or missiles could be rained down upon an enemy. At the other end of the barway another portcullis stood raised, and beyond that the Silver Wolves fared into the lower levels of the city proper and into the broad open market of Rian at Challerain Keep.

The square was teeming with people, and the babble of the throng dropped to whispers as all stood in awe as the Draega moved among them, some people shying back as the great beasts drew close.

Through the crowd passed the 'Wolves, silent as ghosts, and it seemed the only sound in the square was that of the hooves of Captain Ewan's horse clattering upon the pave. And the Draega ears were pricked and their noses took in scents and their amber gazes swept to and fro, as if seeking threat.

They passed out of the market square and moved between the shops of crafters: a cobbler's, a goldsmithery, mills, lumberyards and carpentries, inns and hostelries, blacksmitheries and ironworks and armories, kilns, masonries, and more. And above many of the shops and businesses were the dwellings of the owners and workers. And the cobbled Post Road wended through this industry, spiraling up and around the mont, climbing toward the crest. Narrow alleyways shot off between hued buildings, and steep streets slashed across the road. And yet the Draega seemed alert and to note the way, as if storing the scents and sights for a quick exit from the city should there be need, though more likely they would plunge directly down the slope, as if the walls of the barriers were of no moment whatsoever to them. But for now they followed the well-marked Post Road and padded through clusters of shops and warehouses and work yards.

Again they came to a massive wall and followed the road as it curved alongside the bulwark. At last they reached a gate, and it, too, was guarded but open. Through it and up they went, now among colorful row houses with unexpected corners and stairs mounting up, and balconies and turrets, too, and all with colorful tiled roofs now covered with snow. And everywhere people stopped in the streets or leaned out of doorways and windows to watch the legendary Draega pass by.

Once more they trotted through a barway under a great rampart—the third wall—and again they fared among houses, now larger and statelier than those below, yet still close set.

At last they arrived at the fourth wall, the one encircling the Kingsgrounds. When they came to the portal through, the portcullis was down although the massive iron gates themselves were laid back against the great wall. And as the captain approached with his escort, gears rattled and ground and the barway was raised.

They came within the sector where sat the castle, the land consisting of broad gentle slopes terminated by craggy drops stepping down the tor sides until they fetched up against the massive encircling rampart they had just passed under. On these Kingsgrounds there were many groves, and pines growing in the crags, and several lone giants standing in the meadows, many trees bereft in winter dress. There, too, were several buildings, and the Draega could smell nearby stables. The citadel itself loomed starkly ahead, a stronghold of crenellated granite battlements towering starkly round blocky tall towers.

At the fore, the darker Silver Wolf turned to the larger companion at his side, and they seemed to confer, and all the 'Wolves broke away from Captain Ewan and headed toward one of the lone giant oaks...all but the dark Draega, that is, and he loped ahead and into the now open passageway leading through the final wall, that of the fortress-castle itself.

Captain Ewan rode through and into the forecourt to discover Dalavar waiting for him, but of the dark Silver Wolf, there was no sign.

AGAIN, DALAVAR CAME INTO the council chamber at Captain Ewan's side, but this time he was truly there. And after

Ewan gave his complete report, Cavin said, "Well done, Captain, and though you thought you had failed in your mission, clearly you did not."

"I lost too many good men," said Ewan.

"Yet you brought back a Mage," said Cavin.

"Hear, hear," called out several councilmen, and others added, "Indeed, well done."

Mayor Hein had resumed his seat, having regained what little composure he possessed, though he still seemed to be on the edge of bolting. And, without looking at Dalavar, Hein said, "But, Lord Cavin, can he do that which we ask?"

Lord Raden slammed a fist to the table and, invoking the name of a dead Dragon, bellowed, "Sleeth's teeth, Hein, would he be here if not?"

Hein blenched and dark-haired Aarnson suppressed a laugh, even as Cavin said, "My Lord Dalavar, we seek a rightful heir to the High King's throne, someone to displace the usurper who now foully occupies that seat."

Dalavar nodded and said, "I know."

Mustering what little courage he had, Hein again turned to Cavin. "But is this—this Wolfmage even a Seer? I've heard strange things of him."

With his grey eyes turning flinty hard, Dalavar whispered, "Doubt me not, Mayor Hein, for I am the child of Seylyn." And though he had spoken in but a murmur, Dalavar's voice seemed to fill the chamber with angry thunder, as if somehow a raging stroke of lightning had hammered down among all there.

Councilmen flinched and Hein gasped, his eyes wide in fear, for there were old wives' tales of a mad Seeress by that name who had lived among Elvenkind.

Hein would have fled, but all the strength in his legs had given out, and instead he sat paralyzed and mute.

Dalavar then turned to Lord Cavin and the others and smiled and gently said, "I will seek what you ask for."

Tension fell away, and men sighed in relief, and Lord Raden gruffly said, "Bully."

*   *   *

Sergeant deyer and corporal Lann stood guard outside the great doors of the feast hall, the ensconced lantern light behind them casting long shadows before them.

"Who?" asked Lann.

"They call him the Wolfmage," replied Deyer.

"Those big brutes out on the grounds are his?"

"They say he calls them his companions."

"And the Council opened the long-shut hall just so as he could go inside?"

Deyer nodded. "Someone said that he needed to be where King Valen spent time."

"What for?"

Deyer shrugged. "Who knows the ways of Mages? Not me, and that's for certain."

"Well, he took in one of the King's diadems. D'you suppose he's in there sitting on the throne, crowned?"

Deyer turned up his hands.

Inside the great chamber, Dalavar sat on the floor beside the throne. Rather than a crown, he held a narrow golden circlet in his lap, plain but for the incised griffin at the brow. There was no light in the hall, but the Wolfmage didn't need illumination to see the length of the room. Many tables and benches sat along the floor, and standards of nations limply hung from staffs jutting out from the walls: Rian, Wellen, Jord, and others, each and every realm under the High King's rule.

But Dalavar wasn't looking at the many flags, or at the banquet tables, or the columns and alcoves along the sides, or anything whatsoever in the chamber. Instead his eyes were closed, and he gripped the circlet and muttered an arcane word and his mind flew unto Pellar, unto Caer Pendwyr, unto the day of Valen's death.

He watched a lad come running bearing a bundle, and he saw what it contained.

But Dalavar slipped his mind back to where the lad had come from, and there he discovered catacombs. Down in the spire. Where two men replaced a sarcophagus lid and resealed the join with strips of lead.

Dalavar noted the name and dates carved into the lid, and he smiled, for they were ancient.

He followed the twisting stairwell down and down, until he came to a sealed door. But such was no impediment unto him, and he passed through and out upon the waters of the Avagon Sea.

Silverleaf! And a Human woman. Two children: toddlers. How clever, my friend.

Back along the corridors of time he flew, to earlier moments, where he verified the identity of one of the children: Reyer.

Then he sped forward, across the sea, following Silverleaf's journey; but when he came to Kell: *Blocked. Protected. And by the touch it seems to be that of Driu. Well and good.*

Yet in that same moment Dalavar detected another's touch, a malignant touch, and though no conjoining Sorcerer was there to aid Dalavar to blend his strength with that of Driu's, still he threw all his power into thwarting that of the malevolent being.

Necromancer

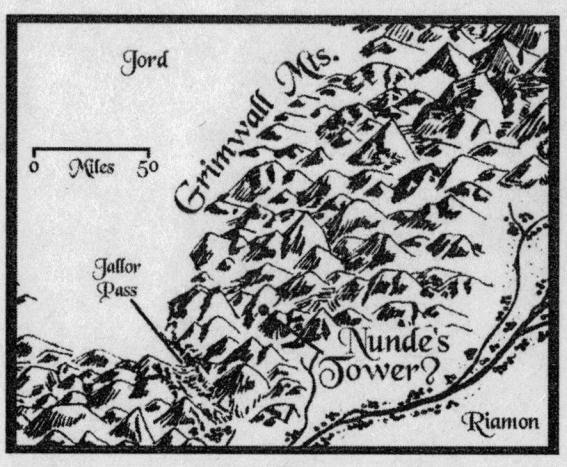

All things leave faint but lasting impressions upon the aethyr, and gaining access to these glimmers can lead toward good or ill. Among those of Magekind who touch upon those nebulous imprints are Seers and Mystics and Necromancers. The Seers generally use rune stones or cards or basins or some such a talisman as a focus to aid them to marshal this tenuous fifth element to perceive past events, or to peer into the uncertain future, or to discover the whereabouts of someone or something. Mystics, however, generally access these dim etchings through trances or dreams or other consciousness-altering means to sharpen their aim. Necromancers, though, use the dead to manipulate the aethyr to whatever ends they desire. And though it is believed by common folk and royals alike that Necromancers speak with the souls of the departed, most of Magekind conjecture that necromancy simply taps into the impressions left in the eternal flux. But Necromancers themselves are certain that they are speaking with the dead, and therefore they use corpses and bones and skulls and other grisly remains as a focus for their spells. Yet dealing with the dead often leads practitioners deeper and deeper into a shadow world, and for some it draws them well beyond the light and into dreadful darkness, a place where awful ambitions lead to appalling acts of murder and mutilation and torture. These monstrous deeds are usually carried out in secret.

Away from discovery.

Away from civilization.

In laboratories arcane.

In places of unspeakable horror . . .

. . . And in one of those hideous sanctums . . .

*   *   *

AMID A STENCH OF blood and feces, of bile and urine, and of rotting corpses, Nunde, his naked body covered with dark and arcane runes, with a rough stone knife ripped open the gut of the shrieking Drik upon the table before him. The screaming changed to a gurgle and dwindled to silence as the Drik thrashed about in its death throes, which swiftly became a feeble twitching, and then naught. All about the stone chamber, wall-shackled Drik and Ghok moaned in fear, for if Nunde did not gain whatever he sought from that victim, then one or more of them would be next. Ignoring their whimpering cries, Nunde shoved his black-nailed hands deeply into the abdominal cavity of the corpse and lifted the steaming intestines free and slithered them into a waiting vat; he would later slice the bowels open their entire length and examine them for signs and omens. But now, his dark eyes glittered in fervid anticipation of the pleasure to come—horribly profane in its manner of acquisition—and he trembled in eagerness, for he would flay the corpse and gain moments of ecstasy as he slowly sliced and peeled skin away from gristle and muscle and bone. He turned to the table littered with his terrible tools—knives, augers, screw-driven clamps, fire irons, rasps, pliers, meat hammers, saws, picks, and other such—all instruments of torture and slaughter and dismemberment. And amid the cloying miasma of death, he selected his keenest flaying knife from among the hideous assortment.

But even as he first set blade to flesh, the massive door directly across the room flew open.

"My master, my master—"

Infuriated at being interrupted, Nunde looked up from the disemboweled Drik to see Radok, glowing with glee, rush into the nekroseum.

But then Radok glanced at his unclothed master and his gaze shifted to the nearby dark cloak hanging from a peg. He began to stutter and back out from the chamber. "O-oh, M-Master, I did not mean to intrude upon y-your, your . . ."

Struggling for control, Nunde carefully set his flaying knife aside. "But you *did* mean to intrude, Radok. And now that you have, I would hear what is so important to come bursting in without my leave."

Peering at the floor at his own feet, Radok said, "The remains of deposed King Valen have arrived—skull and bones, nearly complete, but for the wear and weather."

Nunde took a deep, shuddering breath. This was even better.

Still . . .

Nunde's gaze strayed to the corpse on the table, and he took up his flaying knife and said, "Leave me, Radok. I will be with you anon."

A FEW TATTERED RAGS YET clung to Valen's remains, the bones picked nearly clean by gorcrows and beetles and blowfly larvae and other such feeders upon the dead, though here and there desiccated shreds of flesh still loosely clove. Wind and rain and the weather, along with the sun, had washed and scoured and bleached. With its jaw gaping wide as if in japery, the skull along with two vertebrae from the spine was separate from the rest of the frame. Most of the smaller bones were missing from the feet and hands, but in the main the remnants would serve Nunde well. It would have been somewhat better were the head yet attached and were there more flesh upon the bones, but, in all, these would be but minor impediments.

"Master, can we, will we—"

Nunde glanced up at the tall, thin, bald apprentice. "Yes, Radok, we can and will."

"And my role, Master . . . ?"

"Command more Chun—Drik and Ghok, but not Oghi— to the chamber. I will need much <essence> for the casting, and you will be the instrument to bring desperation and agony to the sacrifices prior to their demise."

"But as to the casting itself, Master . . ."

"You will witness all, and later, after I have recovered, you will perform the ritual yourself, while I provide the fruits of unendurable distress and unbearable pain and"— Nunde took a shuddering breath—"and brutish death." He paused to regain his composure and then added, "Perhaps we can glean even more from Valen to sow great dissention among those who opposed us in the war."

"ANOTHER," commanded Nunde, and Radok jerked one of the white-hot irons from the glowing brazier and jammed the fiery instrument into the flesh of a Drik. Meat sizzled, and the goblinlike being shrieked in anguish, and burning stench rose to join that of previous victims. Other shackled Drik and their larger Ghok kindred moaned in dread at the sight. And at the height of the tortured being's intolerable agony, Radok savagely hacked open the Drik's throat, and Nunde sucked up the magnified <lifeforce> released from the dying Chun.

Filled with ripped-away energy, Nunde turned toward the table holding the skeletal remains.

Nunde's brow was dark with concentration. *"Ákouse mé!"* he hissed, commanding the dead one to listen.

Clenching his long grasping fingers into clawed fists, Nunde imperiously demanded, *"Peísou moî!"* compelling the dead one to obey.

Sweat beaded on Nunde's forehead as he called out, *"Idoû toîs ophthalmoîs toîs toû nekroû!"* commanding the dead one to see what the dead can see—visions beyond time and space.

At a small gesture from his master, Radok stepped to the next shackled Chun and again applied a white-hot iron to the being's flesh and then slew the Drik, and channeled the heightened energy to Nunde.

Power flowed through Nunde's being, and perspiration runneled down his face, and he spoke the next decree, coercing the dead one to utter naught but truth.

Salt stung his eyes, yet Nunde did not wipe it away for to do so would loosen his control; instead, he chanted an unyielding demand for obedience.

Now Nunde gestured for Radok to feed him more <essence>, and so it was that another Chun died, this one a Ghok.

Renewed with power, still Nunde's body was slick with effort. Yet, with trembling hands, Nunde mandated, *"Eipè moî hó horáei!"* compelling the dead one to reveal what it sees or is asked.

Now Nunde's entire being shook, for such arcane workings called for energy beyond that which most could give, yet fed once again by Radok's doings, Nunde chanted, *"Aná kaí' lékse!"* demanding the corpse to rise and speak.

Sweat pouring down, muscles knotted, dark eyes bulging, jaws clenched, mind shrieking for relief, Nunde spoke the final command, *"Egó gár ho Núndos dè kèleuo sé!"* invoking the name of Nunde commanding the dead one.

As of a legion of voices in distant agony, the chamber filled with unnumbered whispering groans, the corpse stirring. Shackled Drik and Ghok quailed in fear. Momentarily, even Radok seemed to cower. Nunde, his ebon eyes burning with a ghastly light, called out, *"Aná kaí lékse; egó gár ho Núndos dè kèleuo sé!"*

One skeletal hand—missing two fingers—clutched a side of the table, and slowly, agonizingly, the other partial hand reached for the far edge. Dry bones cracked. Again there came the massed groans of a multitude, and haltingly, falteringly, the frame hauled itself upward, rib bones falling away in the effort. At last it levered itself to a sitting position, and slowly, vertebrae snapping, it turned what remained of its neck, as if it yet had a head mounted atop, as if it would stare at the one who summoned. Beside it, on the table, rested the skull, and Radok swiftly altered its position so that its empty eye sockets gazed upward at Nunde. And through the gaping jaw, and speaking as one voice, a hideous choir of whispers filled the chamber.

The remaining trapped Chun whimpered at the empty sound, and even though shackled they looked about as if for a place to flee. And the voices spoke in a language the Drik and Ghok did not comprehend, yet it was naught but Pellarian, the common tongue of Mithgar.

"Why . . . why . . . summoned me . . . summoned me . . . summoned me . . . summoned me . . . summoned . . . ?" echoed the ghastly chorus of mutterers, whispers hissing, different voices fading in and out, stronger weaker, rising falling, murmurs on top of murmurs, all asking . . . asking . . . asking. . . .

Nunde answered, threat in his voice, "Seek not to evade me, dead one. Instead, answer me this! What is the most important thing would you not have your enemies discover?"

Still the empty eye pits stared at Nunde, but his own ebon-eyed gaze did not waver. At last, mid the creaking and cracking of bone, and the thin sound of dry ligaments tearing, the skeletal remains turned its neck as if seeking to look at Caer Pendwyr. Radok quickly followed suit by repositioning the skull. A myriad whispering voices hissed answers, simultaneous agonizing echoes murmuring, rustling, mumbling, as if numberless mutterers crowded forward, all speaking, each striving to be heard, murmurers fading in and out, many voices talking at the same time through the same mouth, each whisperer describing a different event, a confusion of sissing babble.

...flay...Black Fortress...catacomb...burn...three... pierce...Queen Ammor...my father...orb...

Nunde carefully paid heed, and he heard several dominant whispers seeking voice over all, yet his mentor, Modru, had told him long past, "It is written that one should trust little the word of a dead soul, for unto the dead time has no meaning. They see the past and the present and the future all at once, all the same. Unless the Psukhómantis—the Necromancer—has the will and energy and endurance, the power to give focus, then the voices of the dead bring words of little use to the summoner, for they may bear a message meant for another entirely. You must listen carefully to find the truespeaker for you. If you can single out that voice, then words of value may come. There is this, however, some spirits seek to keep their secrets or to mislead, and for these you must concentrate, dominate, else what you learn will lead to disaster."

And so Nunde listened warily, trying to choose from among the countless agonized whispers, trying to pick out the voice of slain High King Valen who would answer his questions among the mutterings filling the chamber, among the murmurings, sissings, hissings.

And within the whispering babble, there seemed one reticent voice, as if someone was trying to withhold. And this uncommunicative voice was not easily distinguished from the multitude. Yet it seemed to belong to *these* remains.

At a gesture from Nunde, Radok seared and slew another of the Chun.

Filled with additional <lifeforce>, *"Peísou moî!"* demanded Nunde, adding in Common, "I compel you, Valen, to obey! Tell me: what is the most important thing you would not have your enemies know?"

Unable to resist, yet hiding its words behind the mutterings and whispering of others, the reluctant voice spoke.

But Nunde was a skilled Necromancer, and he winnowed out the unwilling words.

And then he laughed and said, "Oh, how delicious. The Usurper will be in my debt when I tell him this. But first ..." Nunde commanded the corpse to look toward Kell and name the place where the secret dwelt, yet Valen remained mum.

Again Nunde commanded, but Valen spoke not.

"More power, Radok," commanded Nunde, and Radok seared and slew another Ghok, and Nunde sucked up the added energy.

"Peísou moî, Valenos!"

Still, Valen remained silent.

Grinding his teeth, Nunde spat, "Someone blocking. Slay them all, Radok."

And Radok burned and slew and burned and slew until no Chun were left.

And bloated with enormous power, Nunde again commanded, *"Peísou moî, Valenos!"*

And among the many voices and sibilant whispers issuing forth from the skull, it seemed that Valen began to speak—

—yet of a sudden, all voices chopped to silence.

Frustration and puzzlement filled Nunde's features ... and then furious enlightenment, and he cursed, and his fist smashed down on the skull; the fragile weathered bones shattered, shards flying wide. As the skull fell to ruin, so too did the frame, and it clattered back unto the table, its bones scattering as well.

Now it was Radok who cursed, for with the remains broken and strewn, he would not have a chance to perform the rite. Yet why the master had destroyed all, the apprentice did not know. Only that his mentor was enraged. And Radok's own ire passed into dread, for he knew not what Nunde might do. Even so, and with his voice quavering, Radok asked, "Master, what passes?"

Nunde spun toward his flinching apprentice and snarled, "You fool, someone thwarted me. I know not who."

14

Rune Stones

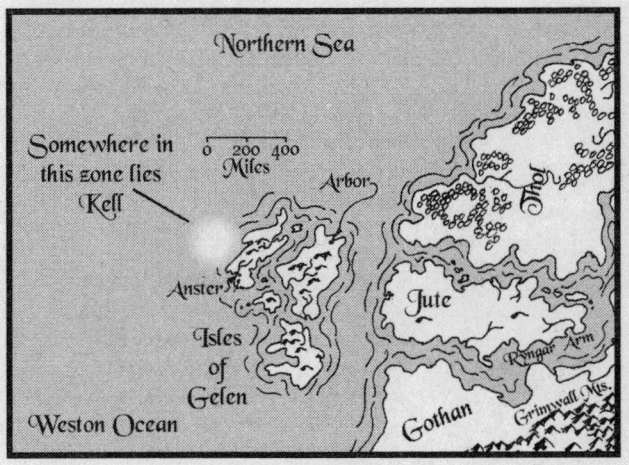

Among the many items Seers use to focus their castings are rune stones. There are many varieties of these arcane objects, and typically they come in sets of twenty-five stones. Yet some sets have more stones, and some fewer. But no matter the number in a given set, the individual stones in all sets have this in common: one side is blank, the other marked with a rune, but for one stone that is blank on both sides.

The stones themselves are usually small, generally no larger than a modest coin—a copper penny or such. And like a coin they are not very thick—perhaps double or triple that of a copper. And rune stones can be circular or rectangular or oblong, with smooth or rough edges and surfaces; all stones in a given set are nearly identical in size and shape, for the Seers would not have them identifiable by feel.

Typically, when reading what the day might bring, the Seer selects sight unseen a number of stones. The number selected depends upon what the Seer is trying to achieve. And, remaining sight unseen, the selected stones are then shaken together and cast before the Seer, to fall faceup or facedown. Whether faceup or facedown, the stones are read as they land, though facedown ones usually mean something that is unknown until revealed.

If some stones land faceup while others are facedown, whatever rune the facedown ones contain, typically they are in opposition to the faceup ones. If all stones land faceup, there is no conflict among the runes. If all stones land facedown, again there is no conflict among the runes. Whether a reading bodes good or ill simply depends upon which stones happen to be selected unseen, and the manner in which they fall. . . .

...And in a farmhouse on the island of Kell three stones lay on a table, one faceup, two facedown ...

"Quick," snapped Conal, holding Driu, "fetch brandy."

As Catlin rushed away, Gretta dipped a cloth in water and wrung it out.

Conal lifted the Seer in his arms and strode to a nearby room, where he gently laid her on a cot.

Gretta placed the cool cloth against Driu's brow.

Even as Catlin rushed in with the brandy and a small cup, Driu's eyelids fluttered.

Conal unstoppered the brandy and poured a jigger of the liquid into the cup. The aroma of peaches wafted up.

"Support her, my love," bade Conal, and Gretta raised Driu just enough for Conal to give her a sip of the bracing liquor.

Driu swallowed and then coughed and gasped.

"Too strong," muttered Catlin. "Should have cut it with water."

But then Driu's eyes flew open and she took the cup and gulped the remainder down and held the vessel out for more.

After a second tot, she sat up.

"What happened?" asked Conal.

"I am not at all certain," said Driu.

Gretta said, "Someone was searching for Rígán, for Reyer; at least that's what you said."

"Yes," replied Driu. "He was evil, abominable, and using <dark power>."

Catlin moaned, and raised trembling fingers to her mouth.

"I managed to hold him at bay," said Driu, "but then his power increased tenfold or more, and I could not stop him."

Conal growled. "You mean he knows were Reyer is?"

"Perhaps, though I think not."

"But you said—" began Gretta.

Yet Driu pushed out a hand to stop her. "Just before I swooned, someone else came and aided me. Whether he succeeded or failed, I know not, though I think he prevailed over the vile one." Driu paused for long moments, gathering her recollection. Finally she said, "Yes, I am certain he prevailed."

"Even so," said Conal, "we must remain on ward. I'll alert the men. The Dylvana, too."

As Conal left the room to speak with the farmhands, Gretta headed for the stables. There she gathered up Rígán and Alric and folded them into her embrace. When she finally released them, she stood and smiled down at the twain. Reassured that things were all right, they grinned up at her with gap-toothed smiles, for each had lost two front teeth, being at that age.

Back in the kitchen, Driu looked down at the three rune stones she had cast for the day. Her set consisted of twenty-seven rough rectangular black stones mined from the heart-stone of the dark mountain the Dwarves called Aggarath in the Quadran, one of the four mountains of Kraggen-cor, or Drimmen-deeve as it is known by the Elves. These rune stones had served her for many long years, for Magekind, with <rest> to restore their youth and vigor, could be as long lived as Elves.

But now Driu peered at the three dark stones lying where she had cast them. Among the meanings of the faceup one was Death or a Soul After Death.

Driu turned over one of the facedown stones: Aid, Strength. And in this case, Hidden Aid, Hidden Strength.

Driu turned over the second facedown stone: Protection. Defense. Both of those hidden as well.

Of the malignant presence, Driu had not a glimmer as to who it might have been. Yet of the one who had come to assist her, there was something familiar about his touch.

And then she smiled unto herself. *Ah. Of course. It would be him.*

Demonspawn

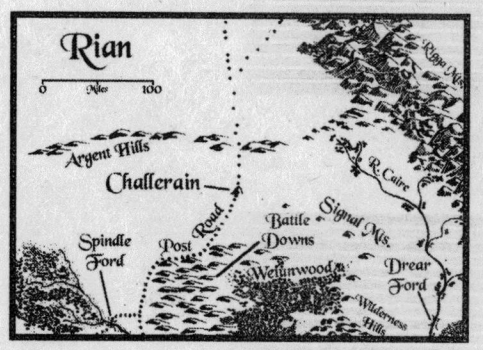

Scholars have long argued over the makeup of the Planes. Are there just three? More? Where resides the world of Vadaria, the world of Magekind? Is it on the High, Middle, or Low Plane? Is it on a Plane of its own? And what of Grygar, where Demons dwell. Or of the Dragon world of Kelgor. And are there many more worlds we know nothing of? Many more Planes? And if there are others, who rules them? Adon? Gyphon? Naxio? Garlon? Some other god?

This much is known: there are three principal Planes—High, Middle, and Low. Adon reigns over all of creation, and certainly the High Plane is His. Gyphon rules the Low. As to the Middle Plane, Adon holds sway, though Gyphon is not without followers. It is the Middle Plane wherein lies the determination of who commands all.

Gyphon is jealous of Adon's rule, and He contrives to have supreme authority. One of His means of trying to conquer Mithgar and thus assume dominance o'er all is to sow dissent and conflict upon the middle world, and He has many agents to do this: Black Mages, Demons, Fiends, others, along with Rûcks and Hlôks and Ogrus and other Foul Folk.

Much is known of Black Mages and Rûcks and Hlôks and Ogrus, and a bit about Demons—after all, a Gargon is of Demonkind—yet a Fiend is the least known of these fomenters of discord and struggle. Some common folk tell that a Fiend is likely the get of a true Demon upon a Spawn of Neddra—whether it mated with Rûck, Hlôk, Ghûl, or some other Foul One, that no one can say. But Scholars believe a Fiend is a commingling of Human, Demon, and Foul Folk blood. No matter the which of it, the creation of Fiends is an evildoing of Gyphon.

On a day long past, such a terrible creature came upon a

Seeress—Seylyn was her name—living alone in a tower in the Grimwall nigh the Elvenwood of Darda Galion. And he took her and spewed some of his vile seed in her, and then turned into a great Fell Beast and flew away upon leathery wings.

And Seylyn went mad.

Yet Lian Elves came upon her, and took her unto their care. But in spite of their healing arts, they could not cure her. Instead they sheltered and cared for her.

And from this horrible mating Seylyn grew large with child, and she bore twins—male and female—yet she never regained her sanity, and died of terror some ten years after, screaming in unassailable dread.

Among the Elves was a Silver Wolf named Greylight, and he "imprinted" both of the twins, and shape-shifters they became. Yet they could see the aethyr, for Seylyn's Mage blood was in them, and so they traveled to the college of Mages in the City of Kairn on the island of Rwn and there they learned many things, <seeing> not the least of them.

The boy remained on Rwn for many long years, growing into his fullness, and he learned even more. . . .

. . . And in the throne chamber at Challerain Keep, this Seer, this Mage, this shape-shifter, this Demonspawn . . .

Dalavar took a deep breath and opened his eyes. He stood, and, bearing the circlet, he went among the dust-laden tables and toward the far end, and, at a small gesture, the doors opened as he approached.

Sergeant Deyer and Corporal Lann turned in surprise, and they bowed to the Wolfmage as he passed.

"Ordinarily, i would at most tell you little of this, but—"

"What do you mean, you would not tell us?" growled Lord Raden. "If you have found an heir, we demand to know just who it is, and where."

"I will say who but not where," said Dalavar.

Hein turned to Lord Cavin. "How do we even know if he's telling the tru—?" Realizing what he was about to ask, the mayor clapped his mouth shut, and, cringing down in his seat, shot a terrified glance at Dalavar.

Lord Cavin took a deep breath and said, "Your reason, Lord Dalavar?"

Dalavar stood and said, "There are those who would slay him, if they but knew. Hence, the less who know, the safer he is, until his time has come."

"But surely we here in the council—" began Viscount Axton of Harth, but his gaze turned toward Mayor Hein. "Ah, I see what you mean."

Hein puffed up as if he had been insulted, and surely he had been. But he spoke not.

"This I will say," said Dalavar. "You asked for an heir, and there is one—someone you do not, did not expect. 'Tis Reyer, King Valen's own son."

A gasp went 'round the chamber, and Hein said, "But he is dead. Reyer is dead. He burned with the Queen."

"Not so. 'Twas a ruse," said Dalavar. "He was spirited away. Yet, heed, Arkov knows, if not now, he will know soon. This I have <seen>."

"Then we must bring him here, where he will be safe," said Raden.

"Nay," said Dalavar. " 'Tis better he stay hidden at a place where he is well protected. When his time comes, he will make himself known, and there will be a call to arms. Prepare for that day, my lords. Stand ready."

"But when?" asked Lord Aarnson.

"And how will we know him?" added Baron Fein.

"You will know him by his birthmark, and he—"

"Birthmark?" asked Mayor Hein.

"The claws of a griffin," said Raden. "Everyone knows that Reyer was born with the right forefoot of a griffin on his own right shoulder."

"The size of a large penny-coin," added Cavin.

"Well, I didn't know," huffed Hein.

"That doesn't surprise me," said Raden.

"Well, birthmarks can be falsified," said Aarnson.

Cavin nodded. "By a skilled needle hand with the right dye." He turned to Dalavar. "Is there aught else?"

"Aye," replied the Wolfmage. "In addition to the mark of a griffin claw, he will bear the King's seal, Valen's ring, and one who is unimpeachable will vouch for him. By those three things you will know him."

Dalavar stood, and Lord Cavin asked, "Who is it will vouch for him?"

"You already know this person, and you will know his word is true. I will say no more." With that, Dalavar strode from the chamber, leaving a babble behind.

Moments later, seven Silver Wolves streaked down the mountainside, ready to be quit of this overcrowded place and back into the clean woodland environs of faraway Darda Vrka.

Arden Vale

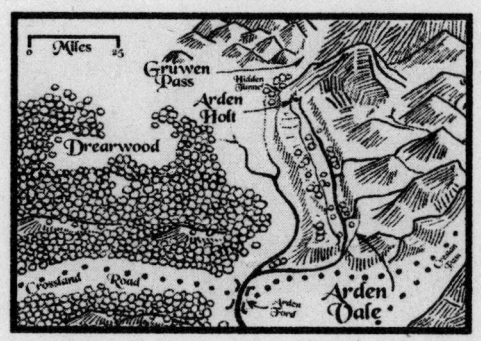

In the north of Rell, the land that once was called Lianion, lies a deep-cloven ravine—a gorge—running north and south along the western edge of the Grimwall. Through this chasm dashes the River Tumble, known as the Virfla by those who dwell in this crevasse. In the north, the rift fetches up against the mountains where a waterfall plummets into the gorge; the river then runs some twenty-five leagues or so to the south, where it exits from the chasm through a narrow cleft. Out from between close-set high canyon walls roars the River Tumble—the Virfla—to cascade over a high linn and plunge into a deep pool, then rushes to crash onward. Mist boils upward from this cataract—a white curtain to obscure the view into and out of the ravine. The falls themselves stretch the width of the narrow slot, and the way in is difficult to see. Yet behind the roaring plunge lies a hidden path, always guarded by those who live within. The mist from the cataract swirls about to dampen those who pass along the wet stone roadway and up through a hewn tunnel and out into the gorge beyond.

And just inside the gorge there towers an enormous tree hundreds of feet upward, as if to touch the sky itself. Its leaves are dusky, as if made of the stuff of twilight, for it is one of the Eld Trees, brought from Darda Galion and to this vale as a seedling millennia upon millennia past.

Beneath the sheltering branches of the behemoth lies the campsite where stays the Arden-ward. And beyond it and northward stretches out the pine-laden gorge, wending alongside the rushing waters of the River Tumble. High stone canyon walls rise in the distance to left and right, the sides of the gorge at times near, at other times two or three miles apart. Crags and crevices are seen here and there, though for the most part the lofty walls are sheer granite. In the places where the canyon narrows dramatically, hewn-rock pathways are carved partway up the side of the stone palisade that forms the west wall of the valley, for in these straits when the river o'erflows its banks, the vale below becomes a raging torrent, and so these routes high along the wall were made for safety's sake. And the gorge continues, at times through narrow, stone-bottomed slots and at other times across wide valley floors of gentle loam, with soft green galleries of shadowy pine forest spreading wide.

Near the north end lie fields and orchards and farmland and range, as well as thatched and whitewashed stone buildings: dwellings and storehouses and an armory and such, as well as a meeting hall.

'Tis the Elvenholt of Arden Vale....

...And at a small table just outside the doorway of one of those thatched-roofed, stone-sided, whitewashed dwellings...

"HE LIVES, Silverleaf, thou sayest? Reyer lives?"

"Aye."

"Then who is it went up in flames at the Queen's side?"

"Trenor, child of King Bain and Queen Sarai."

"Ah. Trenor. Died in the plague."

"Aye, Riatha. That's the one."

"Clever. Was Arkov deceived?"

"So it seems."

Golden-haired and slender, Riatha turned her gaze upon Vanidar Silverleaf, her eyes such a pale grey as to seem almost silver. "Well, then, since Reyer lives, battle will surely come; what said the gathering at Darda Galion? Do we side with Reyer?"

Silverleaf shook his head. "Thou knowest we gave up rights of succession long past, after the Time of Madness."

Riatha nodded, for Vanidar spoke of the days when Elvenkind was yet young, and many were the struggles over power and dominance and the gathering of material things. Endless Wars were fought, and Elves were slain, and long and vicious feuds occupied many in the bitter struggles to rule as Coron—as King—over all of Elvenkind. Adonar itself became a battleground, yet Adon let no gods interfere, for He knew that His creations would ultimately come to their senses. And so they did, after millennia of destruction, for Elves are ageless, and many achieved dominance. And when it became apparent to those who potentially can live forever, they found attaining such ambitions were pointless, where the sweet taste of victory becomes naught but ashes in one's mouth, for, strife led to strife, endlessly. One of Elvenkind finally realized the folly of dominion, for when one controls and subjugates, then free will and freedom of choice and self-determination are lost. And so, he founded a movement of change simply by saying, "Let it begin with me."

Scholars do not know just how long it took for the movement to become the creed of Elves—one millennium, two millennia, ten or more—but eventually Elvenkind turned sane, and the Time of Madness ended.

Elves then became warders of life and the living, protectors of the wild, and keepers of the forests and fields. And they sought after knowledge through art and crafting and long study of nature and its gifts, and they grew with the learning. Finally Adon permitted Elves to come unto Mithgar, for as long as they were mad, they would have done dreadful things to this wild and savage world, but in their sanity, they would cherish it instead.

Elvenkind yet engages in wars, but only if freedom and free will and self-determination are threatened. Hence, they consider Gyphon the greatest evil, and they fought bravely upon the side of the allies against Modru in the Great War. And ofttimes they take up arms when small pockets of the living are endangered with slavery or extinction.

As to the recent events concerning the High King, all the past Corons and Keepers and representatives of the Guardians had gathered in Darda Galion to determine what to do.

Vanidar Silverleaf, a Guardian, was one of the past Corons, and he had heeded the call.

Riatha refreshed Vanidar's goblet with pale white wine. "Well, Silverleaf, what then was decided?"

Vanidar took a sip, and then said, "Each may follow his or her own conscience, to wage war on the side of Reyer, if he lives, or with a rightful successor if not, or to stand aloof from this matter of Human succession to the crown."

"I see," said Riatha. "Fight or no, no matter the which of it, in the course of seasons it will eventually pass."

Silverleaf nodded, yet added, "But there is this: Arkov has emissaries from Chabba and Sarain and Hurn in his court, and there are Chabbains now on the soil of Pellar, there nigh the site where Gleeds once stood."

"Worshippers of Gyphon, all," said Riatha.

"Aye. And though in the whole of things those in the High King's lands are not many, still . . ."

They sat for long moments in silence, and only the gurgle of the Virfla and the songs of birds broke the stillness of the surround.

Finally, Riatha said, "For me, unless the followers of Gyphon become a factor, I believe 'tis a matter for the Humans to settle among themselves. What dost thou intend, my friend?"

Silverleaf's infectious grin brightened his face. "Me? I think I will unlimber my bow and wait for the announcement that Reyer is alive."

Ruefully, yet smiling, Riatha shook her head. "Thou and Aravan: ever the ones for adventure, neh?"

Silverleaf laughed, then looked about. "Speaking of Aravan, where has that rascal gotten to?"

Riatha sighed. "He has news of a yellow-eyed man in Thyra."

Silverleaf's face now fell glum. "I see. He is ever after Galarun's killer."

Riatha nodded and added, "And the Silver Sword."

Kraggen-cor

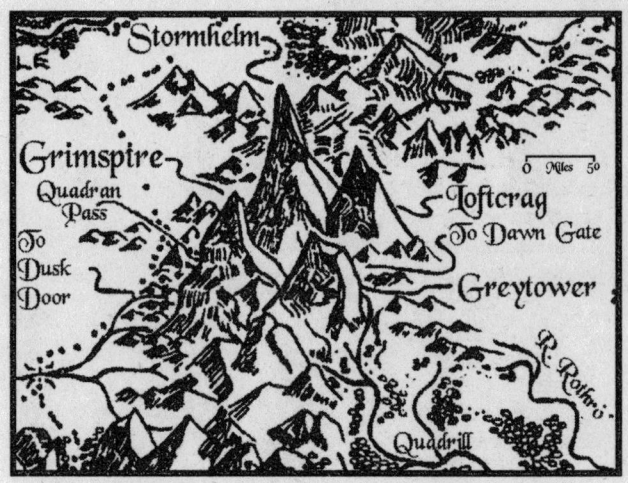

Known as Drimmen-deeve by the Elves and as the Black Hole by Men, under the four mountains known as the Quadran the mighty Dwarvenholt of Kraggen-cor is delved. There, among other ores, precious starsilver is mined, called silveron by Men. Higher prized than jewels, no metal is more dear on Mithgar, and many seek the wealth of it, and in very few places on this world is it found.

Yet starsilver and the things that can be made of it are not the only goods produced in this holt, for the Dwarves—the Châkka—are quite clever with their crafts, and the variety of items fashioned therein abound.

As to Kraggen-cor itself, its full extent none know, not even those who live there, for the Quadran is riddled with natural caverns carved by water throughout countless years. Why, Durek himself was lost within the vastness of these endless corridors, until, that is, he was rescued by one of the Utruni—giants who can part stone with their fingers, and seal it behind seamlessly.

After his rescue, Durek led his line of Châkka from the Isles of Gelen to this newly discovered place, and they set about smoothing the tunnels into hallways and shaping chambers to live within. In general they enhanced the stone, even though they cut and hammered and drilled and carved and clove to do so.

It became the greatest Châkkaholt on Mithgar, and a place of wide renown.

To all outsiders there are two established ways into Kraggen-cor—the Dawn Gate, named the Daûn Gate by the Châkka, and the Dusk Door, called the Dusken Door by the Dwarves—and these two entrances lie on opposite sides of the Grimwall, for that's where the Quadran sits, with the nation of Rell to the west, and the wold above Darda Galion to the east. These two entrances are some forty-six miles apart by the most direct route within, and perhaps forty miles apart as a crow might fly, were it able. And the way between the Door and the Gate has been a trade road for millennia, and the Dwarves charge high tolls for its use. Yet it provides a way through the mountains when winter grips the land, and the passes are blocked by snow.

But other than these two known entrances, 'tis rumored there are many secret ways into Kraggen-cor, Dwarven delved and hidden. True or not, only one secret way—the High Gate—will become known to outsiders millennia or so from now, for it will be mentioned in subsequent histories, after the War of Kraggen-cor. But that time was yet to come, and this time was now.

And some four years after the overthrow of High King Valen, at each of the entrances into Kraggen-cor, visiting Châkka arrived, to be led through the corridors to the chambers within....

...And when all had come and were well quartered and rested and fed, in one of those chambers ...

THE DELFLORDS HAD GATHERED.

They stood about a large stone table as if waiting.

Just then leaving were lithe creatures dressed head to foot in swirling veils, their countenances and forms unseen. These were Châkia—trothmates, mothers, healers, precious females—who had sung welcoming greetings to the Châkka lords and had asked Adon's daughter Elwydd for Her blessings and Her wise guidance to be present during these proceedings.

The Châkka did not watch the Châkia depart, for to do so would be rude beyond measure.

Instead, the DelfLords waited in silence.

They were a varied lot, these eight, though they did have much in common: all stood somewhere between four foot four and four foot eight; all wore beards braided in twain; all were sturdily built and broad shouldered, a span nearly half again as wide as those of Men; and all were armed and armored, for this was a council of war.

Yet they spoke not or looked at one another and stood with eyes downcast.

And some moments later, a distant chime rang.

DelfLord Bekk of Kraggen-cor cleared his throat and raised his gaze from the table and glanced 'round at the gathering.

The other DelfLords also looked up, and at a word from Bekk, they placed maces and axes and morning stars before them and took their seats. Yet Bekk, as host, remained standing, his own double-bitted axe in hand.

In a voice sounding much like gravel sliding from a hod, Bekk said, "Normally, we do not interfere in the squabbles of Men unless it somehow threatens us. Yet this time might be different, hence we are gathered to decide whether to go to war against Arkov when the time comes."

Bekk then laid his axe to the table and released his grip and took a seat.

The DelfLord of Skyloft reached forth a hand and gripped the helve of his mace.

Bekk nodded and said, "Borri."

The ginger-haired and youthful Borri said, "Say what this Elf told you."

Bekk said, "Silverleaf is his name—Vanidar in the Elven tongue—and long has he been Châk-Sol . . . from well before the times of any of us, perhaps even back unto the days of Durek himself."

A murmur rustled 'round the table at Bekk's words, for rarely did an outsider become Châk-Sol—Dwarf Friend. And yet, given that Silverleaf had been Châk-Sol since the time of Durek, he had been a Dwarf Friend for thousands of years.

Bekk let the whispers settle and then continued. "Silverleaf says that there is a rightful heir to Valen's throne, and in the days to come, he will make himself known."

Many reached for the helves of their weapons but white-haired Velk, DelfLord of Blueholt, was the first to speak. "Just as we would not welcome Men interfering in Châkka affairs, I ask: why should this concern us?"

"Because it involves the High King, to whom we swear

fealty, and Arkov is a usurper," gritted Kerek, DelfLord of Kachar, the redheaded grandson of Baran, brother of Thork Dragonslayer. "And this usurper, this *Arkov,* is of the line of Borik the Oathbreaker, and has no honor whatsoever, and I will not swear allegiance to him."

"Even so," replied Velk, "even though we do not swear fealty, this is a matter for Humans, I would think."

All eyes turned to Bekk, but it was Regga of Redholt who said, "Arkov has let the Chabbains take land in Pellar."

Oaths and shouts and questions erupted: *Kruk! What? Chabbains on the High King's soil?*

Bekk let the uproar subside and then nodded to Regga to continue. And with his dark eyes glittering in fury, Regga said, "Arkov let these worshippers of Gyphon have the site where the battle of Gleeds took place. They are driving crofters out. Many of the dispossessed have passed by the Red Hills on their way to refuge elsewhere."

"Do not the Pellarians rise up?" asked fair-haired Degan of Blackstone.

"Nay," said Regga, shaking his head. "They are scattered and unorganized, and should they gather they would be crushed by Arkov's armies, which are swollen in ranks by mercenaries from Alban and Hurn and Sarain."

"Kruk!" cursed Vrenn, DelfLord of the Quartzen Caves. He made a fist in his mailed glove and stared at it. "Mercenaries from Sarain? Fists of Rakka?"

"Aye," said Regga.

"Rakka is but another name for Gyphon," said Vrenn. "And these Fists: I thought we destroyed them all in the War of the Ban."

Bekk shook his head. "They are like a foul weed, a thistle of thorns, and the moment you think them gone, they spring up elsewhere. This time in Arkov's ranks."

"Next we know, Arkov will enlist Modru to his side," said young Borri.

They sat in silence for long moments, and finally white-haired Velk said, "What of this rightful heir? Who is it and when will he come?"

"Silverleaf did not say," replied Bekk. "This I believe, however: the heir is not yet of an age to rally Men to his side."

"I do know the Northern Alliance stands ready," said Degan, whose Châkkaholt—Blackstone—lay in the Rigga Mountains along the borders of Rian not far from Mont Challerain.

"Have they assembled an army?" asked Belek, DelfLord of Mineholt North in the Rimmen Mountains of Riamon.

"Nay," replied Degan, "yet my emissary at Challerain Keep tells me that all nations north and west of the Grimwalls have pledged to support this unknown heir."

"Pah! Unlike we Châkka, pledges are easily made by Men and just as easily broken," said Regga.

But Degan turned to Velk. "What says your emissary in the royal halls of Gelen?"

Velk shrugged and said, "The king of the Isles of Gelen, too, has pledged support to the Alliance at Challerain. Yet, it is as Regga says, Men easily break the pledges they make."

"What of the Elves?" asked Vrenn, turning to Bekk. "Where do they stand in this?"

The DelfLord of Kraggen-cor sighed and said, "The Council of Corons has decided to remain neutral. They do, however, give permission for any Elf desiring to do so to stand with the Northern Alliance against Usurper Arkov."

"Elves, pah!" spat Regga. "Pussyfoots all."

"Nay," said Bekk. "None would I call pussyfoots. Yet in this matter, Silverleaf said that in the long march of time successions mean little to Elvenkind. Hence, for the most part they take but vague interest in who rules among Men and who does not."

Young Borri said, "Even though worshippers of Gyphon despoil the soil of the High King's realm? Still the Elves will not engage?"

"Some will," said Bekk. "Others, not. The Council of Corons has chosen to let each Elf decide for himself."

"Faugh!" said Regga, disgust in his voice. "And they name themselves Guardians."

*   *   *

OVER THE NEXT THREE days the Council of DelfLords met, and Old Velk did point out that the Châkkaholts were far-flung from one another, and should they decide to march to war, it would take considerable time to assemble. But Regga said, once this rightful heir had revealed himself, should war be in the offing, they could come together as swiftly as the nations of the Northern Alliance.

But the issue at hand was not how quickly they could gather, but rather whether to gather at all. Unlike Humans, Châkka did not reproduce swiftly, and they had not yet fully recovered from their losses in the Great War of the Ban, even though that had occurred nearly two millennia agone. Nevertheless, they had ever marched to war on the side of right, and this would be no different, or so Regga claimed.

In the end they decided that if the worshippers of Gyphon became a greater threat, then they would throw in their lot with the Northern Alliance. But if Gyphon's followers did not become a significant factor, then each Châk could decide for himself. It was a position that Regga and Belek and Vrenn and Kerek disagreed with, saying that it was no better than what the pussyfooting Elves had settled on. Yet in the end they yielded to the other four, for, as Bekk said, much could change between now and the time the rightful heir revealed himself.

On the following day, after being sung farewell at meeting's close by the veiled Châkia, the DelfLords departed for their separate holts.

All gathered at the Daûn Gate, through which Vrenn, Belek, Regga, and Kerek went:

Vrenn to the gold-rich Quartzen Caves in Riamon.

Belek to Mineholt North and its ores of copper, in Riamon as well.

Regga to the armories of iron-laden Redholt in the Red Hills lying along the border of Jugo to the south and the abandoned land of Ellor—sometimes called Valon—to the north.

And Kerek to Kachar in the Grimwalls between Aven to

the south and Jord to the north, there where a mother lode of zinc lay.

After those four and their entourages had ridden eastward down the slope of Baralan, Bekk and the others headed for the Dusken Door, a two-day journey westward along the trade road linking the two entrances.

When they arrived, and after spending the night, out through the Dusken Door went Young Borri, Old Velk, and Degan, and their bands:

Young Borri to the silver mines of Skyloft, lying in the Sky Mountains between Basq and Gothon.

Old Velk to Blueholt in the Blue Hills of the North Isle of Gelen, where tin lay rich.

And Degan to jewel-laden Blackstone, the holt recovered at last from Sleeth the Orm by Foul Elgo, stealer of treasure, and his warband of thieves. With his thievery and his insults it was Elgo who started the war between the Châkka of Kachar and the Vanadurin of Jord, a war that ended in disaster for both.

As these three DelfLords and their accompanying warbands fared down Ragad Vale, setting out on the long treks to their separate holts, Bekk and his own entourage turned eastward to follow the hallways back.

THEY SPENT THE NIGHT in a small chamber some twenty-one miles along the northeastward corridors from the Dusken Door, but none rested well. Even the ponies seemed unsettled.

"I am uneasy in this part of my realm," said the DelfLord to his armsmaster, Dekon.

Dekon nodded and said, "They say that ever since the Great War of the Ban, something of dread haunts these halls nigh. Yet none can say what it might be."

"It is as if some horror died nearby and its ghost yet lingers," said Ferek, the keeper of ponies.

"Mayhap it is something that dwells deep under, something disturbed by our delvings," said Ranak, one of the warriors in accompaniment.

"Pah!" snorted Bekk. "Legends and fables. I deem it but a damp drift of air or an odd smell, or even a slight venting of a strange gas that causes such disquiet. Let us press on."

And they took the rightmost fork of the four corridors before them and left the small chamber behind, all in the band dismissive of the subtle warning of a dire terror that would one day be loosed in these very halls.

Emissary

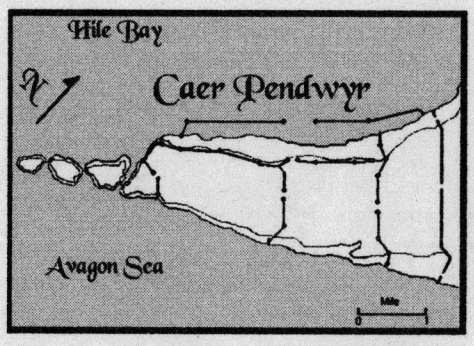

The realm of Chabba lies along the southeastern shores of the Avagon Sea. Dwellers in that land are dusky-skinned, though not as dark as those who live on the plains and in the jungles far south of the Karoo. The Chabbains are a nation of traders, with their long trains of camels plying ancient roads leading south and west and east, faring as far toward the sunset as the land of Hyree, as far below the midline as the jungle land of Tchanga, and as far toward the sunrise as Jinga on the waters of the Yellow Sea. This latter trade route is the longest of all and quite valuable and coveted. It is made even longer by the mighty Jangdi Mountains, which stand in the way of a direct easterly road to Jinga; and so the Chabbains first fare northward, through Sarain and Hurn and Alban and Aralan to come to the Grey Mountains, where they then turn eastward and go far overland to reach the silks and porcelains and jades of that distant realm. Yet the Northern nations also trade with Jinga, mostly by sea, but at times by overland treks. And much of the route the Chabbains follow flows through the High King's domain. And when Rolun became High King, Chabba and Pellar did dispute ownership of this trade route with one another, and the Askars of Chabba crossed the Avagon Sea in ships and burnt the young city of Gleeds to the ground, and many an innocent died: women, children, babes, oldsters. Yet High King Rolun's army did entrap the invaders and, but for a niggling few, slew them one and all, even though many had surrendered. Not only because of that act of retribution, but also because of other deeds in other wars, ever did and do the Chabbains clutch hatred unto their breasts and swear to avenge those who are so slaughtered, be it soon or late. To not take such oaths is unthinkable, for they venerate the ghosts of their kindred and carry hatreds on, believing that all dark deeds need redress, whether done of recent or of long past. Were the living to forget their duty, the ghosts of those so slain would find no rest, no solace, and their wailing would inflict misery upon any kindred yet alive.

And the deeds of the Askars and of Rolun millennia ago generate hostility between the nations still.

Yet in the third year of the Usurper's reign, in order to gain the allies to buttress his own forces, Arkov was forced to halve the levy upon the Chabbains for use of the trade route to Jinga, and he also had to allow the Chabbains to occupy the site of the massacre of their army of Askars who had invaded Pellar long past. And in return Arkov gained the promise of a sizable force of Askars to aid in the overthrow of the Northern Alliance.

And as new-made allies, the Chabbains sent ambassadors and emissaries to the court in Caer Pendwyr....

...And some two years later on a day in the sixth year of Arkov's reign, from a distant tower in the Grimwalls far north, a dark bird flew to one of these emissaries....

"My lord," whispered Counselor Baloff, "Ambassador Mosaam bin Abu seeks a private audience. He says he has news of critical import."

Arkov looked up from the map he and the others studied. "Critical?"

"Yes, sire. He specifically said critical."

"What does that dark bastard want now? Less tolls? More land?"

"He does not say, my lord, only that it is a matter of import."

Growling, Arkov looked 'round the table at his commanders. "Wait here. I shall deal with this Chabbain and then return. In the meanwhile, come up with a plan to discover those who are behind these village uprisings. We'll make an example of them and put this foolish unrest to bed."

Arkov turned to his counselor and said, "Where did you put Abu?"

"In the blue chamber, my lord," said Baloff, gesturing the way to the door. As they strode beyond hearing, in a low voice he added, "I thought you would wish for me to listen to what he has to say."

"Indeed, Baloff. Observe and make a written record."

"Aye, sire."

They passed through several halls, with sentries at every turn, and finally they came to a warded door.

Arkov stepped to the side of the portal and commanded one of the guards: "Announce me."

Moments later Arkov swept into the chamber, and a tall dark Chabbain turned from a sideboard and bowed, though not half as deeply as Arkov would have liked.

"Ambassador Abu," said Arkov.

"Sire," replied the man.

He was dressed in a yellow robe, the bright color making his dusky skin seem even darker. He wore a like-colored turban, which made him appear still taller than his considerable height. He had a hawklike nose and his eyes were such a dark brown to be almost black. His fingers were long and slender, and he held a cup in his right hand.

"My lord," he said, his voice a silky baritone, "someday I will have to teach your staff how to make a better brew of *khawi*."

"Psht!" Arkov's face twisted in revulsion as he moved to the sideboard. "Vile liquid, that swill. No matter what one does with it, I deem it still would be undrinkable." He poured himself a dollop of golden brandy, and then gestured at two leather chairs angled toward one another, a small low table between.

As they took their seats, Arkov glanced at a wall-hung tapestry depicting distant ships on a storm-tossed cobalt sea, dark clouds swirling above, a driving rain hammering down. On the opposite wall hung another tapestry, this one showing a deep blue indigo sea, its waters calm, its ships at sail, a cerulean sky above.

A faint smile twitched upon Mosaam's dark face, for surely beyond one or the other of the varicolored designs, or perhaps both, someone watched through a spy hole.

Arkov took a sip of his brandy. "What is it this time, Abu?"

The ambassador did not correct Arkov. After all, the one who entitled himself "High King" was an ignorant infidel, hence would not know that Abu was Mosaam's father's name.

Stupid Garian.

Mosaam set the *khawi* aside, the drink so poorly brewed that it was nearly unpalatable. He steepled his fingers and said, "I believe what I have to tell you is worth reducing our trade toll in half again."

Arkov nearly choked on his brandy. "What? What could be so important that I would— You've already accepted our bargain, Abu. And speaking of bargains, where are the main of your Askars, your jemedars, your commanders? We need to march on those northern rebels."

"My lord, we are still gathering the armies we promised. Harvests and such interfere. Besides, you said they would not be essential until you quelled the unrest that—"

"Yes, yes, Abu," snapped Arkov. "I know what I said. I know our agreement. But to halve the tolls once more is unthinkable."

"But this information, my lord, is a threat to your very rule. It is something you must deal with before—"

"Don't tell me what I have to deal with. Just spit out what you've come to say, and then it is I who will decide."

Mosaam raised his hands in surrender and smiled, his teeth pearl-white against his dusky face. "My lord, I will tell you the news. Yet I will withhold the proof and a location. And should you decide it worthwhile, I will give you the proof, but only if I have your word that you will halve the toll after you see for yourself. Then I will give you the location."

"I should have you murdered right now, Abu."

"Then you would lose any hope of a Chabbain army, and I suspect that means in the long run you would lose your throne."

"Dark bastard!"

Mosaam merely smiled.

Arkov stormed to the sideboard and served himself a large spill of brandy. He gulped it down and then poured another. He returned to his chair and sat.

"Tell me and we shall see."

"You accept my terms?"

Grinding his teeth, Arkov gritted, "Aye. But only if what you say is worth what you ask."

Mosaam nodded, all the while wondering if Arkov would keep his word. Yet if he did not, then he would lose the support of the Chabbains.

As if to impart secret knowledge, the ambassador leaned toward the Garian, knowing that he would bend forward to hear. Then, of course, Arkov would have to look up at the taller ambassador. It pleased Mosaam when, like an unwilling puppet, Arkov followed suit, glancing up like a supplicant to receive a blessing or alms. Mosaam then lowered his voice and said, "My lord, King Valen's child, Prince Reyer, Valen's heir, is alive."

"Pah!" snorted Arkov, leaning back, now looking down upon the ambassador. "I saw Reyer's corpse myself, lying on the pyre of his mother. The child is naught but ashes."

"No, my lord. What you saw was not Reyer. My master, my *m'alim*, himself knows what passed, and for this news he will one day ask for a boon, and I would not gainsay him, were I you."

"Your master? King Fadal? For misinformation?"

"Not King Fadal, my lord. The *m'alik* and I both answer to one higher."

"Gyphon? Ha! He is beyond the Planes. Trapped in the Abyss. Nay, Abu. I will not fall for this scheme of yours."

"'Tis no scheme, my lord. Were I to give you proof, would you then halve the toll as well as owe my master a service?"

Arkov looked at the ambassador, and paused. "Luba's teats, but you're serious."

"Indeed, my lord, for this is serious business."

"Who is this master of yours?"

"He is a Mage, my lord. As to his name, I know it not, yet I do know his ... <mark>."

Arkov stood and went to the sideboard and poured himself another brandy. Then he turned and said, "All right, Abu. You give me the proof, and I will honor your wishes, but only if you also give me the location as to where this so-called Prince Reyer can be found. —But mind you, if what you tell me turns out false and this pretender is not who you say, then, for the trouble you put me to, tolls will not be reduced but doubled instead. Not only that, but you will still provide the force of Askars I desire, and I will owe your Mage naught. Agreed?"

Without hesitation, Mosaam inclined his head. "Agreed."

"Then the proof, Abu. The proof."

"My lord, it lies in the catacombs below."

Arkov was taken aback, for he knew of no catacombs below the castle. Swiftly recovering, he said, "Go on."

Smiling to himself, Mosaam continued, "There you will find an empty sarcophagus, the lead seal removed and then replaced. The name on the tomb is Prince Trenor, child of King Bain and Queen Sarai. It was Trenor's corpse you saw upon the burning pyre, while Reyer himself was whisked away to safety."

"So you say," declared Arkov.

"'Tis not I who tell you this, but my master instead."

"A Mage, you claim," said Arkov.

"A most powerful one, my lord."

"Even so, this 'Reyer' could be an imposter," said Arkov.

"Not so," said Mosaam.

"Imposter or no, give me the location and I will see to him."

"The location of Prince Reyer will be forthcoming when you have halved the toll."

Growling, Arkov downed his brandy and said, "First I will see to this tomb of yours."

"The island of kell, that's all we know?" asked Baloff.

"That's what he said," snapped Arkov.

"My lord, that narrows it but little. And what if this is a trick? What if Mosaam somehow spirited away the corpse of the one buried in the sarcophagus? Perhaps he has agents within the palace. Perhaps he found a way to reach the catacombs from the outside. What if—?"

"Enough, Baloff! Think you that I have not considered all those things you ask and more? The proof one way or another will come on the Island of Kell."

"And should we find him, what proof?"

"Mosaam says he has the griffin claw birthmark and bears the King's seal."

"Even so, who is to say it is truly Prince Reyer? Rings can be forged and birthmarks falsified."

"Reyer or not, the seal alone will convince enough fools that Valen's line yet survives. And the birthmark will cinch it for them."

Baloff shook his head. "I think this but a ruse to halve the tolls. This so-called prince might be nothing more than Mosaam's plant, his dupe. And should we lose the war, then Mosaam will be the power behind the—"

"Silence, fool!" raged Arkov. "By damn, we will *not* lose the war!"

"Yes, my lord," quavered Baloff, shrinking back.

The counselor waited until Arkov's seething abated. Finally, Baloff said, "Indeed, we will not lose the war, yet this trumped-up Prince Reyer still could be a sham."

Arkov grunted and nodded. "Nevertheless, send assassins."

"The last time we sent assassins anywhere, my lord, they vanished."

"Deserters, I would think," said Arkov.

"If these vanish, then what, my lord?"

"Then we will have Abu arrange for assassins from the Red City."

"Nizari," murmured Baloff.

"You disapprove?"

Baloff sighed, then said, "My lord, at every turn it seems we get deeper and deeper into the debt of these men of the South. Their memories are long, sire, and with a Chabbain army upon our shores, who is to say whether or no they plot some vengeance for Rolun's doings as well as revenge for the demise of their men during the War of the Ban?"

"Without them, I think I cannot defeat the Northern Alliance, especially should the current unrest turn into a full revolt. So I need the Chabbains and our other allies from the South. —Or would you have me simply abdicate?"

"No, sire. It's just . . ." Baloff's words fell to a whisper and then naught.

"Besides," said Arkov, "should the Chabbains attempt to carry out some violent plan of retribution, we control the food supply. Our sources in the East have provided us the means to deal with Askars in that event, yes?"

"They have, my lord. Three days after ingestion, the entire Chabbain army will be no more."

"Well, then, fear not these necessary but temporary southern catspaws," said Arkov. "Once we dispose of this pretender, and settle the growing unrest, and put down the Northern rebels, then we will rescind our treaties with those dark bastards and either throw them out of our land, or bury them under it."

"As you will, my lord," said Baloff. Then he glanced down at the map depicting the Isles of Gelen and touched the area in which Kell was said to lie. "As to this Prince Reyer, what would you have me do?"

"Given a choice, I would invade the isle and kill every person there, but I am not yet ready to take on the Northern Alliance. Instead, arrange for men of stealth and guile to search out the one who claims to be Valen's child. I would have this so-called 'rightful heir' dead and the seal recovered. The sooner the better."

"As you will, my lord," said Baloff. "I shall form a death squad."

"No, send not a squad, Baloff. Individuals instead. Disguised as ordinary traders or tutors or some such. Choose from among our better spies. And they do not all have to be men, for to do in the pretender, perhaps a woman's gentle hand is better suited to the task."

Sjøen

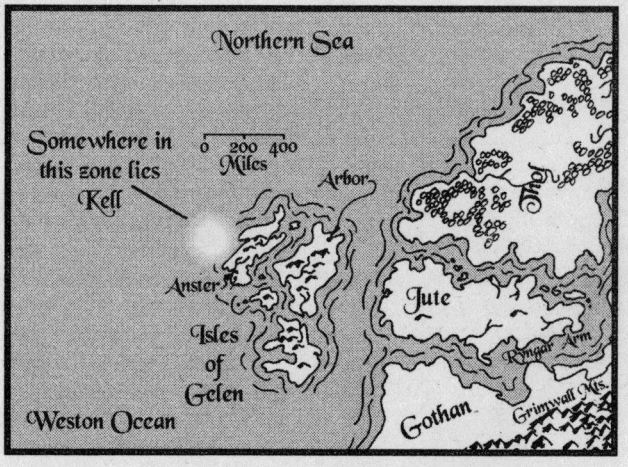

In the north of Mithgar along the waters of the Boreal Sea lies a coastal nation known as Fjordland. With its narrow, steep-sloped, ocean-mouthed ravines filled with deep and dark and chill waters along which the towns and villages lie, its very name describes this land. The inhabitants—strong and yellow-haired men; buxom, yellow-haired women—are fishermen and traders and sea merchants and craftsmen of various stripe as well as fierce mercenaries, and in times past were raiders who preyed upon the innocent. Yet since the days of Egil One-Eye, their raiding days dwindled as more and more of the men came to realize the harm they did to the blameless as they took from them that which their own labor fashioned not. Even so, their hawklike ways remained, and many became warriors for hire in causes their jarls deemed just. Still others sailed forth to find fabled lost riches in distant lands, as did Arik and others who accompanied Elgo of Jord and his men on their mission to slay the Dragon Sleeth and claim his treasured hoard.

And these ventures were made in Dragonships, long and slender and open-hulled, clinker-built to give them flexibility and nimbleness and speed as they clove through distant seas.

Yet they were not the only realm that plied the waters in such craft, for their ancient enemies, the men of Jute, also sailed the oceans in Dragonships, but they had not given up their plundering ways, especially when it came to raiding Fjordlander settlements.

And retaliation begat retaliation . . . over and again throughout time.

And on a day long past, three ships bearing Fjordlanders returning from a far distant endeavor sailed past the Island of Kell, and there at a place on the western shore smoke rose from burning buildings, and four Jutlander ships were beached and raiders despoiled the town.

The Fjordlanders, though outnumbered, landed on the shingle and entered the small seaport and fell upon the men from Jute. None of the raiders escaped alive.

With most of the townsmen slain, the women gratefully tended the wounds of their rescuers, and the Fjordlanders remained for a while.

Winter roared in, and the storms were fierce, and the Northern Sea as well as the Boreal became too dangerous to ply. Yet spring finally came, and the Fjordlanders sailed on. Yet a goodly number of the warriors remained behind, and they settled down with their new wives and families, and became fishers and crafters and took up other such occupations.

And that's why that small town in Kell is now called Sjøen—Seaside, in the Fjordlander tongue—and why many of its inhabitants are tall and blond and speak three languages altogether, and the men are handy with shield and axe.

And it was this coastal village to which Silverleaf had come some nine years past, bearing a wet nurse and two children, one of whom was a boy with the birthmark of a griffin's deadly talons on his right shoulder, a mark that assassins would seek. . . .

. . . And on a summer morn in the tenth year of the Usurper's reign, when Rígán and Alric were eleven summers old, into Sjøen they came riding . . .

THEY WERE DOUBLE-UP ON Alric's steed, Rígán's horse trailing behind on a tether, a roebuck draped across the saddle. Each of the lads had a bow slung on his back along with a quiver of arrows. It was Rígán's green-fletched shaft that had brought the buck down, and not Alric's white-feathered one.

The sun had not yet cleared the forest to the east, and a heavy low fog swirled out from the sea and into the lanes of the town, to curl up the slopes and over the crests and into the greenery beyond.

Down at the docks and dimly seen, the fishermen readied their nets and oars, for with the wind lying still this dawn like so many other daybreaks they would have to row out on the flat sea, and wait for the offshore breeze to come rolling down from the land.

And craftsmen and shopkeepers stirred through the streets and prepared for the oncoming day.

And a stillness blanketed the village just as did the morning fog.

All of this the lads noted without comment in passing, for it was like other dawns when they and Da Conal and Mother Gretta and some of the hands had brought beef and pork to the market.

And now they were taking a roebuck to the butchery, hoping for the coppers, perhaps even a silver, it would bring.

"You turned him right past me," said Rígán.

Alric nodded. "I ride better. You shoot better."

"Someday I'll catch up," said Rígán.

"Ha! You think so. Mother tells me that I am a born Vanadurin, and we are riders supreme. But you, you are just a Pellarian."

"A Pellarian who can shoot the eye out of a partridge in flight," shot back Rígán. "Let me see you do that."

Alric's voice took on a portentous tone, and he said in Sylva, ["'Tis not seemly to brag, little one."]

Both boys broke out in guffaws, and Rígán said, ["Yes, Alor Halon, armsmaster."] And they broke out in laughter anew.

They rode a bit farther and then Alric said, "What say we stop at the tea room and have a bracing cup?"

"We did sneak out before sunup," said Rígán, "and I could use a scone or two."

"With clotted cream!" exclaimed Alric.

"And red-berry jam!" added Rígán.

"We'll put it on Da Conal's tab," said Alric, "and pay him back with what we get for the deer."

As they were making their plans, a form darted through the fog and across the street in front. It was a dark-haired girl, about their age. She skidded to a stop before them and smiled and dipped in a curtsey, and then dashed on, heading into the milliner's shop.

"What was that all about?" asked Rígán, staring after her.

"I don't know," said Alric. "Maybe she's daft."

Rígán laughed. "Well, to curtsey to you she'd have to be."

They passed by the cooper's, where out to the side at a small forge Rolf was heating an iron hoop for a herring keg. They called out a hello and Rolf waved at them, and they rode on.

"Oh, look, Alric, a tinker's cart," said Rígán, as they rode past the gaily festooned canvas-covered waggon. "We'll have to tell Mother Gretta. Perhaps she has a pot or two needing mending."

"Or knives to sharpen," said Alric.

On they rode, not noting the black-bearded man who leaned out from the cover to watch the two lads disappear into the fog.

Finally they came to Tessa's; her tea room was still closed.

"Rats," said Alric, "I was looking forward to a—"

"Here she is," said Rígán, looking back over his shoulder.

Bearing a lantern, the light blooming in the drifting vapor, a tall blond-haired woman hurried along the wooden walkway, mist swirling in her wake.

Rígán hopped down, followed by Alric. They tethered the horses to the hitching post, and, unshouldering their bows, up to the stoop they went.

"Well, well, but haven't you grown," said Tessa as she reached the lads.

"I'm right at six stone seven," said Rígán.

"And I'm just under," said Alric.

"And we are now taller than the armsmaster," said Rígán.

"He's four foot ten and I'm four nine," said Alric. "Rígán and me, I mean. Not Armsmaster Halon."

"Ninety-one pounds and o'ertopping a Dylvana? I'm impressed," said Tessa, who herself stood some five foot eight, tall even for a Fjordlander-Kellian woman.

"Here now," said Tessa, "hold this lantern as I unlatch the door."

"As you will, my lady," said Rígán, placing one foot behind the other and bowing.

"Your wish is our command," said Alric, grinning and bowing also.

Tessa laughed and handed the lamp to Rígán and said, "My, but aren't you the princely ones. Your court manners are impeccable."

"Mother Gretta is teaching us," said Rígán.

"Not that we are ever likely to be at court," said Alric, "pig farmers that we are."

"You never know, pig farmers or not," said Tessa. "But whether or no you ever are there, it's good to see that someone in this town has manners. Many could learn from your mother. I mean, all the women in town say you two are ever the nicest. You both should be proud of that."

"Yes, ma'am," they mumbled in reply.

The latch gave way, and as they went in, Tessa said, "You lads light the lanterns while I stir up the stove and put the water to boil."

Shucking their bows and quivers, Rígán and Alric went about lighting the lamps, filling the place with a cozy yellow glow. By the time they were done, Tessa had the fire going, and so she set them the task of laying the tables. When that chore was finished, Tessa asked, "Now what can I do for you two handsome warriors?"

"Tea, please," said Rígán.

"And scones," said Alric.

"With clotted cream," added Rígán.

"And red-berry jam," said Alric.

Laughing, Tessa said, "Coming right up, as soon as the kettle boils."

The boys took seats at one of the just laid tables.

"What's new at the farm?" asked Tessa.

"Not much," said Rígán.

"With Alor Halon's help, Durgan is training Steel for combat," said Alric.

"Combat?"

"Aye."

"Well, what with the Northern Alliance getting ready to go up against the Usurper, I shouldn't wonder if it doesn't come to that," said Tessa.

For some unknown reason, at Tessa's dour words Rígán's heart skipped a beat, or so it seemed to him. This talk of an oncoming war and the search for a suitable heir was a daily conversation in town and on the farm as well. And neither Conal nor Gretta nor Driu nor Armsmaster Halon ever spoke of just who this rightful heir might be. Even the tutors who lectured on royalty and the history of the nations— their foes and wars and alliances and treaties—did not seem to know who might replace the Usurper, should the Alliance win, though many thought it should be someone from the royalty of Jord, while others held it should be a prince from Riamon. After all, those were the nations involved at the root of the dispute, and given that Arkov of Garia had overthrown Valen, he had forfeited any right to the crown.

To change the subject, Rígán said, "We got a buck."

"I saw," said Tessa, spooning tea into a pot, and then pouring hot water over it. "I also saw that you met Caleen."

"Caleen?" asked Rígán.

"Well, you didn't actually meet her."

"The dark-haired girl in the street?" asked Alric.

"That's the one. A pretty little thing, she is, too. She'll be a stunner when she grows to a lass. I shouldn't wonder if you'll both be chasing after her, along with all the men in the village."

"Us? Chase after a girl?" Rígán shook his head.

Tessa merely laughed.

"Besides," said Alric, "she's daft."

"Daft?"

"Didn't you see how she stopped and curtseyed?"

Again Tessa laughed. "At that age, every girl hopes to meet a prince. And so, to bob a curtsey at passing . . . um . . . warriors upon a high horse, such as yourselves seem to be, well, I shouldn't wonder."

"She's new in town?" asked Rígán. "I mean, there are not many dark-haired girls in Sjøen, or so it seems."

"Ah, lad, you are just like every man. Looking for one who is an exotic stranger, rather than the beauties he sees every day."

Rígán shook his head and turned to Alric and murmured, "Girls."

The tea having steeped enough, Tessa poured and then fetched a plate of scones along with a small bowl of clotted cream and another of red-berry jam.

"Hers is a sad tale," said Tessa.

"Whose is?"

"Why, Caleen's. About nine moons past in the middle of the night, she and her aunt washed ashore. Thrown from a Jutlander ship, she said, the aunt, Britta, I mean. Her husband slain, she herself repeatedly ra— er, treated badly, and then, like fodder tossed to the cattle, she and little Caleen were pitched into the sea. Fortunately, they managed to catch hold of some flotsam, and the tide brought them to Sjøen. The men who found her took up axes and shields and set out in a Dragonboat, but the Jutlanders were long gone. And so any revenge must wait till another day."

"Jutlanders," spat Alric.

Rígán remained silent, and spooned some more cream and jam on his scone and took another bite.

Tessa sighed, and then looked at the boys. "Ah, me, but I didn't mean to spoil your bit of a nibble and all, what with the talk of Jutlanders."

"You didn't," said Rígán.

A silent moment or two passed, and finally Alric said, "We passed a tinker's waggon."

"Aye. He came down the north road just yestermorn, looking to fix any pots and pans, sharpen knives and scissors and the like. And he has a goodly supply of needles and thread, and a bit of cloth."

"Mother Gretta might be interested," said Rígán.

"I'll tell him," said Tessa. "He'll be glad, for he was asking around for news of anyone who had come in the years since last he was here—looking for new customers, I suppose—though for the life of me I can't remember him at all. Perhaps he didn't have a beard then."

*   *   *

Just after dawn, Driu cast her runes to see what this foggy day might bring. Frowning, she took up the five stones and put them back in the bag. After shaking them again she said a <word> and withdrew nine without looking, and, cupping them in her hands, she rattled all together and said another <word> then cast them to the table.

Moments later, out in the barn: "Conal, where's Rígán? Alric?"

Conal looked up to see a harried Driu. Then he glanced down the row of stables to see two empty stalls. "Ahorse somewhere."

"They said they were after a stag," piped up Cuán. "Rode out way before dawn."

"Then find them," snapped Driu. "Peril looms."

Taking up their bows and quivers, Rígán and Alric bade their farewells to Tessa and stepped out into the early morn, the sun just then peeking over the forest to bring light to the yet drifting fog, though down in the street it was still enshadowed.

Appearing out from the dimness, a bearded man grasping a long-knife stepped before the two lads. His gaze flicked from one to the other, as if momentarily confused, but then he grabbed the closest, Rígán, by his jacket and snarled, "Princely ones, eh? Let me see your shoulder, boy."

"Sir?" Rígán jerked back, but the stranger held fast.

"Your shoulder," the man snarled again. Then he raised his knife for a slashing throat-cut. "Ah, Neddra, I'll just kill you bo—"

Thock!

A white-feathered arrow sprang forth from the man's left eye, and he pitched over backward, jerking Rígán down atop him, the man dead before he hit the ground.

A shrill scream sounded nearby.

Alric nocked a second arrow and spun to his right. There stood Caleen, her hands clasped to her terrified face.

Behind Alric a door banged open, and Tessa rushed out from the tea room.

Rígán finally broke the man's death grip and jumped up and backed away and turned about see Alric with a nocked arrow, the lad's face gone ashen in the lantern light.

THE SUN HAD RISEN a hand or two and the fog was nearly gone, when riders, weapons drawn, thundered into the streets—Dylvana, Conal, men from the farm, Durgan in the lead on Steel.

They had come to rescue the boys.

Enlightenment

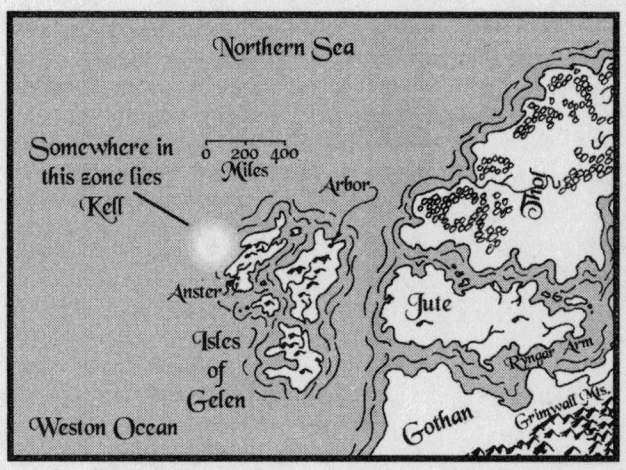

Throughout the Eras, birds have been trained to swiftly bear messages from one place to another. It is easiest to teach these messengers to travel a one-way flight—that is, from wherever they find themselves to wing from that place to their home cote. So, usually the birds are carried in cages to a remote location, and when they are released they simply fly home, just incidentally carrying the message to a receiver at the far end. Yet with persistence, a good trainer can teach the bird not only to fly from a distant location to home, but to also fly back to that faraway point.

Typically pigeons are given the task; rock pigeons from North Gelen are especially good at it, as are their kindred from the distant Islands of Stone. But at times a pigeon bearing a message falls victim to a bird of prey, or to a hunter's arrow or sling. To better ensure that dispatches get through, other birds are taught to be bearers of tidings as well, birds that do not easily become quarry, birds such as falcons, kestrels, and goshawks, and the like. Usually, though, these raptors can be pressed into service only by Magekind, yet there are a few particularly gifted trainers who also can succeed in turning these hunters into carriers.

Too, in the far north in a long chain of dark mountains lives a black bird known as the Grimwall Corvus. It is a strange bird, a raptor, one that at times does its master's bidding by bearing messages from place to place. And so it must be included in the number of carriers, yet never has anyone but a person of Magekind ever compelled this particular bird to heed to the task.

In the tenth year of the Usurper's reign, a swift pigeon with a coded message in a capsule tied to its leg set out from the Island of Kell. The message was simple and reported a fiasco, with the recommendation that someone better skilled at execution be sent on the mission rather than another agent like the ham-fisted ruffian who had failed so miserably to carry out an undemanding task.

Not long after that missive arrived at Caer Pendwyr, a Grimwall Corvus flew northward, aiming for a distant tower. The black bird bore quite triumphant news, for the message noted that the failure meant the recipient's plans would once more begin moving apace.

Yet at a pig and cattle farm back on Kell, the root object of the messages stood in disbelief. . . .

"WHAT?" HE ASKED. "What did you—?"

"I said, the man was an assassin sent by Usurper Arkov, for you are King Valen's rightful heir."

"No, Da, *that* I understood. What I want to know is, what did you say my new name is?"

Conal held grim laughter in check, for he had just told the lad that he was the true High King, and that assassins would be hunting him, and all the boy really wanted to know was his "new" name. Ah, to be eleven again.

"Reyer," said Conal. "It's Reyer."

"But that is not in fact a new name for you," said Gretta. "Instead, it's your true name, your given name. Rígán is what we—Silverleaf and I—decided to call you so that no one would know who you really are. Silverleaf got the name from Aravan."

"The Elf with the spear?" asked Alric.

"Krystallopŷr?" said Driu.

Alric nodded and said, "The one that burns Foul Folk."

"It doesn't really burn them," said Driu. "But, yes, Aravan is the one with that spear."

"And why did the man—the assassin—want to look at my shoulder?" asked Reyer.

"To see your birthmark," said Driu.

"My birthmark? What does that have to do with anything?"

"It resembles the right forefoot of a griffin," said Driu.

Gretta said, "When you were born and the midwives and I and the King's healer saw the mark, we all thought it a great portent."

"Portent," said Reyer, looking at Driu for enlightenment.

A faint smile flitted across Driu's face. "The High King's seal and his flag bear his golden sigil—a griffin rampant—as do you, Valen's firstborn . . . or at least the right foreclaw of the griffin—a most perilous part of that fabulous beast."

"And on your right shoulder, too," said Gretta. "The right-hand claw upon the strong right arm."

Driu nodded and said, "Your mark was taken to mean that you will be a mighty High King in your time, one as fierce as a griffin, for you carry those deadly talons."

Alric laughed, and when Reyer shot a puzzled glance his way, Alric said, "I always thought it a chicken foot."

Gretta gasped in horror at Alric's breach of etiquette, but Reyer laughed, and so did Conal.

But then Conal sobered and stepped to the fireplace in the sitting room and worked a small stone loose from near the edge of the outer hearth. From the gap revealed, he took an even smaller object tightly wrapped in leather, and out from that he took a man's ring. "Here is the High King's seal." He handed it to Reyer. "Your father gave it to Silverleaf to give to you one day, and Silverleaf gave it to me for safekeeping."

The ring was gold and set with a sparkling scarlet stone with a Golden Griffin rampant somehow incised thereon.

"The griffin's forefeet hold talons much like those of an eagle, though greater and a deal more lethal, and the full claw of the right foot matches your birthmark," said Conal. Then he knelt upon one knee and said, "You are Reyer, son of Valen, and are the true High King."

Driu then added, "And by this ring and your birthmark, they shall know you."

Conal sighed and stood and said, "We were to tell you when you turned twelve, but events now intervene."

Reyer sat down, a bit stunned. He peered at the ring, and said, "I don't think I want to be King." He looked up at Alric as if seeking his opinion.

"Ha!" said the dark-haired lad, barking a laugh. "Better you than me."

"You have no choice, Reyer," said Conal.

"But I like my life here, tending pigs, herding cattle, fishing, hunting, running through the woods, training with the Dylvana, living a good life."

"It is your duty to be King," snapped Gretta. "Let's have no more of—"

"Gretta," said Conal. "This is all new to the boy. Give him time to come to terms with the facts."

A silence fell upon them all, but then Reyer said, "This is why we are schooled in courtly manners."

"I'm not going to have to call you 'my lord,' am I?" asked Alric, grinning.

Reyer smiled back at his blood-sworn brother, and then drew out a long "May-be." Then they both laughed.

But Conal looked sternly at Alric and said, "Lad, you will call him 'my lord' when the time comes, as shall we all."

"Aye, Da," replied Alric, chastened.

"But not in private," said Reyer. "None here shall call me that in private. It would just make me feel the goose."

Gretta beamed proudly at Reyer and Alric and said, "But in public you shall call each other 'my lord.'"

"I am a pig farmer and not a lord," said Alric.

"You are Harlingar," snapped Gretta. "Your father—" Of a sudden her voice chopped to silence, and she said no more.

Both Alric and Reyer glanced from Gretta to Conal and back, but neither adult gave further word to Gretta's outburst.

Finally, Alric shrugged and looked at Conal and said, "Do I call him Rígán or Reyer?"

"Rígán," said Conal. He swung his gaze to Reyer. "We will not use your real name until the right time. Instead, you'll be Rígán till then. It might keep you safer."

Driu added, "And we will not bow nor otherwise recognize you as High King until that time."

Reyer reluctantly nodded, and then asked, "When will *be* the right time?"

"A few years from now," said Driu.

"When you take command of the Northern Alliance," said Conal.

Again Reyer looked at the ring and then up at Alric. "I am to lead the army in a march upon Caer Pendwyr." His words were a statement—not a question.

"That's why we are practicing at arms and learning strategy and tactics," said Alric, looking at Conal.

"Training in warfare," said Conal, nodding in agreement. "Preparing for the day."

Tears welled in Gretta's eyes and spilled down her face.

Alric then turned to Reyer and said, "Vanadurin have ever ridden to the High King's aid, and I will be no different."

"Then we ride together," said Reyer, and in that moment both he and Alric seemed well beyond their years.

Gretta looked from one child to the other and then back again, and she burst into sobs and rushed from the room.

Conal watched her go, pain in his gaze.

Reyer started to rise, but Driu laid a hand on his arm; her gesture kept both lads in place. "She has known this for nine years, Rígán, Alric. Nevertheless, it still comes as a blow. No mother likes to see her children stand in harm's way, yet you have little choice but to do so."

"I THOUGHT I WAS GOING to be sick," said Alric, as he and Rígán, under the shade of the oaks, shoved upon the fat sow, trying to get her off her side and to her feet and to move her back to the gap in the fence and toward the sty.

Straining, Rígán grunted, "Up, Molly, up."

They both paused, and Rígán said, "Sick?"

"When I feathered that—that tinkerman," said Alric. In spite of the adulation he had received from their would-be rescuers and Tessa and later from the farmhands, it was the first Alric had said about the killing.

"Well, I'm glad you did so, else we'd both be throat cut."

"The thing is, Rígán, I almost shot that girl, too."

"Caleen," said Rígán.

"Uh-huh, Caleen."

"Good thing you didn't," said Rígán, grinning, "else she wouldn't have been breathlessly hanging on to everything you said after."

"Pfaugh!" snorted Alric. "It was you she looked at all googly-eyed."

"Girls," said Rígán.

"Girls," agreed Alric.

Rígán looked about and stepped away, to return moments later with a finger-thick stick. He showed the stick to the sow, and she eyed the lad with suspicion. "Up, Molly, up, or else." Replete with acorns, she grunted but otherwise did not move, though she did keep an eye on the stick. "All right," said Rígán, and with a *Whap!* he struck a sharp blow to her rear. Squealing, Molly bolted to her feet and took off running the wrong way.

After a long chase, they finally got Molly headed the right way. And as they followed the sow through the broken fence and toward the sty, Alric said, "She is pretty, you know."

"Molly?" asked Rígán.

"No—no, you dolt, Caleen."

"Oh. Right. And yes: she is pretty."

They walked on a bit farther, and finally Alric said, "Girls."

"Girls," agreed Rígán.

And they continued on in silence, each one's thoughts his own.

Assassins

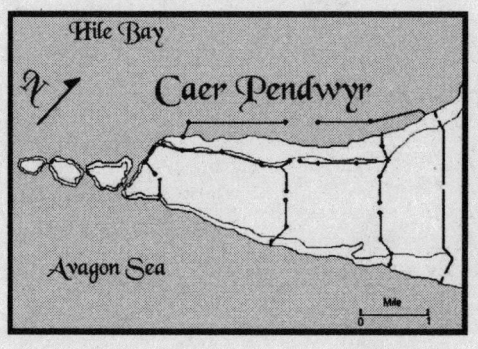

Some twenty-four hundred miles across the indigo waters of the deep blue Avagon Sea nearly due south from Caer Pendwyr lies the city of Sabra. It is a principal port city, but it also rests on the edge of the great desert known as the Mighty Karoo. If one journeys from Sabra and bears south-southwest across the hot shifting sands and salt-encrusted wadis, then some sixteen hundred miles as a crow flies a traveler would fetch up against the walls of the Red City of Nizari. But if one were to make this trek from Caer Pendwyr to Sabra to the Red City, the actual journey across both the ocean and the desert would be much longer than that which any bird might fly, for ships must tack in the shifting winds to fare the ocean waves, and camels must stride from various water holes to verdant oases to deep-sunk wells to survive the crossing of the ever-changing dunes to reach that distant goal.

Nizari itself lies at the foot of a rust-red mountain, the bastion guarding the mouth of a pass running through the range to the west. And *that* is why the Sultans of Hyree claim the city, for it sits across the principal trade route through the Talâk Mountains—the corridor providing passage between the harsh Karoo and the green realm of Hyree—and caravans and other travelers pay a toll to greatly shorten their journeys this way. These tolls are one of the measures the city uses to maintain its coffers, yet it is not the principal means.

The city consists of crimson buildings clutched against dark, ruddy mountains, and a high red wall encircles the town entire.

Individual structures are made of bloodred rock carved from the range behind, and for the most part are flat-roofed buildings, though here and there pitched-roof edifices stand.

Jutting up among the constructions are scattered high, slender minarets or soaring obelisks. Here and there long stairways rise up and tilt down and the streets fare past merchants' shops and through bazaars and across alleys reeking of garbage and sewage, over open squares, past community wells, among dwellings rising high to either side. And everywhere there is noise—shrieking children at play; haggling storekeepers and customers arguing; strident mothers shouting for sons and daughters; drovers cursing pack camels, the beasts *hronking* in return; merchants hawking their wares—the city awash in a hubbub.

The arrangement of the whole seems to follow no regular pattern, for the city streets twist and jink throughout, the red brick roads slanting this way and that, lanes and alleyways shooting off at odd angles, jerking 'round sharp corners to disappear beyond seeing, the entirety a maze, like runs in a rat's warren. And this jinking and twisting tortuous tangle reflects the immoral fiber of the city.

Dominating all is an adjoining citadel, its scarlet dome rounded and coming to a tall spire, the whole of it onion-shaped ... or perhaps shaped like the abdomen of a dreadfully poisonous malevolent red spider. The dome is set in the center of a massive rectangular building, which itself sits in a wide courtyard. It is from here the heart of evil beats. The fortress is walled about with looming battlements—twice as high as those surrounding the town as a whole—and one of the high ramparts of the fortress abuts against and towers above the southwest wall of the city.

And just outside the citadel bulwark lies the *Ahmar Madrasi*—the "Red School." It is in that place where the students are trained in the arts of assassins—stealth, poisons, silent kills, and the like. These courses are deadly, and those who survive to graduate are called *Sukut Khayâlîn*—Silent Shadows. Only the *Kinzuru-na Gakko*—the "Forbidden School"—of Ryodo produces assassins equal to or perhaps even better than those of Nizari. Even so, the principal industry of the Red City is the training of these Khayâlîn, and the hiring of them to those in need ... that and the selling of toxins and venoms, common and exotic alike. Whether hired or bought, assassination is a means by which jealous lovers and heartless others remove a rival or someone thwarting their desires, and it is especially used as a recurrent tool of callous and wicked statecraft, be it against the many or the few or, more likely, against but one.

From the seventh through the eleventh year of the Usurper's reign, Arkov sent individual Garian killers disguised as workaday tradesfolk to the island of Kell, seeking to end the life of a single boy. . . .

. . . For Arkov was threatened by the very existence of the child . . .

WRINGING HIS HANDS, Baloff stood before his master. "How many must we kill to slay just one?"

"As many as it takes," snarled Arkov.

"But, my King, our agents have butchered lad after lad without success. None have borne the mark of the griffin. And now all the Kellian ports are forbidding entry to tinkers and shoemakers and other traveling trades. And all wayfarers are looked upon with suspicion, even though many are well known by those of the isle."

"Idiot! You think I don't know that?"

Baloff took a step back, for when his master was in such a mood . . .

Arkov ground his teeth and shouted, his voice echoing off the walls of the throne chamber: "Is there no one in my entire kingdom who isn't a ham-fisted fool?"

"It seems there are none in Garia," said Baloff, and then blanched when he realized he had said it aloud.

Arkov gripped the arms of the throne so tightly his knuckles turned white. But of a sudden he slapped his hands down on the armrests and burst out laughing.

Baloff loosed his pent breath and smiled in return.

"I am beginning to think you are right, Baloff, just as said my agent in Sj-Sjo—"

"Sjøen?" supplied Baloff.

"Yes. Sjøen."

Looking inward, Arkov shook his head and growled, "Incompetent fools."

Baloff nodded and said, "They've left a trail of corpses across the scapes of Kell, a number of the boys not even the right age. Some of our agents have been caught by mobs and beaten to death or hacked to pieces. Gutted, quartered, hanged, burned."

"Serves them right, the bunglers."

"Sire, they have pointed the finger at you."

"Baloff, we will continue to claim my innocence, and say I am an easy target."

"Still, my King, we need to succeed. The child will be fifteen within a year or two, and he will then be announced, even crowned by the Northern Alliance."

"You assume there *is* such a child," said Arkov.

"So said Mosaam bin Abu's unnamed Seer," replied Baloff.

"Actually it was only Abu's word we took for truth," retorted Arkov. "For all we know, that ebon bastard lied about the Mage."

Baloff remained silent, not wishing to gainsay his King.

But then Arkov sighed again and said, "Still, in our most recent message, our agent in Sj-Sjøen says that two boys are being trained in courtly manners."

"Aye, my King. And they are being taught by a lady who has spoken of Caer Pendwyr. And she did come to Sjøen with two babes—two toddlers—which would make them of the right age."

Arkov nodded and said, "Send for Abu."

"My lord?"

"Are you deaf? I said send for that dark snake Abu."

Baloff frowned in puzzlement, and Arkov said, "I intend to have him hire assassins from the Red City. Surely they will succeed where others have failed."

Baloff groaned, for they were being drawn further and further into the debt—or perhaps the clutches—of the men of the South.

THAT EVENING, in this, the tenth year of the Usurper's reign, two dusky birds took to the air from the Chabbain embassy: one—a Grimwall Corvus—winged north toward a hidden tower, its message triumphant; the other—a black gull—winged south-southeast across the sea, its message a command.

It took a sevenday for the Grimwall Corvus to deliver its coded slip to the dark tower, but the Black Gull was on the wing for nigh a fortnight altogether. When it finally came to rest in the port of Sabra, an agent there read the message and then transferred it to another bird—a desert kite—and that carrier headed south-southwestward to land at the scarlet, onion-domed fortress a tenday after.

YET FOLLOWING THE ORDERS in the message capsule, it was a full two years ere, from the port city of Khalísh in Hyree, three lateen-sailed ships, their canvases crimson, set out in darkness along the southern arm of the Straits of Kistan, heading northwesterly. The passengers were highly trained . . . eradicators. Their destination: a modest seaside village on the Island of Kell.

Arms

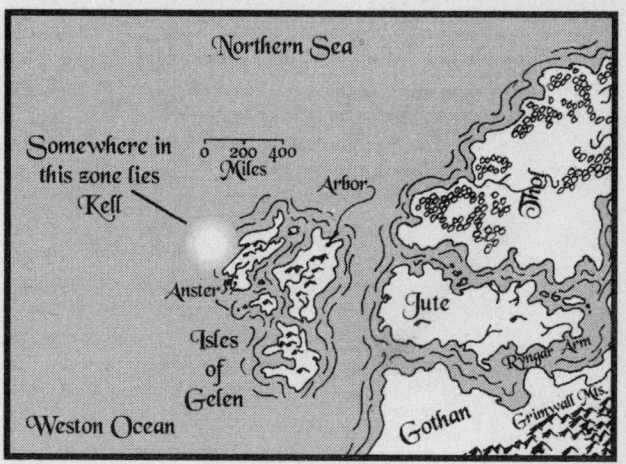

Northern Sea

Somewhere in this zone lies Kell

0 200 400 Miles

Arbor

Thol

Anster

Jute

Isles of Gelen

Ryngar Arm

Weston Ocean

Gothan

Grimwall Mts.

Cleaving, Slashing, Bashing, Piercing, Burning: These Are the Things That Mithgarian Weapons Do. From Axes to Swords to Maces and Morning Stars and Flails, to Poniards and Arrows and Quarrels and Long-Knives, to Fireballs and Stones and Other Such Missiles Hurled from Trebuchets and Catapults and Ballistas.

Yet these are not the only ways of death in war and battle, for there is also strangulation by garrotes and nooses and choke holds and even bare hands; and there are poisons and venoms and other such toxins smeared on blades and points and even vile potions slipped into food and drink; devastating plagues and other diseases are sometimes used against a foe by sending the ill and infected into the enemy ranks.

One can also drown an enemy by breaking dams or rerouting streams to send wild and rushing waters raging over the foe. Likewise, landslides and rockfalls and loosed log piles and burning brushes and other such can thunder down on the adversary, and even wild or tamed herds are stampeded to trample the enemy underfoot, as do well-trained warhorses.

These and other things are merely the earthly means of inflicting fatality upon enemies, for in Mithgar there are also death-dealing castings and spells, should one be a Mage.

Yet for the most part, great wars and large battles come down to arrow flights and missile castings and the combat of one on one, with foe facing foe and eye looking into eye, whether it be ahorse or afoot, where lances and spears and swords and maces and morning stars and axes pierce and slice and hack and slash and crush, and blood spurts and flies wide and bones break and brain matter splatters and intestines spill and lopped limbs flop and severed heads tumble aimlessly o'er the rough ground.

And all of it with men and horses screaming midst the clang and clangor of steel on steel and shrieks of fear and shouts of battle and cries of shock and pain and calls for aid and the unheard sighs and whimpers of the dying.

At times the outcome is decided by sheer numbers, though often it is simply the overmatching skills of one side that defeats the other, and still at other times it is the strategy and tactics that determine the winners and losers, whether it be by flanking move or ambush or feint or coming upon the foe unawares.

Strategy, tactics, weaponry, and skills: these are the tools of war....

... And in a forest clearing nigh the edge of a farm upon the island of Kell, two lads, of ages nearing fourteen, were given new metal swords....

RÍGÁN THUMBED THE EDGE. "I say, Armsmaster, this isn't even sharp—just like the one I gave up."

"Mine's dull, too," complained Alric, gazing at his sword and then Rígán's. "These are no better than the wooden training swords we used as children. In fact, those might have been even sharper than these."

Halon smiled and said, "I wouldst not have ye lop off a hand or e'en a finger of the other, and that goes for me as well. And think on this, too: whether clad in leather, chain, scale, or plate, oft the foe dies of battering, whether or no the weapon striking is sharp-edged or dull."

"Huh?" said Alric.

"The armor," said Rígán. "If the sword doesn't cut through the armor, then the blade is no better than hitting the enemy with a warbar."

"Ah, I see," said Alric, grinning at Rígán, then turning to look at the Dylvana armsmaster for confirmation.

Seeming to be no more than a slender, dark-haired youth, though he was millennia old, Halon turned up a hand and raised an eyebrow in equivocation and said, "Rígán is right, and yet he is wrong."

Rígán's eyes flew wide in puzzlement. "I am? How so?"

"Well, lad, tell me this: what is a warbar?"

As if reciting a litany, Rígán said, "There are a number of so-called great weapons, most of which are two-handed in wielding. The exact number is in dispute, but among them and well recognized are the battle axe and war hammer, favored by the Dwarves; the lance and the spear, favored by the Vanadurin; the great sword, favored by many; the flail, and the warbar, favored by the—" Rígán's recitation stopped well short. "Oh, I see. The warbar is a Troll weapon."

Halon nodded and queried, "And as such . . . ?"

"And as such," blurted Alric, "to wield a warbar is almost impossible for someone of lesser strength than a Troll."

"Aye," said Halon in approval. "Were someone to strike another with a Troll warbar, 'twould be no love tap."

Rígán nodded and said, "More likely would break every bone in his body."

Halon laughed and said, "Not quite, but close."

"So, with a sword striking someone armored in leather, chain, scale, or plate, and not cutting through, that would be somewhat akin to hitting him with a cudgel."

"Favored by the Rûcks," said Alric. "—Cudgels, I mean."

"Perhaps a bit sharper than a cudgel blow," said Halon, "yet that is the idea." Then he turned to Alric and said, "Now about thy complaint as to these being no better than training swords, though we tried to make the wood hew as close to the action of the steel as we could, still there were differences. And with your first metal swords, they were fitted for young children, and had not the heft of these. But now ye have swords fit for youth of thine ages, and as such your training changes once again." The armsmaster took his own sword in hand and gestured for Rígán and Alric to follow suit, as he stepped the boys through various learned moves to illustrate his words, saying, "Heed the distinction in balance, the difference in heft, the alteration in the way the wrist feels in merely holding it or when starting a strike, the shift in the forearm adjustment during the swing, the divergence in shoulder action during a thrust, the variance in the way of the parry and . . ."

* * *

EVEN AS RÍGÁN AND ALRIC with their new swords followed Halon's slicing strokes, quick lunges, stabbing thrusts, and rapid parries, Gretta and Catlin with knives in hand sat at a yard table and scraped and chopped the freshly plucked and washed parsnips, preparing them for the noon meal soup. At a distant whistle, they both looked westward in the late-morning sun and peered toward the far end of the clearing, where, just emerging from the forest, Conal came riding.

" 'Tis the tiarna," said Catlin. Then she glanced at Gretta and added, "Your man."

"Aye, it is," replied Gretta, worry now knitting her brow.

"He's riding slow," said Catlin. "No need for concern."

"Still," said Gretta, "what with all these doings . . ."

"Shameful and wicked," said Catlin, and she took up another pale root to prepare.

Driu stepped onto the porch and walked down into the yard and took a seat next to Gretta.

Conal rode to the barn and dismounted and gave over his horse to the stable hand, Cuán. Moments later he came to the women and stood, a distracted frown on his face as if pondering what next to do. He took a deep breath and looked at Driu and said, "You were right, Seer. Another boy dead up north in Glasbaile last week. They caught the one who did the deed, just as he was about to slit a second child's throat."

Gretta's eyes welled with tears. "Arkov's man?" she asked.

"Aye. He confessed even as they gutted him."

"Wicked!" spat Catlin. "Wicked."

"Is there naught we can do?" asked Gretta.

"Not without exposing Rígán and Alric to concentrated peril," said Driu. "The whole of Kell is now on alert against these killers. It remains up to the families to be on watch against any stranger who comes into their midst."

Conal nodded and said, "Just as we now send armed escort with Rígán and Alric whenever they go into Sjøen, so, too, must all others do the same with their children."

"Armed escort or no, I would rather they not leave here at all," said Gretta.

Conal moved around the table and sat beside his wife and put an arm about her. "Ah, love, we can't keep them prisoner. And surely once Reyer is announced, his life will be at hazard no matter where he is." Then Conal grinned and said, "Besides, I'd rather they go with an escort than to sneak off on their own to see that dark-haired girl—what is her name?"

"Caleen," said Catlin. "And a pretty little thing she is, too. They're both after her, you know."

"Rígán and Alric?" asked Gretta.

"Aye, but Caleen seems to have eyes only for Alric," said Catlin. "Or so it is Tessa tells me."

"Tessa of the tea room?" asked Gretta.

"The very same," said Catlin. "Tells me that Caleen thinks Alric is the finest warrior who ever strode this green, green isle, what with him doing in that vile tinkerman, who would have killed them all, or so Caleen says."

"And she's after my Alric and not Rígán?" asked Gretta.

"Aye. Oh, she thinks Rígán is a fine lad, but Alric fills her heart."

"But she won't be able to marry my Alric, just as she wouldn't be able to marry Reyer."

Catlin shot Gretta a puzzled frown, but Gretta said no more. On the other hand, Driu smiled knowingly, yet kept her knowledge to herself.

"Are the men in Sjøen ready?" asked Driu.

"What?" said Conal, who hadn't been listening, but instead had fallen into a deep thoughtful state.

"I asked if the men in Sjøen are ready."

"They are," replied Conal, nodding.

"And the Dylvana?"

"Them, too."

They remained in silence for long moments, but for the scrape and slice of knife against parsnip. Finally Conal asked, "Do you know when it might occur?"

"Not yet," said Driu.

"Peril from the sea," said Catlin. "Jutlanders, I would imagine."

"It is not clear," said Driu.

"And you think they are coming after Rígán?"

"I do."

"But why?" asked Gretta. "Aren't the Jutlanders part of the Northern Alliance? If so, why would they be after Rígán?"

Catlin turned her head aside and spat on the ground, growling, "Jutlanders. Who knows what their mad king will do? Mayhap he's made a pact with Arkov."

OVER THE NEXT WEEK OR SO, in the clearing where they trained, steel rang against steel, as Rígán and Alric took turns sparring with Halon. Occasionally, the Dylvana faced them both, and yet they could not get through his guard, even though they split wide and came at him from both sides.

And when left to themselves, Rígán and Alric took up blade against one another, and in this they were evenly matched: each fairly skillful for thirteen-year-old lads, yet clumsy on occasion, though hardly at one and the same time.

And though they would rather stay with the swords, Halon made them practice with bow and arrow, with long-knife and dagger, and with spear and lance.

And he spoke of other weapons: curved swords— cutlasses, scimitars, shamsheers, and the like—instead of the straight blades they now wielded. "Suitable for slicing cuts," said Halon, "for the curve keeps the blade in contact with the foe throughout the sweep of thine arm, throughout the arc of the stroke." He looked at Alric and said, "Your folk— the Vanadurin—wield a somewhat curved and heavy blade from the back of a horse. Very effective, these Harlingar, when atop a steed, be it with a lance or saber.

"Now the Fjordlanders favor the axe, and the East-Isle Gelenders the falchion, but as to the men of Gothon, they take up the . . ."

And so the drilling went on, and Alric could not wait to get on the back of a horse with a lance or a saber in hand, whereas Rígán favored the bow and arrow as well as the light and swift rapier.

*   *   *

No sooner had driu looked up from the runes and said, "This is the day," than a rider arace came shouting the alarm: "Red-sailed ships, Tiarna. Red-sailed ships have landed, and slaughter fills the streets."

An Elven horn rang throughout Darda Coill, and Dylvana girded weapons and took to horse, and rode to the distant sound of battle.

"Rígán, Alric, stay here," ordered Conal, as he and Durgan and the men of the stead mounted up to follow. As Rígán and Alric protested, Conal snapped, "I command you to stay: do not disobey me. Here you will be safe."

Even as the riders galloped away and into the forest to the west, a red-sailed ship landed down the coast. Twelve dark-clothed, dark-skinned men, who named themselves *Sukut Khayâlîn*—Silent Shadows—disembarked and soundlessly slipped into the woodland, heading for a nearby cow-and-pig farm.

23

Astral

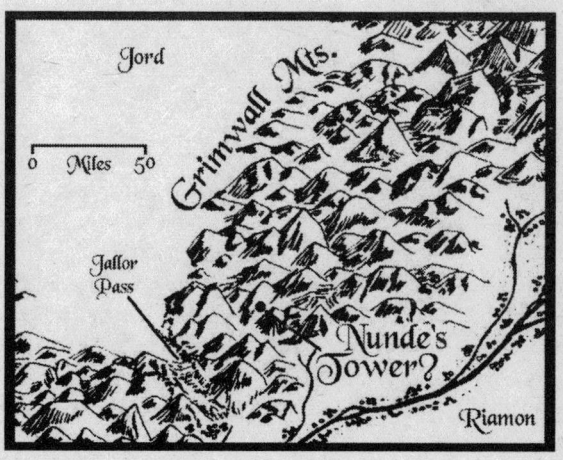

There are many ways to travel across the lands of Mithgar: walking being the slowest common means and perhaps the most used, for not all folk have animals to ride or to draw carriages or waggons—animals such as horses and ponies and oxen and donkeys and mules ... or camels. ... or even the great tusked animals of Bharaq, there in the land south of the great Jangdi Mountains. Then again, in Ryodo and Jinga and other lands of the East, oft travelers are borne through the streets of the cities by jinricksha and palanquin and sedan chair, the bearers of which are little better than draft animals. And in the far north, journeys are often made by sleds drawn by dogs and reindeer. And in Darda Erynian, Pysks ride Foxes.

As to travel by water, one can swim or be borne by boat or canoe or raft or some such, or by ship, of which there are many types—from scows to the swift *Eroean*, though that fabled Elvenship has not been seen since the days immediately after the sinking of Rwn.

So, travel by land and water is common in Mithgar, yet travel by air is rare indeed. It is said that the Phael—a type of winged Hidden Ones—are able to fly ... as are Dragons. Too, there are legends of other Hidden Folk—Sprites, Pixies, and such—as having wings—just as it has been said that the Pysks, being small, not only travel by Foxes but have traveled by bird as well, eagle being the rumor. Hearth tales speak of sighting Witches and Warlocks in flight, yet those are difficult to believe, for they would number among Magekind, and Mages deny their existence. And speaking of Magekind, only few can master the castings needed for such transportation, yet we do know that some Seers and Mystics dreamwalk or use the astral plane to fly across the 'scape, and, uncommonly, a handful of Necromancers have been known to travel via this occult domain—Andrak was known to be among these latter, ere he was slain by a token of power hurled by a Warrior Maiden to save her beloved.

It is not startling that Seers and Mystics use dreams and the astral realm to journey thither and yon, but that a Necromancer might do so comes as a surprise. For Necromancers fear betrayal by the folk they grind under heel—Rûcks, Hlôks, Ghûls, Ogrus, and the like—as well as their very own apprentices. And to travel by the mysterious sphere means separating the essence of being from the body, leaving it completely defenseless. On the other hand, to slip the soul out from the physical being is rather much like death, and death, of course, is the province of the Necromancer indeed.

And in a tall tower hidden deep within the Grimwall, one of these Necromancers became impatient to see for himself whether or not his plans moved forward. . . .

. . . It was time to make ready for a flight. . . .

"RADOK," said Nunde, wiping his hands on the blood-smeared apron.

"Yes, Master," replied the tall, thin, bald apprentice.

Nunde gestured at the massive corpse on the table. "I would have you raise this Ogh, and march him up to the battlements. Leave him standing until sunrise."

"But, Master, that will mean—"

"I know what it means, you fool," snapped Nunde.

Flinching, Radok said, "Yes, Master. I meant no offense. I am merely mystified."

Somewhat placated by Radok's cringing, Nunde said, "I would have you study his frame, and what better way to do so than to have Adon's own cursed light reave the flesh from these bones."

"Ah, I see," said Radok. "And as the rabble say—"

Nunde interrupted: "Yes, yes, Troll bones and Dragonhide: both escape destruction by the sun. Still, the Ogh bones will fall apart from one another, for the tendons and cartilage will vanish along with the flesh in the light. Nevertheless, I would have you reassemble them as part of your study."

"As you will, Master," said Radok, inclining his head in obeisance.

Nunde turned to go, but Radok said, "Yet, Master, for me to raise this Ogh, I will need to slay a number of—"

"Of course, of course. It will take <fire> to get this behemoth up to the banquettes. But reft no more than six Drik to do it, for I would have you stretch your abilities."

"Yes, Master. Will you observe?"

"No, Radok, I plan on retiring."

Radok frowned in puzzlement, for the nighttide was yet young; still he said naught.

Now certain that his apprentice would be occupied the rest of the dark—*The pusillanimous fool trying to get the slain Ogh up to the battlements using the <fire> of only six Drik. Ha!*—Nunde stepped down the dark-granite torchlit hallway to the apothecary. Quickly selecting the necessary ingredients, with mortar and pestle and flask and flame, soon he had brewed a bitter concoction. And as he did so, the Necromancer contemplated what he might do about Radok, for Nunde trusted him not. *Perhaps I should take on another apprentice—fat Malik is a candidate. Yet the two of them might plot against me. No, instead I will keep a wary eye upon Radok, and should he betray me . . .*

The potion finished, Nunde poured the resulting dark liquid into a vial. Even as he stepped from the chamber, a deep thud, one that Nunde felt through the very stone of the tower, sounded from the hallway behind.

Mayhap the Ogh has fallen from the—

A second thud followed, and then a third, and another.

Nunde raised an eyebrow in surprise, for the slain Ogh was afoot. Yet on down the dark corridor Nunde went, and into his quarters.

He bolted the massive bronze door, with latches and turn-locks and the heavy slide-bar. And he cast a shutting upon it as well. Then he took to his wide bed, and, ignoring the corpse at his side, Nunde drank the fresh-brewed acrid concoction. In but moments he fell back as if dead, and his aethyrial self flew free, his body completely helpless.

He soared overland, and to his astral sight all shades and colors were reversed: dark was light; light, dark; crimson shone viridian; sapphire shone ocherous; amethyst, amber; ebon, alabaster; and the reverse. The night skies were bright and speckled with dark stars; the moon, black, reminiscent of Neddra. Faster than any eagle he soared, swifter than even a shooting star. And when he reached his destination, dawn was yet some long candlemarks away.

He was nigh the isle of Kell, yet not too close, for he would not have that cursed Seer somewhere near discover even his astral form. Still, from his height he could see the isle afar.

And he searched the bright pallid orange sea below.

Long he spent scanning the luminescent black-topped waves, and yet he did not espy what he was—

Yet wait! There they are!

Far below fared three lateen-rigged ships, their sails pale green, their hulls grey-lavender to his aethyrial sight.

Yet one was on a diverging path.

Nunde frowned, for he knew not why they—

He sighted their near-distant destinations—a seaside village was the goal of two, but the third was headed for a shingle somewhat south.

Mosaam bin Abu, you fool! This is not my plan!

Enraged and cursing, Nunde railed at this ruse, for it might actually succeed. Yet in aethyrial form he had no power to stop it. And he could not wait to see the outcome, for dawn would arrive ere then, and even though he traveled the astral plane, Nunde did not dare to defy Adon's Ban.

Back across the sea he sped, back toward his Grimwall sanctum.

Even as he neared and flew in among the bright mountains, the skies were beginning to darken with the approach of dawn. And fleeing the oncoming day, Nunde raced to the battlements and down and in and to his body lying supine in his bed, his corrupt soul slipping back into place.

And he started up and cursed, for not only had Mosaam

bin Abu stupidly deviated from the design, but up there on the wall and awaiting the rending of the sun stood the corpse of the slain Ogh.

In spite of having the <fire> of but six Drik to aid him, Radok had succeeded.

Nunde would have to take care indeed.

24

Gambit

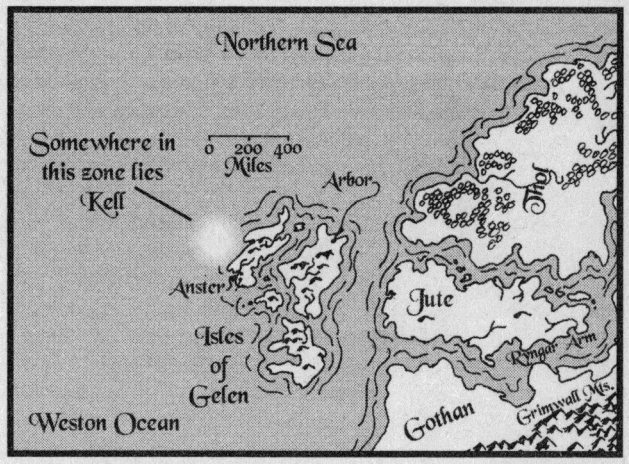

Northern Sea

Somewhere in
this zone lies
Kell

0 200 400
Miles

Arbor

Anster

Isles
of
Gelen

Jute

Ryngar Arm

Thol

Gothan

Grimwall Mts.

Weston Ocean

A mong the terrible things about war, battle, combat, are the unintended consequences, the side effects, the collateral damage, not only to persons, places, animals, and things, but also to the mind, to the spirit, to the heart, for the wounds are seen and unseen as well. And the veiled injuries are perhaps the most damaging of all, for they are driven by fear and rage and loss, and they leave hidden scars behind in the ones so hurt. Some never recover, and the festering hate, unremitting grief, everlasting dread, and the like, profoundly affect their very existence, and at times lead them to take excessive measures. Others rebound swiftly, though the harm is not forgotten. Most who survive war and battle and combat fall somewhere in between these two extremities, for life goes on. Yet, waking or sleeping, on occasion remembrance engulfs them again, and the violence and harm sweep through their presence once more.

And as to outcomes of battle: at least the dead are dead and escape the follow-on torment.

Whether they served in the midst of the conflict, or on the fringes, or at a place far away, those who live on are the ones who suffer the unintended consequences, the aftereffects, the collateral damage; they are the casualties who pay the irreversible price, be it everlasting or fleetingly swift or lying somewhere in between. . . .

. . . And upon a farm in Darda Coill, several survivors fretted and stewed even as another one came flying toward them. . . .

As ALRIC STOICALLY WINGED arrows toward a target on a cord-tied bale, Rígán, his own bow in hand, paced back and forth and seethed.

Off to one side Catlin and Driu sat at a yard table, and

snapped green beans from a large tub at hand, using the common labor to keep their minds off the events in Sjøen, whatever they might be.

As the dark-haired lad loosed another shaft, "We should be there, Alric," declared Rígán. "At least, I should be. I mean, after all, I am the one who brings this danger down upon everyone. I should be in the forefront rather than cowering back here at the farm."

"Not so," said Alric, stepping forward to recover his arrows. "At least not until you are declared."

Rígán groaned in frustration, and Driu said, "Alric is right, Reyer. We would like you to reach the throne, more apt to happen if you don't mix in the thick of it."

The tall, nearly fourteen-year-old Rígán stopped his pacing and glared at the Seer and angrily countered, "Then what good is it to be trained in combat if I don't use any of it? It's my fight, too!"

Driu opened her mouth to reply, but a distant, high-pitched shout interrupted her: *"Alric! Alric!"*

A horse came hammering out from the trees and across the far field, and on its back—

Alric slipped the last arrow into his quiver and turned even as came another piercing cry of *"Alric!"*

"That's Mór Dearg," said Alric, moving swiftly back to the table.

"Mór Dearg? The tiarna's horse?" blurted Catlin, as she and Driu leapt to their feet.

Again the girl cried out for Alric.

Rígán frowned. "Caleen?"

"It *is* Caleen," said Alric.

On she came, her dark tresses flying out behind. Her legs were too short for her feet to reach the stirrups, yet the girl managed to hang on to Mór Dearg.

"Arrows!" barked Rígán, and he and Alric nocked shafts and searched the tree line for following foes.

In moments the gelding reached the sward. The girl haled back on the reins, and Conal's horse slid to a stop, squatting on its haunches. Caleen lost her seat and flew over the pommel and tumbled to the grass. As Alric scrambled to the girl, Rígán managed to grab the reins of Mór Dearg, the gelding wild-eyed and snorting.

Cuán came running from the stables, and Gretta stepped out from the house, and when Gretta saw Conal's horse, she cried, "Oh, no!" and the strength went out from her legs and she slumped to the porch.

"Steady, Big Red, steady," soothed Rígán, calling the gelding by its common name as he tried to calm the horse, yet it sidled and snorted and stamped and pulled back, clearly on the verge of bolting.

Alric got Caleen to her feet and away from the tramping hooves of Mór Dearg. And the girl clung to Alric and wept, her dress torn, a smear of blood across her face.

Cuán reached the mount and took the reins from Rígán, and spoke to the animal, his cooing words in old Kellian, and in but moments Big Red settled somewhat.

"They killed her, Alric," wailed Caleen. "They killed her. And they wanted to kill me, too."

"Someone tried to kill you?" blurted Alric.

"Who are the enemy? And is there fighting?" asked Rígán. "I knew we should have been there!"

"Who did they kill?" asked Alric.

"What of the tiarna?" demanded Catlin. "And the men?"

"And the Dylvana?" added Rígán.

"Stand back," commanded Driu, and she shushed them all and knelt at Caleen's side and motioned for the boy to sit her down.

Cuán led Big Red away toward the stables, and Rígán turned and saw that Gretta, her legs folded to one side, was crumpled down in the middle of the porch, stricken, weeping. He rushed to her. "Mother Gretta?"

She looked up at him. "He's gone, Rígán. He's gone."

Rígán knelt. "We don't know that, Mother Gretta."

"But the horse—"

"All we know is that Caleen rode him here." He stood and held out his hand. "Come, let us hear what Caleen has to say."

"I haven't the strength to listen," said Gretta, yet she took Rígán's grip and stood, and he fetched her to the table, where she sat.

"—villagers," wailed Caleen.

"The people of Sjøen? They killed your aunt?" asked Driu.

"Why?" asked Alric.

"The birds. Aunt Britta had birds."

"I don't understand," said Alric, looking at Driu.

Driu took Caleen's hands in her own and said a <word>. A moment later, Driu said, "She was an agent of Arkov's."

Alric shook his head. "An agent of—?"

"Never mind that," blurted Rígán. "What of the battle? What of the foe? And what of our men?"

"It's over, it's over. The killing is over," said Caleen. "They came in two ships, and—"

"Two?" demanded Driu. "Two ships?"

"Jutlander Dragonships?" asked Catlin.

"No, they were—"

"There should have been *three*," exclaimed Driu.

From the sty there came a loud squealing, which abruptly chopped to silence.

"Molly," said Rígán, and he turned to see dark men in dark clothes—seven with tulwars, five with crossbows—come running, spread wide.

Even as he raised his bow and stepped in front of the women, "Driu, Catlin, into the house!" snapped Rígán. "Alric, the ones with the crossbows first!" And he loosed at an onrushing man at one end of the line. Beside him, and yet kneeling, Alric took up his own bow and let fly at another.

Two arrows; two men down. Yet ten more continued to charge.

Driu grabbed Caleen, and she and the girl and Gretta bolted for the house, but Catlin snatched up a large knife from beside the bean pan and stood her ground with the boys.

Rígán kicked over the table, shouting, "Alric. Shield!"

"My beans!" snarled Catlin, even as the tub went clanging to the ground and Alric and Rígán stepped to the table to use it as cover.

Cuán, Big Red in hand, had just reached the barn, and he turned and gasped at the unfolding scene. Then he vaulted to Big Red's back and charged empty-handed.

Two more arrows; two more men down.

Crossbowmen stopped and took aim, yet coming at an angle, Cuán on Big Red ran over them even as the quarrels were loosed—two to thunk into the table, two to fly wide, and one to bring down one of their own men—and the remaining men were scattered, one to die under the hooves of Big Red.

Alric and Rígán brought down two more of the disarrayed attackers.

Two of the men came on, shouting, *"Nihna Issukut Khayâlîn!"* Tulwars raised, they had nearly reached the table, yet neither man survived the next two arrows.

Even as those arrows were loosed, Catlin, screaming some prolonged and unrecognizable cry, leapt toward one of the men who had been knocked down by Big Red, and as that foe floundered, trying to regain his feet, she slashed her blade through his throat. Blood spurting, he fell back slain.

A man behind her swung his sword, but Alric's white-fletched arrow took him in the neck, and the blow never landed.

Cuán on Big Red swung the horse about to make another charge, yet all the attackers were down, and he looked at Rígán for what next to do.

"Stay sharp," said Rígán. "We know not whether these are the last," and he motioned for Cuán to circle about and see if the threat was through.

Rígán, Alric, and Catlin waited long moments, and Cuán on Big Red went wide 'round the house and the outbuildings, seeking enemy, yet no more foe appeared. Cuán returned to the foreyard, and, finally, Rígán said, "This battle is over."

Cuán nodded and headed Big Red for the stables, but one by one Catlin stepped to each of the fallen men and cut their throats just to make bloody certain they were well and truly dead. At the man pierced by the crossbow bolt she called out, "This one is yet breathing."

"Save him for—" began Rígán, even as Catlin slashed the knife across the man's neck.

"Ah, well," said Alric, "so much for capturing a prisoner."
Then he turned to see Driu and Gretta and Caleen peering
out the doorway, and said, " 'Twas good we remained here
instead of riding to battle in Sjøen, else the women might
now be slain."

Rígán looked at Catlin, just then striding back from the
farthest dead assassin, blood dripping from her kitchen
knife, a satisfied savage grin on her face, and he said, "Then
again, perhaps not."

Both he and Alric broke into gales of laughter, relief, not
humor, pouring out of them—the aftermath of the slaughter.

25

Revelations

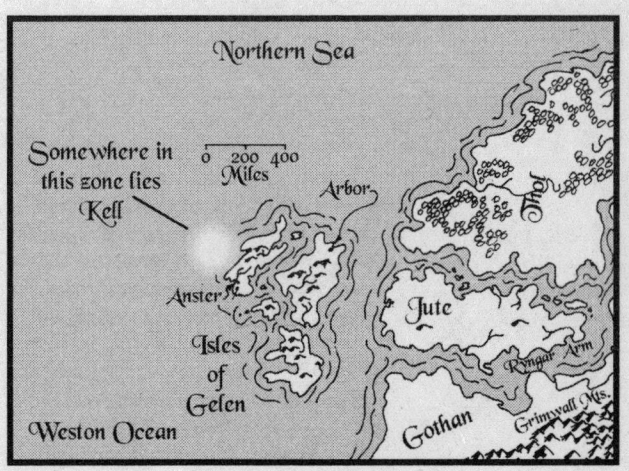

For the most part, heroes are commonplace people who manage to rise to the occasion when they are caught up in extraordinary circumstances. They do exceptional things to meet the crucial needs of the moment. Typically, they themselves do not consider what they have done to be heroic, but rather it was simply what had to be done, and, without much forethought, they did it.

Cowards, on the other hand, flee from these moments, or shrink in hiding or commit some heinous acts to keep themselves safe from harm, be it physical or mental or otherwise.

It is said that the seeds of heroism and cowardice exist in the everyman, and a hero one day might be a coward the next, as well as vice versa—spineless Alos, a simple sailor and drunkard, is an example of this latter, for, in spite of his cravenness in perilous circumstances, he became a linchpin in the Quest of the Dragonstone.

That is not to say that all heroes and cowards are commonplace people. Many throughout the history of Mithgar are in fact quite far from being run-of-the-mill. Elgo of Jord was certainly the opposite of an everyday person, as was his sister, Elyn, and her eventual companion, Thork.

But when one considers Tipperton Thistledown—an ordinary miller who was called upon to deliver a coin—who could be more normal than that? A Warrow he was, yes, one living among Humans, but otherwise he was completely indistinguishable from any other ordinary villager. Yet had he not taken up the cause at the onset of the Great War of the Ban ... well, who knows what the outcome might have been?

And so, heroes come in all stripes, be they ones of special abilities or ones without, be they unsung or not. What sets them apart is their steadfastness in the face of peril, their acts of courage or nobility or purpose, and their ability to rise to meet the occasions. And even though they do not see themselves as heroes, it is in the eyes of others that they become such. . . .

. . . and on a farm in a forest in Kell . . .

"Alric!" Caleen broke free from Driu's grasp and came running toward the lad. She clasped him in her embrace and said, "Oh, Alric, you were so very brave. Even more so than when you saved us all from that tinkerman."

"Um . . . er," mumbled Alric. Then he managed to say, "Rígán and Catlin and Cuán on Big Red—"

"Yes, yes, they must have helped you," interrupted Caleen, "but Alric, you were so brave."

Driu smiled, but Gretta frowned and sighed in exasperation, both women now out on the sward. And Gretta said, "Here, now," and reached for the girl. But in that moment and from the barnyard, Catlin loosed an anguished howl.

"Wha—?" barked Rígán, nocking another arrow even as he turned and ran toward the pigsty.

Alric broke away from Caleen, and ran after, an arrow set to string as well.

"They killed her," wailed Catlin. "They killed my Molly."

Rígán arrived at the pen to see Catlin sitting in the mud, with the sow's head in her lap. Two quarrels jutted out from Molly's side. A pair of abandoned crossbows lay nearby.

Catlin, tears streaming, looked up at Rígán and said, "Oh, Reyer, they killed her to keep her quiet, to keep her from sounding a warning. But she called out the alert in spite of them."

"Oh, Catlin, I—" began Rígán, but at that moment Molly gave a grunt and opened her eyes and struggled to get free of Catlin, but squealed in pain and flopped back down.

"I'll get Cuán," said Alric. "He'll know what to do."

When the men and the Dylvana came riding back on the land of the farm, they found Driu and Gretta and Catlin and Cuán kneeling in the mud of the sty and treating the wounded pig, with Alric and Rígán and Caleen sitting on the top fence rail and watching.

Working out from the midst of the band and riding a black horse, Conal said, "Men dead in the fore yard, women down in the sty, what passes, Rígán?"

"*Conal!*" shrieked Gretta, "You live!" Yet, while Cuán cat-gut-stitched up the other wound, Gretta kept the pressure against the dressing on this one and did not leave her place at Molly's side.

"Of course, I live, woman," said Conal. "Did not Caleen tell you so?"

DYLVANA CAME RIDING BACK onto the farm, and one, a lithe female named Ris, leapt down from her horse and touched hands with Halon, her consort. Like all the Dylvana, her shoulder-length hair—hers chestnut colored—was held back from her face by a rune-marked headband.

"Dara," he said.

"Alor," she replied. Then she turned to Conal and said, "We followed their tracks back to the shore." Ris glanced at Driu and shook her head and said, "The third raider was not moored there. But we espied crimson sails dwindling in the distance, just then going o'er the rim of the w'rld, sails like on the other two ships."

Conal growled. "The raid on the town was a ruse."

At Conal's words, Halon nodded and added, "To get us away from Rígán so the assassins could reach the farm unimpeded. We cannot let this happen again."

As Conal nodded his agreement, Caleen frowned and leaned over to Alric and whispered, "Why would they want to harm Rígán?"

Alric looked at her, but said nothing.

"I mean, *you* are the one who slew the tinkerman," murmured Caleen, "not Rígán."

Alric merely shrugged.

Conal glanced at Caleen and away and said, "Well, it did reveal Arkov's agent in Sjøen, or so I believe."

"Aye," said Halon. Then the Dylvana shook his head and said, "Yet only because she released that bird." Halon looked at his beloved.

"I thought it a messenger back to Kistan," said Ris, fingering her bow. "That's why I brought it down."

Rígán looked at Conal. "Why think you it was headed to Arkov instead?"

"The message, though coded, was in a script I recognized," said Conal. "One I came across when I was a kingsguard. Garian, it was, with those backward letters sprinkled here and there. Then again, though it was written in Garian runes, she might have been another's agent, mayhap someone in Kistan."

"Have you the message still?" asked Driu.

Without comment, Conal handed the tissue-thin strip over to the Seer.

Driu said a <word>, and moments later, she nodded and said, "It is to Arkov and says that the raiders have landed, but all were killed and the boy survives."

"Then she did not know about the third ship," said Conal.

"No, she did not," said Driu.

"Too bad she did not live long enough to be questioned," said Ris.

Conal sighed and said, "I let slip that she was Arkov's spy, and that's when the women of Sjøen tore her apart." He looked at Caleen and said, "They would have killed you too, lass, but I stopped them."

"Thank you for putting me on your horse, Tiarna," said Caleen.

"I knew he'd run right here," said Conal, "where I thought you would be safe. Little did I know . . ." He shook his head and stared out across the field at the pyre where the twelve assassins' corpses now burned.

"Even so," said Gretta, glaring at the girl, "the child needs to be questioned. She might be an agent as well."

Driu shook her head. "She is not. I looked into her past when I held her this day. Instead she is an innocent, used by her so-called aunt as a ploy to garner sympathy."

"So-called? So-called aunt?" said Rígán. "You mean Britta is, er rather, *was* not really Caleen's kindred?"

"Nay, she was not," said Driu.

"She wasn't?" asked Caleen, her eyes wide in shock.

"Nay, child," said Driu.

"But she said—"

" 'Twas a lie," said Driu.

"Oh, Alric," said Caleen, stricken and looking at the lad, tears streaming down her face, "she was a spy. My aunt was a spy. Or rather the person I thought was my aunt."

Alric reached out and took Caleen's hand, and Gretta gritted her teeth to see such a thing.

"What about these raiders?" asked Rígán. "They don't, or rather, didn't look like Garians. And what does *'Nihna Issukut Khayâlîn!'* mean?"

"Nihna Issukut Khayâlîn?" asked Driu.

"That's what one of the men shouted as he came running toward us," said Alric.

"It was a boast," said the Seer, "a battle cry. It means 'We are the Silent Shadows.' "

"They certainly are silent now," said Ris, a grim smile on her face, a glint of satisfaction in her grey eyes. Then she inclined her head toward Rígán and Alric and Catlin and said, "Nicely done."

"Don't forget Cuán and Big Red," said Alric. "Without them we would be the ones on the pyre instead of the Silent Shadows."

"Oh, my," said Caleen. Then she added, "No, Alric, you wouldn't be on the pyre; you would have found a way to save us all."

"Silent Shadows," said Conal. "I've heard of them. They are from Nizari, the Red City of Assassins. And with this attack upon Reyer—Rígán—it means that they are in league with Arkov."

As Caleen looked toward Rígán and blinked in confusion, "Then the rumors of Arkov making alliances with the Southers must be true," said Halon.

"Damn his eyes!" spat Catlin. "Siding with our enemies of old."

A silence fell upon all of them, but finally the Seer looked at the others and then back to Caleen. "Why not tell us when you first met her—Britta, I mean."

"All right," said Caleen. She took a deep breath and began: "It was just before we came to Sjøen," said Caleen. "I was in the workhouse—"

"Where?" asked Rígán.

"In Caer Pendwyr," said Caleen.

"The children's workhouse in Caer Pendwyr?" asked Gretta.

"Yes," replied Caleen. "Until Britta took me, it was where I had spent most of my life."

Gretta nodded to herself, but did not again interrupt.

Alric smiled at Caleen, encouraging her to go on, and she said, "One day they had all of us girls to stand in a row. A woman came—Aunt Britta—and she went up and down the line several times, looking closely at everyone.

"Finally, she stopped at me and said I had good bones and promising features, and would be acceptable when I grew up. Then she told me she had found me at last. She said she was my mother's sister, and that I was now free to live with her." Caleen looked at Alric and said, "I was so glad she had found me that I cried, for I had a family at last."

"You never knew your mother?" asked Rígán.

Caleen shook her head. "Nor my father."

"Neither did I," said Rígán. "Neither mother nor father."

For the first time Caleen looked at Rígán with sympathy in her gaze.

"I never knew my father," said Alric.

Gretta sat silent.

"Go on, child," said Driu.

"We sailed away on a ship."

"What kind of ship was it?" asked Catlin. "Jutlander, like Britta said?"

"Yes," said Caleen, while at the very same time Driu shook her head and said, "No."

"No?" asked Caleen, looking at Driu. "But Aunt Britta said—"

" 'Twas another of her lies," said Driu.

"What kind was it?" asked Conal.

"An Albaner," said the Seer.

"One of Arkov's allies," said Gretta. "They aided him to overthrow King Valen."

Morosely, Conal nodded, and again a silence fell upon them all.

Timorously, Caleen smiled at Alric and entwined her fingers with his.

Gretta noted the gesture and glowered at Caleen and said, "You do not speak like the little guttersnipe you are."

"Gretta!" snapped Conal.

Alric looked at his mother in surprise. Gretta turned her face away from the girl, but said no more.

"On the ship," said Caleen, a bite in her words, "Aunt Britta schooled me in the proper way to speak Common, and in table manners, and other such things. And when we got here, she continued teaching me, including how to read and write."

"At least she did that much good," said Catlin, now glaring at Gretta.

"What of this tale of your aunt, of Britta, being . . . molested?" asked Gretta.

"Molested?" asked Caleen.

"She means being hurt by the men on the ship," said Driu.

"Oh, I think it must have been terrible, though she bore no scars afterward. But when they tortured her, it was when she went to the captain's cabin and I could hear her moaning."

Conal barked a laugh, and Halon and Ris and Catlin smiled in understanding.

"What of this tale of being thrown overboard?" asked Gretta, still not looking at the child.

"Oh, that's true," said Caleen, and Driu nodded in affirmation.

"They tossed us into the sea, but Britta kept me from drowning and she found a floating plank nearby. We paddled away, and the ship turned and sailed off."

" 'Twas to make the story ring true," said Driu. "After all, Caleen, believing the lie, would buttress her aunt's tale."

"Then what about the birds?" asked Gretta.

"All I know is that she kept three," said Caleen. "One night a man came, and the next day was gone, and after that Aunt Britta had three birds. I liked them; they were pretty. Now and again she would let me feed them. They were nice and gentle."

Caleen fell silent, and finally Conal said, "We need to give her shelter."

"What?" asked Gretta.

"I mean," said Conal, "she cannot stay in the village, not with tempers as high as they are. They are like to kill her out of hand simply because of her 'aunt.'"

"Well, she cannot stay here," said Gretta. "She is nothing but a Lowborn—"

"Gretta," warned Conal harshly.

Gretta clenched her teeth and finally said, "I cannot let her turn Alric's head, nor for that matter, Reyer's."

Caleen frowned and looked at Rígán, as if wondering why anyone would call him Reyer.

"She will stay with us," said Halon, with Ris nodding her approval.

"Stay with the Dylvana?" asked Caleen, her voice rising with hope. "You want me to stay with the Elves?"

"Yes, child," said Halon. "We will raise you as our own."

Schemes

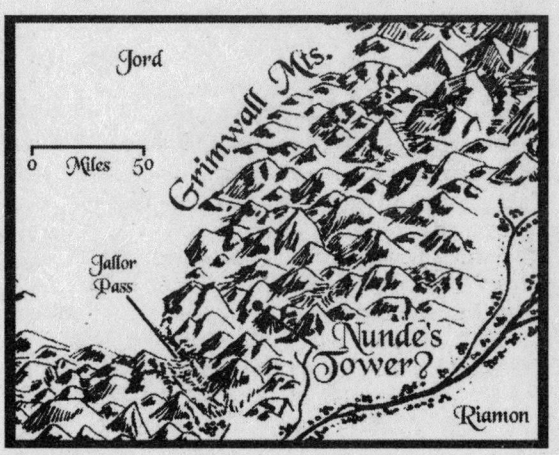

In the Grey Mountains in the Realm of Xian there sits an ebon Wizardholt. 'Tis Black Mountain, where at the time of this tale, Mages <rest> to recover the life force given up during the Great War of the Ban. Were they on their home world of Vadaria, they would have already recovered what they had spent. Yet with the destruction of Rwn, the only known crossing had been lost; but e'en could they return to Vadaria they would not go, for with the Sundering they could not get back to Mithgar. And so the Mages <rest> and recover, there in the dark stone mountain, a place of infinite possibility.

And somewhere within this fortress there exists a great spherical chamber, in the middle of which is a huge globe rotating slowly on a tilted axis. It is not told just how large is the orb, yet it is certainly several times man-height. A catwalk leads to a sturdy, latticed framework enclosing the sphere, and on one wall of the chamber is a lensed lantern in a housing affixed to a track marked with days and seasons running full 'round the room.

Designed by the Mages but crafted by the Dwarves, the globe is an accurate map of Mithgar, and the lantern represents the sun. The moon itself is missing from this depiction, but it will be added some day.

That the world is a ball might surprise some, but not the members of Wizardry, for they ken the truth of the matter.

Yet not only are the lands and waters delineated thereon, but the globe itself is riddled with glints—some dazzling, some dark. Each bright spark represents one of White Magekind, and each dark glimmer one of those of the Black; one might speculate how this is done, yet only the Wizards know for certain.

And at the place of one of the shadowy gleams, there in the depths of the Grimwalls ...

* * *

"Master," cried Radok, clattering down the stone stairwell, "a message, a bird, from Gelen, from Kell."

But Nunde was not in the laboratory, and so Radok's call went unheeded.

Whirling, Radok stepped back into the corridor where stood a Hlôk on guard. [Where is the Master?] snarled Radok in Slûk.

Cringing in fear and bobbing in subservience, the Hlôk grunted wordlessly and pointed toward the end of the hall where lay Nunde's chambers.

Now it was Radok who cringed, for to disturb Nunde in his quarters . . .

Yet the message was vital, and so, dreading what might happen, Radok crept toward the far end of the hall, while the tongueless Hlôk behind him smirked, now that the tables were turned.

Lightly, Radok tapped at the heavy bronze door, and whispered, "Master?" Yet he knew the sound did not penetrate.

Screwing up his courage, he reached for the speaking tube and spoke into the funnel. "Master, a message, a bird, from Gelen."

With his ear pressed against the bell of the horn, again Radok cringed as he heard Nunde curse. But then Nunde bade him to enter.

Lifting the latch and grunting with the effort, Radok pushed open the door and stood on the sill, waiting. And sitting on the edge of the wide dark bed in which a fresh female corpse lay splayed, Nunde gestured the apprentice to enter.

Radok passed by the altar with its still warm basin of blood and handed the message capsule to his master.

A moment later, Nunde gave a triumphant laugh. "The boy survived the raid of the fortnight past. Good! Now my plans go forward in spite of that blundering fool."

"Blundering fool, Master?"

"Mosaam bin Abu, you idiot. Had the raid succeeded, then Arkov would no longer be my unwitting catspaw."

"Catspaw, Master?"

"My ignorant dupe."

With this latter remark, the apprentice did not know whether his master referred to Arkov or to Radok himself.

Smiling, Nunde looked at Radok, and the apprentice cringed in response. "Radok, let me explain my glorious design."

Clothed only by his own waist-length hair, Nunde paced back and forth, elaborate gestures punctuating his words, his voice glowing at his own cleverness.

Radok stood speechless, not only because to interrupt his master might be fatal, but also because of the deviousness of Nunde's plan.

And when Nunde finished, Radok said, "Oh, Master, how, how . . ."

"Ingenious?" supplied Nunde.

"The very word, Master, the very word."

"Yes, it is," said Nunde, preening. But then his face twisted in a scowl. "Yet first, I must deal with the one who nearly wrecked all my plans."

Still unclothed, Nunde stepped to a small escritoire and quickly penned a note on a tissue-thin strip. He then stood and slipped the message into a capsule, all the while looking at the corpse on his bed. He handed the capsule to Radok. "This goes to Chabba, to the m'alik himself."

"Fadal, Master?"

"Of course, idiot," snapped Nunde, and he turned toward the bed. "Now go, and leave me to my pleasures."

"Yes, Master," said Radok, glancing at the black satin sheets and the throat-cut female thereon. Then he spun on his heel and raced toward the cotes, for the sun would soon rise, and he would dispatch the bird ere then, for he would not delay his master's order.

Within moments, a black Grimwall Corvus winged on its way, the message tied to its leg.

And heartbeats later the sun rose, yet it found no one on the dark ramparts above, for all those so banned cringed in the chambers below, shut away from Adon's light.

Allies

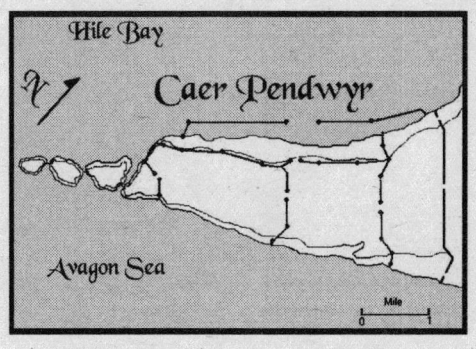

As an eagle might fly, it is just over four thousand miles from the Island of Kell in the Weston Ocean to the city of Khalísh in Hyree. But by Kistanian ship the journey is much longer, for a bird wages over both water and land, whereas the oceangoing vessel must sail the brine. Hence, by water, a craft would first fare southerly from Kell to reach the Straits of Kistan and then southeasterly to reach the goal of Khalísh, a journey of some five thousand miles. But given the fickleness of Ruella, the goddess of the winds, there are calms and doldrums with "irons" to escape, or storms and blows with shrieking winds to battle, and the tacking alone adds at least half again as many miles as one would think. Even so, the surviving crew of the Kistanian Rovers sailed into port some fifty days after the raid on the farm. A black desert kite was immediately dispatched to the capital of Chabba, and shortly thereafter a dark gull flew across the Avagon Sea, aiming for cotes of the Chabbain embassy in Caer Pendwyr.

And from that embassy the new ambassador, Kaleem bin Aziz, called upon King Arkov.

And in the throne room emptied of all but three . . .

"I BRING NEWS FROM KELL, my lord."

"At last," growled Arkov.

"The raid failed; the boy yet lives."

"*Sranje!*" cursed Arkov, slamming his fist against the arm of the throne. He leapt to his feet and strode to a window and looked out upon the Avagon Sea, where sheets of rain fell from the somber skies above.

Counselor Baloff turned to the ambassador. "And you know this how?"

"The Kistanian ship docked in Khalísh a fortnight past,

and messenger birds were sent. It confirms what M'alik Fadal has known for weeks."

Arkov whirled about. "Fadal has known this for weeks?"

"Aye, sire."

Arkov stalked over and glared down at the short dark man. "And yet you withheld that knowledge?"

Kaleem inclined his head in assent and said what he had been instructed to say: "We waited for confirmation, my lord." Then he spread his fine-boned hands wide. "We thought surely your own agents in Kell would have sent you word."

Arkov ground his teeth in frustration. "Out! Leave my presence!"

Kaleem bowed and backed away. "As you will, my lord. As you will."

Baloff accompanied the ambassador to the door of the chamber, and when they had stepped clear of it, the counselor asked, "Is there aught else you would tell us?"

"Just this," said the small dark man. "If the boy is truly Valen's heir, that he has survived will make the Northern Alliance even stronger. I think your own forces are woefully inadequate to meet them in combat, and the army we are assembling to send to your aid must be strengthened."

ARKOV ONCE AGAIN STOOD at the window overlooking the sea. The skies continued to weep, wind-driven rain sweeping across the white chop below. "Did you hear what that little brown pile of *gnoj* said?" Arkov took on a mincing tone: " 'Surely your own agents in Kell would have sent you word.' As if we had any agents left on that cursed isle."

Baloff shook his head. "Even so, my lord, he was right. If Petja yet lives, she should have sent a bird."

"Think you she has turned against us?"

"Perhaps, my lord. Perhaps she has joined with the people of Sjøen, she and that little girl."

"I am besieged by traitors and fools," growled Arkov. He turned away from the window and strode to the throne and flopped down. "At least we know why Abu suddenly and mysteriously died."

"Mosaam bin Abu?"

"Yes, Baloff. That's what I said."

Baloff made no comment, for it seemed Arkov was intent on not recognizing the difference between any Chabbain's given and surnames.

As Baloff took his customary seat at the side of the dais, he said, "My lord, what I meant was that I don't understand why he died, though rumors say he was poisoned."

"Abu failed, Baloff. First, it took two years just to get the mission under way, and then his so-called Silent Shadows bungled the assignment; they did not slay the child. Fadal has known Abu's blunder for some time, and so the m'alik had that incompetent killed."

They sat in silence for long moments, each lost in his own thoughts. Finally, Arkov said, "As much as I hate to admit it, this new ambassador, Aziz, has a point: it will make the Northern Alliance stronger. We should ask Fadal for more aid."

Baloff groaned softly and said, "I think it will cause the unrest in Hoven and Jugo and Riamon to grow."

"Let it," snarled Arkov. "After we destroy the Alliance, then we will deal with them."

Again a stillness fell upon the two, finally broken by Arkov, who murmured, "Fadal is a good ally to have."

Baloff wondered whether Arkov meant for his thought to be silent or said aloud.

WITH RAIN FALLING FROM a dismal sky, Kaleem bin Aziz, from the covered carriage in which he rode, marveled at how the tile roofs of Caer Pendwyr channeled the precious liquid into the cisterns and wells below. He would make a note of this and pass it on to his superiors in the palace of M'alik Fadal. As much as the Chabbains loathed the Pellarians, still this was a good way to gather such a harvest against more arid times.

Kaleem then smiled to himself, for the meeting with Arkov had gone just as planned. Then he laughed aloud, but quietly, for he knew that the fool of a usurper and his aide would draw an erroneous conclusion over the news of

Kaleem's predecessor. But Kaleem had deduced the truth behind the m'alik's decision, and, no doubt, that of the *m'alim* in the dark mountains far north. For Kaleem had perhaps determined the master's grand scheme, and so would not make the same mistake: Mosaam bin Abu had been recalled and eliminated not because he had failed to kill the boy, but rather because he had nearly succeeded.

Escort

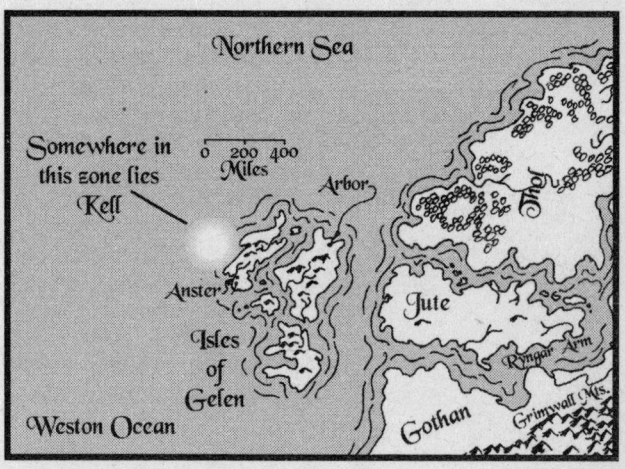

When adversaries of old with millennia of bad blood between them unite against a common foe, the wrongs of yore simply do not vanish but instead lie smoldering 'neath. The antagonists keep wary, vigilant eyes upon one another, seeking signs of betrayal, treachery, duplicity. There lies no trust twixt the two, for their past encounters with one another most often have been in brutal retribution. Even so, when faced with a mutual adversary, there is an old saying: the enemy of my enemy is my friend.... At least for a while, that is.

In Mithgar, even among nations within the High King's realm, bitter is the blood that often fills the cups of individual warring monarchs. And one of the High King's roles is to settle such disputes fairly. Yet when the Usurper took the throne for himself, seldom did any bring their grievances to him, for though they trusted one another not, they trusted Arkov even less.

And among ancient and recurrent antagonists, the nations of Jute and Fjordland seemed ever in conflict—not continuous war but sporadic assaults instead. It began centuries agone, when both were in the same ravaging pursuit—the business of looting and pillaging and raiding, plundering from others that which they themselves had not earned, neither by the labor of their hands nor the sweat of their brow. Each raided the seaside villages and river cities of Thol and Rian and Gothon and Basq and Vancha and the Gelen Isles. Each in their Dragonboats, each with swift and lethal strikes. At times their raids brought them into conflict with one another, when, on rare occasion, they came upon a town being raided that they themselves had come to spoil. At other times they found their intended victims had already been sacked by their rival. But one side then made the mistake of marauding a town of the other—just which one did this first has always been in dispute. Yet, given that instance, there began the assaults and killings of reprisal, of vengeance, retaliation, and of settling scores both new and old. And in spite of the efforts of various High Kings down through the centuries, the enmity and revenge never ended.

Yet following the Quest of the Dragonstone, of Arin Flameseer and Egil One-Eye's union, Fjordland slowly became a seafaring nation of trade: they left their old plundering ways behind. Oh, they still sought vengeance against the Jutes—answering incursions with incursions, raids with raids, and killings with killings, for even the great Fjordlander Egil One-Eye could not let such things go without answer. And as for the Jutes, they, as well, let not such things pass . . . especially with their mad monarchs sitting on the Black Throne, Hadron being the first to do so. Even though he began his reign perfectly lucid of mind, he slowly went insane, gradually coming to believe all those about him—as well as those afar—were plotting his downfall. And all who have sat upon the Black Throne since then, they have gone mad in their turn. It was and is commonly believed that a curse or bad blood in the Jutland royal line did and will always lead to an irrational occupant of the Black Throne. But the dukes, counts, and viscounts, even down unto the barons of that realm, use this madness to promote their own ends, feeding the monarch's unfounded fears and suspicions of the Fjordlanders and others to play upon the fixation, hence furthering the ambitions of the members of the royal court. And thus, with one side driven by a madman and perceived persecution, and the other by ancient hatred and vengeance, no High King of Mithgar had ever managed to settle once and for all the adamant hostility between the two.

Yet using the enemy-of-my-enemy argument, Lord Aarnson of Thol managed to tentatively unite these two implacable foes in the cause of the Northern Alliance for the duration it would require. Even so, in Reyer's fourteenth year, it took Vanidar Silverleaf the full of it to negotiate an escort to ferry the fifteen-year-old true High King of Mithgar on the first leg of his investment journey. For they would be sailing through the northern reach of the Ryngar Arm of the Weston Ocean there along the border of Jute, and Silverleaf trusted not the mad king.

During these long negotiations, birds flew—some to Challerain Keep, others to Fjordland, and still others to Kell—all messages couched in an obscure code, all citing the painfully slow progress of the talks.

Yet occasionally a bird would fly from Jute to Caer Pendwyr, followed by a dark bird winging to the Grimwall Mountains and another to Chabba. And once in a while a bird would fly from Challerain Keep to the Usurper's royal towers in Caer Pendwyr, followed by a flurry of birds flying from Arkov to allies in Alban, with birds flying in return.

But at last the negotiations came to an end, and on an appointed day in the fifteenth year of Reyer called Rígán, in the seaside city of Sjøen . . .

. . . FRANTICALLY THE ALARM SOUNDED—the striking of sledge on the great hanging loop of iron—the clangor calling all to arms. A hammer of running feet pounded on the wooden sidewalks, and men shouted and pulled their war axes from wall racks and headed for the seaside docks. Women wailed and gathered their children, and headed up the inland slopes toward the reaches of the Elven forest above.

Tessa stepped out from her tea room and grabbed a lad flying past by the arm, swinging him about to face her. "What is it, Ragnar? What's—"

"Jutlander Dragonships. A fleet. Coming from the south. A hundred or more."

Tessa's heart leapt to her throat, but ere she could ask further, Ragnar jerked loose and fled. Tessa hiked up her dress and belted it anew so that the hem fell just to her knees. Then she ran into her shop and to a back room and slipped into a heavy leather vest and snatched up her Fjordlander-style fighting axe. As she sped toward the docks—*What would a hundred Dragonships want with the likes of Sjøen?*

When she reached the wharves, some men were there

and more came running, along with a handful of women. With axes in hand, all were dressed for battle: leather vests—some with small bronze plates affixed like scales on a fish. A few had the iron helms of their ancestors, and many bore round, metal-bossed shields.

None gainsaid the women, for, like Tessa at her five foot eight, they were as tall as many of the men and certainly taller than some. Besides, this was the Isle of Kell, where women oft fought at the sides of their men.

"Has anyone sent for the Elves?" Tessa asked.

"I think so," said a smaller man at hand.

"What of the tiarna?"

"Him, too. I sent Ragnar to the stables to ride to Conal's holt."

No wonder he jerked away.

"Good," said Tessa, now braiding her long yellow hair.

"I count twelve!" called the lookout on the watchtower.

Twelve?

"No more?" shouted up Tarl, the unofficial mayor of Sjøen.

"Just twelve."

Better than the hundred Ragnar reported. Even so, 'tis more than we alone can handle. Tessa turned and looked upslope toward the distant tree line. *Without the Elves we are lost.*

"Do they all fly the double eagle?" called up someone.

"Aye," came the response.

Jutes, all right.

Tarl leapt upon a large keg and turned to the assembly. "Gather 'round."

As he began reviewing the battle plans and calling out assignments, Tessa kept an eye toward the woodland above, yet no Elves appeared.

Where are they?

While some of the men ran back to their homes to fetch bows and arrows and crossbows and bolts, barricades were erected, and the Jutland Dragonships drew on.

The men returned with the missile casters and were stationed atop several buildings nearby.

And still the fleet neared. Single-masted all and square sailed, with their hulls clinker-built they swiftly cut the waves.

And the Elves did not appear.

Nor the tiarna.

Within a candlemark the Jutes reached the small bay, where, instead of beaching their craft and leaping ashore with weapons in hand, they struck their sails and dropped anchor and remained out in the cove just south of the town.

"What are they doing?" asked Tessa, peering over the newly erected bulwark.

"I don't—" began the man who had stayed by her side, but just then the lookout called, "Sails ho! From the north. Fjordlanders!"

This brought a cheer from the people of Sjøen.

"How many?" shouted up Tarl.

"Looks to be twelve, all flying the Red Dragon."

"By Garlon, there's something afoot here," declared Tarl.

Tessa shook her head, a rueful grin on her face. *I shouldn't wonder, Tarl old sod.*

And they waited . . . as did the Jutes.

Whispered conversations murmured throughout the townsfolk—speculations, rumors, wild guesses.

And still the Elves did not appear.

Soon, and just to the north of the town, the Fjordlanders struck their own sails and dropped anchor as well.

And even as they did so, a sloop rounded the headland. And high on its mast flew the gold and white standard of Thol.

The sloop headed for a pier and struck its sails to glide to a stop dockside.

The lithe helmsman threw a rope to a waiting hand, and then leapt from the ship to the wharf.

'Twas an Elf. 'Twas Vanidar. 'Twas Silverleaf.

And from the forest above, armed and armored Dylvana slowly came riding down.

Silverleaf now sprang to the top of the barricade and gestured toward the Jutes to the south and the Fjordlanders to the north and called out to the townsfolk: "They come in peace to escort the High King on the first leg of his journey to his castle at Challerain Keep."

High King?

Challerain?

"Are you talking about that Usurper?" shouted someone.

Someone else spat on the ground and snarled, "That Arkov bastard?"

More shouts followed.

Silverleaf threw up his hands and waited until the cursing died down. "Nay! Not Arkov. But King Valen's own son."

What?

King Valen's—?

Just who—?

Again Silverleaf threw up his hands, and when quiet was restored, he said, "You know him as Rígán, yet his true name is Reyer. He is the rightful High King."

Tessa's hand flew to her mouth. *Rígán? The High King? Oh my, but wouldn't you know? And here I've bossed him about, telling him to wipe his feet and such, and not get jelly all over. Him and that Alric. But now it wouldn't surprise me if Alric himself isn't a high lord or some such.*

Once more questions and shouts erupted, but then the Dylvana arrived and quietly rode in among the gathering, and their presence seemed to calm the assembly.

" 'Tis true," said Silverleaf. "Rígán is Reyer, the son of Valen, and we are here to escort him to Challerain for his investment. The Northern Alliance stands behind him, and he will one day soon assume rule o'er all the nations under the High King's sway."

Tessa shivered. *War is coming.*

Mired in the death and destruction of the times she herself had been in battle, she lost track of what was said over the next few moments, but came to the dialogue again when Silverleaf said, "The Jutes and the Fjordlanders are united in this, and they come in peace, so call your women and children down from the forest, they are in no danger."

"I will fetch them," said Elissan, one of the Dylvana.

As Elissan turned her grey about, Silverleaf looked at

Tarl and said, "Now if I might, I'll signal the captains to bring their crews ashore." Tarl nodded, and Vanidar raised a silver horn to his lips and sounded a call. At the signal the individual crews of the Jutes and the Fjordlanders began raising anchor and deploying oars, preparing to beach the craft. Vanidar turned to Tarl and added, "Try to not let them mingle o'ermuch, else they're like to renew their old strife."

Tessa broke out into laughter.

DRIU TURNED TO CONAL AND SAID, "They are here."

"Both?"

The Seer nodded and took up her rune stones and slipped them back into the bag.

"I'll call in the family and hands," said Gretta. She stepped to the side porch and took up the metal rod and began ringing the iron triangle. Soon all were gathered in the foreyard, and Conal, standing on the stoop, said, "The ships are here"—he glanced at Driu—"and Silverleaf?" Driu nodded. Conal smiled. "Yes, Silverleaf, too. Well and good. Anyway, as we have discussed these last few days, some of us will stay and mind the farm, while others accompany Reyer on his journey."

Alric grinned, as did Durgan, for they would be in Reyer's train. Catlin frowned, Cuán, too, for they were among those who would remain—Cuán to manage the farm; Catlin to manage the house. Catlin turned and spat on the ground, and mumbled, "I wouldn't want to be in the company of them Jutlanders, anyway." Then she turned to Conal and said aloud, "You mind them Jutes, you hear me. Treacherous swine that they are." She glanced at the sty and added, "I mean no offense to Molly and hers."

In that moment, calling at the top of his lungs, a lad on a roan came galloping out from the woodland. He was too far away for the words to be understood, all but "Tiarna," that is. Arriving at last, he haled the steed up short, and leapt to the ground and ran through the gathering toward Conal, his words tumbling over one another to get the message out; the blowing and snorting roan pranced and sidled, adding an unspoken urgency to the lad's errand.

"Slow down, Ragnar," said Conal, as the boy came running up.

"Two hundred Jutland ships, Tiarna," babbled the lad. "Come to murther us all."

"I told you," shrieked Catlin, and empty hands reached for weapons absent from their sides.

Startled, Conal looked at Driu, and the Seer shook her head, a faint smile playing at her lips. "Twelve, no more, as agreed. Twelve from Fjordland, too. And one from Thol, with Vanidar aboard." Then she laughed and said, "Methinks Ragnar, here, took to horse ere a proper count was made."

"Ah," said Conal, and all in the gathering relaxed, all but Catlin, who muttered under her breath, her words unheard.

Conal looked at the boy and said, "Ragnar, the ships are here in peace. Come into the house. We'll get you a bite to eat, and then you can ride back at a leisurely pace; I have a message I would have you deliver into Silverleaf's hand. That, and you can tell everyone the High King will arrive three days hence; we have packing to do."

Ragnar's eyes flew wide. "The High King? In Sjøen?"

"Indeed."

"Pardon, Tiarna, but I think none will welcome Arkov."

"No, no, lad, not Arkov." Conal glanced at Reyer and smiled. Then he turned back to the boy and said, "No, Ragnar. Not Arkov. The true High King instead...."

ON THE THIRD MORNING, just after dawn, an entourage of Dylvana Elves and Humans rode into the streets of Sjøen. With the ring of his father now on his left hand—the scarlet stone winging crimson glitters to the eye—Reyer rode in the lead, Alric at his left side, Durgan on Steel on his right, and Durgan bore a standard planted in his stirrup cup, with the flag of the High King wafting in the morning breeze: a Golden Griffin rampant on a scarlet field. The flag was one borne into battle by Conal when he was a new cadet in the High King's service, and it had lain in a chest for many long years, furled and unseen. Yet its time had come once again.

The streets were lined with the citizens of Sjøen, and with the crews of the Dragonships, several of whom had bruises and one or two with broken noses and some with black eyes. Yet no one had been slain, and all had finally been brought to task by the various captains of Jute and Fjordland.

And all men bowed and all women curtseyed as Reyer rode past. Reyer smiled and nodded, yet when he fared by Tessa and she raised her gaze from her deep curtsey, he winked. She did not respond in any manner, for this occasion was overwhelmingly solemn to her. He was, in the end, gangling lad or no, the High King of them all.

The lading of the ships began—with goods, water, food, grain, horses, and other such, along with those who would be going.

As that got under way—ships docking, filling, pulling back—down from the woodland rode Ris, and at her side fared black-haired Caleen dressed in Elven garments—pale blue and white—and riding a dappled horse, and though but a maiden in her first teens she was striking in her silken raiment.

She curtseyed to Reyer, but she embraced Alric and whispered something in his ear.

Off to one side Gretta looked on, her gaze somehow less unfavorable, for perhaps Caleen wasn't a guttersnipe after all. Even so, Gretta was determined that Alric would not marry a Lowborn—slender and beautiful or no.

At length all stood ready—the ships fully laded and their captains anxious to catch the good wind that had come.

Finally, and last, Reyer—fifteen and nearly six feet tall—stood on a keg before the assembly and said, "Thank you for my safekeeping. I shall try to serve well. Someday I will return and we shall all have tea and red-berry jam-spread scones at Tessa's Tea Room."

This brought a quiet smile to Tessa.

Reyer was about to step down, but Conal gave a nearly imperceptible shake of his head. And then unofficial Mayor Tarl called out, "Three cheers for High King Reyer! Long may he rule!"

When the echoes of the shouts died away, Caleen again curtseyed to Reyer and kissed Alric, tears in her eyes. And then the two lads stepped aboard the sloop, and Silverleaf cast off.

THE LATE-MORNING TIDE and the brisk wind carried all ships out to sea, a few fishing boats riding along with the flotilla to see them away. And all the Dragonships as well as the Tholian sloop flew the scarlet and gold, for it was now a King's fleet that sailed into the deep.

Both Reyer and Alric sat in the back of the craft and watched Sjøen recede, Caleen now but a small figure standing on the dock. And though neither lad would admit it, their hearts seemed like unto choke them.

29

Ryngar

The Ryngar Arm of the Weston Ocean is a bight that loops 'round three sides of Jute, the wide sea occupying the fourth; hence one might say that Jute itself is an island, though no one thinks of it that way, for it is embraced by the continent, with Thol just across the channel to the full of the north, Gothon to the whole of the south, and Wellen and Trellinath completely occupying the east. These waters are not without dispute, for some small islands lie in the midst of the northern and eastern reaches of the bight, the islands not only claimed by Jute but by Thol as well, though a few are claimed by Trellinath. In the past, High Kings have affirmed that most of these isles lie outside the offshore limit of three sea leagues from any of these lands and thus are free and independent of anyone's domain but for the inhabitants themselves and, of course, that of the High King. But those isles that lie within the traditional three sea league bounds of a nation, then those lands are within the rule of the associated domain. Yet the islanders themselves— mostly fishermen and farmers and a few craftsmen—are banded together by what they call the Confederacy. A loose-knit union, it is, of all the isles, whether they are within or without the three sea leagues. In general, the Confederacy has but meager business to conduct, except for trade carried out by the independent islander boats selling their fish. Still the scattered members fly a unified flag—a field of blue dotted with white stars, one for each of the isles. As for any given island, it is presided over by an Überbergermeister, elected by the people of the villages thereon. Typically, it is but an honorary appointment, with little or nothing to do except to attend or to host a gathering of all of the Überbergermeisters in an annual meeting of the heads of the Confederacy. On these occasions, each one acts as spokesman for his isle. Most of the union's inhabitants think that these meetings are simply an excuse by the Überbergermeisters to get together and drink a copious amount of ale. The Überbergermeisters themselves do not deny this.

And in the Mithgarian year 3E1999, the fourteenth year of the Usurper's reign, the fifteenth year of Reyer's life, toward these islands, and to go beyond, a unified fleet of ancient enemies set sail from the island of Kell.

They did not then know what awaited them at one of the tiniest of these dots in the water. . . .

"WHAT DID SHE TELL YOU, Alric?"

Alric looked at Reyer and shook his head.

"She's sweet on you, you know," said Reyer.

Alric nodded, yet remained mute, and though he could not see her, his gaze yet dwelled in the direction of the girl in the village of Sjøen, now beyond the horizon.

Gretta looked to the left and then to the right, and she turned to Silverleaf and said, "Fjordlanders and Jutes in the same fleet. But they are ancient enemies. Why those two, when Fjordlanders alone are mighty enough to protect Reyer and Alric? Besides, we of Jord have long been allied with Fjordland. Our ancestors are a common link. And so I would favor the ships of Fjordland alone to protect us."

Reyer shook his head and smiled, and he said, "Mother Gretta, don't you think that a Fjordland fleet sailing in the waters of the Ryngar Arm wouldn't be considered a threat by Jute?"

"You have learned your lessons well," said Conal, nodding his approval. "Yet it goes deeper than that, all thanks to Silverleaf as well as Lord Aarnson of Thol."

"Goes deeper?" Gretta cocked an eyebrow.

"Aye. You see, by showing that we have joined these two in common cause to seat Reyer and overthrow the Usurper, then all lesser dissensions between other realms will remain in abeyance until those deeds are done."

"Then they will be yours to solve, Reyer," said Alric, breaking into laughter.

Reyer scowled at Alric and then turned to Conal. "You

mean they will go back to war with one another, enemies again? —Fjordland and Jute, I mean."

"Most likely," said Conal. "The enmity between them is entrenched. They trust one another not."

At the tiller Silverleaf said, "That's why the Jutes sail on the starboard and the Fjordlanders on the larboard."

Now it was Alric who frowned. "I see not why."

"Trust," said Silverleaf. "The Jutes sail on the right hand because that's where Jute will lie once we gain the north Ryngar channel."

"Ah, yes," said Reyer, "for that puts the Jutland ships between their own realm and the ships of the Fjordlanders."

"In case of treachery?" asked Alric. "But they escort the High King—or at least the High King to be—and an act of treachery would cast the Fjordlanders into disfavor."

Silverleaf smiled. "As I said, 'tis a matter of trust."

"Well, at least they are united behind Reyer," said Conal.

"For the nonce," said Silverleaf, then he burst into laughter.

NORTHWESTERLY THEY SAILED, northwesterly, a fleet of Dragonships surrounding a sloop, to fare beyond the Isle of Kell and into the uncertain waters 'tween the Weston Ocean and the Northern Sea. The day was sunny, and the wind brisk, and the King's ship and its convoy clipped through the gentle waves, and they came to a point where, on this day, the view aft was one of a mist concealing what lay beyond. It was the mystery of Kell, reborn—that which hid the isle from prying eyes—though all sailors of worth knew the isle lay beyond.

"What is it, Driu?" asked Reyer.

"What is what, Reyer?"

"That—that fog, that mist. When I look forward, it is not there, but looking aft it is. And we did not sail through any of it, or any that I could see."

Driu smiled. "I think it was made just for you, Reyer, on this most auspicious of days. And whoever is responsible, I know not."

"For me, you say?"

"Aye, for you are the High King, and they do it in your honor."

"Long past," said Silverleaf, "it kept the isle hidden. Mage-made, god-made, or other, none knows, I think. Yet resurrected it is this day, for you are on the first leg of your investment journey, and whoever is responsible made it in your honor."

" 'Tis not Mage-made," said Driu, "no ordinary illusion, though an illusion it is. Yet those of us of Magekind do not understand how 'tis done. <Wild magic>, we think, though just the how and what of it, we know not. Nor do we know the one or ones who brought it about. Mayhap Adon knows, but not we."

"Hidden Ones?" asked Alric.

"Mayhap," said the Seeress. "Mayhap the Children of the Sea."

"Children of the Sea?" said Gretta. "But I thought they are naught but a fable."

"Nay," said Driu. "They are quite real and are the Hidden Ones of the Sea. Seldom do they show themselves to mortals or aught others, though now and again one might get a glimpse."

"Their magic <wild>?" asked Reyer, his gaze now upon the watery surround.

"It is," replied Driu. "Yet we know not whether they are responsible for the concealment of Kell."

"It's not on any map," said Conal. "It seems that pilots cannot bring themselves to place it thereon."

"Indeed," said Driu, and the King's ship and convoy sailed onward.

Given braw westerly winds, the swift sloop and the even swifter Dragonships took but three days to come to the northern extent of the Gellian Isles ere turning easterly to round the reach of that realm. Another three days they went toward the dawn before turning a bit southerly to head in the general direction of the upper channel of the bight known as the Ryngar Arm of the Weston Ocean, flanked by the shores of Thol to the north and those of Jute to the south.

Another two days passed before the coast of Thol rode up o'er the horizon, and they spent a sevenday ashore in the city of Frihavn enjoying themselves—bathing, resting, eating, drinking, exercising the horses—all making the most of their freedom from the confines of the boats. Even the Jutes and the Fjordlanders did not squabble overmuch, for they, too, were glad to be aland again.

Under the command of Riessa, the Dylvana though were ever vigilant in their warding of Reyer, and seldom did anyone get near without thorough scrutiny.

Even so, the Tholians seemed overjoyed to have King Valen's heir in their midst, and they gladly hosted the fleet.

Driu, though, seemed discomfited, for her runes showed peril lay in their near future, yet what it might be, she could not scry. Yet, as she had explained in the past, seeking to see into the future is a chancy thing at best, and the further one tries to look, the less certain the results. Besides, peril is simply a part of being a High King, Reyer's life no exception. Not that she shrugged it off, for every day she told Conal and Reyer and the others just what her runes revealed.

In the dawning of the eighth day, again the ships were laden with the animals and people and new supplies, making ready for the journey ahead. And on the evening tide they set sail once more.

"THIS IS THE DAY," said Driu, looking up from the rune stones. "Ships ahead. Lying in wait."

Silverleaf raised an argent horn to his lips and sounded a complex call. The Dragonships carrying animals and passengers and supplies fell to the rear, while the Dragonships bearing warriors of Jute and Fjordland and Kell, including Dylvana, surged to the fore.

A tiny isle came into view.

"A dark cast lies upon Øysmå," added Driu.

"Øysmå?"

"'Tis the name of the small island yon, Reyer," said Silverleaf, pointing.

Reyer, at the tiller, and Alric, at the sheets—both lads having learned much from Silverleaf during eight days asea—shaded their eyes from the morning sun and peered eastward at the craggy but green dot of land lying to the fore.

"Starboard, Reyer," commanded Silverleaf. "Quarter to the wind. Alric, make ready with the sheets."

Alric's mouth dropped agape, and he said, "What?" even as Reyer echoed Alric's "what."

"You both heard him," growled Conal. "Quarter to the wind."

Reyer shook his head. "But then we'll miss—"

"Exactly so," said Silverleaf.

"We will not expose the future High King to any battle," said Driu.

"Nor my Alric," said Gretta. Then a distressed look came over her face and she added, "At least not yet."

Even as Reyer swung the tiller hard over and Alric tightened the sheets to trim, Reyer said, "But we've already been in combat."

"Not at sea and not a full battle; 'twas a land skirmish instead," said Conal.

"Skirmish, battle?" shot back Alric. "We are blooded, no matter what name."

"Even so," said Silverleaf.

With the lads yet fuming, the sloop came to the new heading, and but for the warrior-laden ships now ahead, the full of the remaining fleet turned with them.

They watched as the Dragonboats, flying flags of the High King, neared the small isle, and 'round the shoulder and into view sailed six Albaner barks—each three-masted and square-rigged.

Fire flew from the decks of the larger craft, most to splash ineffectually into the brine. Yet one burst upon the sail of a Fjordland boat, and the canvas flared with flame. Instead of fighting the fire with water, some of the men cut the sail free to cast it into the sea while others shipped oars from the trestles and out through the oar ports and began swiftly rowing toward the ship that had set it ablaze.

And still more fire arced toward the Dragonboats, and wooden wales were set aflame and men as well. Some, so stricken, leapt into the sea to quench the blaze, while other warriors poured water on the fiercely burning gobs of tarry substance clinging to the ships.

And the Dragonboats closed with the foe, while arrows winged from craft to ship and vice versa, the Dylvana shafts flying long and true, while those of the barks fell short. Soon the Dragonships—some afire, others not—drew alongside the Albaner barks, Jutes on one side, Fjordlanders opposite. Grapnels flew as Elven arrows met those from Alban. Albaner crews chopped frantically at the hook lines, but Elven shafts drove them arear. Shouting bloodthirsty cries, battle-hardened veterans swarmed up the ropes and over the rails, for this was their kind of war. Even as cutlasses and falchions met the boarders' embossed shields, axes hewed and Albaners fell slain or maimed, as did fighters of the yet-uncrowned High King.

Fiercely raged the struggle, yet bark after bark fell to the ferocious Dragonship warriors. And during the shipboard battle, two of the Fjordland craft went down aflame, while one of the Jutland ships was burnt beyond salvage.

At last the fighting came to an end, and all ships turned toward the shores of Øysmå, the prisoners of the Fjordlanders and the Jutes sailing their barks toward the beaches. Some of the Dragonships paused to take up their comrades who had gone into the sea, several Dylvana among them.

"DEAD? They're all dead?"

Conal nodded. "Yes, Reyer, all the islanders were slaughtered."

"None survived?"

"None," said Conal. "The Albaners, they butchered all— all the women and children, babes and oldsters, the halt and the lame, as well as the hale and fit."

"They must have taken the islanders unawares," said Alric.

"Aye, lad, they did at that," said Captain Alfdan. "They sailed under false colors. We found these on their ships." The Fjordlander held up a flag of a white falcon on a blue field.

"Wellen," said Alric. "That's a Wellener banner."

"I suspect the people of Øysmå welcomed the Albaners with open arms, not knowing 'twas a serpent they greeted," said Alfdan.

"Damn Albaners," spat Durgan.

They sat in the common hall of the village situated on the shores of a small cove. The Dragonships had been beached and unladed of animals and crew and others. The barks were moored in the little bay, and the sloop was tied to one of the fishing docks.

As they had entered the town, they had come across weeks-old corpses—sword-hacked and gull-stripped and crab-eaten—lying in the streets. Silverleaf had dispatched warriors to look for any survivors . . . yet there were none.

Conal turned to Silverleaf. "What else do we know?"

"Twelve Fjordlanders, nine Jutes, and three Dylvana are slain—"

Shock registered upon Reyer's face. "Riessa?"

"She lives. 'Twas Dyel, Fener, and Varin who fell."

Even in relief over the news that Riessa had survived, still tears slid down Reyer's cheeks, and he looked to Mother Gretta, but she too wept. All others fell mute, for to know that ageless lives had been quenched seemed sorrow beyond relief.

Finally Silverleaf took a deep breath and said, "We also have wounded—twenty-one of the Jutes and but eight of the Fjordlanders. Yet some of these cannot go on . . . or, rather, they will have to be left at the next isle for the Confederacy to succor back to health."

"What of the Albaners?" asked Conal.

"One hundred and twenty-three survivors, thirty-one of which are walking wounded," said Alfdan. "We and the Jutes took mercy on the severely injured Albaners and put them out of their misery. Three of the captains survived, along with a few of the officers."

Reyer finally shook out of the depths of his misery and asked, "What know we of the mission they were on?"

"Most of the Albaners were following the orders of their captains," said Alfdan. "The officers, though, knew the full of the mission, and that was to slay thee, sire. They were acting under the command of one of the captains, and he was following the directive of King Malak—"

"Arkov's lackey," said Gretta. "I imagine he has designs for Amani to be Arkov's mate."

"Amani?" asked Durgan.

"His youngest daughter," said Gretta.

"And this Malak is . . . ?" asked Durgan.

"King of Alban," said Reyer.

"Ah."

Conal turned to Reyer and said, "Sire, 'tis time for your first judgment."

Reyer frowned. "Judgment?"

"Aye. What to do with the Albaners."

"Oh," said Reyer, paling slightly.

"Kill them all," said Gretta. "They would have slain the full of us—Alric, you, the rest, all."

Alric looked at Conal. "What has been done in the past?"

But it was Reyer who answered. "Those who swear fealty to the High King are spared. But those behind the plot, or those who know the full of it, that is another matter."

GRIM-FACED AND FLANKED BY HIS WARRIORS, at the docks Reyer stood upon a wooden platform before the assembled Albaners, and the standard of the High King was held by Durgan at Reyer's side. Arrayed directly before the stand were Riessa and the captains of the Dragonships; though smaller than the men, she seemed no less in stature. And a chill wind blew from the sea, swirling flag and cloak alike, and silence reigned, but for the sough of the ocean and the sigh of the curling air.

Finally, Reyer took a deep breath and called out:

"You have slain Our liegemen, immortal Elves among them.

"You have sided with the foul Usurper and have sought to take the life of Us, the rightful heir of Valen.

"And you have committed unforgivable deeds upon the peoples of this isle.

"Hear Us now, for this is Our judgment.

"Because they commanded you to do these heinous deeds, your officers are to be hanged by the neck until dead and their corpses left for the birds to pick.

"The remainder of you will see to the burial of the townsfolk you slew.

"Under the command of Our warriors, you will sail your ships to the next isle for the verdict of the Confederacy, for the citizens you slew were of that domain, and, by right, they will determine your fate.

"Any who are spared will swear fealty unto Us, to ever be at Our command."

Reyer then raised his right hand, his fist clenched, and Durgan stamped the butt of the standard to the platform.

"So do We say," said Reyer.

Again Durgan struck the standard.

"So do We say," repeated Reyer.

Once more the standard stamped.

"So do We say," said Reyer, a third and final time, and he lowered his right arm and unclenched his fist.

A FULL SEVENDAY PASSED ALTOGETHER ere the fleet got under way again, this time sailing with six barks trailing after.

The Albaner officers had been executed, the townsfolk had been properly buried, the Fjordland and Jute dead had been solemnly burnt upon a common pyre, as had the slain Dylvana, their spirits sung into the sky.

It took but half a day for the ships to reach the next isle of the Confederacy—Øygrøn, its name. Another four days were spent being feted thereon by Überbergermeister Karlton.

When the fleet sailed on, they left behind the six barks to be sold for wergild, for many of the relatives of the people of Øygrøn had lived on the isle of Øysmå. As to the Albaners, all were now dead, for the verdict of this isle of the Confederacy was harsh.

SOME EIGHT DAYS LATER the Wellen port of Roadsend hove into view.

It was the fleet's final destination.

Progression

Oft in Mithgar a king and his court will take to the road and visit the cities and the nobility in that king's realm. The king will not leave his castle unmanned or the country unled, but instead the king's appointed charge shall rule—a prince, a princess, a steward, or at times an armsmaster. While the king is away, the chosen ward will sit in judgment on all matters brought before the court, with exceptions as outlined by the king—capital cases being one.

But the king himself will dine elsewhere—with dukes and earls and barons and mayors and such—at the royal houses throughout the land as well as those of the mayoralties. Often, though, the retinue will stop by a village inn for refreshments during travel, and pity the poor taverner who might just barely be scraping by, for in the main it seems neither the king nor any of his attendants ever pay for aught. There are exceptions, of course, but many kings consider it a royal right to simply take and not give.

The dukes, earls, viscounts, barons, mayors, and other hosts of the king and his coterie see these sojourns as both a bane and a boon, for on the one hand the visits deplete their larders—and thus their treasuries—but on the other hand they have the king's ear to press for favors—lands, rights, alleviations, beneficial marriages, king's grants, and such.

Thus across their realms fare king's progressions, or so they are called. . . .

Yet in some lands they are known by other names, one of which is . . .

"A RAID? We are going on a raid?"

"No, Reyer, not r-a-i-d, but r-a-d-e," said Conal. " 'Tis a fine old Kellian word, meaning a special kind of ride, one where the people can see you . . . you and your entourage. And we are going on a rade."

"Is that why we didn't sail directly to the city of Ander in Rian, there on the Boreal Sea?" asked Reyer. "—So that we could go on this rade, I mean."

Conal smiled and nodded. "Aye. That and other reasons."

"What other reasons?" asked Alric.

"This time of year the Boreal is too tempestuous for safe passage. Too, we would be exposed on a longer sea voyage, and should the Kistanian raiders come at us for a second attack, they would have more opportunities to do us in."

"Them, or the Albaners who did come at us," said Alric.

"Just so," said Conal. Then he smiled and said, "By the way we go, not only will Jute, Fjordland, and Thol have had a hand in your journey, but also will Wellen and the Boskydells, and a bit of the Wilderland, along with Rian."

"Ah," said Alric, "more countries involved."

"Indeed," said Conal. "More invested in the High King, in Reyer. Hence, we are going on a rade."

Reyer looked across a short expanse of water toward the town of Roadsend, where they were to make landfall. "A rade to Challerain Keep," said Reyer, his words not a question.

"Yes, where the Northern Alliance will invest you as High King, now that you are of an age to be so named."

"Will we be visiting every city in Reyer's sovereignty?" asked Alric.

"Oh, no," said Conal. "We haven't the time."

Reyer nodded and said, "Besides, we have a war to fight ere visiting some parts of the realm."

Distressed at the thought, Gretta glanced at Alric even as Conal sighed and said, "Ah, yes, there is that to do."

"Still, 'twill be nice to ride a horse again 'stead of this rolling craft," said Alric, "especially out front with the forerunners."

Gretta shook her head. "You will ride at Reyer's right hand. It is the proper place for you."

"But I am Harlingar," protested Alric. "I should be in the vanguard, with lance and saber, and even a bow."

"When you are fifteen you may make your own choices, but until then you will do as I say."

"But, Mother, I *am* fifteen."

At her son's words, stark realization flashed over Gretta's face, but then she said, "Even so."

An unspoken plea in his gaze, Alric looked at Conal.

Conal said, "Gretta?"

Her jaw jutted out and she said, "Fifteen or no, just as we must protect Reyer, so, too, must we protect Alric."

Conal pursed his lips and nodded, and the air went out of Alric, and he muttered under his breath, "It's not fair."

At Alric's side, Reyer said, "To be sure."

Alric hissed, "When you are King, set me free of these shackles."

Reyer nodded.

At the tiller Silverleaf called out, "Alric, wouldst thou like to bring her in?"

"What?"

"Wouldst thou dock the *Gull*?"

Alric's glower was replaced by a smile. "Aye, Captain, I would."

"Then thou to the helm and Reyer to the sheets."

Reyer laughed and said, "All hands, prepare for ramming."

ROADSEND WAS MORE THAN pleased to host the High King and his retinue, and the White Falcon Inn provided room and board for the King's immediate party. The Fjordlanders and Jutes instead took to the Broken Spar—an inn, a tavern, and a bordello—where they jointly celebrated their victory over the Albaners. News traveled like wildfire, accompanied by rumors—

—*Fjordlanders and Jutes celebrating together? Must be th' end of the w'rld.*

—*The High King's fleet sunk the entire Alban navy?*

—*Nar, but a goodly portion of them—ten, twenty ships, I hear.*

—*Old Malak is like t'have a fallin' down fit when he gets the news.*

—*Malak, y'say? No, I say that Arkov'll be the one who falls down in a foaming rage.*

—*Did y'see all them Golden Griffins flying high on the masts? Liked to burst my heart with joy.*

—*Yar, but I hear the Albaners were sailing under our flag?*

—*Under the falcon, you say?*

—*That's what one o' th' Fjordlanders said.*

—*Then I hope they all died in agony.*

—and so the stories went.

A SEVENDAY LATER, ere departing on the first leg of the rade to Challerain Keep, and in spite of Gretta's protestations that it was not a suitable place for Reyer and Alric to be, accompanied by a cordon of Dylvana, the lads went to the Broken Spar. There, Reyer stood upon a table before the Dragonship captains and crew, as well as the women of the Spar, and he thanked the Jutes and Fjordlanders for their gallant service. Unfortunately, he also wished them well in their unity, which caused jostling and shoving among them, until Riessa snatched up a metal stein and hammered for quiet, declaring, "You stand before your High King!"

Sheepishly, the men came to order.

Someone called for three cheers for King Reyer.

All gladly complied.

It was after Reyer and his party left that the barroom brawl broke out.

ON THE MORNING OF THEIR DEPARTURE, Silverleaf sent a bird winging easterly for Challerain Keep, a message capsule on its leg, bearing news of the King's rade, and telling the Northern Alliance to expect them within four fortnights or so.

As the entourage rode from the town, the streets were

lined with those who would see their High King, for like as not he would never be here again. And, with Alric at his side, as Reyer passed, men bowed and women curtseyed, and then they cheered him on.

Armed with bows strung with nocked arrows, the Dylvana escort—leading, flanking, trailing—kept sharp eyes out, scanning the crowds lining the street as well as the windows and balconies and rooftops, seeking any who would betray their King, but none did.

Reyer smiled and nodded to the greeters, but at his side Alric scowled, for he would rather be some distance ahead, there with the vanguard to the fore. After all, they would be first to meet any foe, and here he was, lagging to the rear.

"Cheer up, Alric," said Reyer. "Soon or late you'll be riding with the lead warriors."

Alric growled low in reply.

And on they rode.

At last they passed the outskirts of the city and fared into the rolling farmland beyond. The fields were green and fertile and burdened with crops that had not yet come into fullness. Orchards bore fruit, some, such as those growing cherries, had already seen the harvest, while others were still to mature—peaches would be next, apples last.

In some pastures, cattle and sheep and horses grazed, while in other fields horses or yoked oxen drew wains filled with bales of hay, while men with sweeping scythes and children with sickles harvested the crop, and others raked the largesse to spread it out to dry.

Up on the slopes beyond the farms and fields, thickets and woodlands lay scattered in patches, some large, others small, though here and there forests stretched on beyond seeing. And at places among the trees, men hewed with axes or plied saws, while oldsters collected long-fallen dead branches into rough bundles of sticks and kindling.

And as the retinue passed, dogs barked and alerted the workers, and the farmers and foresters stopped in their chores and watched from afar, though now and again, while their mothers would step from the houses and cottages and shade their eyes and look on, children would run to the fence lines and climb the rails or stone walls and gape in awe as the Elves and others passed.

The King and his escort followed the Crossland Road, a mighty passage that reached all the way from Roadsend— there on the Ryngar Arm of the Weston Ocean—to the Crestan Pass in the remote Grimwalls lying leagues upon leagues to the east. The route itself continued on beyond those mountains, but its name changed to the Landover Road, and it went all the way to far Xian ... and some say even farther: to distant Jinga on the far-off shores of the Bright Sea.

"But we won't be taking that route to Jinga," said Driu, as they set up camp that eve. "Instead, we'll follow this way into the Boskydells, where we'll turn northwesterly and travel along a route to the Post Road, and thence to Challerain Keep."

They were at the small hamlet of Greensward, nine dwellings all told, entirely too small to put up the High King and his party. Yet the villagers did slaughter a hog and roasted it on a spit, and, along with cooked beans and greens and vinegar-wilted lettuce, it made tasty fare.

THEY MADE CAMP ALONGSIDE A SMALL LAKE, and Reyer and Alric cut poles and fetched line and hooks from their packs. Together they strolled alongside the bank, now and then stopping at a likely spot to cast in, a wriggling leaf-hopper on each barb.

When they were well away from the others, Reyer heaved a sigh.

Alric looked at him, an unspoken question in his gaze. Finally he said, "What?"

Reyer jiggled his line, and then said, "I am not certain I am up to being High King. Who am I to lead an army? I would much rather be a pig farmer. Much rather be out hunting, fishing, riding through Darda Coill, even snapping beans than to be sitting on some throne."

Alric said, "I think I know how you might feel. Thank Adon, I will never be a monarch. Such is not in my bones.

But list, we've trained for battle, for war, though for much of the time we did not know it was coming, or how we might fit in. Nevertheless, heed me: I will ever be at your beck, should your events dictate."

Reyer smiled and said, "Spoken like the Harlingar you are."

Alric grinned. "I say, that *was* rather noble of me, right?"

They broke out into laughter, carefree for the moment.

Little did they know what lay ahead.

A FORTNIGHT AND THREE DAYS LATER, and some four hundred miles east of where they had begun the rade, Driu summoned Durgan unto her side.

"My lady?"

The light from their campfire illuminated the Seer's face, now lined with age, for she had been casting a spell every morning for the past thirteen years, ever since Reyer had arrived at Kell. And to cast spells meant the spending of her \<essence\>, burning a bit of her youth each and every time. One day she would have to \<rest\> and regain the full of her \<fire\>. But Durgan and the others had seen her every day of those thirteen years, and so she simply looked the same to them, as if she had not aged at all.

"Durgan," she said, "on the morrow I would have you ride swiftly ahead and to the Boskydells."

"There where the Warrows live," said Durgan.

"Aye. I would have you tell them that we are coming. We should reach the Thornring some eight days hence. Do not press Cruach beyond bearing; you need but to ride him such that you precede us by a day, yet no more."

"Were it necessary, Steel and I could reach it in but a twoday or three, though it would be hard on him."

"No, Durgan. Your getting there in a sevenday is sufficient."

"As you will, my lady. What then?"

"I would have you ride on to a village called Rood, there at the center of the Seven Dells. It is on the Crossland Road."

"Rood."

"Aye. It lies some thirty-five leagues from where you first enter the Dells. Tell them we will be in Rood six days after you yourself reach it."

Sensing there was more to come, Durgan looked up from the fire and into Driu's lined face and said, "And . . . ?"

"And I would have you ask the Captain of the Thornwalkers if he could spare us seven or so of his best archers. I would have them accompany us to Challerain Keep."

"Thornwalkers? Warrows? Riding with us?"

"Aye. You see, in the Great War of the Ban, 'twas a Warrow—Tipperton Thistledown—who saved the High King and all of Mithgar from Modru the Vile, and we would have Thornwalkers with us. —Ah, but heed: 'tis important that you show them this." Driu held up a small pewter coin with a hole through the center and threaded on a leather thong. "'Tis a Gjeenian penny, by which they will know it comes from the High King. Yet I would have you say we ask not the entire Bosky to muster, for it is not their fight to join. But for an honorary presence of a handful of the Warrows in the company of the High King, we would have the remainder dwell in peace."

"Gjeenian penny," said Durgan, taking the coin and holding it up in the firelight.

"Someday I'll tell you that tale," said Driu.

"As you will, my lady." Durgan looped the thong about his neck, the penny to hang at his throat.

"Oh, and this, too, Durgan." Driu opened a small satchel and lifted out a folded crimson tunic. "This tabard bears the Golden Griffin of the High King. It will look well upon you." Driu handed the garment to the young man.

Durgan's mouth fell open, and he took the surcoat in hand and shook it free of its folds. The griffin glowed auric in the firelight. Finally he breathed, "I will wear this in honor, my lady, and do nothing to disgrace the symbol thereon."

"I know," said Driu, the Seer smiling.

* * *

THE NEXT MORNING DURGAN on Steel set out before the others broke camp. Gretta and Conal stood and watched as he rode away, Gretta with tears in her eyes. And Steel galloped up to the crest of the next hill just as the sun rose. And over the crest and down beyond ran Steel.

In a scarlet flash, Durgan was gone.

Rage

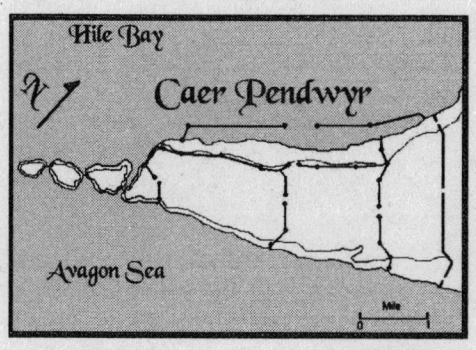

Hile Bay

Caer Pendwyr

Avagon Sea

Mile
0   1

The fastest way in Mithgar for news to travel a distance is from a Mage to a Mage afar. Yet since the Great War of the Ban, most of Magekind now <rested>, gradually recovering the <life essence> spent in their hidden struggles during that conflict. And so, only in the direst need is Magetalk used, is <fire> spent, for millennia must pass before Magekind will be fully recovered, and each iota of <essence> is to be husbanded dear.

Hence, the next swiftest way to send word from place to place is by messenger bird. But even with birds, news travels slowly in Mithgar, and without birds, word of distant affairs simply creeps across the land from one realm to another, its progress maddeningly slow. In some of the smaller villages, it can be weeks, months, years ere knowledge of a happening comes to light, and in some—if not most—areas, decades and centuries pass without anyone knowing aught.

Likewise, any needed responses to distant events also can take weeks, months, years to occur. And during the Usurper's reign, skirmishes and rebellions rose and were put down by Arkov's mercenaries ere the news reached Caer Pendwyr weeks later. And no sooner would one fire be extinguished than another would spring up—in Riamon or Jugo or Aven, or in Hoven or Tugol.

It had taken some six years of sitting on the throne ere Arkov had learned of a potential heir of Valen, a child who might not have burned atop a pyre but was perhaps living on Kell. Subsequently, four years elapsed, during which Kellian children were murdered by Arkov's agents without any confirmation that a child with the griffin-claw birthmark was among the slaughtered. And it seemed that none of the slain children had had a royal upbringing. But then his spy in Sjøen sent word that an assassin disguised as a tinker had failed in an attempt to slay a pair of lads, one of whom might be that heir. And both seemed to have the carriage and manner of those who have had courtly training.

Two more years slipped into the past ere the *Sukut Khayâlîn* from the Red City of Nizari made an attempt upon those particular children's lives, and it was weeks ere Arkov learned of the result: utter failure.

Hence, even though news borne by a messenger bird takes but days, any response can take months in the making, for plans must be conceived, and resources gathered, and distances must be traveled—on foot, or by horse, or wind-driven ship, or combinations thereof.

Yet Arkov laid more plans, their execution delayed by the slowness of means to carry them out.

And in what the Alliance knew to be the lad's fifteenth year, a bird from the port city of Roadsend in Wellen arrived at Challerain Keep. It bore a message telling of the seaborne attempt upon the true heir's life. It also spoke of an intended rade of the heir easterly along the Crossland Road to the Boskydells, and then northerly to the Keep.

Not a day had passed at Challerain ere another bird winged south from the Mont toward the halls of Caer Pendwyr....

...and when that bird arrived...

"DAMN, DAMN, ALBANERS!" hissed Arkov, reading the coded slip. He shoved the missive at his counselor. "Davich promised me that he would get the task done, but they proved no better than those Nizari pigs. I am surrounded by incompetent fools."

"Though I hate to admit it, we could have used the Rovers," said Baloff, unrolling the flimsy scroll.

"Did you not hear me? I said Nizari pigs were worthless, and that includes their Kistanian kin. Besides, ever since Abu's failure, I do not and did not trust his replacement, that dark bastard Aziz, to properly carry out my wishes."

"Then, my lord, mayhap we should not allow a Chabbain army to—"

"Silence, Baloff. When the day comes, you know we will need them to face the Northern Alliance. Besides, many are already asail. Some of the ships should be here within a fortnight, ere returning to Chabba to transport others. Then we'll march on those upstarts ere the snow flies."

Baloff read the pigeon-borne tissue-thin strip. "Fjordlanders and Jutes . . . Dragonships allied? No wonder the Albaners lost. Who could have anticipated—?"

"I *told* you we needed agents at the mad king's court," snarled Arkov, "but, oh, no, you said, the demented whims of the mad king himself are better than a hundred spies. Imbecile!"

Arkov stalked to an opening overlooking the Avagon Sea. He stood for long minutes peering out at distant sails and muttering. "Ships. Sailors. I never should have trusted those bunglers. Give me a good strong army, instead. And horses. Yes, horses."

"What will we do, my lord?" asked Baloff. "I mean, given the date of his birth, if he is the true pretender, the boy is fifteen. And if he reaches Challerain Keep—"

"I know, Baloff. No need to remind me. Fear not, for other plans are afoot."

NOT LONG AFTER THE bird-borne news of the Albaner defeat arrived at Caer Pendwyr, from the embassy towers of Kaleem bin Aziz a Grimwall Corvus winged north and a black seagull winged south.

Fury

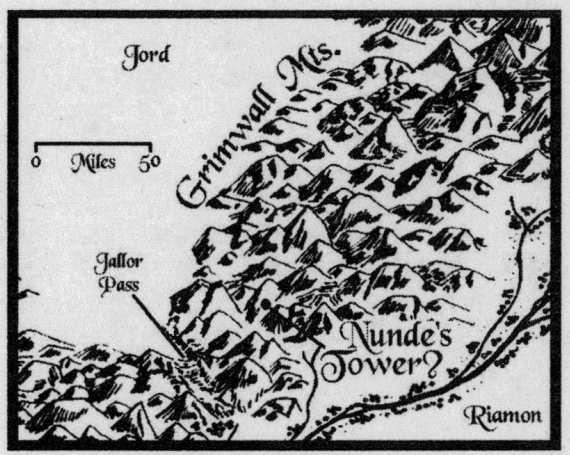

A mong the birds of Mithgar there are many members of the Corvidae family, in particular the Corvus. They are clever and trainable for the most part, but only if one begins when they are young—that is, from nest onward. One must beware these Mithgarian birds when encountered in the wild, for they are raptors all, with claws that snatch and beaks that shred.

They come in many forms:

The raven is the largest of all, and black as midnight itself, its voice consisting of knocks and creaks and harsh calls, and its manner a blend of curiosity and cleverness and savagery.

The gorcrow is an atrocious bird—a seeker of carrion and a lurker of battlefields, picking among the slain and severely wounded, choosing the choicest of meat.

Then there is the grey crow, with its ebon head and wings and tail, and a splash of black on its breast, but the bulk of its body is a ghostly grey; it is said to be a harbinger of death, for it haunts battlefields as well, rising up wraithlike from the blood-soaked soil if disturbed, only to return.

Rooks gather in mobs—called "buildings"—and fill the air with their calls, as if each is trying to outshout the other. At times on radiant days they preen and strut as if showing off to all, with their black feathers casting an overlying sheen of bluish-purple in the bright rays of the sun.

Jackdaws are the smallest of all, but are raptors still. A gathering of these Corvuses is called a "clattering," for they seemingly chatter incessantly. And, like others of the Corvus family, they oft steal shiny things and gather the plunder in their nests.

There are many other members of this extended family, the common crow being one, yet perhaps the most predatory of all and the most difficult to train is the Grimwall Corvus, a vicious raptor nearly as large as a raven and more brutal than a gorcrow.

And in a dark tower hidden among the Grimwalls, there is a cote of these hostile birds. They are trained as messengers, sent forth from the tower by a whispered word of a Black Mage and bearing a small capsule with a tissue-thin strip on which coded words are laid. They take the messages to the places commanded, where they wait for a reply—sometimes for weeks, sometimes for days, sometimes immediately. Being vicious hunters and carrion eaters, they can feed along the way, yet the Dark Mage has embedded them with an urgency to make haste.

In the hutches at either end of their flight, there are trained cote-masters, who tend to the care and feeding of these rapacious birds—tend them cautiously, that is, for they are savage....

...and in that dark tower well-hidden in the Grimwalls...

SLEKK WAS AWAKENED by the clang of the gong announcing the setting of the sun. Pushing, jostling, elbowing, cursing, he shoved his way among the flood of other pushing, cursing Drik—Rûcks all—lunging toward feeding troughs filled, as usual, with a thick slurry of meal, enriched with gobbets and shreds of grey meat floating throughout, some of it yet oozing. As usual, after gulping down his fill, he scurried with others toward the defecation chamber—food in, feces out, was a morning rite. Among Drik he squatted astraddle the common sluice in the floor and emptied his bowels and bladder. And as he did so, though he did not have deep thoughts, still he wondered about two things: was it true that upon Neddra—that haven upon the Low Plane—there was rutting all day long? And was he the only Drik who actually had a name? Not that either question really mattered, for—rutting or no—he was trapped here on Mithgar, unless of course the Master or someone else with power took him across in the night. And as far as his so-called name—Slekk—he had made that up himself. Even so, he didn't know anyone else who had a name—among Driks, that is. But for some inexplicable reason, Slekk wanted a name of his own. After all, the Ghok and Gûk—Hlôks and Ghûls—had names: the Ghok simply to self-style themselves after their own masters, the Gûk—besides the Ghok needed to have names so that a Drik would know whose squad he was assigned to, or who to go to with a message. Like the Drik, the Oghi—the Trolls—behemoths that they are, didn't seem to have names. Perhaps that was because they never ran things, but were around to simply do the heavy lifting, or to crush the enemy, and to follow orders, just like the Drik.

But the Mages—oh, Gyphon—they had dreadful names, names to strike fear and terror, to stab deep into the very heart of anyone.

Though Slekk's thoughts and desires were quite primitive, animalistic at best, still he knew about rutting and names . . . and he knew dread.

It took only moments to dump his bowels and bladder, and, fearing the lash of the overseeing Ghok, he fled the defecation chamber and made his way toward the stairs. He stopped long enough to pick up two buckets of putrefying hacked-off arms and sawn-off legs and split viscera—there being no shortage of such in Nunde's tower. And then he headed up the stone spiral toward the cote high above.

Huffing and wheezing, he at last reached the top, where the hostile black birds awaited, *rawking* and *gracking* at Slekk's appearance, demanding to be fed.

Slekk chopped up the severed limbs and ropy lengths of intestines and threw the rotting bits into the cages, where the Grimwall Corvuses shredded and ripped at the grey meat and gulped it down.

Slekk watched them rend and tear, and his mouth watered at the sight of frenzied feeding. He had often thought of reaching into a cage and snatching up one of the birds and biting off its head and crunching it to pulp and gulping it down. That would be followed by eating the rest of the fowl—bones, feathers, all—and he wondered what it might taste like—certainly it would be fresh. But dread of the

Master stayed his hand, for the birds were more valuable to him than any Drik alive.

And as he turned to take up the scraper to clean away the steaming piles below the cages, a glimmer caught his eye.

A capsule.

Tied to the leg of a feeding Corvus.

Taking great care to avoid sharp claws and rending beak, Slekk managed to get the capsule free, and he bolted from the cote and scrambled down the stairs.

As always, Radok would reward him with a ration of fresh meat.

But as Slekk entered the lower corridors—Nunde! Master Nunde!

Blubbering in fear, Slekk fell groveling to the floor.

Nunde peered down at the Drik's outstretched, trembling hand. Then he stooped over and took up the capsule.

He did not give Slekk his ration of meat.

Instead, he opened the capsule and read the coded words within, his face turning black with fury.

"Fool!" he shouted, and he ground his teeth, his jaw clenching and sawing. And then he burst forth: "Damned fool! With my plan nearing fulfillment, that *imbecile* sends ships to slay the heir! He could have ruined *everything*!"

Nunde swung about, glaring, looking for someone, anyone to—

But only a Drik lay blubbering and groveling upon the cold stone corridor floor.

Nunde muttered a word and reached out a clawed hand and slowly squeezed it shut, as if crushing a still-beating heart.

Thus was slain the only Drik with a name in the dark depths of that well-hidden tower.

33

Thornwalkers

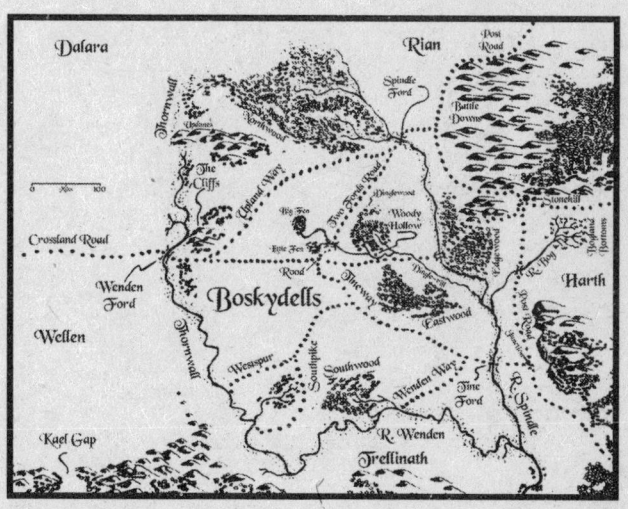

Being a small folk, of Warrows it is said that they make the finest of scouts, stepping lighter than an Elf and blending into the 'scape. And they are cat quick when faced with danger, especially when cornered. Yet list: in times of strife Warrows are not given to swords and spears and shields and bucklers and other such accoutrements of war. No, they are missileers: slings and bows and arrows being more suited to their kind. Oh, some have mastered the art of knife throwing, and a few can shy a rock with deadly accuracy, but in the main, it's slings and bows that make them deadly in battle. Other folk might cast arrows and bullets farther than Warrows can, yet in all of Mithgar one would be hardpressed to find better archers and slingsters.

They come by these skills through tradition and hard practice, for most young buccen—that age between twenty and thirty—train to become Thornwalkers, guardians of the Seven Dells. They are called Thornwalkers because among their other duties they patrol the bounds of the Bosky, there where the Thornwall lies, though in times of peace only few are needed. Still, now was not a time of peace, though as of yet neither was it a time of war. Even so, war was coming, but whether the Thornwalkers would join the Northern Alliance or merely defend their own borders . . . well, that debate was not yet settled. Regardless, the ways through the Thornwall were now plugged, and Warrows guarded these entrances.

And then one day on a steel-grey horse a rider wearing the scarlet and gold tabard and bearing a Gjeenian penny showed up at the western bound. . . .

THE MAN HELD UP a coin on a thong and looked up at the small archers atop a stand just beyond the barricade of thorns obstructing his way ahead.

"He's come from the west, not south," whispered Banley.

"So as he ain't one of Arkov's lackeys," added Graden.

"We'll see," said Norv, and he turned toward the rider and called down, "It's true then, what the Red-Coach drivers said?"

"Aye," replied the man. "King Reyer will be here in a sixday."

"That's what they said, they did," hissed Graden. "Told us flat out that Valen's boy was on his way."

Banley nodded his agreement. "They did at that."

Graden turned to Norv, who seemed to be the Warrow in charge. "Do we open the barrier?"

"Of course, you jobbernowl," growled Norv. "Can't you see he's got the penny?"

"A penny from the true heir, too," said Banley, " 'stead o' that Arkov Usurper."

"Well, hop to," ordered Norv, "we can't keep the King's herald waitin'."

Warrows scrambled down from the stand and swung the barricade aside.

"Better take a torch," Norv called down to the rider. "You'll need it to see."

As they moved the wall out of the way, the man warily looked at the gloomy tunnel through the Spindlethorn barrier. "How far to the other side?"

"It's half a league to the river and then another half league beyond."

"Then perhaps I'd better take two torches," said the herald.

"Nah. One'll do. You can fetch another at the river ward, and it'll last the rest of the way. Banley!"

The Warrow named Banley took up one of the oil- and pitch-soaked brands and lit it and handed it up to the man.

"Hup, Steel," said the rider, urging his mount forward. And he took the torch and called, "King Reyer," and then rode into the shadows beyond.

"REMEMBER, REYER, YOU DO not expect Warrows to kneel. King Blaine gave them leave to acknowledge all of royalty, no matter the realm, by nothing more than a simple bow."

Reyer nodded at Driu's words. "I remember. 'Twas a promise made to Sir Tipperton Thistledown."

"And to all Warrows everywhere," added Alric. "Not that it'll mean aught to me."

Gretta raised an eyebrow, but said naught.

Driu merely smiled.

A DAY OR SO LATER, Reyer scowled and shaded his eyes and peered easterly. "Looks to be a storm coming."

"What?" said Alric, who had been rapt in a conversation with Riessa.

Reyer pointed. "There. Low on the horizon. Dark clouds gather."

Alric looked ahead and then groaned. "I hate riding in the rain."

"'Tis not storm clouds," said Riessa, her sharp-eyed Dylvana gaze taking in the view.

Alric frowned at her, an unspoken question on his lips.

"'Tis the Thornwall."

"Looks like clouds to me," said Reyer, Alric nodding his agreement.

"Besides," said Alric, "for that to be a wall of thorns, it must be—"

"I believe here it's something like fifty, sixty feet high," said Conal, riding on the opposite side from Riessa.

"Adon!" exclaimed Alric.

THE PASSAGE THROUGH THE thorns was open when the entourage reached it, and as the rade passed the ward, Warrows stood agog at the sight of Dylvana Elves riding among the Big Folk. And all the buccen bowed when the lean-limbed High King rode past, though neither Norv nor any of his squad mates knew which of the two lads might be him.

And as the torchlight faded away easterly, the west ward closed the barrier once more, and immediately began arguing as to which was the young King and which his youthful companion.

*　　*　　*

THEY STOPPED AT THE River Wenden to stretch their legs and let the horses drink. A slash of blue sky shone above, light filtering down between the great walls of thorn on either side of the waterway.

Alric breathed deeply, as if glad to be clear of the tunnel behind, though it seemed he was not looking forward to passing through the one ahead.

Reyer, on the other hand, marveled at the massive tangle, great-girthed plants twisting and twining out from the soil, the thorns themselves ranging from dagger to long-knife length.

"I say, one would be quite bloodied were he to attempt that maze," said Reyer. "It looks to be better than the best of moats."

"Moats don't burn," said Alric. "And though it might take a long, long while, were it mine to breach, I would simply set it on fire."

"Flame cannot seem to get purchase," said Driu.

"It doesn't burn?"

"One might set a blaze to going, yet it cannot sustain itself. Hence your plan is doomed to fail."

Reyer laughed and said, "See: better than a moat."

They stood without speaking for a moment, then Driu said, "We'll stay at the Cliffs this eve."

"The Cliffs?"

" 'Tis a series of dwellings, Reyer, carved into the face of a limestone bluff rising up from the surround just beyond the Thornwall. A village of Warrow scholars, I am told."

"Scholars?"

Driu nodded. "Keepers of a great library. I am looking forward to visiting its halls."

Reyer frowned and peered at the squad of buccen across on the opposite bank, waiting for them to fare onward. "It's hard to think of this wondrous small folk being other than the salt of the earth."

"Nevertheless, they are," said Driu. "—Scholars, I mean. And I was told by one of my mentors that if events unfold as he has seen, sometime in the distant future the ones who will be living here at that time will have a significant role to play. What it might be, he did not say."

Nearby, Riessa laughed, and when Alric glanced at her, she said, "Mages—always speaking in mysteries and riddles and hints."

"Indeed," said Alric and he and Reyer both laughed.

Driu smiled and said, "How else would you have us be?"

Reyer looked at her and grinned and said, "I, for one, wouldn't change a thing."

In that moment Conal whistled, and soon all were mounted up, and they rode into the shadowy tunnel beyond.

WHEN THE RADE REACHED ROOD, just as did the people of the other towns and villages along the way, the streets were lined with those who had come to see the heir ride through. And it was here at last that they discovered which lad was the King and which his companion, for Reyer stood on the steps of the town hall and thanked Mayor Bradely and all the Wee Folk for the welcome they brought.

And when they rode away two days afterward, everyone agreed that the fair-haired boy would make a splendid High King, for unlike Arkov, Reyer hadn't expected them to kneel.

AND WITH THE ENTOURAGE were seven pony-mounted Thornwalkers—archers all—Digby Thimbleweed and Alton Periwinkle among them, for it seemed Driu had asked for them by name.

Stonehill

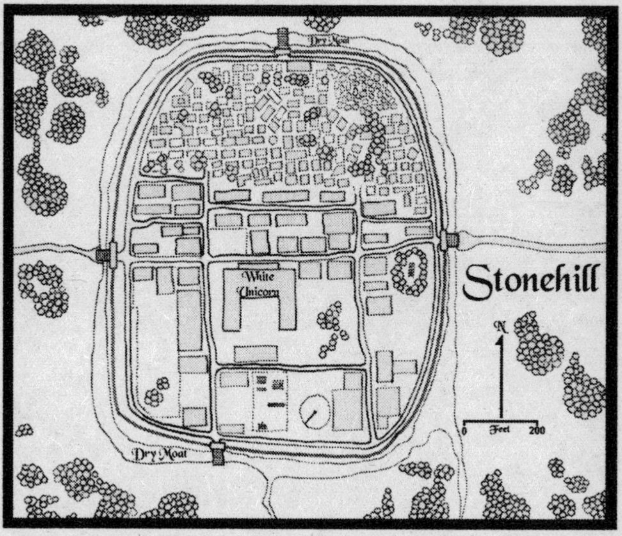

Fifty-five leagues east of the town of Rood—twenty-three leagues beyond the borders of the Boskydells—the east–west Crossland Road and the north–south Post Road intersect. Nearby sits the large village of Stonehill; it is a compact town on the western fringes of the sparsely populated Wilderland, with a hundred or so stone houses perched upon the hillside above. For the most part, Humans occupy the village, though a few Warrows do dwell nigh the crest of the hill in the northeast corner of the town.

Where the two main roads form a junction, the terrain is quite level, and a spur from that intersection runs into and through the town itself, lying just north and east of the crossing. The village straddles the spur, and for protection a dry moat and a high stone wall completely encircle the town. There are two primary ways into Stonehill: a causeway over the moat to the east and another one to the west. In spite of the moat and wall, during the Great War of the Ban a Horde of Foul Folk, marching westerly from the Drearwood, broke through the heavy gates and overran the town and set afire as much as they could, though most of the buildings were made of stone and did not burn. Still, a great deal of Stonehill had been destroyed, and had to be rebuilt afterward. As to the villagers themselves, they had retreated into the nearby Weiunwood, for the Warrows of the forest had warned the inhabitants that the Horde was coming.

Because the town is situated at the junction of two main roads, until a few years past, strangers and out-of-towners were often present—in fact, were welcomed. It was, after all, a layover point for the Red Coaches, traveling as they did between Roadsend in Wellen, and Caer Pendwyr to the south, and Challerain Keep in the north. It was as well a gathering point for merchants and travelers heading east along the Crossland Road and through perilous Drearwood, and the greater their numbers and guards, the less likely Foul Folk and brigands would attack. Too, it was a resting point for those coming west along the Crossland, a place where wounds could be healed, wounds taken within that dreadful wood.

And so Stonehill would bustle with traveling crafters and traders and merchants and the like, and every now and then there would be a royal—a Duke, Viscount, or other such personage—passing through, at times traveling with their own retinue, at other times accompanying the High King on his springtime trip going north or his autumnal journey faring south. And there were days when *real* strangers came, such as a company of journeying Dwarves, or King's-soldiers from the south, or a Guardian or two, and they would invariably stay at the only inn in town—the White Unicorn, Wheatley Brewster, Prop. And when these special strangers came, the local folk would be sure to drop in to the common room to listen to them and hear the news from far away.

Yet that was before the Usurper seized power. Now however, since there is no commerce between the Northern Alliance and the Usurper's domain, the Red Coaches are infrequent, and with this source of trade absent, the town has fallen upon ill times.

Even so, these days the White Unicorn, with its many rooms, hosts a wayfarer or two, or perhaps a nearby settler who might be staying overnight.

And on the same eve that Reyer and his retinue entered the Boskydell town of Rood, hard men—twenty in all—rode into Stonehill, the hooves of their horses ringing on the cobblestone streets. Grim-faced and silent, they stabled their horses and entered the inn. . . .

WITH HIS FAST HANDS working on his apron, Wheatley Brewster—large and rotund with salt-and-pepper hair—bustled out from the kitchen as the men tromped into the inn, chain mail ajingle, swords slapping at thighs, saddlebags and bedrolls in hand.

"Welcome, welcome," he said, his blue eyes atwinkle and his rubious face breaking into a wide smile. "Welcome to the White Unicorn. How might I serve you?"

"Rums," said one, his accent heavy.

"Rums?"

"Slip," replied the man.

Wheatley frowned, but then enlightenment dawned. "Oh, I see: rooms. A place to sleep."

"Dà. Rums. Slip."

"Pa hrána," said another, his cold gaze sweeping the common room as if seeking hidden threats.

The spokesman glanced over and with a deferential bob of his head said, *"Dà, povêljnik."*

He then turned to Wheatley and said, "Fud," as he made eating motions. Then he added, "Um... *píti.* Er, drank," now acting as if taking a drink.

"Food. Yes. I have a great side of beef sizzling on the spit, and plenty of drink—tasty brown ale, cool spring water, bracing dark tea, hearty bloodred wine—and tubers and fresh-baked bread and, well, I am sure I have enough for you all." Wheatley turned and bellowed, "Hops!" And he smiled at the man, the delegated spokesman, and added, "My son."

From a distant somewhere within the inn there came the clatter of footsteps speeding down unseen stairs.

"Sounds like a horse," said Wheatley, "but he's really a nice young man. —Oh, and by the bye, would you and your company like baths? We've bathing rooms out back, and large tubs and plenty of hot water. Get rid of the grime of travel, don't you know."

The delegate frowned at Wheatley and turned up a hand.

"You know, baths," said Wheatley, now pantomiming washing and bathing motions.

"Ah," said the man, nodding, and he turned to the one who seemed to be the leader, a captain perhaps, given his military bearing. *"Kopél?"*

Barking a laugh, the leader turned to his comrades and rattled off something entirely too rapidly for Wheatley to catch even a single word. The room rang with the harsh

laughter of the men. Then the captain said to the spokesman, *"Ne kopél."*

"Dà, povêljnik," said the interpreter and then turned to
Wheatley and said, "No beth."

"Ah," said Wheatley, his face falling, for he knew the grime
would take extra soap to get the bedding clean. "No beth."

Again the leader spoke up: *"Stroškóvna cerna."*

"Dà, povêljnik," said the delegate. *"Stroškóvna cerna.
Kovánec."* He sighed, and looked at Brewster and said,
"Kovánec. Um—" He frowned, but then, lighting upon a re-
membered word, he brightened and said, "What coin?" Then
he mimed eating, drinking, and sleeping. And once again said,
"Coin."

"Oh, the cost," said Wheatley. "Well, then . . . harrumph . . .
a silver each for room and board, twenty silvers all told. Flagons of ale or goblets of wine, extra."

The delegate turned to the leader. *"Dvájset srebó."*

The captain, if he was a captain, shook his head and said,
"Desét."

"Ten silver," said the interpreter.

At that moment, a young, dark-haired man, even taller
than Wheatley, though considerably less rotund, popped
into the common room. His eyes widened as he took in the
sight of so many rough, unshaven men, with all of them
armed and armored, too. But the youth stood by as Wheatley and the interpreter haggled, finally settling on eight coppers for each of the twenty men for room and board, a total
of sixteen silvers.

Now that the bargaining was done, "Yes, Da?" said the
young man.

"Hops, show these guests to the rooms. It seems they
speak little Common. This dark one here"—Wheatley gestured at the interpreter—"is the spokesman, though I think
that one over there is the captain of this squad. In the meanwhile, I'll get Tansey and Sam to hopping; these men seem
to be hungry."

WORD OF THE VISITORS quickly spread through the town, and
many came to catch the latest news. But for the most part

the twenty men were grim-faced and silent, and when they did speak it was in a tongue the villagers did not ken. And so, with naught forthcoming, after a pint or two, most villagers returned to their own doings.

As to the soldiers—as Wheatley considered them to be—they whispered among themselves, falling silent when food or drink was borne to the tables by Wheatley or Hops, and at times by broad-beamed, ruby-cheeked, bustling Tansey—Wheatley's wife—or tall, stick-thin Sam, the cook.

As soldiers do, they wolfed down their food and drink, and as Hops and Wheatley were delivering more flagons to the men, "What nemm plece?" asked the delegate as he took up a tankard, the man well into his cups.

"Eh?" asked Wheatley, setting more flagons down.

"What nemm plece?"

"Oh, Stonehill. This is the village of Stonehill."

"Willage?"

Wheatley nodded. "Village. Town. Hamlet."

"*Ne. Ne vás.* No willage." He pounded on the table and gestured about and said, "This plece. *Róg kònj.* Horn horse."

"Ah. The White Unicorn. It's not really a horse, but a Unicorn. Some think it a fabled beastie, but me, I think it's real. I mean, of certain there's a lot of old wives' tales about them, and the bards are always singing of maidens and true love and Unicorns, and who would know better than the bards, eh?"

It was clear that the man didn't at all follow Wheatley's words, but he smiled widely and said, "Horn horse."

Pausing in his taking up of empty flagons, Hops said, "I say, where are you and your men bound? Up to Challerain Keep, I expect, right?" He glanced at his father and said, "I wish that I could go."

Wheatley sighed, but did not reply.

"So, where are you bound?" asked Hops again. "Challerain Keep, I would think."

The man frowned.

"Challerain Keep?" repeated Hops, miming riding motions.

"*Ne. Ne.*" The man shook his head. Then he owlishly

looked about, as if seeking eavesdroppers and lowered his voice and said, *"Tájnost."*

"Tájnost?" Hops turned up his hands.

"Bíti molčeč!" snapped the captain.

The interpreter cringed. *"Dà, povêljnik,"* he mumbled. A moment later, full of too much ale, he vomited on the floor, and then fell over, passed out.

THE NEXT MORNING, with some worse than others for their drinking, all the men laded their horses and fared out the western gate and over the causeway and toward the Post Road, where they turned north.

Watching them ride away, Hops turned to his father and said, "Looks like they are bound for Challerain."

Wheatley nodded but said naught.

After a moment, Hops said, "What do you think *Tájnost* means, Da?"

Without a moment's hesitation, Wheatley said, "Secret, I shouldn't wonder."

Drearwood

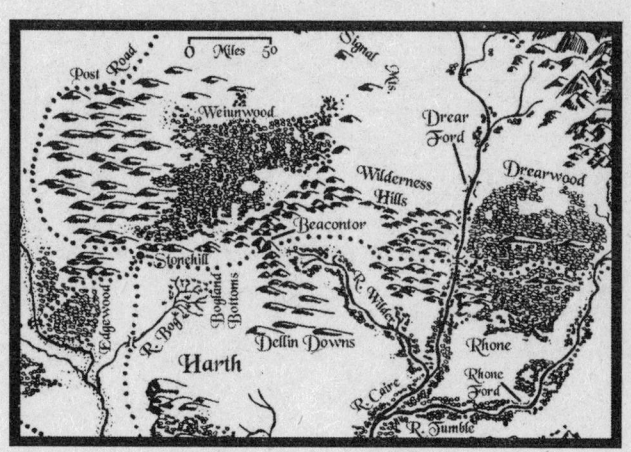

As the gorcrow flies, some sixty-six leagues farther east of Stonehill there crouches the dark fringes of a dreadful woodland. But by the slow meander of the Crossland Road it's another six leagues ere a traveler aground would reach the sinister edge. The tangled mass fills the stony hill country twenty-five leagues north to south and thirty east to west, and it squats astraddle the route, where it imperils anyone who would think to travel through. All within the enshadowed mass, blackness musters in ebon pools, and a dismal sky seems ever to hover above this malevolent place. To either side of the way, stunted undergrowth clutches at the rocky ground, and gnarled trees twist upward and into gloom-cast darkness. Jagged branches seem ready to seize whoever or whatever comes within reach, while runs of thorny growth stand ready to rend to bloody shreds any victim who would dare their grasp.

Long has this ill-cast clutch been a region most dire. Therein Foul Folk lair—in cracks and crevices and caves and holes, anywhere out of the radiance of day, for they fear the Ban, and rightly so: any who are caught in Adon's light suffer the Withering Death, leaving husks to crumble into dust in the stirring wind. But between dusk and dawn they are free to roam, and woe betide any who would be within that tangle when the Foul Folk are abroad.

But Spawn are not the only dread things to fear, for other grim monsters are said to dwell within, *things* all: some hulking, larger than Trolls; others massive and long and thick like snakes, but no snakes these; there are the multilegged, spiderlike, some creeping, some swift; and yet others, unseen but heard, their squalls and clickings and mewls and hisses driving terror deep within.

Many are the tales of lone travelers and small bands who

have followed the road into this dismal woodland never to be seen again. And rife are the stories of large caravans and groups of armed warriors who have beaten off grim monsters half seen in the night, and many have lost their lives to these grisly creatures. This land is shunned by all except those who have no choice but to cross it, or by those adventurers who seek fame, most of whom do not live to grasp their glory. Yet the main trade route—the Crossland Road—splits through this dread realm, and so traders and travelers mass together, and armed escorts hire out their axes and swords and bows and arrows and other such weaponry to see them safely through. Even so, casualties are high, though the larger the caravan, the less likely a full attack from the cowardly Spawn.

It is the Drearwood, this awful haunt, and perhaps some day, Men or Dwarves or Elves or others, or combinations thereof, will purge this tangle of these dire inhabitants. Perhaps someday, but not this day ...

And at sunset on the eve that Reyer and his retinue reached the Boskydell town of Rood, in the faraway Drearwood a Grimwall Corvus came to rest in the gnarled branches of a shadow-wrapped tree nigh the hide-covered mouth of a dim-cast cavern deep in that dreadful place....

THE CORVUS SOUNDED A sharp *graak!*

There was no response.

Hopping to a lower branch, again the Corvus called.

Still there came no response.

Agitated now, the bird began a sound much like that of knuckles rapping on wood. *Knk! Knk-knkk!* ...

With the Corvus knocking and skrawking and gracking, finally, the hide gave a faint twitch aside, enough so that whoever, whatever was within could see that twilight had fallen, and out stepped a Hlôk. [Shut your beak!], he snarled in Slûk at the bird. Then he saw the capsule upon its leg. *A message!* Perhaps it bore news of a caravan or merchant or someone else coming through. Thoughts of horseflesh and plunder raced across the Hlôk's limited mind. Then he turned and stepped back to the entry and pushed the flap aside. [One of you slugs bring meat, now!], he shouted.

Rûcks within the cavern looked at one another, but otherwise did not stir.

The Hlôk ground his teeth and pointed and said, [You!]

Moaning, the designated Rûck scrabbled to one of the buckets and withdrew what appeared to be a thick gray worm. And, trembling because he knew what was coming, cowing and whining, he stepped to the cover and the Hlôk shoved him outside, snarling, [Feed it and bring me the vial.]

The Corvus flew down to the mewling Rûck and landed on his flinching forearm and dug in its claws, and blood spurted. It snatched the gobbet of meat from the yowling Rûck and permitted the screamer to detach the capsule. By this time a second victim, bearing another wad of gray meat, stepped out to the bird's eager rush.

A third Rûck slipped a fearful look out from behind the hide flap and saw that the message capsule was free, and then, grinning at the other two, he stepped forth with a third chunk of meat and threw it on the ground, and the Corvus leapt from another bleeding perch and snatched up the wriggling morsel.

The first Rûck, his arm dribbling dark ichor, bore the capsule to his leader.

Snatching it away from his whimpering minion, the Hlôk opened the tiny vial and extracted the tissue-thin strip from within. There was no writing upon the slip, but even had there been any, the Hlôk could not read, for, as with nearly all Foul Folk, he was illiterate except in the crudest sense: a rude drawing or no more than a symbol or two was the limit of Spawn enlightenment. Yet no writing was needed on this missive, for it had come from a Dark Master, and the message it bore stabbed directly into the small wit of the Hlôk.

He groaned.

What he was told to do was perilous in the extreme.

That much he understood.

He loped swiftly to another crevice, where he let a second Hlôk hold the missive, and then to a third hole, and then a fourth, where the final Hlôk was commanded to join the first three.

They gathered up their respective Rûck lackeys, along with weapons and rations, and, fifty-two in all and led by the first Hlôk, north to the Crossland Road they went and began loping westerly along its course.

All night they ran, starting out under the light of the half-moon, but it set at mid of night, which left only starlight to see by. Yet they did not slow, for to do so would mean death.

And the world slowly turned in its track until false dawn came.

Rûcks began to whimper, yet onward they sped, now at a faster pace—they were running for their lives.

The east began to lighten, and still they ran; the Dark Master had told them where safety lay, and toward this hold they galloped.

And just barely before the rising sun lipped the eastern horizon behind, away from the Crossland Road they sped south and into the Wilderness Hills, where they jammed into a tiny cavern. All but one laggard, who withered away and crumbled to dust in their wake.

THE NEXT EVE THEY continued westerly along the road, and this time just ere the sun rose, they found refuge in a deep crevice at the far fringes of the hills.

The night after that they splashed across the River Wilder and found safety barely ere dawn in the cracks of Dellin Downs.

In the following darkness they made their way to the Bogland Bottoms, where, in that mire, as day arrived they squirmed under the roots of black cypresses and gray willows to escape the sun, and the gnawing wrigglers and razor-mouthed leeches and boring worms feasted.

They remained off the road the ensuing night, as things all about them slithered and plopped or frantically sped off in splashing flight. Midst clouds of biting midges and ear-crawling gnats and blood-sucking mosquitoes whining all 'round they slogged their way through the marsh, for they would not have their presence discovered, as close to the Weiunwood and Stonehill as they had come.

The Weiunwood itself was certain death, for Warrows and Hidden Ones dwelled therein, and the Spawn would not dare their wrath. As to Stonehill, wayfarers coming to or going from that town might see this band and sound the alert, and their mission would end then and there. And so, when the sun again rose they spent another miserable day burrowed into the swamp at its far western extent, and once more lost blood and flesh to the denizens within.

When the next night fell, the sixth of their undertaking, they sped across the open plain south and west of Stonehill, first crossing the Post Road and then the Crossland to finally reach the southernmost extent of the Battle Downs. But they lost two more Rûcks to the first rays of sunrise, their withered dry husks lying behind to crumble to dust throughout the day.

Over the next three nights, they ran north through the Battle Downs, where they searched for their quarry.

As to just exactly where within those hills their prey might have been, even their Dark Master did not know. For it was the Battle Downs, and Magekind, both dark and light, held no sway therein.

Battle Downs

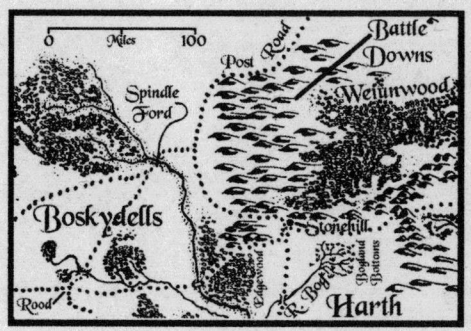

Some hundred miles long south to north and fifty miles wide west to east, a low run of hills starts just outside of Stonehill and runs north toward Challerain Keep. The range fares all along the western border of the Weiunwood, and sits somewhat east of the eastern border of the Boskydells. These hills are known as the Battle Downs, a name gotten from the raging combat therein during the Great War of the Ban. Here it was that the allied Men of Rian and Dalara, of Harth and the Wilderland and Stonehill, and Warrows from the Boskydells and the Weiunwood—along, some say, with the Hidden Ones from the Weiunwood—all met and did battle with one of Modru's great Hordes of Foul Folk that had spilled out from Drearwood and Gron to throw down Challerain Keep and rule the lands all 'round.

For days the battle raged, with Rûcks and Hlôks and Ghûls and Trolls in combat with Men, Warrows, Hidden Ones, and a handful of Elves. Long were the struggles, the Allies using the hills themselves to strike and withdraw, harass and harry, and to stand and fight the Foul Folk.

Many fell on both sides, but in the end the Allies prevailed, and long were the days of mourning after.

Yet what is not known by common folk is why none of Magekind—neither light nor dark—fought on either side. Surely, one might say, their aid would have been invaluable to Foul Folk and Allies alike. Yet none participated at all. . . .

At the time of King Reyer, those days of combat lay some two thousand years in the past, yet the name of this region and how it got to be that way is well known by many and well remembered by some.

And it was this range of hills that Reyer and his entourage would pass alongside on part of their journey northward toward the city of Challerain Keep.

But that lay some days in the future, for on this day the King's rade had just left the Boskydell town of Rood. . . .

AT THE INSISTENCE OF DRIU, Alton Periwinkle and Digby Thimbleweed rode in the company of Reyer, Alton to the left of the young High King, and Digby to his right, the place where Alric would normally be. Yet that young man, at his own insistence and at the pleasure of the King, now rode in the vanguard, some hundred or so yards ahead of the main body. Gretta was not happy with this arrangement, but Alric had finally convinced Reyer that a Vanadurin, one in whose blood stirred the spirit of Strong Harl, needed to be on point, and as the only Harlingar warrior in the company of the King . . . well, who better to ride out there with lance and saber and bow?

As to just why Driu had supported Alric in his quest, and had insisted that these two particular Thornwalkers ride with Reyer, she did not say. Only that it was important that they do so. And as the High King's Seer, she was not questioned, though Gretta seemed like to burst from keeping her mouth shut.

And so, Alton "Perry" Periwinkle, and Digby "Diggs" Thimbleweed quickly became known as the High King's Thornwalkers, his personal handpicked Warrow guard.

They had ridden out from Rood along Two Fords Road, and easily settled into the journey. Nigh midday, they crossed a sparkling stream, pausing long enough for the horses to take on water and the riders to dismount and stretch their legs.

"What flow is this?" asked Reyer, turning to Digby, the little Thornwalker who had been chattering away for the full of the seventeen miles they had thus far come on the journey.

"The Dingle-rill," said Digby. He waved vaguely to the west and added, "It comes out of Big Fen and is joined by a stream out of Little Fen; together they make this part of the Rill. It streams on east, through Woody Hollow and Budgens and Raffin and other towns to join the Spindle River somewhat south of Eastpoint. This crossing is known as West Ford."

"Hmm . . ." mused Reyer. "Tell me this, then, Diggs: if the Dingle-rill flows eastward, then why is the road called Two Fords?"

"Oh," said Digby, "because here we cross through the Dingle-rill, and some leagues on up the way we'll ford the Spindle River, up north."

"At Spindle Ford," clarified Perry. "The road crosses out from the Bosky at Spindle Ford."

"And that's where we are headed?" asked Reyer.

"Yup," said Digby. "Just over a hundred and ten miles from Rood to the Spindle along this way."

"Thirty-seven leagues," said Perry.

"Four days, then," said Reyer.

"Thereabout," said Perry.

"Oh, oh," said Digby, "but by the Red Coach, it's more like two days."

"It runs this route?" asked Reyer.

"Not so much any more," said Digby. "Mostly, folks going from Wellen to Challerain Keep follow the Upland Way through the Bosky."

"Mother Gretta suggested we take the Upland Way," said Reyer. "She said it would be quicker."

"Well, it would be and is," said Digby.

"Runs through Northdune," said Perry.

"But you came to Rood instead," said Digby.

"Driu insisted," said Reyer.

"Why?" asked Perry. "I mean, Rood is just a tiny place compared to Challerain Keep, or so I am told."

"Perhaps because Rood is the capital of the Boskydells," said Reyer. "And since we are on a rade, well . . ."

Perry snorted, but Diggs nodded and said, "I am glad you came this way instead of that."

Reyer smiled at the Wee Ones. "Me, too."

A silence fell upon them, but then Diggs said, "You see, there are seven major roads through the Dells: the Crossland, the Upland Way, Southpike, Westspur, the Tineway, and the Wendenway, and Two Fords." Digby waved westerly. "The Upland is over yon." Then he vaguely gestured southward, "And the Tineway and Southpike and the Westspur . . ."

Diggs was still chatting away about routes and spurs and footpaths and trails through the Boskydells as the company once more got under way.

NORTH-NORTHEAST THEY RODE, north-northeast for three days, and at mid of day on the fourth day from Rood they saw in the distance ahead a lone hill, its shape somewhat irregular—lumpy, one might say. As they neared they could make out that it was a great jumble of rocks—large boulders and small—rearing up into a pinnacle.

"I say," said Reyer, "looks like a Giant were playing here."

"It's Rook's Roost," said Diggs. "And you just might be right about a Giant piling them up. I mean, Old Gaffer says so."

Perry snorted, but said naught.

"It's right at the junction where the Upland Way and Two Fords come together," said Digby.

"Rook's Roost?"

"Yar," said Perry. "You don't want to be here at sunset and after."

Reyer frowned. "Why's that?"

"The clatter'll drive you batty," said Perry. "All that scrawking and chatter as the rooks come back to roost. It's even worse than listening to Diggs."

Reyer laughed, but Digby drew himself up in his saddle and said, "Worse than—?"

"You heard me, Diggs," said Perry, now grinning.

To fore and aft, Dylvana burst into quiet laughter, and Riessa, smiling, turned in her saddle and said to Digby, "'Tis but a tease, Wee One. Fear not, for thou art well loved."

"Oh, I know that," said Digby. "Perry and I are best friends and he's always twitting me."

And in good humor, they fared past the tall spire of stones, to join the Upland Way. They went along this road awhile, and, after a league or so, in the fore they could see a Red Coach rumbling toward them. They moved off the road to let it pass, the strangers within peering out at this odd company of Men and Elves and Warrows. And of course Diggs thought those inside the coach were an odd company as well, being all Humans accoutered in merchant finery, and not a farmer or Warrow among them.

The King and his entourage spent the night at the Thornwalker encampment at the edge of the Spindlethorn Barrier, the company there treating them to a hearty meal of coney soup and roasted lamb and steamed vegetables and cheese.

THE FOLLOWING DAY IN a drizzling rain they continued along the Upland Way, the road into Rian, and they passed through the long thorn-barrier tunnel to reach Spindle Ford, and thence through the Barrier again to slowly emerge up and out from the Spindle Valley to come to a rather featureless plain, with naught in view but tall grass bowing in the swirling mist.

They rode in somber silence, but for the clop and splash of hooves and the faint patter of rain, yet ere the noontide, the falling tictac dwindled and dwindled to finally let up, yet the overcast remained. Even Digby said little, his chatter stilled for the nonce, and Reyer as well as Perry missed his continuing stream of fact and fancy and his wild-hare schemes.

And even as the unseen sun—naught but a dim glow in the west—lipped the horizon, they came to where the Upland Way ended at the Post Road, that major thoroughfare running to north and south alongside a low range of grassladen hills.

They had come to the Battle Downs.

THEY HAD INTERCEPTED THE range not quite midway on its south to north run, and it was there they settled for the eve. And in camp that night, Driu assembled the company and said, "Keep a sharp eye, for if unknown peril lurks, I know not when it might strike. All I can say is not this day."

"Wait," said Alric. "Can't you just cast the runes?"

"Nay, I cannot, for we are in the grip of the Battle Downs."

"And . . . ?" said Alric.

"And the aethyr is roiled."

"Roiled?" asked Gretta, alarm showing on her face.

"Constantly roiled," said Driu. "Here, Magekind's arts are useless."

"I say," said Digby, "then the old tales are true?"

"What old tales, Diggs?" asked Perry.

Digby threw up his hands in exasperation. "Don't you remember what the Gaffer said?"

"Oh, that! Hogwash," said Perry.

Driu turned to Digby. "What said this, um, Gaffer?"

"That in the Battle Downs lodestones spin wildly, cannot tell east from west, north from south, just as likely to point down or up. He said that even Dwarven feet get tangled in these parts. And if there's a lightning storm here, stay low, 'cause the strikes sometime leap from hilltop to hilltop stead o' from sky to ground. And he said there be strange fluxes in the aethyr here, but what that might mean I haven't a clue, only that he did say the word 'aethyr.'"

"I still say, poppycock," said Perry.

But Driu shook her head. "Your Gaffer is at least partly right, Diggs. The aethyr here does have strange fluxes, and it cannot be brought to bear."

Digby grinned at Perry and said, "See there, Mister Smarty-pants Alton Periwinkle, the Gaffer was right."

"She said 'partly right,' Mister Know-it-all Digby Thimbleweed," huffed Perry. "Lady Driu said the Gaffer was *partly right.*"

"Wull," said Digby, "if we just had a lodestone, or if we could get some lightning, then we'd see."

"Yes, we would," shot back Perry.

"Enough," snapped Conal. He then turned to Driu and asked, "You cannot see aught of what is to come?"

"Nay, I cannot," she replied.

"Not even danger?" asked Gretta.

"Not even that," said Driu.

"Then we double the ward," said Conal, looking at Riessa, the Dylvana nodding in return.

"And we scout the surround in the dark," said Windlow, captain of the Thornwalker squad accompanying Reyer.

"Oh, I want to go," said Digby. "Perry, too. No one steps softer, moves quieter, manages to remain unseen as well as Perry and I do."

"Nay," said Driu. "Perry and Diggs will remain at Reyer's side."

"Why?" demanded Perry. "I mean, guarding the King is necessary, but so is scouting."

"Aye, but this I ken," said Driu. "Though I am blind to what is to come, I do know that you two have a key part to play in Reyer's safety. What it is I cannot say."

"Wull, that key part could just as well be played by us being scouts," said Perry. "And another thing—"

Conal threw up a hand to silence Perry's words. "Driu has guided us well these past thirteen years. I see no reason to change that course. Hence, you will stay nigh Reyer and keep watch from there."

Gretta looked down at the two buccen, and then at the other five Wee Folk. "But wouldn't it be better to have Dylvana on ward. I mean ... *Warrows*?"

"I'll have you know, Lady Gretta," said Captain Windlow, rising up to his full three foot seven, "there are no better warriors than those of us you dismiss out of hand."

"I am sorry, but you are so small," said Gretta.

"Small, yes, but no one is more perilous than a buccan with a bow," said Riessa.

The Dylvana's words seemed to settle the issue, and the council continued debating the pros and cons of various actions, including whether or no to leave the road and ride westward to be free of the aethyr churn. They also debated whether to go east and to the Weiunwood, where the Wee Folk and the Hidden Ones could provide protection. Yet Driu said the extent of the roil was considerable, and that to carry on north along the Post Road would perhaps set them free of it the soonest. It was late in the night when they called the meeting to a close, for too many were the unknowns as to what might come, and in the end only vigilance seemed to count.

THE NEXT DAY THEY turned northward along the Post Road, and that eve they camped again along the marge. Buccen ranged outward in the gathering darkness to look for danger lurking.

None was found.

That evening, Diggs and Perry took turns at watch, along with Riessa and others, and naught came in the night.

The following day, they took up the trek again, and Driu said, "One more eve and we'll be free of the churning aethyr. Then I will see what I might."

On they rode and on, Alric and the vanguard especially alert, though Perry and Diggs took turns dozing in the saddle, making up for lost sleep.

The sun set, yet they continued riding in the dusk, hoping to reach the far edge of the downs ere making camp. The bright full moon had just risen, shining its clear light aglance across the scape, the Battle Downs somehow lending vitality to the glow, and even the lunar-cast shadows seemed curiously . . . vibrant.

Yet just as full nighttime fell, from ahead and within the vivid flux-ridden hills they heard shouting and cursing, and the hum of bows and the ring of steel on steel, mingled with shrieks and cries. Voices howled, some guttural, some clear. "Those are Men in battle!" said Conal. "With *Spaunen*," said Riessa.

"Alric!" screamed Gretta, for, with swords drawn and lances lowered, the vanguard had charged through the moonlight and toward the battle.

Viper

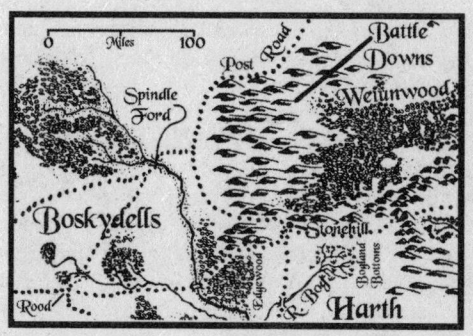

Among the many gifts of Elvenkind is an ageless life. How this came about, perhaps even the gods do not know. Still, Elves are born as helpless babes, and in this they are like Humankind and others. And over the next twenty-five or thirty years these fey children, these Lian and Dylvana, become tall and lithe and graceful, and from that point on they simply do not physically age beyond, but instead live in eternal youth.

It is their nature.

And no matter how many years an Elf has lived beyond that beginning—be it ten or a hundred or a thousand or more—the number of seasons behind each one represent but a single step, the first step, upon an ageless life ... though the journey itself might come to an end for a given Elf.

One might think that with the prospect of countless years before them, Elves would greatly fear death. After all, they would be losing a particular form of Forever. Yet it is not true: they do not fear their own demise any more or less than other Races, for, like them, they also seek out the challenges of living ... to do otherwise would be like unto death itself.

Even so, Elvenkind has learned that to strive for dominion—power over others—is a false goal. This they came to realize in their "Time of Madness," when they fought bitter wars with one another, struggling for command, struggling for rule. Yet one among them in the long view realized such bitter fights were all for naught, for once such transient goals are achieved they turn to ashes in one's mouth. And so this enlightened one set aside those ambitions and spoke to others of what he had envisioned—a better way of living. And he said to them, "Let it begin with me."

And so it did.

And thus did Elves one by one gradually throw off their madness to finally become sane.

Yet that does not mean Elvenkind refuses to engage in battle, for some things must be settled by force of arms, especially when there are those who try to control others' lives.

Hence, as a Race, they fought in the Great War of the Ban, when Gyphon and his minions threatened the existence of all—all the worlds, all the Planes ... all.

Likewise, Elves champion lesser causes: some with force of arms, some with gentle persuasion, some with diplomacy, some with education, some by example.

In the time of the Usurper, to restore the rightful High King was certainly a lesser cause, for it involved just Humankind, and not all of Humankind at that. Even so, as always, individual Elves could choose to aid or not.

Riessa and her band had chosen to aid.

And on this particular night, in this particular place, *Spaunen* were involved. . . .

Reyer put spurs to his horse, his steed leaping forward in response. Likewise did Conal and Riessa follow, as did the remaining escort—Elves, Humans, and Warrows alike—all except Driu and Gretta, who remained back, along with their personal guard—Jame and Jace Brownleaf—the twin Thornwalkers, nocking arrows to bowstrings and seething at not being with the others.

Racing alongside Reyer, Conal called out, "Take care, my boy, I will guard your left."

With but a nod did Reyer reply, and sword in hand he charged ahead, hoping that Alric and Durgan and the others in the vanguard were faring well in the battle. He did not note that Riessa and the Dylvana, who appeared to be randomly galloping toward the conflict, were actually running in a protective ring about him, more to the fore than aft.

And in the vivid light of the bright risen moon, ahead they could see a swirl of men and Rûcks and Hlôks afoot in mêlée, and the King's vanguard on horses charging through—lances piercing, sabers hewing, hooves trampling.

Rûcks with twisted bows loosed arrows, the black shafts and their dark-slathered points finding victim after victim. Other Rûcks hammered with wicked iron cudgels at men and mounts alike, felling them with broken limbs, and the agonized screams of the horses were liken unto those of terrified women. Rûcks swung scimitars and Hlôks hewed tulwars deep into human flesh, and men afoot slashed daggers and long-knives and broadswords at the foe.

Slain and wounded lay in deep moon-shadows, while fighters stumbled over corpses and injured alike, and hooves crushed bone underhoof.

Horses ran loose, their eyes rolling in panic, some galloping away. It was as if the Spawn had come upon these men leading their animals, and had attacked them ere any could mount.

And into this swirl of combat, Reyer and the others charged, with the out-galloped Warrows on ponies coming last.

"Target their archers," shouted Captain Windlow, even as he felled a Rûck.

And Perry and Digby, along with Billy Buckbell and Arlo Loosestrife and the captain flew arrow after arrow into the bow-shooting Rûcks, and one after another the Foul Folk fell to the shafts of the buccen.

And Reyer's blade hewed and chopped and slashed, and blood flew and Rûcks and a Hlôk died screaming.

On Reyer's left, Conal fended off strike after strike, his own saber now slathered with grume.

Alric on the far side of the mêlée now hewed with saber as well, his lance broken in twain. The blade end of the long wooden shaft had pierced deep through two very dead Rûcks who had had the misfortune of standing nigh one another when Alric skewered the first through and through and his charge had carried him into the second one ere the lance snapped with both on the shaft.

And the Dylvana, graceful as dancers in a ballet of motion, glided their horses among the *Spaunen* and felled them as if reaping wheat.

Yet one Rûck and then another took aim at Reyer, but

ere either loosed black arrows, two shafts pierced each of their hearts, and the Rûcks fell slain even as Digby and Perry nocked arrows to protect their King.

And in that moment the Foul Folk broke and fled into the moon-shadows, with Alric and three Elves in pursuit.

Astride his barely controlled half-mad steed, the animal driven so by the reek of death and the tang of blood and the screams of downed herd mates, Armsmaster Conal called out amid the aftermath, "Are any of you wounded? Any take hurt?"

As his mount skittered this way and that, Conal looked about, waiting for a reply.

None said aught.

"Well and good, then," he said. He turned to Durgan and said, "The downed horses: I would have you put them out of their misery."

Durgan paled, but nodded. "Aye."

Next, Conal turned to Riessa. "Dara, would you have some of yours round up those loose-running steeds?"

"I will do it myself," said Riessa, and she signaled to two other Dylvana.

"Take care," said Conal, "more Rûcks are about, those that fled."

As the three Dylvana rode away, Conal dismounted and soothed his horse and said, "Captain Windlow, while Reyer and I check the fallen, would you fetch Driu and Gretta. Mayhap they can help these men, any who are wounded."

Windlow turned to Digby and Perry and said, "Stay with the King, lads. Keep him safe." Then the captain headed toward the road.

Both Conal and Reyer turned their steeds over to a Dylvana to take them from the carnage, and Perry and Digby gave over their ponies to Billy and Arlo to do the same.

And Reyer and Conal, with Perry and Digby following, strode among the downed combatants. Now and again they passed by Durgan at his grisly task, the young man weeping as he slit throats. The armsmaster and King found none of their own lying dead, but they did count some forty-two slain Foul Folk—three of them Hlôks, the rest Rûcks—thirteen of them pierced by Thornwalker arrows.

But as to the men first attacked by the Spawn, only three survived—two of them badly injured. Seventeen others lay slain. The one man who had come through unscathed seemed to have a military bearing, and he looked coldly at the two who lay wounded. He turned and said something to Conal, but it swiftly became clear that he spoke no Common. Instead his language was rather harsh, guttural. Conal, by what little he had heard of these kinds of tongues in the past, knew that this man probably came from one of the nations in the northeastern part of the High King's realm—perhaps Garia or Khal or even Naud.

Driu, who by this time had come with Gretta to the field, said, "I will talk with him as soon as we are free of these cursed Battle Downs, with its roiled flux."

Conal nodded, for he knew that she simply had to cast one of her Seer's spells to speak any tongue whatsoever.

He turned to the standing survivor and said, "You and your injured will come with us to Challerain Keep."

The man looked at one of his wounded, and that man groaned out, "Challerain Keep, *Povêljnik. Mi jahati med jih.*"

At the word *"Povêljnik,"* Conal took Reyer aside and said, "'Ware, Reyer. I recognized that term. 'Tis a military rank. This man is a Garian commander."

Trailing after, both Digby and Perry overheard Conal's warning.

ALRIC, ALONG WITH THREE Dylvana—Ralen, Aliser, and Ianne—rode back into camp. As they dismounted and unsaddled their horses, Alric said to Conal, "Well, Da, we got three more, but I think four, mayhap five escaped. We just couldn't run them to earth. Oh, but we did find where these men had been camped." Alric turned and pointed. "Just yon, on the far side of that hill. From the looks of it, they had been here for two, three days."

In that moment, Gretta came running and embraced Alric. "Oh, my child, my child. Don't ever go running off like that aga—"

"Gretta!" snapped Conal. "He is a blooded warrior now, as is Reyer. They are of age."

"Mother," said Alric, pushing away, his voice cold. "Would you have a Harlingar shirk his duty?"

"It's just that— Fifteen is not—"

"Strong Harl rode to combat when he was fourteen," said Alric. "Would you have me do less?"

Gretta burst into tears. Alric's mien softened and he embraced her and whispered, "Mother, be strong, as all Vanadurin women are."

Her voice muffled by Alric's chest, Gretta said, "You're right. You're right. I will worry, as all Jordian women do, yet I will endure." Then she pushed back from Alric while yet holding on to him and then pulled him close and kissed him on the cheek.

To one side, Conal nodded and said to no one in particular, "I believe Gretta has finally come of age."

Reyer leaned over to Conal and whispered, "I don't think she heard you, and it's better she did not," then he laughed aloud.

"You're right, my boy," Conal replied, and he joined Reyer in his laughter.

"THERE WAS NAUGHT WE COULD DO," said Driu.

" 'Twas *Ruch* poison," said Riessa. "From arrows. We had no gwynthyme to counteract it."

"Then only the *povêljnik*—the commander—survived," said Conal. "Riessa, set ward on Reyer's tent. I trust not this Garian."

Reyer shook his head and said, "No, Da. I think I have a better plan."

IN THE WEE HOURS after mid of night, at the back of Reyer's tent, a keen blade slipped under the edge and quietly sliced upward through the silken fabric. Moments later a face peered in at the King lying lax. The figure moved forward.

From the darkest shadows, "Now!" hissed Perry.

Th-thock! Two arrows took the *povêljnik* through the eyes. He fell dead half in, half out of the tent.

Reyer, yet accoutered in his mail, rolled out from under the covers, his sword in one hand, his dagger in the other. "Nicely done, Perry, Diggs. I say, nicely done."

Perry spat on the slain would-be assassin and growled, "Arkov's viper."

Digby looked at the dead Garian and sighed and said, "And here we saved him from the Rûcks and such. You'd think him a bit more grateful for all that."

Of a sudden the three burst out in laughter, and Conal, Riessa, Alric, Gretta, Durgan, and Captain Windlow found them howling like loons.

Enigma

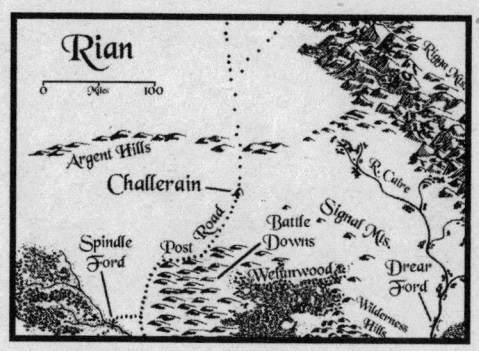

Most things move at a slow measured pace throughout Mithgar: days seep by, as do weeks, months, years. The seasons turn slowly. Crops are planted, sprout, grow, ripen, and are at last harvested. Mortals are born, take years to mature, and age throughout their lifetimes, some much longer than others, ere they finally pass away. And in many places time itself is measured by the movement of the sun, the cycles of the moon, the wheeling of stars, the onset of the dry season, the rainy season, the flooding of the river, and other such indications, gradual or annual; while, in places more advanced, time is gauged by marks on a burning candle or other such incremental measures.

Even though the pace is slow and perhaps but barely noticed, still there are those in Mithgar who puzzle over the very basic elements of time, pondering its nature, wondering if it is a flow streaming o'er the world, or if the world itself moves forward through the essence of time. Too, some wonder if time and fate are continuous, spilling from the future through the present and into the past, washing over all on the way to the Sea of Oblivion, and, if so, are future events predetermined, or can one truly guide one's own fate? Lastly, one wonders if what one has done affects what one will do. Do the events of the past shape those of the future? And since the events of the past seemingly occur *before* those of the future, then is not the future mutable? In which case one would think the past—even though it is gone beyond recall—is merely prologue for that which is to come.

Mayhap a Seer can set to rest some of these musings, yet, to date, none have.

But if one assumes time itself moves forward, rather like a meandering river, it seems to drift slowly until, in moments of immediate crisis, critical events squeeze together to form a constricted channel of urgency, like a high, narrow gorge through which the river plunges headlong. And whether or no the critical events are dire, perilous, or merely overwhelming, in those places for those involved, they say time runs at a breakneck pace.

It is only afterward that any survivors can pause, when the River of Time returns to its slow meandering.

Such as it did in the very dark hours one night in the Battle Downs. . . .

CONAL AND DURGAN HAULED the corpse of the Garian commander out from Reyer's tent.

Riessa fetched a horse from nearby. At Reyer's questioning gaze, " 'Twas his," the Dylvana said, tilting her head toward the dead would-be assassin. "Saddled and provisioned and ready to flee once the deed was done."

"We watched close at hand," said Alric, "though I could but barely stop myself from cutting him down like the cur he was. Yet Driu said, 'Nay,' and so I was forced to do naught."

Windlow barked a laugh and said, "You jittered about like a trembling goat. 'Twas only my firm hand that kept you back."

Cocking an eye, Alric looked down at the Thornwalker captain. "Jittering goat?"

"Or some such," replied Windlow.

"More like a hawk getting ready to swoop," said Alric, grinning.

"Well," said Windlow. "Maybe." Then he laughed again, Alric joining him.

Then Alric sobered and clapped Reyer on the shoulder and said, "I really wanted to be in there with you."

"As did we all," said Conal.

"Well, you couldn't get an entire army in the tent," said Digby. "It would have tipped our hand. Besides, Perry and I were enough."

Driu nodded, but said naught.

Conal and Durgan lifted the carcass up and slung it bellydown over the saddle.

"What do you intend to do with him, Da?" asked Reyer.

"I think I'll haul him out among the slain Rûcks and such and leave him for the crows."

"Not with our arrows you won't," said Perry, and he stepped to the opposite side of the horse and—with a liquid sucking sound—jerked his and Digby's shafts out from the Garian's skull.

"Eew," said Gretta.

"Now you can throw him anywhere you please." Perry handed one of the arrows to Digby, who looked at it askance.

"I'll do it, Da," said Durgan, taking the reins.

"Strip him and search him for any papers he might have," said Conal. He turned to the others and said, " 'Twould be nice to have proof of Arkov's perfidy toward the true High King."

A faint smile twitched the corner of Riessa's mouth. "The proof of his perfidy occurred on the day he broke down Caer Pendwyr's door."

Conal nodded and said, "Nevertheless . . ." Then he added, "We'll strip and search each one when the day comes."

"And then leave them all for the crows?" asked Alric.

Gretta sighed, but otherwise remained silent.

"Indeed," said Conal.

"What about the Foul Folk?" asked Perry. "What'll we do with them?"

"Come dawn," said Digby, "Adon's light will deal with those deaders. But I suppose we can look through whatever's left."

"Ah, you're right, Diggs," said Perry. "I forgot about the Ban."

Riessa looked at the wheel of stars and said, "There are not many candlemarks left ere the coming of day, and I think the company too stirred to gather much sleep ere then. I suggest we all have a meal and make ready to leave soon after sunup; perhaps we should stop midafternoon to then make camp and recover the rest we lack."

All eyes turned to Reyer. He covered his surprise, for it

seemed that he was to make the decision. "Well and good," he said, and so it was settled.

The sun rose, and the Withering Death turned three Hlôks and forty-two Rûcks to husks, three of them away from the others, where Alric and Ralen, Aliser, and Ianne had run them down. The Warrows recovered their arrows, even as the remains gradually collapsed to dust in swirling wind.

Of the Garians, all now lay on the battlefield, where Perry had described them as "dead snakes in the grass, waiting for the crows." Driu looked over at the stripped corpse of the commander. "Perhaps this is why, back at Rood, I asked for Digby and Alton to be among the Thornwalkers."

"Call me Perry," said Alton. "I never did like my given name."

"All right, then: Perry it is. Even so, I knew that I needed you and Digby, but I didn't know why."

"An unforeseen Seer's gift?" asked Riessa, smiling.

"Mayhap," said Driu, grinning back at the Dylvana.

"—Oh, I get it," said Digby.

Perry looked at Diggs. "Get what?"

"Unforeseen Seer," said Digby.

Perry turned up his hands in confusion.

"I'll explain it later," said Digby.

"Well, unforeseen or no, anyone could have killed the Garian viper," said Perry, "so I don't think you needed us specifically for that. On the other hand, Diggs and I slew two Rûck archers before they could spit King Reyer."

"You did?" asked Driu.

"We did," said Digby. "First one, then the other; they each had dead aim on him."

"But we took them down before they could let fly," said Perry.

"Good thing, too," said Digby, looking at Riessa, " 'cause you, my lady, said we have no gwynthyme to counteract the Rûck arrow poison."

"Slaying those two Rucha might have been why Driu chose ye," said the Dylvana. "Still, the reason lies unknown, and in fact might not yet have occurred."

"Oh," said Digby. "I didn't think of that."

Of a sudden Perry broke out in laughter.

Surprised, "What?" asked Digby.

"Unforeseen Seer," Perry managed to say. "I get it."

Smiling, Digby clapped his friend on the shoulder and said, "I knew you would."

They stood and watched as the remains of the Garians and the Foul Folk were searched along with their goods, and Durgan found a message-capsule strip in the clothing of one of the crumbling, Ban-withered Hlôks. He handed it to Driu.

"I'll see what it might say when we are free of the wretched aethyr roil of this place," said Driu.

No orders at all were discovered among the remains of the Garian troop, neither on their bodies nor in their saddlebags and supplies, though Aliser did find a crude map of the Battle Downs in the saddlebags of the Garian commander's horse. He brought the drawing to Riessa.

"How did they know we'd be coming this way?" asked Perry.

"Spies, I shouldn't wonder," said Captain Windlow.

"Not in the Dells, surely," said Digby.

"No, Diggs," said Windlow. "Probably someone who discovered the route Reyer would take."

"Someone in Challerain Keep, I would think," said Driu.

"Or mayhap at Roadsend in Wellen," said Riessa, "though Challerain is more likely."

"We did send a message by bird to the Northern Alliance headquarters," said Reyer.

"So," said Perry, "Diggs and I will have to keep a sharp eye out when we get to Challerain, in case someone there has plans to do away with you, Sire."

"Even before then, Perry," said Digby. "And perhaps after."

Perry nodded and then said, "The Keep: how far from here is it anyway?"

"Thirty leagues or so," said Driu.

"Three days, maybe four," said Reyer.

"Four, I would think," said Riessa, "since we are cutting this day short."

"Steel and I could make it in one," said Durgan, running his hand along the neck of his horse.

"You could?" asked Digby, looking up at the grey. "How fast is that horse, anyway?"

"It's not only speed that's needed, Diggs," said Durgan, "but also endurance, and Steel is gifted with both."

"Even so, Durgan, I'd still like to know just how fast he is."

Durgan shrugged and said, "Well, sired by Iron Bobbie, he's out of Brown Lady, the two fastest horses in all of Kell, and ..."

On the second day out from the Battle Downs, the rade came upon a small roadside camp, and waiting there were Vanidar Silverleaf and Dalavar Wolfmage and six pony-sized Silver Wolves.

After hailing one another with greetings all 'round and introductions following, Silverleaf said, "We thought we'd go the rest of the way with ye, that is if ye'd like our company."

"You are most welcome," replied Reyer. "Besides, I understand from what I was told back on Kell, Dalavar and you will vouch for me."

"That, and thy birthmark," said Vanidar. Then he grinned and turned to Dalavar and said, "Should be enough, neh?"

"More than enough," said Dalavar.

"Lor," said Digby, gazing in wonder at the Draega. "These 'Wolves, they're like the ones Beau rode?"

"They *are* the ones Beau rode," said Dalavar. "Or at least Shimmer is."

"These are the ones from that time?" asked Perry. "All of them?"

"Indeed," said Dalavar.

"But that was—what?—two thousand years ago."

"Even so," said Dalavar.

"Seven Silver Wolves," said Digby. "Greylight, Shimmer, Beam, Seeker, Trace, Longshank, and Shifter, or so the old tales say. —But wait, there are only six here."

Silverleaf laughed, but Dalavar smiled and said, "Shifter will be along by and by."

Alric glanced at the campsite and said, "I see you have but one horse, and there's no need to ride double. We have plenty of extra mounts—Garian, most likely."

Silverleaf cocked an eyebrow. "Garian?"

"There is a tale here for the telling," said Dalavar.

"Indeed," said Reyer.

" 'Tis nigh the noontide," said Riessa. "Let us break for a meal and we will speak of dark deeds done."

As THEY TOOK FOOD, Driu fetched the message-capsule slip recovered from the Hlôk and said to Dalavar, "We are free of the Battle Downs, yet I cannot seem to break the seal on this message. Would you try, Wolfmage?" She handed him the tissue-thin strip.

Dalavar frowned in concentration. Then he said, " 'Tis powerful, and I've felt this presence before. The latest being some few seasons past, when he was trying to overcome you, Driu."

"I thought that was you who aided," said Driu, smiling. "That one was attempting to discover Reyer's exact whereabouts."

Dalavar smiled and glanced at Reyer and said, "Ah, I see. Someday I will have to deal with that Mage more directly."

Then Dalavar stared at the message and whispered a word. After a moment, he closed his eyes and whispered another . . . and then another. Finally he opened his eyes and grinned at Driu. " 'Tis not written, but spoken in Slûk."

"Ah, no wonder," said Driu, taking the slip back from Dalavar. Then she murmured a word, and cocked her head as if listening, and a puzzled frown came over her features.

"What is it?" asked Reyer.

" 'Tis a command to the Spawn we slew, Reyer, telling them to go to the Battle Downs and seek out the Garians and kill them all ere they could spring their ambush upon you."

"You mean the Foul Folk were aiding us?" blurted Perry. "I don't believe it!"

"Besides," said Digby, "they tried to kill Reyer."

*   *   *

DALAVAR REFUSED THE HORSE, saying that he had a better way to travel, and over the next day and the one after, a seventh Silver Wolf, seeming darker than the rest, joined the pack to lope alongside the rade: two out in front of the vanguard, one right, one left; two each alongside flanks of the main body, and one trailing. With a bit of help from Silverleaf, all the Warrows quickly learned the names of the individual Draega, Shifter being the dark one.

Of Dalavar there was no sign, though he would be among the troop when they camped at night.

And this way they traveled to Challerain Keep.

And all along the route, they speculated as to why a Dark Mage would aid Reyer to avoid an ambush, yet the *Rûpt* themselves would try to kill him. None knew the answer, yet many were the conjectures put forth.

WHEN CHALLERAIN KEEP CAME full into sight, Alric dropped back from the vanguard to ride alongside Reyer. Perry moved over to give these two blood-sworn brothers a chance to converse the last league or so.

"There it is," said Reyer, "at the very top."

Reyer stared at the craggy mount rising up eight or nine hundred feet above the surrounding plain. At its very peak stood a castle, not tall-spired and airy, like one from a fairy book, but rather blocky and rugged, much like a stronghold, a fort.

"'Tis the High King's seat in the North," said Alric. "Your seat, Reyer."

Reyer's heart hammered in his chest, as the weight of a kingdom came crashing down upon him. And he said, "Oh, Alric, events are rushing headlong at me, and I am like to drown in them."

Ascendancy

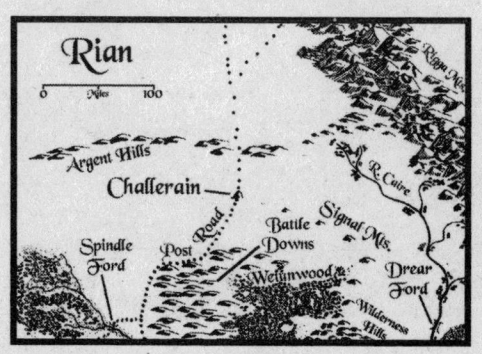

Throughout the whole of Mithgar there are many ways of choosing a king—some simply by inheritance, others by conclaves of various sorts, some by rather strange traditions:

In the mountains of Jangdi, upon the death of the ruler the mantle is passed on to the male child born soonest after. Often this has led to conflict—quite bloody at times—when competing claimants appear.

In the dark southern lands below the Great Karoo, there is a tribe that will let no male who is not physically perfect to sit upon the throne. In this case, the women of the tribe sit in judgment, and the candidate is brought before them and is stripped naked and examined. Sometimes this candidate is aroused by the females' admiring gazes. It is considered a good thing that he has responded so.

In other lands it is the priesthood who chooses a successor to the throne. Some believe this allows the religious leaders to maintain their power in that manner.

In yet other places, it is the royal guard who choose the successor to the throne. They decide who they would guard and who they would not. After all, if they are to protect the royal personage, it had better be someone they are willing to die for.

There is a humorous legend about a small group of islands widespread in the Shining Sea, where navigation and boating and swimming are paramount, and fish are often taken by underwater spearing. In the tale, the leader is chosen through a test of endurance. Candidates submerge themselves in the warm waters, and the one who stays under the longest becomes the next king. At times the one who succeeds drowns during the ordeal, and, after a proper period of mourning for the King Under the Water, the islanders test all candidates again. The truth is: those islands are ruled by women, and the queen is chosen once every five years in trial by combat, their weapons naught but clubs embedded with bits of coral. Most of the queens are well scarred.

And that is another way kings are chosen: trial by combat—either in duels or in mêlée or through battle in war.

And at Challerain Keep . . .

To WRENCH HIS MIND away from the burden that awaited him, Reyer studied Challerain rising up in the near distance. Below the crenellated granite battlements and blocky towers of the grey castle itself, gentle slopes terminated by craggy drops stepped a short way down the tor sides to fetch up against a massive rampart rearing up to circle the entire mont. These slopes were the Kingsgrounds, and there were small groves on that land, as well as pines growing in the crags, and several lone giants stood in the meadows, the trees in full summer dress. There, too, were several buildings on the encircling slopes, perhaps stables or warehouses.

Below the Kingsgrounds began the city proper, falling away in tier upon tier of bright-colored buildings, of stone and wood and brick, all ajumble in terraced rings descending down the grade: varied in their shapes, they were homes, shops, storehouses, stables, and other structures, and threading among them were three more massive defensive walls, stepped evenly down the side of Mont Challerain, the lowest one nearly at the level of the plain. Only a few permanent structures lay outside the bottommost wall.

"It's a real city," said Digby, his voice filled with awe. "Bigger'n Rood. Bigger'n Stonehill. Bigger'n—"

"Diggs," snapped Perry, "of course it's bigger'n. It's the northern capital."

"D'y' think it's bigger'n Caer Pendwyr?" asked Digby.

"How would I know? —Though I can't imagine a town any larger than Challerain."

"Nay, wee one," said Riessa. "Caer Pendwyr is a port city as well as the prime capital of the High King's realm. 'Tis much larger than Challerain."

"Then I wish I could see it, too," said Digby.

"Fear not. Thou and Perry and the rest of us are likely to do so."

"You mean when we overthrow the Usurper?" said Perry.

"Aye," said Riessa.

"Nay," said Reyer, shaking his head. "I would not ask Warrows or Elves or aught others to join in this fight. It is a thing to be decided by Humankind and—"

"Poppycock!" shouted Perry. "You are my King and I—"

"Take care, Alton Periwinkle," said Riessa, her voice pitched to stop his outburst. "Moderate thy words. As thou dost say, Reyer is thy King."

Alric broke into laughter. "Silence a Warrow, would you? 'Twould be like unto silencing a chattering finch."

Reyer smiled and cocked an eye toward Perry. "All should have a Warrow in their Court."

"'Twould be one way to hear the truth," said Riessa.

Now in control of his wayward mouth, Perry said, "You are my liege lord, King Reyer, and times are troubled, and in such days Diggs and I will follow you to the ends of the world should needs be. Besides, Driu says that you need us: Captain Windlow and Billy and Arlo and Jame and Jace ... and especially me and Digby—Warrows all."

Reyer glanced at Riessa, and she said, "Thou wouldst not turn away the Dylvana, nor any Lian, nor, were they to come, any of the Drimm. 'Tis not just a Human conflict, though there are those who might think so and would not encroach upon a Human affair. Yet, heed: turn away not any who wouldst be thine ally in these days of thy need, for none knows what might tip the balance in the end to come."

"Except maybe Driu," said Digby.

"Not even she," said Riessa. "For Driu herself says that the threads of now run off in many directions in the times ahead, some more likely than others."

"Do you think—" began Digby, but Perry growled and said, "My King, I would you resolve this matter here and now. Whether or no you accept our aid, you have it. And I, for one, would rather you accept it."

Reyer smiled and inclined his head. "As you will, my stalwart wee ones. As you will."

"Good," said Perry. "That's settled."

Finally, in the noontide, as Reyer's vanguard fell back to join the main body, the company reached the fringes of the city. And there stood a guard captain and a company of men, and horses were arrayed with them. The soldiers saluted—a clenched fist to the heart—and knelt, and the captain, upon one knee, said, "My liege, though you have your own warband, we would escort you to those who are waiting."

Reyer smiled to himself, but graciously said, "As you will, Captain."

The guard company mounted and wheeled toward the tor, now leading Reyer's rade. They rode up among the sparse buildings flanking the Post Road to come at last to the open city gates laid back against the first wall, with a portcullis raised high. As they came to the opening the captain of the escort raised a horn to his lips and sounded it. An answering horn replied, and soldiers at the gate and the wall above saluted by striking clenched fists to their hearts.

Led by the escort, in through the twisting cobblestone passage under the wall the escort and the company fared, with two Draega—Shifter and Greylight—at the fore. Silverleaf and Riessa and the Dylvana followed the 'Wolves, and Durgan and Conal and Captain Windlow and Billy and Arlo rode just after, two more Silver Wolves among them. Reyer came next, flanked by Alric, bearing the High King's standard, and those two flanked by Digby and Perry. After them came two more Draega, followed by Driu and Gretta, with the Thornwalkers Jame and Jace to each side.

Trailing rode a handful of Dylvana, one Silver Wolf with them.

Of Dalavar there was no sign.

As they rode into the tunnel, "Diggs, keep a sharp eye out now," said Perry. "Don't let that scatterbrain of yours get distracted by— Oh, my goodness, look there."

Perry pointed up at the machicolations through which

hot oil or missiles could be rained down upon an enemy. With hooves of the horses and ponies echoing loudly, and with Perry and Digby gazing up in awe, through the barway they went. At the other end of the passage, another portcullis stood raised, and beyond that Reyer's company rode into the lower levels of the city proper, where the smells and sounds and sights of the city assaulted them. They had ridden into an enormous bazaar, the great open market of Rian at Challerain Keep.

Both Perry and Digby were overwhelmed, for the square was teeming with people—buyers and sellers—farmers from nearby steads with hams and beef and sausages, bacon, geese, duck, and fowl of other sorts; carrots and turnips and tubers and leeks; grain, and other commodities. And many customers crowded around the stalls, purchasing staples. Hawkers moved through the crowds selling baskets, walking sticks and staves, hats, brooms, pottery, and such. A fruit seller peddled fresh cherries and peaches, with a sign that said apples were to come in the autumn. The odor of fresh-baked bread and hot meat pies and pastries wafted o'er all. Jongleurs strolled, playing flutes and harps, lutes and fifes, timbrels, and some juggled marvelously. Here and there soldiers and townsfolk drank cool drinks, and talked among themselves, some laughing, others looking stern, or nodding quietly, some gesticulating.

But the moment that the horns had bugled, the sounds and stir began to wane, and people looked about, finally settling upon the escort and warband now moving through the crowd.

"Elves!" cried some. "Dylvana!" cried others. And someone called out, " 'Tis the High King's heir," while someone else shouted, "Not heir, but the rightful High King himself."

People turned and surged toward the road, for they would see this lad. Yet the sight of the Silver Wolves made most timorous, and they flowed toward and ebbed away as these great beasts went by.

And silence fell, and men and women and children bowed as Reyer passed, and someone began a cheer. In but moments the whole of the square burst into loud acclaim.

"Get used to it," said Alric, but Reyer did not hear him above the roar.

Through the crowd rode Dylvana and Humans and trotted Silver Wolves, but then someone espied the buccen on ponyback, and like unto Elven children they appeared, yet most folk there realized just who they were—the Wee Folk of legend with their jewellike eyes and mayhap distant kindred of Tipperton Thistledown himself. And another cheer broke out, this time calling out "Warrow!"

At last the column rode out from the market square, leaving the people behind, but for a few young lads running after. Just beyond the square were the shops of crafters: cobblers, a goldsmithery, mills, lumberyards and carpentries, inns and hostelries, blacksmitheries and ironworks and armories, kilns, masonries, and the like. And above many of the shops and businesses were the dwellings of the owners and workers, and these folks, too, came out to see what the hubbub was all about. And they looked on in wonder, and bowed when the High King passed.

The cobbled Post Road wended through this industry, spiraling up and around the mont, climbing toward the crest. Narrow alleyways shot off between hued buildings, and steep streets slashed across the way, making the whole of the city rather like a maze. Yet they stuck to the Post Road, 'round and up.

Again they came to a massive wall and followed the route as it curved alongside the bulwark. At last they came to a gate, and it, too, was guarded but open, and horns sounded and soldiers slapped fists to hearts.

Through this gate and on they rode, now ascending among colorful row houses with unexpected corners and stairs mounting up, and balconies and turrets, too, and all with colorful tiled roofs to harvest the frequent summer rains and winter snowmelts and channel them into catchments. People stopped in the streets or leaned out of windows to watch the procession ride by.

Once more and following a flourish of horns they passed through a barway under a great rampart—the third wall—

and again they wended among houses, now larger and more stately than those below, yet still close-set.

At last they arrived at the fourth wall, the one encircling the Kingsgrounds. The two leaves of a massive iron gate laid back against the great barrier, and even as they approached, the portcullis clanked upward, and once more the horns sounded, for the King was passing through.

The column rode into the passage under the wall and waited until the second portcullis was raised, too, and at last rode out into the Kingsgrounds

Now the fortress in all of its massive strength could be seen: it was grey and ponderous, with great blocky granite buildings with high windows and square towers. Crenels and merlons crowned the battlements; massive groins supported great bastions outjutting from the walls. Stone curtains protected hidden banquettes where would stand defenders in the face of attack.

Along the cobbles of the Post Road they clattered, at times riding up and across the faces of craggy looms, drawing ever closer to the Keep.

They came to a fifth and final wall, the last loom ere the castle itself, and the massive main gate ground open with yet another fanfare of horns. Through a last jinking passage they rode and into the forecourt. As they emerged, Silverleaf fell back to ride alongside Reyer, Digby pulling his pony aside to let the Lian Elf do so. And into the courtyard they rode.

There awaiting them, with the flags of many nations unfurled, stood the members of the Northern Council.

The military escort split in twain and formed a corridor, through which the King's warband rode and stopped before the awaiting council. The Draega, however, moved off to one side and gathered in the shadows along a massive abutment, and there among them now stood Dalavar.

And ere anyone dismounted, Silverleaf called out, "My lords, I present to ye Valen's heir, High King Reyer, Lord of all of Mithgar."

And the Council members knelt, all but one, an ambassador from Jute—Baron Hoffstra.

Lord Raden looked up at him and muttered, "Down, man. The High King is before you."

Hoffstra glanced at the kneeling lord and then up at Reyer and said, "My own liege, King Viktor of Jute, bids me to see the griffin claw before acknowledging you as the rightful heir."

"Just like the Mad King to do so," muttered Alric.

Gretta started to protest, but with a word Driu silenced her.

"Take care, my lord," said Silverleaf, though it was uncertain whom he addressed: Hoffstra or Reyer.

"Keep your seats," called out Reyer, and only he dismounted. And the crimson stone bearing its Golden Griffin on the ring he wore cast back a glitter of scarlet rays from the sun. And as Reyer strode toward the assembled lords, both Digby and Perry quietly nocked arrows and stealthily eased their ponies to places for clear shots.

Reyer stopped before Baron Hoffstra and gritted, "This is the only time you, my lord, will see the mark of my birthright."

Then he said to the others: "Rise."

As Reyer peeled out of his vest and jerkin and tossed them to Hoffstra, as if the baron were naught more than a lackey, the members of the Northern Alliance got to their feet: Raden glaring at Hoffstra, Mayor Hein trembling and eyeing the Wolfmage and his Draega across the yard and in shadows, dark-haired Aarnson with a sardonic grin on his face, and all the others looking at Reyer with respect in their gazes, for the lad had of certain put the Jutlander in his place.

And in the bright sunlight, the griffin claw shone starkly on the front quarter of Reyer's right shoulder, matching the one on the flag and the ring. And one by one Reyer stepped before each member of the council so that each in his turn could see the mark. And each in his turn nodded his approval.

Finally, Reyer circled back to Hoffstra, and, glaring, he looked the baron in the eye, but said naught.

Quickly, and taking care to not let Reyer's vest and jerkin touch the ground, the baron knelt and said, "My lord." And, head bowed, he held up the clothes for Reyer to take.

"Well, now, that's the end of that," muttered Alric, smiling. Then he looked down at Perry and over at Digby and noted for the first time that they had been ready to slay Hoffstra.

Then he ruefully grinned and said to himself, "May I never make an enemy of a Warrow."

40

Muster

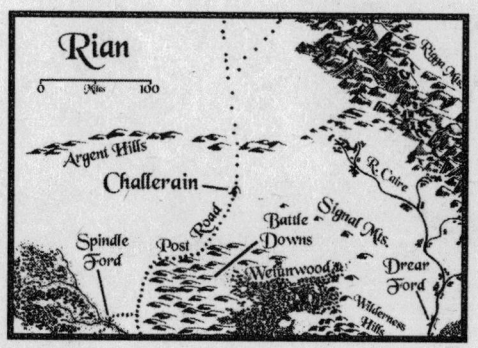

There is little need for an army to gather but at the site of battle, arriving early enough to get there first and take whatever tactical advantage might be yielded by the terrain. Of course, that seldom happens, for armies are usually mustered at distant places and at inconvenient times.

Too, mustering an army from widespread points is no small feat, especially when travel is by foot and horse and wain and boat.

There is this as well, for the old saying is that an army travels on its stomach, hence, unless they are living off the land, food and supplies need be readily at hand. Yet feeding a host through many days—to say naught of months—of a campaign is no small task. Hence, foodstuffs must be gathered, laded, made ready for travel, and even perhaps staged along the army's route ... food not only for the men of the army but also for the animals with them. Nothing perishable, of course, hence waybread—most likely crue—and grain and beans and well-cured meat and feed are the fare of the campaign. And, oh yes, forget not the tea. Some animals for slaughter—cattle, for example—are gathered and driven ahead before the army begins its march, since livestock are usually the slowest of the slow. And sources for water must be carefully considered, plotting out which rivers, lakes, streams, and springs lie upon the proposed route, and what water must be hauled or carried by the army itself.

Both the Northern Alliance and Arkov's forces must take care and plan well, for lack of good forethought will in all likelihood lead to defeat.

Each side in this oncoming conflict had had more than a decade to prepare for such: one side waiting for the rightful heir to the kingdom to lead them; the other side harassed by local revolts, and by the frustrating delays in the gathering of the southern allies needed to assure victory.

And on the day after Reyer arrived at the northern capital and had told his tale of the journey from Kell, birds bearing messages winged south and west and east and north, bearing the news. . . .

IN A DARK TOWER deep in the Grimwalls a Necromancer chortled with glee, and yet somehow simultaneously fumed with rage:

"Good! The boy is safe, yet those fools I sent to thwart the ambush stupidly attacked him. He might have been killed. Radok, I would have you root out the surviving Chun and bring them to me. It will give me much pleasure to . . . well, you will see."

"Yes, Master Nunde."

"And send this message to Fadal. It is time to let the full of the Chabbain forces cross the Avagon Sea."

Radok accepted the capsule and bowed his way from the chamber and headed for the birds high above. How clever Nunde's plan and devious . . . and should it come to pass, then it would tip the balance and Gyphon would have to be released and the Ban rescinded and Nunde would be elevated, taking Radok up with him.

ARKOV WAS ENRAGED. Not only were some nations of the Northern Alliance already on the march, but Foul Folk had ruined his carefully planned ambush. Where had they come from and why then and there? Arkov did not know. It was almost as if the boy were charmed, or that Arkov himself were snakebitten.

BENIR MIN ALIK, the new ambassador from Chabba, requested an audience with Arkov. Benir had replaced Kaleem bin Aziz, who had died unexpectedly of a stomach ailment shortly after the Dark Master had learned of Arkov's planned ambush. Benir believed that Kaleem had been deposed because he had not discovered the plan soon enough to suit the Dark Master. Benir resolved to never make a like error.

The new Chabbanian ambassador was escorted into Arkov's chambers by Counselor Baloff.

"What is it, Alik?" asked Arkov. Once again the nuance of the Kabla tongue evaded Arkov, for he mistook Benir's birthplace for the ambassador's given name.

"The full fleet is under way, my lord," said Benir, smirking to himself at this king's willful ignorance. "The entire army will be on your shores ere the full of the moon."

"At last!" shouted Arkov, clenching a fist and hammering it against the arm of the throne.

The Chabbainian ambassador merely smiled in return.

"In Gûnar?" asked Reyer.

"Aye, my lord," said Steward Cavin.

"Actually, just outside Gûnar at Gûnar Slot," said Lord Aarnson, stabbing a finger down at the map, the Slot at the south end of Rell, "here along the Grimwall, not far from the west entrance into the Black Hole."

Perry frowned. "Black Hole?"

"Drimmen-deeve," said Silverleaf.

"Kraggen-cor," said Dalavar.

"Yes," said Aarnson, "Gûnar Slot is a few leagues south of that Dwarvenholt."

"I see," said Perry.

"Why there?" asked Alric. "Why at the Slot?"

"Should we get enough of a march upon Arkov, then we think we'll meet his army somewhere either in Gûnar or in the abandoned land of Ellor," said Raden. "Hence, the Slot is the best place to assemble. And in the event Arkov is first on the march, the Gap is a bottleneck where we can best use our forces."

"Barring that," said Lord Cavin, "should we be enough ahead of Arkov, next we will try to use Gûnarring Gap as a choke point."

"And if not there, then along the Red Hills in Ellor," said Raden, pointing at the place named.

"And how many troops will we have?" asked Conal.

Cavin moved a hand across the map, noting each nation as he replied, "Ten thousand each from Gothon, Jute, Rian, and Thol. Five thousand each from Gelen, Dalara, Wellen, and Harth, which includes the Wilderland. And a smattering of others from Trellinath and Basq."

"Some sixty thousand, then," said Reyer.

"What of Jord?" asked Alric.

Raden growled and glanced across at Silverleaf and Riessa. "Like the Elves and Dwarves"—his glance flicked to Captain Windlow and Digby and Perry—"and others, the Jordians have decided to remain neutral."

"Adon, tell me this is not so," said Alric.

"Sorry, lad," said Cavin, "but it is all too true."

Alric gritted his teeth and said, "Well, this Harlingar isn't going to sit this one out."

Reyer looked at Alric and smiled. Then he turned to Cavin. "What of the foe? —Arkov's forces."

Cavin again pointed at the map as he spoke. "In addition to his joint Garian Albaner army, he is allied with Hurn and Sarain, and—"

"The Fists of Rakka!" blurted Digby. "He is allied with the Fists of Rakka?"

"Huh?" said Perry.

"Oh, Perry, don't you remember the tale of Arin and Egil One-Eye?"

"Sort of," said Perry. "But what's that got to do with this?"

"When Arin Flameseer was searching for the Dragonstone, one of those who would aid her was the 'Cursed Keeper of Faith in the Maze.' She found him in Sarain, but also in that land were the Fists of Rakka, dreadful people."

Perry shook his head. "So . . . ?"

"Rakka is another name for Gyphon," said Riessa.

Enlightenment dawned, and Perry said, "You mean Arkov is in league with Gyphon's faithful? Enemies of old?"

Cavin sighed and nodded. "It is so."

"But that is not all," said Lord Raden. "Arkov also has a small contingent of Chabbains on Pellarian soil."

"Askars," said Riessa. "They and the Fists of Rakka sided with Modru during the Great War of the Ban."

"This history is all well and good," said Conal, "but Reyer's question is yet to be answered. What of Arkov's forces? What are their numbers?"

"We should be evenly matched," said Aarnson, "for though his total is considerable, much of his Garian army is tied up in policing Jugo and Hoven and especially Riamon and Aven, putting out fires, putting down local revolts."

"When we face off against Arkov," said Alric, "are these locals likely to rise up and aid us?"

"Perhaps," said Aarnson, "yet they are disorganized; their aid will result in ineffective harassment of Arkov at best."

"Even so," said Alric, "every little bit will assist."

A silence fell around the table, and finally Reyer said, "When do we march?"

"Even now, the nations are on the move," said Lord Cavin. "Farthest to come are those in the west: Basq, Gothon, Gelen, Jute, Thol. They began their march even before you set out from Kell. The livestock and food wains were under way long before then."

"That far ahead?" asked Reyer.

"This plan has been in the making for thirteen years," said Lord Raden. "And we began its execution months back."

"Huh," said Digby.

"Huh, what?" asked Perry.

"No armies came through the Bosky," said Digby. "And if they were marching from Wellen and beyond they should have."

"Nay," said Riessa. "As planned, those coming from the west followed the Crossland Road through much of Wellen, then angled south through Trellinath and headed east from there toward Gûnar Slot. It's shorter than traveling through the Bosky."

"Ah," said Digby, nodding, then he turned to Lord Cavin. "I say, what if — Adon forbid — what if something had happened to Reyer? What of your plans then?"

Lord Cavin smiled and glanced across at Silverleaf and Riessa and Driu and Dalavar. "I had every reason to believe that King Reyer would arrive safely."

"Besides," said Perry, as if explaining all, "from the Bosky onward he had Warrows in his band."

Amid a roar of laughter, "Ah, right," said Digby, grinning.

When the humor faded to chuckles, Reyer said, "What I am asking, Lord Cavin, is when do we here in this room set out for the rendezvous?"

"As soon as we have had a proper crowning ceremony," said Cavin.

Reyer sighed and shook his head. "There is no time for pomp, my lord. But if we must have pageantry, we will do so when I take the throne at Caer Pendwyr."

"Then a simple ceremony must suffice," said Cavin, "for we of the Northern Alliance would have our crowning."

Again Reyer sighed, then said, "If you must."

"On the morrow, then, the city bells will ring," said Cavin. Then he covered up the map and said to an aide, "Summon Mayor Hein."

"NEUTRAL? The Harlingar remain neutral?"

"Yes, Mother," said Alric.

"Then you can't go," said Gretta.

"You will not stop me, Mother," said Alric. "I shall be at Reyer's side, for he is now my king."

"King Ulrik of Jord is your rightful king, and if Jord is neutral, then so must be you."

"Mother, I am going, whether you say yea or nay. And were King Ulrik himself to forbid me, still I would go. I might be the only Harlingar in Reyer's march, yet I will be in his host."

Gretta broke into tears.

LATER IN THE DAY, Gretta spoke long and passionately with Lord Cavin, who finally said, "I will send a bird to Ander. Perhaps we can have a Dragonship waiting."

*　　*　　*

THAT NIGHT AND BY CANDLELIGHT, Gretta sat at a small escritoire and penned a long note. She read it over several times, and finally sealed it with a dollop of red wax embossed with the sigil from the ring on a chain 'round her neck, a ring given to her by her sire on a day long ago when she set out from Jord to serve as a companion to Queen Mairen in King Valen's court.

It was a ring she had not used for the past sixteen years.

"SHE IS PENNING A LETTER," said Driu, lying abed.

"Mayhap there is a chance," replied Dalavar, lying beside her.

"If so, they will need a guide," said Driu.

"Indeed," replied Dalavar.

THE BELLS OF CHALLERAIN Keep rang out on the morning of Reyer's crowning, and when a curious crowd following the rumors of yester gathered before City Hall, Mayor Hein made his way out to the front steps and announced that Reyer had been crowned High King.

Later that day, as promised by Hein, Reyer and the Council rode into Market Square, where Reyer, nearly six feet tall and verging upon manhood, and with naught but a simple gold headband upon his brow, stood upon the back of a produce waggon and promised that he would serve as best he could. Eyes sharp, soldiers moved among the gathering, yet naught untoward happened. Instead, in recognition, all knelt before the newly crowned King, all but seven Warrows, that is.

After the ceremony, Gretta, at her stepson Durgan's side, said, "I need you to deliver a letter."

"Gladly, Mother Gretta. Where and to whom?"

"Jord."

"Jord? The nation of Jord?"

"Yes. They must not remain neutral. They must come to Reyer's aid."

"But, Mother Gretta, I ride with Reyer."

"You will, yet you must bring Jord with you."

"Please, Mother Gretta, send someone else. I am no diplomat to persuade them to come."

"Durgan, you have the only horse that can make the ride in time."

"Steel, Mother? Steel?"

"Aye, Steel."

"Send someone with remounts."

"Even remounts cannot outrun and outlast Steel. I recall on the journey here you said Steel had not only the speed but also the endurance to make a journey such as I propose. And you have also been our herald and the one to bear our messages, and no message that you have ever borne is more vital than this." Gretta thrust her night-penned letter toward Durgan. He looked at it a long moment, and then reluctantly accepted it.

"You have told me where I should go, Mother Gretta, but not who should get this letter."

Gretta gave him a map and a set of instructions as well as the name of a person and where in Jord he would be found.

With Durgan now committed to delivering her letter, Gretta watched as Lord Cavin released a bird bearing a message to the Harbor Master in the city of Ander on the shores of the Boreal Sea.

GRETTA THEN WENT TO her quarters and unwrapped a long-held token. She sat and stared at it awhile, tears in her eyes. Then she rewrapped it and set out for Alric's quarters. She tapped on his door, and when he answered she said, her voice quavering, "My son, you are heading to war. 'Tis meet you have this." She thrust the silk-wrapped gift into his hands.

Alric looked at her in 'wilderment, then unfolded the cloth.

'Twas a black-oxen horn, ever borne into battle by Jordian warriors.

"Mother, I—"

Gretta embraced him, then, weeping, fled away.

THE VERY NEXT DAY under dark skies above, Reyer and a small host rode south and away from Challerain Keep.

With regret lurking deep in his eyes, Durgan watched the warband leave. Then he mounted up on Steel and said, "Hup, laddie buck, we've a long way to go and not much time...." And he rode away to the north.

And high up on the castle-keep wall, in the chill blow Gretta pulled her cloak tighter 'round and wept, despair in her gaze to the south, hope in her gaze to the north.

41

Northward

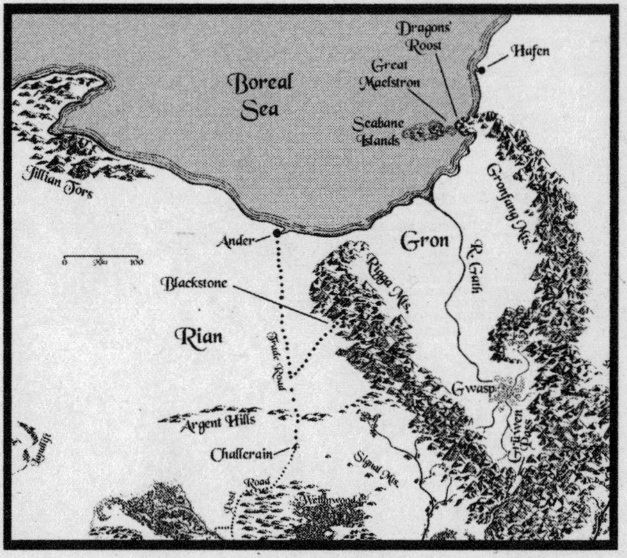

Among the various messengers in Mithgar are King's Heralds. They might come afoot or ahorse or in a coach or by ship or boat to deliver their messages from their liege lords to whomever that lord has sent the message. Generally speaking, a King's Herald is a diplomat and should be treated accordingly, with food and shelter and protection from harm. It is not often that a King's Herald is assaulted or even murdered out of hand, though such has been known to occur, generally to make a statement to the king who sent the message. No, most often, a King's Herald delivers his liege's word, and might or might not await a reply, depending upon his instructions.

Usually, King's Heralds are given free room and board, and at times free passage, though some kings provide their heralds with coinage for token payments.

When Durgan set out from Challerain Keep, he had a modest purse to pay for goods and services, especially for Steel....

LATE IN THE EVE of the third day after setting out, Durgan and Steel rode into Ander, Steel's shod hooves clattering upon the cobblestones of that port city.

They were some two hundred sixty-five miles north of Challerain Keep, having covered the distance in but three days. Surely Steel was a horse beyond compare, yet Durgan's words concerning the charger's speed and endurance proved to be true.

They had traveled from dawn to dusk, and sometimes a short way into the night. And every eve, Durgan took care of Steel's needs before his own. During the days he made certain the horse was well fed and well watered, and he varied the gait as well as walked to give Steel respite from any single pace.

The map that Gretta had given to Conal's eldest had proved to be true, for Durgan had come to the streams marked thereon, and to the villages and hamlets along the way, where he resupplied his and Steel's provisions, and traveled lightly, not being burdened with food and feed. He had followed the Trade Road north out of Challerain, passing through the Argent Hills in a cold drizzle midmorn the first day, and for the rest of that day and the next two he had ridden across rolling plains. Always on the road or along its verge in the rougher places, for that road led directly to Ander.

On the eve of the second day out, he camped with a small trade band of armed and armored Dwarves, heading crossland from west to east, for they were going toward Blackstone, their holt in the Rigga Mountains. They and their ponies just happened to be settled for the eve alongside Durgan's route, and they welcomed him gruffly, for that is the manner of Dwarves. Yet they fed him well and provided pleasing company, and they thoughtfully stroked their braided forked beards and spoke of war and marveled at the distance Durgan had traveled in but two days. When Durgan suggested that they trade their ponies for horses, they shook their heads and fell silent, and Durgan wondered why such a redoubtable people, though they used horses to draw wains, would fear riding upon such beasts.

It was a mystery that perhaps one day would be resolved.

But that was yester, and on this night, Durgan made his way to the docks in the chill seaport town of Ander, there on the verge of the frigid Boreal Sea. He found the harbormaster, a white-haired, white-bearded old sea dog of a man, who told him that he was expected, and the Fjordlander Dragonship, *Slagferdig*, had been waiting, and would sail with him and his horse on the morning tide.

Durgan made arrangements for food and feed, and, after taking good care of his mount, that night Durgan slept in a warm bed, while Steel slept in a warm stall.

*　　*　　*

"JA, WE OFTEN TAKE horses with us on our, er, inland forays as well as our trade missions."

Durgan nodded and glanced over at Steel, who stood in a simple pole stall on the deck in the wales of the Dragonship.

"And the ship's name—*Slagferdig*—what does that mean in the common tongue, Captain Jarn?"

"'Ready for Battle,'" replied Captain Jarn, who, like the other members of the crew, was tall and yellow-haired and blue-eyed. "It also means 'Quick Witted,' but we prefer 'Ready for Battle.' Though, since the truce with the Jutes, we haven't seen much battle."

On a chill morn, they had sailed on yester's dawn tide, all nine members of the crew dressed in fleece jackets and leather breeks and well-insulated boots, proof against the icy swirl of air coiling up from the frigid Boreal.

Durgan, too, was dressed as the crew, Captain Jarn having lent him the warm garb, though it was somewhat overlarge on Durgan's slight frame.

As for Steel, a heavy fleece blanket covered him, reaching down to his fetlocks.

In steep contrast to the wild tales told 'round warm tavern hearthstones, life aboard the Dragonship had proved to be rather humdrum, or so Durgan thought.

They relieved themselves over the sides as necessary, and Durgan did scoop up Steel's droppings and heave them over as well.

Yet the winds were favorable—on the aft starboard quarter of the beam—and they had sailed in nearly a straight line across uneventful waters, no land in sight whatsoever, with only the sun and stars to guide them, though Captain Jarn now and again did use a device he called an astrolabe.

"If this keeps up," said Captain Jarn, "we'll make port in three days."

On the eve of the second day out, distant land—just a smudge on the horizon—came into view.

Captain Jarn swung the ship to the port, making ready to pass them by.

"We're not going to stop and take on water?" asked Durgan.

"'Tis the Seabanes, lad, and no good will come of landing on those dire shores."

"Dire?"

"Aye, boy. See that bare top of a peak to the right and far far ahead, just now lit up by the setting sun? That be Dragons' Roost, and the Seabanes be in their domain."

"In the Dragons' domain?"

"Aye, lad. And should ye be foolish enough to challenge them"—Jarn's laughter roared across the waters—"then I pity the fool ye be."

Moments later, Jarn grew serious. "There be a shift in the wind. Ah, Garlon, but Ruella toys with us; we'll be tacking 'gainst her blow."

Durgan frowned. "Garlon? I seem to recall—"

"He is the god of the sea," said Jarn, "but she is the goddess of the winds."

Sailing first this way then that, they slowly made their way past the Seabanes, first in the dark and then in the day, while low clouds gathered above, and now Jarn sailed by dead reckoning, though with the islands generally off their beam, his dead reckoning was not that much of a marvel.

But then Ruella began to smile and the wind shifted into a more favorable quarter, and the skies cleared above, and with only starlight on high, gleaming scintillant, in the wee hours of the third night at sea they cleared the last of Seabanes.

Durgan, who had risen to relieve himself over the starboard, asked Bjorki, second in command, "What is that green glow afar?"

"Shh . . ." whispered the mate, a finger to his lips. "Listen."

In the distance, whence the glow lay, there came the faint sound of a low constant rumble.

"Thunder?" murmured Durgan.

"Nay, boy. 'Tis instead the fire and growl of the Great Maelstrom, both glow and grumble. Any ship caught in its drag be wrenched down into Hèl itself. Only the *Longwyrm*, with Captain Arik and Elgo and the men aboard, e'er escaped its dread suck."

Durgan nodded, for even on Kell they had heard the tale of Sleeth and Elgo and the Curse of the Dragongield.

Bjorki sighed and said, "And in the Maelstrom itself, there be the monstrous Krakens, Dragons' mates, they say."

"And the green . . . ?"

"Spinning witch fire," said Bjorki. "And cursed it be as well."

Durgan stood for long moments, his gaze captured by the far-off glow. But finally he turned away and bedded down again, the plash of the Boreal against the clinker-built sides intermittently interrupting the faint and distant rumble of the monstrous churn.

LATE IN THE EVE of the fourth day at sea, the *Slagferdig* sailed into the port of Hafen. Taking care for Steel's slender legs, Durgan offladed the steed. And that night they spent in the warm comfort of the Sea Horse Inn, Durgan in a soft bed, Steel in the adjoining stable.

The next morn Durgan set out for Jordkeep, and as he had done every morning, Durgan walked Steel for a while to warm up the steed for the day. Then he checked the saddle cinch and mounted up and set off for his goal lying six hundred miles away.

And they flew across the vast grassy plains of Jord, the gallant steed holding up for the long days of travel and gaining his needed rest at night. And Durgan found holdings with water and feed to spare, for this was a horse kingdom. They passed by herd after herd along the way, and here Durgan had to ride with a firm hand, often steering Steel wide and away from the mares and the occasional stallion.

And on the seventh day out from Hafen, and with six hundred miles lying behind him, Durgan espied in the distance ahead a broad splash of buildings lying across the green rolling plains: 'twas Jordholt, capital city of this realm, and therein should be the one who was to receive the letter he bore.

Southward

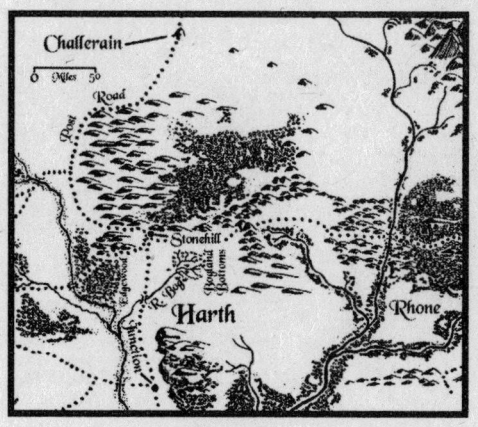

As the raven flies, it is some four hundred and thirty miles from Challerain Keep to the northern end of Gûnar Slot, there where the Allied Army would gather ere marching south and then east. And also as the raven flies, it is nine hundred and thirty miles from Challerain Keep to Jordkeep, the capital city of Jord.

Yet men are not birds, but must travel by other means: afoot, ahorse, by waggon or ship. And Reyer and his warband would ride altogether some six hundred and fifty miles from Challerain to the Slot, while Durgan and Steel would need altogether to cover some thirteen hundred miles to reach the capital of Jord—four hundred of those by sea.

And as each set out from Challerain Keep, reluctance in their hearts—Durgan, for he was not riding with Reyer, and Reyer for he was taking men to war—a cold wind swept down from the Boreal Sea, bearing dark clouds and drizzling rain.

And in Reyer's company, Digby wondered . . .

"D'Y THINK THIS IS AN OMEN?"

"What?" asked Perry.

"I said, d'y think this is an omen?" replied Digby.

"I heard that," said Perry. "What I meant is: what might be an omen?"

"Well," said Digby, "an omen is a—"

"Blast it, Diggs, I *know* what an omen is. What I want to know is what did you see or hear that caused you to ask the question in the first place?"

"Oh," said Digby. "Well, what I meant was *this*," and he broadly gestured toward the grim sky and the drizzle falling 'round.

"You mean the rain?"

Digby nodded, and then added, "And the darkness."

"Bah," said Perry. "It's just rain."

"Yes, but it's cold," said Digby, slightly offended, "and here autumn hasn't even come. Just how do you explain that, bucco?"

"It came down from the north," said Perry.

Digby nodded. "And . . . ?"

"Well, if it's an omen every time rain blows in from the north," said Perry, "then, let's see, I think we would have long ago succumbed to deep dark doom."

Digby laughed.

And they rode the next few miles in comfortable silence, now and again smiling unto themselves.

THREE DAYS LATER, the warband reached the edge of the Battle Downs. Conal ordered the number of scouts doubled, and extra care be taken in seeking ambuscades and sign of Foul Folk.

And though both Digby and Perry would like to have joined Billy and Arlo and Captain Windlow on the scouting mission, still, hewing to their assignments, they stayed by Reyer's side, just as Jame and Jace stayed with Driu.

No sign either of assassins or Spawn was found, and so they made camp nearby.

That eve Conal posted extra sentries, mostly Dylvana, for their eyes and ears were sharper than those of Men.

'Round the campfire, Alric turned to Reyer and said, "Think you that Durgan will bring my folk, the Harlingar?"

"I know not," said Reyer, "and I'd rather we not hold false hope."

Alric nodded, but said naught, though his brow was knitted in puzzlement. Finally, he sighed and said, "Still . . ." and then lapsed into silence as Reyer nodded in unspoken agreement.

AND IN JORD, King Ulrik and his brother, Valder, said naught as well, each wrapped in his own thoughts about the upcoming conflict between an untested boy and a brutal veteran somewhere far away, each with a claim to the throne. In the past Jord had remained neutral in matters concerning squabbles between Royals in distant nations, but in this case they were not certain that neutrality was the wisest course. And many were the arguments that went first this way and then that. Still, they had little at stake in the outcome, though if Arkov tried to levy unwarranted taxes upon Jord, he would find a formidable foe in the Harlingar.

Of course, Arkov knew this, and he had made no such move in the nearly fourteen years since overthrowing Valen.

Having nothing at stake is a profound deterrent to entering any war.

REYER AND HIS WARBAND DECAMPED, and they traveled southward along the Post Road, Digby chattering about this and that, Perry snorting in skepticism at some of Digby's claims, especially when Digby brought up the topic of Giants.

"Pah! Giants? You must be joshing, Diggs."

"Oh, no, they are real, or so I believe. I mean, why would there be stories of them, if not based in truth?"

"They are eld dammen's tales, Diggs. Told to keep their younglings in line. I mean, 'Behave, else the Giants will grind up your bones for bread.'"

"Well, Perry, let me ask you this: would you call an Ogru a Giant? I mean, they're ten, twelve feet tall. So, would you call them—?"

"Of course not. They are Ogrus, Diggs, and not Giants."

"But they're big, Perry. And you act like—"

"Giants are Giants and Ogrus are Ogrus," snapped Perry.

Digby grinned. "Well, let me ask you this, bucco, if Giants are Giants, then that must mean they're real."

Reyer laughed, and Perry threw his hands up in exasperation.

Digby looked over at Riessa and said, "Do you believe in Giants?"

Riessa smiled to herself and said, "Of course I do, Digby."

Digby's eyes flew wide. "You do?"

"Oh, yes," replied the Dylvana. "You see, they are indeed real."

"What?" asked Perry, astonished.

"I am speaking of the Utruni, the Stone Giants," said Riessa.

"Oh, them," said Perry. "Well, everyone knows *they* are real."

"But, my Wee One," said Riessa, now grinning, "dost thou know that thee and thy Kind have something of them flowing in thy veins?"

"What?" asked Digby, stunned, his mouth agape.

"Aye. The jewellike eyes of thy Folk: they gleam as does the emerald, sapphire, and topaz."

Perry shrugged. "And . . . ?"

"And Stone Giants are said to have real gemstones as eyes," replied Riessa. "Rubies, diamonds, sapphires, emeralds, and the like."

Digby snapped his jape shut. "Really?"

"'Tis true," said Riessa.

"Oh, my," said Digby.

They rode in silence for a while, and finally Digby said, "I wish I could meet one."

"A Stone Giant," said Perry.

"Yes, Perry, a real Giant."

Perry snorted, but said naught, and on they rode.

They camped that eve and the next four, and on the sixth eve after leaving Challerain they reached Stonehill, where they put up in the White Unicorn Inn, to be welcomed by proprietors Wheatley and Tansy Brewster. After a warm meal and several rounds of ale, they remained there that night as well as the next, resting.

And the news flashed through the village as would a lightning bolt, and all the townsfolk, Human and Warrows alike, came to the inn to see and pay their respects to the true High King and hoist a stein to him.

REYER AND HIS WARBAND set out from the White Unicorn Inn. Southward once more on the Post Road they fared.

They had been fed a hearty breakfast provided by Wheatley and Tansey and their staff, and so the members of Reyer's train were in a good mood, even though they had started their ride late in midmorn.

"Barn rats," said Perry, "I wish I had brought my lute. We could have a merry jingle."

"You play a lute?" asked Riessa.

"I do."

"He's rather good at it," said Digby.

Perry frowned. "Well, I wouldn't go so far as to say—"

"Pishposh," said Digby. "He *is* rather good."

"Mayhap we can get a lute in the next town," said Riessa.

"I don't know what that would be," said Perry.

"Junction, I believe," said Digby. "Oh, there are some hamlets 'tween here and there, but none with a lute maker, I would think."

On they rode, speaking of singing and music and various instruments, Riessa admitting that she was a fair hand at the harp.

In midafternoon on the second day out from Stonehill, they crossed over the bridge above the River Bog. "I think we should ride a bit farther ere making camp," said Conal, "else the gnats and mosquitoes and other such might be a trial, the River Bog being what it is."

"Sludgy," said Digby, "or so I hear."

Conal laughed and said, "Not exactly, but a breeding sluice for pests. At least it was, back when I was in service to High King Valen. I mean, the river has its origin in Bogland Bottoms, a midge swarming pit itself. Oft we traveled twixt Challerain and Pendwyr, and each time we made certain to camp elsewhere, far from this river's banks."

"Ah, balderdash," said Perry. "I mean, how bad can it be?"

"Perhaps not bad at all," said Reyer, "yet I say we ride on a mile or so to avoid the worst of it."

The next morn as they broke camp, Perry scratched at his collection of night-swarm bites and growled, "If where we camped was supposed to get us shed of the Bog River's midges, then I say at the river itself it must be unbearable."

"As I said," replied Conal, "Valen and I never camped e'en this close, and so you must be right. But think of just how much worse off it is in Bogland Bottoms."

Six days after leaving Stonehill, the warband reached the town of Junction, there where the Tineway, out from the Boskydells, met up with the Post Road.

Junction itself was a main waypoint on the routes of the Red Coach. Yet with the hostility between the Northern Alliance and Arkov's sphere of influence, few and far between were the Red Coaches now.

But the town, though pressed by the lack of travelers, still served as a place for wayfarers to stay, and with open arms they welcomed Reyer and his band.

And Perry strode into the nearest shopkeeper's store and said, "I say, where might I find a lute?"

Even as Perry found an establishment—Harver's Notions— with a lute for sale, Digby, all aflutter, came running into the store.

"Did you hear, Perry? Did you hear?"

"Hear what? And stop that jittering about."

"Rood has sent forty Thornwalkers to accompany King Reyer."

"Forty Thorn—?"

"Volunteers all," crowed Digby.

"Why did they, uh—"

"The Gjeenian penny," said Digby. "It came, and even though Reyer says it's a matter for Humans, still we Warrows couldn't ignore the penny. After all, you've got to remember: Tipperton promised and—"

"I know what Tipperton promised," snapped Perry. "I'm just disappointed."

"Disappointed?"

"Rood should have sent more," said Perry.

"But we can't go against the King, 'cause he said—"

"I know what Reyer said," growled Perry. "It's just that—well, Rood should have sent more."

"Captain Windlow is happy, and he is in charge," said

Digby. "He's promoted Billy and Jem to be squad leaders, blooded in battle as they are."

"What about us?" asked Perry.

"You wanted to be a squad leader?" asked Digby.

"Nah. I just want to know where we fit," said Perry.

"At Reyer's side," said Digby.

"Barn rats!" said Perry. "That means we won't get to go on any scouting missions."

"Oh, I dunno," said Digby. "I think Riessa can spring us for a mission or two."

"D'y' think?"

"I do."

"You be riding with the King hisself?" asked the store-keeper, a tall, stick-thin, bald Human with a sparse moustache and a frazzled beard.

"We do," said Digby.

"Do you think he'd mind if I made a sign that says I provided the High King's minstrel with a lute?"

Digby frowned, "What? Wait. I mean, Perry's no min—"

"Right now I am," interjected Perry, and he beamed and said, "Of course High King Reyer would not mind at all, Mr. Harver."

"Wull, then, this is yours, free of charge," said the man, handing over the lute.

Perry grinned and put on his best look of innocence and asked, "You wouldn't by any chance have any extra strings, now, would you?"

43

King's Herald

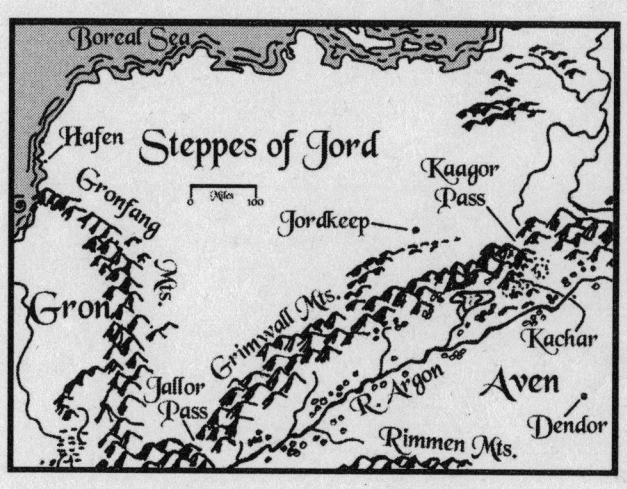

Jord, a nation of horsemen, is divided into four Reichs—known in the Common Tongue as Reaches—each one governed by a Hrosmarshal, the equivalent of a duke. The Reichs themselves—North, East, South, and West—start at their respective borders and form long but irregular wedges that come together at a single point not far from the geographic center of the nation. But the capital—Jordkeep—lies not at the site where the four Reichs converge, but quite a distance to the east, at the place where Strong Harl was born. Occasionally, Jordians argue that the keep should be moved to that central point, yet, much like the blood of Harl himself, tradition flows keen in the veins of these men, especially in the Vanadurin—the warriors of Jord. Hence the capital has never been moved: so it has been for millennia, and so shall it be for many more.

And into that city of horsemen rode Durgan on a steed the likes of which they never had seen. . . .

"I AM A HERALD OF High King Reyer," called Durgan, "and I bear a message allied to his cause."

The gate captain looked down at this youth, who was a man perhaps in his twenties, though his slight build belied his age. He was mounted on a sweat-stained grey horse, streaks of salt striping its flanks.

The gate itself stood open, and traffic flowed to and fro. Yet Durgan, as the High King's herald, was bound by protocol to announce his position, and he would wait for an official escort.

"High King Reyer?"

"Aye, the true High King, son of King Valen himself."

"Valen, you say?"

"I do."

A grin split the features of the captain. "Sleeth's teeth, boy! The rumors be true, then?"

"Captain, no rumor this," said Durgan, smiling up at the man in return, "but fact instead."

Passersby stopped at this declaration, and soon the streets would be afire with the news.

"Wait where you are," said the captain. "I will escort you to King Ulrik myself."

"My message is not meant for him," said Durgan.

The captain frowned. "Then who?"

"Prince Valder," replied Durgan.

"Ah," said the captain, "then we go to both, for the King and his brother are together, out in the grass. Wait till I fetch my horse."

Moments later, the captain rode through. As he led Durgan toward the north and away from the city, "I be Captain Hann," said the Jordian. "What be your name, lad?"

"Durgan."

Hann glanced at Durgan's horse and said, "Ridden hard, I see. Your message must be of import."

"It is," said Durgan, "for the Northern Alliance marches against the Usurper, and this message bears on that, or so I believe."

The captain clenched a fist and said, "Aye!" But then his face fell and he sighed. "We remain neutral."

"Mayhap not, if what my lady has written is of such import as to cause me to ride from Challerain Keep into the east of your land."

"Challerain Keep? When did you start?"

Durgan frowned, adding up the count. "Three days from the Keep to Ander. Four days at sea. Then seven from Hafen to here."

The captain smiled, for oft did riders use a relay of horses to cover such distances in haste. And he looked at Durgan's steed and asked, "Who lent you this mount?"

Durgan shook his head and reached forward and patted Steel on the neck. "No one. This is my horse."

The captain was astonished. "Your horse? You rode your

horse all the way? This horse? Seven days from Hafen to here? No remounts?"

"No. No remounts," said Durgan. "Steel bore me all the way."

"And Steel be the name of your horse?"

"It is, though in Kellian, his name is Cruach. He is the foal of Iarann Rob and Uasal Donn, er, Iron Bobbie and Brown Lady, the two fastest horses in all of Kell. But Steel is better than both, for not only does he have speed, but endurance as well."

"Aye, 'tis a champion steed, you have, lad. I think a legend be born this day."

"Legend?"

"'Durgan's Iron Horse,' they'll call it, for he must be made of iron to have come so far in such quick time. A name rightly deserved, I ween. By the bye, the king will want to get his bloodline in our herds. Does your iron horse stand at stud?"

"Well," said Durgan, "given his head, he would...."

Durgan and Hann were still talking of bloodlines when they reached King Ulrik's cloth pavilion, and the captain led the youth out to where Ulrik and Valder sat at their ease in camp chairs, both with tankards in hand and leaning back with their feet propped on stools. They, along with a handful of attendants, were watching a herd grazing in the grass in the near distance, half-grown foals racing to and fro, gaining their legs, now and then nipping at one another, seeking dominance or yielding submission.

"My lords," said Hann, "this be Durgan, herald of High King Reyer, Valen's son. He has a message."

As Durgan knelt upon one knee, Ulrik sat up and said, "Rise, boy. A message?"

"Aye," said Durgan, standing to fish in his dispatch bag, "for Prince Valder." Durgan withdrew the letter.

Valder dropped his legs and sat up straight. "For me? Who, by Hèl, in Reyer's court would be writing to me?"

Without answering, Durgan stepped forward and handed the prince the missive.

"Boy, your lips look parched," said Ulrik. He turned to an attendant and said, "Give the lad a drink," and in a trice a grateful Durgan held a foaming stein.

"Do you recognize this seal?" said Valder, holding the letter so that Ulrik could see the impressed wax, but then saying, "Ah, wait, it's Hrosmarshal Röedr's."

"His sigil but not his personal seal. Too dainty," said Ulrik. "A child of his, I would think. Most likely one of his daughters. Which, I know not."

Valder looked up at Durgan, an unspoken question in his gaze.

"Lady Gretta," said Durgan.

"Gretta?" said Valder. "Why, it's been, um, sixteen years or so since last I saw her. Caer Pendwyr, it was."

Valder broke the seal and opened the letter and quickly scanned it. Then read it again. He turned to Ulrik and handed the missive over, saying, "I have a son. Alric, she named him. After our own sire. He marches with King Reyer."

Even as astonishment flashed over Durgan's face, Ulrik cocked an eye and said, "A son?"

"Aye."

"With the Iron Duke's daughter?"

"She did not tell me," said Valder.

"I remember her," said Ulrik. "Third girl child of Röedr. A pretty thing. And you and she . . . ?"

"We had too much wine," said Valder, as if that explained all. "Then you and I set sail the next day." Valder pointed at the letter. "She thought I abandoned her, yet had I known . . ."

Ulrik read the letter a second time and then handed it back to Valder and said, "So there she was in the Queen Mairen's court, both she and the queen with child, and—"

"And Gretta's was the bastard," said Valder. "My bastard. My son." He took a deep breath and let it out, then said, "And having given up her virtue to drunken me, she was unsuitable for—" Valder turned to Durgan. "Has she wed?"

"Aye. To my own sire, Conal. He was a captain in Valen's

court ere retiring to Kell. That was before Valen fell. But then, in the immediate aftermath of Valen's downfall, Lady Gretta and Silverleaf came to Kell with Reyer and Alric in tow. And three or four years after that, Mother Gretta and Dad wed."

"Silverleaf, the Elf?" asked Ulrik.

"Aye," said Durgan. "He rides with Reyer, now."

Valder scanned Gretta's words once more, then asked, "When she gave you this letter, had she aught else to say?"

"Only that I bring Jord back with me," said Durgan.

Ulrik stood and stepped forward and gazed long at the distant herd.

Valder, yet seated, looked out at the herd as well, the colts and fillies yet at gambol and frolic in scant concern. Finally, Ulrik turned and said, "We thought we had little or nothing at stake, yet now we know 'tis not true. A royal heir of Jord is at risk."

"Sire, what be your command?" asked Captain Hann.

Ulrik looked down at his brother and grinned. "Light the bale fires. Fly the red flags. Sound the black-oxen horns. We Vanadurin ride to war."

44

Bards, Minstrels, Jongleurs

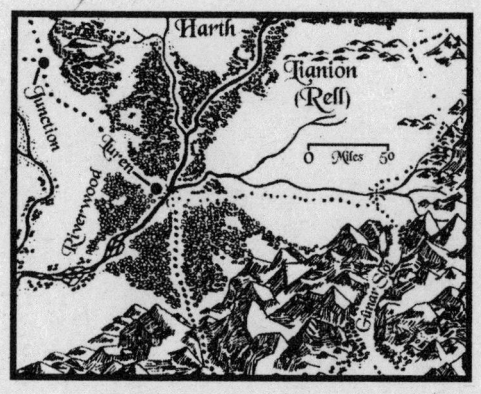

Of the many professions in Mithgar, none is as welcomed into a town as is a good bard. Of course, minstrels rank nearly as high as a bard. And the lowliest of the allied professions, yet still highly respected, are the jongleurs. All are wanderers, and many come to see them perform. Bards quite often play before a royal house. Minstrels and jongleurs are more oft found in taverns and city squares.

And then there are those who simply sing and play lutes and harps and flutes and other instruments for their own amusement, or those of close family and friends.

Perry was of this latter kind. . . .

ACCOMPANIED BY PERRY'S JOLLY TUNE, the next morn, Reyer and his warband left Junction, and, yet on the Post Road, they headed southward. At the end of the third day of travel they reached the city of Luren, charred buildings on the outskirts yet evidence from the great fire that killed so many and destroyed the town in 3E1866. Even though the fire had occurred some hundred thirty-four years past, still it dampened the spirits to see the remains of such ruin. But, spurred on afterward by the trade of the folk riding the Red Coach, some of the town had recovered, especially near the river with its wide ford. Yet over the past decade, the town once more had fallen upon hard times, for now the Red Coach seldom came. But with the King and his entourage passing through, the citizens welcomed them with open arms. And that eve there was much merriment in the Yellow Lantern Inn.

The next morn, Reyer and his comrades crossed Luren Ford, splashing through the waters just below where the Rivers Caire and Frith and Hâth came together and were then called the Isleborne on west-southwestward.

And now they turned east, away from the Post Road, to follow instead the Old Rell Way. And they traveled on this route for five more days. On the fifth day of that journey, in midafternoon amid a thunderous ovation, they rode into a broad encampment of a large army flying many of the flags of the nations of the Northern Alliance.

They had reached the upper end of Gûnar Slot.

45

Red Flags and Bale Fires

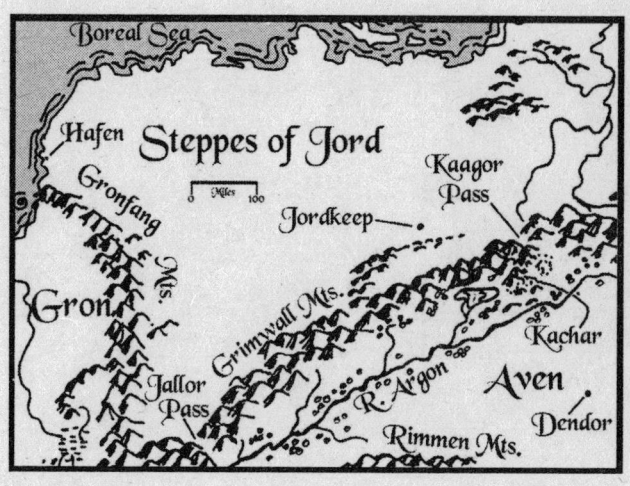

The pace of war creeps at times, while at other times rushes headlong. Yet, even though a war itself might crawl, for those involved in the *readying*, responsibilities engulf the ones engaged. They know some wars are lost at the outset if preparations are not thorough . . . in particular if provisions are lacking and measures are not taken to support the warriors both before the battles and after. Food, drink, medicines, transportation, mustering points, intelligence, and the like: all must go in the advance planning and execution, whether or no a nation has warning ere the fight begins or are victims of surprise.

Even so, resilience, brilliance in battle, or luck oft determines the outcome, no matter the preparation.

For the Northern Alliance the arrangements had been in the making for the years it took for Reyer to come of age to be recognized as High King. For Arkov, his network of spies had excelled at keeping him abreast of the Alliance measures, but his own plans were largely in the hands of the Chabbains, for they would form the bulk of his army. And for the Vanadurin, they were a nation of warriors, with plans ever on standby, even in very long times of peace. And though it might take days or a week or three for the Harlingar to be ready, ne'er would it take months or years.

EARLY THE MORNING OF the day after Durgan arrived at Jordkeep, bale fires blazed atop pinnacles and spires and towers across the grassy steppes of Jord with the call to war. Riders hammered over the plains, red flags flying, summoning. And, bearing messages, birds flew from Jordkeep to the four Hrosmarshals—the four Dukes—of the four Reichs, telling them where the assembly would occur:

"In Jallor Pass," said Ulrik to Durgan, pointing at the map.

"My lord, how far?" asked Durgan.

"From here, some two hundred leagues," said Valder.

"And to the land of Ellor?" asked Durgan.

"You are certain the Alliance plans on meeting Arkov's forces in Ellor?" asked Ulrik.

"So I was told," said Durgan.

"Where in Ellor?" asked Valder.

"Last I heard," said Durgan, "they plan on going through Gûnarring Gap, but as to where any battles might take place, I know not."

"Aye," said Ulrik. "It depends upon Arkov, though, if we can, we'll choose the battleground."

"Regardless," said Valder, "let me see." He unrolled another map and made quick measurements. "Hmm ... from Jallor to the Gap: that would be some three hundred to three hundred fifty leagues, depending on which way we go from this crossing—Landover Road Ford." Valder stabbed a finger to the map at the place where the east–west way crossed the River Argon.

"What are our choices?" said Durgan.

Valder's finger traced the routes: "We can go down the Argon alongside Darda Erynian, or over Crestan Pass. The longer way is through Darda Erynian, but crossing the Rissanin River here"—his finger stopped its trace, then moved on—"and then making our way down the Great Escarpment and finally crossing the Argon into Ellor will not be easily done, and the journey will be a day or two longer, I ween. The shorter way is up and over Crestan Pass, where we then follow the Old Rell Way southward to the Gûnar Slot, and thence on to the Gap ... but Crestan Pass poses the danger of landslides, and, should one occur, we could lose the entire army."

Ulrik nodded and said, "Yet, Crestan Pass, though hazardous, will get us there the quickest."

Durgan sighed and said, "Ah, me. A total of five hundred leagues, fifteen hundred miles. Yet no matter which route we take, I think even Steel cannot keep up the pace needed to arrive in a timely manner. Even the champion as he is, Steel is weary."

"Lad, we are not going to gallop all the way," said Ulrik. "Your iron horse will last."

Durgan looked at Ulrik. "How so?"

The king smiled and said, "We will all ride remounts 'tween here and Jallor Pass. If you decide to take him with us, Steel will be unladen and trailing behind. And so, he should be fit for the long-ride when we go beyond."

"As will each of our mounts," said Valder, "for all of us will leave the remounts behind and ride fresh horses provided by the Hrosmarshals of the South and West Reichs."

"And all—horses and men alike—will be eating the Dukes' provender as well," said Ulrik, smiling.

"Won't that drain their larders and ricks?"

"Aye, it will, but even now the North and East Reichs are sending resupplies, yet they are wain-borne and slow, while we ride in haste."

"Well, then, given that Steel will make the journey to Jallor unladen," said Durgan, "he will go with me, for he is battle trained, and I would have him as my mount in combat. When do we leave?"

"On the morrow," said Valder.

In the dawnlight, Durgan and Ulrik and Valder, along with several hundred Vanadurin, set out from Jordkeep for Jallor Pass, each with a string of remounts in tow. And on Durgan's tethers ran Steel, the grey unladen; he would remain so until the muster was complete and the ride from the Pass to the Gap began.

And over the days as they rode, Durgan told Valder of Alric:

"Though he has his mother's eyes," said Durgan, "I would say that now he looks much like you, sire."

"A handsome devil, eh?"

"If you insist," said Durgan, and Valder roared with laughter.

When he got control of himself, "But what is he like?" asked Valder.

"Steadfast, brave, a bit smaller than Reyer, but quite a bit more adventurous than the High King."

"Adventurous?"

"Daring, perhaps, I mean," said Durgan.

"If he's like his sire, then I say you mean foolhardy," said Ulrik.

"Who, me? Foolhardy?" said Valder.

"You heard," said Ulrik.

"Alric is not foolhardy," said Durgan. "But likely to take some chances."

"Well," said Valder, "we Vanadurin have a saying."

Durgan cocked an eye at the prince and said, "And that would be ... ?"

Valder looked at Ulrik and said, "Lady Fortune favors the bold."

"Indeed," said Ulrik, "indeed."

"That might describe Alric," said Durgan. "Still, at times it seems his heart rules his head."

"Impetuous, then?" said Valder.

Durgan shrugged a shoulder. "Perhaps."

They rode without speaking for a while, but then Durgan said, "He saved Reyer's life, you know."

"What? Saved Reyer's life?"

"Aye. Arkov sent spies into Kell, and one of these was an assassin disguised as a tinkerman."

"Go on," said Valder.

"The tinker was all set to cut Reyer's throat, but Alric spitted him in the eye with an arrow."

"Sleeth's teeth, boy, when was this?" asked Ulrik.

"Let me see. I think it was when they were eleven summers old."

"Eleven?" Valder turned to Ulrik. "By Elgo, Ulrik, Alric was just eleven when he became blooded."

As they changed over to one of the remounts, Durgan told of the attack by the assassins from the Red City—the *Issukut Khayâlîn*—the Silent Shadows. "Reyer and Alric slew most of them, with a bit of help from Cuán on Big Red and from Catlin."

"Catlin? Big Red? Cuán? Tell more, Durgan."

They mounted up and continued onward, and Durgan said, "We were in Sjøen, Aoden and I and some of our hands, along with the axe-wielding men of Sjøen, battling two boatloads of these Silent Shadows, when a third boat landed elsewhere, and . . ."

ON THE FOLLOWING DAY, Durgan told of the ambush in the Battle Downs: "Alric was on point in the vanguard when they heard men battling Spawn, and without hesitation, he and the Dylvana charged into the fray. It turns out that the men had been jumped by the Foul Folk, before the men themselves could spring their own trap on Reyer. Well, we killed all the Spawn, and rescued a few men, but they were poisoned by Ruch arrows and we had no gwynthyme and they died. But their leader had escaped any blade or arrow smeared with that bane, and so he survived. Yet that night he made an attempt upon Reyer, but the Waerlings slew him in the act."

"Waldfolc?" blurted Ulrik. "You have *Waldfolc* in your band?"

"Aye. Seven. Thornwalkers all, from the Boskydells. Still, it's just seven."

"Ah, yes," said Ulrik, "but seven *Waldfolc* are as good as seventy men. Would there were more."

Valder nodded and then said, "And Dylvana? Forest Elves? They are in your band as well?"

"Aye, them too. Riessa is their leader, and she is"— Durgan took a deep breath—"wonderful."

"Methinks his heart has been Elfshot," said Ulrik.

"Aye," said Valder, emitting an exaggerated sigh, adding mournfully, "he is like to die of love." He and Ulrik laughed, while Durgan reddened. But then Valder said, "So Alric led the charge into battle?"

"He did," said Durgan.

"Foolhardy, I told you," said Ulrik.

"Daring," countered Valder.

"Adventurous," said Durgan.

Then all three laughed, and Valder sobered and clenched a fist and declared, "My boy, my only son, is a true Vanadurin."

*   *   *

IN BUT EIGHT DAYS they reached the palisaded town of Jallorby, lying not far from the northern extent of Jallor Pass, and there assembled were half the men they expected, for many had farther to come, and the supplies for the long-ride ahead were yet to arrive.

And so they waited.

Altogether it was another eleven days ere the muster of horses and packhorses and supplies and ten thousand men was complete.

"Tomorrow we ride," said Ulrik.

"At last," said Durgan and Valder together.

Then Durgan's gaze strayed toward the Grimwall and into the shadowed depths of Jallor Pass, and a cold shiver ran up his spine.

Complication

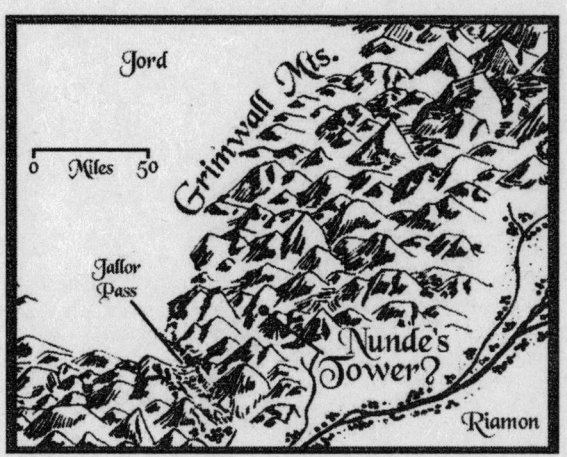

Always in war it seems the best-laid plans are disrupted by unexpected events. Generally, it is a scramble to deal with whatever the disturbance is ere the unbalance unhinges all: a surprise attack, a slain commander, a debilitating disease, food rot, bad water, or other such calamities. Disasters both great and small can upset even the most careful of plans. In fact, one of the tactics of war is to create such ills for the enemy.

There are times, though, when the actions of an unaccounted-for participant threaten to cause ruin, such as a random and unexpected bystander who somehow interferes with the execution of a plan.

Such things happen in war....

...And in a dark fortress high in the Grimwalls east of Jallor Pass ...

"My master," said Radok; the apprentice stood in the door of the laboratory.

Nunde, unclothed and with his face twisted in a rictus grin, hovered over his latest victim. Without looking up from vivisecting the Drik, he said, "What is it, Radok? Can you not see I am in the middle of an augury?"

"Indeed, my master, yet I bear news of import."

Nunde paused, neither lifting his knife nor his avid gaze from the steaming entrails. "Well."

"A scout reports the Jordians are assembling at the north end of Jallor Pass."

Now Nunde looked up.

"Assembling?"

"A great many of them," said Radok.

"*Ghah!*" snarled Nunde, and he hacked and slashed the blade through the bowels before him, feces and other matter flying wide. With the knife yet clutched in his grume-slathered hand, he whirled upon Radok.

The apprentice shrank back, cringing.

"Summon Kothar!" shouted Nunde, hurling the knife aside and reaching for his cloak. "They threaten to ruin all."

Within moments and throughout the hidden bastion, the walls resounded with the clangor of a great brass gong.

Jallor

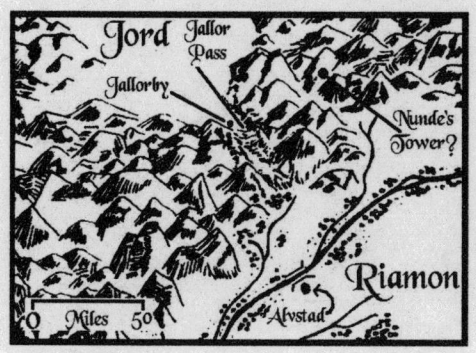

There are a number of ways in and out of Jord. By water there is the Boreal Sea, which runs the full length of the northern border of Jord and beyond. In the east one can travel overland and cross the River Judra to go to and from Kath or Naud, though they are both enemies of old of Jord. But to the south lies the formidable Grimwall, and on the west there upjut the Gronfangs, and passage through these two mountain ranges is limited.

Beyond the western range lies the fearful realm of Gron, peopled by Spawn and ruled by the dread Black Mage, Modru, though at the time of this writing, the master himself is absent, having fled to the Barrens after his defeat in the Great War of the Ban; since then he has not stirred from his bolt-hole—some say he is brooding, while others speculate he is waiting for something to occur, yet what that might be, who knows? Regardless, through the Gronfangs an unnamed passage cleaves, to debouch on the opposite side somewhere near where a dreadful sprawl, the Gwasp, oozes and belches and heaves. And to the north of that grasping mire lies Claw Moor, where, at its far extent, Modru's Iron Tower squats like a malevolent spider lying in wait. It was there in that nameless pass Agron's Army met its doom at the hands of Modru. It was there that Tipperton Thistledown nearly died. It was there that Beau Darby and the Wolfmage and his pack found Tipperton, and Beau saved him from certain death. Yet there are other passes through that range, all secret, some underground, known only by the Spawn.

As to the ways through the Grimwalls, that range is also peopled by Spawn, and so the paths through are at times hazardous. Nevertheless, across that chain there are two main routes in and out of Jord:

In the southeast corner of the Harlingar realm, Kaagor Pass runs through the range, and faring southward through the cleft will bear one into the Silverwood, beyond which Aven lies. Yet, if one is of a mind, upon debouching the pass a turn westward will take one through the woodland to the Dwarven realm of Kachar, there where the Vanadurin and the Châkka fought each other in deadly combat . . . until, that is, the dread Dragon Black Kalgalath came and assailed both sides.

And in the southwest corner of Jord lies Jallor Pass, a fissure through the Grimwalls, leading southward into the realm of Riamon. Spawn dwell on both sides of the hazardous rift, and not very far from there and up among the crags a hidden sanctum houses a terrible Necromancer, Nunde.

Jallor Pass is rugged and some thirty miles in length, and through much of it the walls rise sheer and close.

And as the quickest way for the Jordians to join the High King's army, it was through this pass that King Ulrik had decided to lead his men, his Harlingar, his Vanadurin—ten thousand strong. . . .

. . . and Durgan.

IN THE WEE HOURS ERE DAWN, Aksel, lantern in hand, wakened Durgan.

"We go, now," said the tall rangy redhead.

"It's not light," said Durgan, glancing at the window, stars glimmering in the sky.

"The *fördömlig maskfolk* will be fleeing for caves with the coming of the sun, and so, even as they abandon the walls for safe haven, we enter the pass."

"Fördömlig maskfolk?"

Aksel searched his memory for the meaning in Common. He finally settled on "damnable maggot-folk."

"Ah, the *damanta crimuh-daoine*."

Now it was Aksel who frowned in puzzlement.

"The Spawn," said Durgan.

Aksel grinned. "Yes. The Wrg. —Now hurry."

Swiftly, Durgan donned his garb and took up his gear

and, leaving behind the warm comfort of the White Horse Inn, he headed for the Jallorby stables.

Though large, the stables could not possibly hold all of the mounts and packhorses, who in the main were tethered or kept in rope pens beyond the palisades at the north end of town. Yet Steel had a stall, for Durgan had ridden in with the royal party.

The whole of the force was astir, and a flurry of activity filled the lantern-lit stables.

Swiftly, Durgan had Steel fed and watered and saddled, with Durgan's bedroll behind the cantle and his bow in its saddle scabbard. The Vanadurin had offered Durgan a lance, yet the young man had declined, saying that his weapons of choice were the saber and bow. Besides, with his slight frame, he doubted his effectiveness with a horse-borne spear.

Hrosmarshal Röedr, leading a gelded bay, passed by Durgan and Steel. "You know where you ride?"

Durgan, inspecting one of Steel's hooves, looked up to see a tall, yellow-haired man in his midfifties, with sapphire-blue eyes matching those of his daughter Gretta. "Aye, Hrosmarshal, with the Sixth Brigade, following the pack train and the Fifth."

"I would rather you ride at the front, with the First or Second Brigades, or even with the pack train. It should be safer there, and your Mother Gretta would have it so."

Durgan nodded. "Aye, she would, yet I think I ride where I can do the most good."

The Hrosmarshal nodded. "As you will." He glanced at Aksel, one of Röedr's own men, and received a bare nod in return, then led his mount away.

Durgan watched as the Iron Duke, King Ulrik's war commander, walked onward. And though Durgan was the Hrosmarshal's step-grandson by marriage, the duke had let Durgan ride where the lad wished, with King Ulrik and Prince Valder and Captain Hann, in the midst of several thousand Vanadurin.

Röedr had arranged the column with the First and Second Brigades—two thousand Harlingar, in all—riding in the lead in the event there was an attack just ere dawn. The Third and Fourth Brigades—some two thousand riders, all told—would follow and form up the supply train—no waggons, only packhorses—each man with several tethered behind, for it was likely that dawn would arrive before the train was very far up in the pass. As Röedr had said, it was vital to protect the provisions, and so those two brigades, towing pack animals, would go when they would enter the slot after the Spawn had fled the oncoming day, and where the pack train would clear the pass before nightfall, ere any maggot-folk might return. As to those riding in the rear—some six thousand Vanadurin—should darkness fall ere they exited the pass, they would take the brunt of whatever the Wrg might try, be it an assault or no . . . though with a Jordian force so large, an attack was unlikely.

It was yet dark when they set out from Jallorby, though the sky held the first hints of the day to arrive. All about them, the citizens of that town in good cheer rallied to see them off.

Leading their horses, up into the pass walked the first group, warming their mounts for the day, and then they checked the cinches and mounted up for the ride. And three or four abreast in a long column upward they fared, and ere dawn came, black-oxen horns rang and echoed from the crags and signaled the all clear to those following as well as to those below. Dawn was just breaking when the packhorses started up, and still the oxen horns, deep and mellow, passed the signal back, the crossing yet safe.

To Durgan it seemed midmorn by the time he and the third group got under way, yet it was not quite that late, as up into the slot the Sixth Brigade started.

And the black-oxen horns sounded.

Durgan and Aksel rode side by side, not far behind Valder and Ulrik. Even so, the full of the Fifth Brigade—a thousand Vanadurin in all—led the Sixth up the slope.

Four more brigades would follow, and horns would continue to peal.

Durgan rode in deep thought. Surely the Sixth Brigade would see battle if any came ... or so he hoped. And he wondered if this was a futile journey, for they were some eight or nine hundred miles from Gûnarring Gap. Would they arrive too late?

AS THEY RODE UPWARD, Durgan looked at the cliffs towering to either side. Noting his gaze, Aksel said, "We are well into the Grimwalls, my friend, where the *fördömlig maskfolk* dwell. Should it come to combat, there are places where we would be hard pressed—the walls too near for many to act in concert. If so, then a lance will be of little use, close combat as it will be, yet a good bow or saber will do."

Durgan said, "I haven't a lance anyway." He patted his bow in its saddle scabbard and then the saber at his side. "But these, I well understand their use."

Aksel's freckled face broke into a grin and he said, "Stick with me, then, for I can use a good hand."

Durgan smiled in return as up through the cloven slot in the mountains he fared, with one of Hrosmarshal Röedr's most trusted men at his side.

The higher they climbed, the cooler became the wafting air, and though grasses and small trees grew in the pass, as well as an occasional flower, and even though summer lay on the land, here and there deep crevices and cracks held snow, the dark shadows within too far for the sun to pierce, the clefts too narrow for warm breezes to reach. Winter had been harsh at these heights, and ice had split the stone above and had caused rockfalls. The going was rough, and in places even rougher, the long column threading its way through boulder-laden twists and turns. Still they pressed onward, hooves clattering over the stony route. Now and again soldiers would dismount, and walk beside their steeds, giving respite to the horses as they moved over the uneven ground. Durgan found these strolls to his liking, for during his long, long journey on his ride to Jordkeep, he had had little relief from the saddle, and so he relished the chance to stretch his legs.

As the column progressed, the sky darkened with heavy

clouds, and Durgan gathered his cloak around to ward off the growing wind. The sky continued to darken, and a dampness filled the stirring air.

"Rain," grunted Aksel.

"Aye," said Durgan.

And on they pressed.

Shortly ere the noontide they topped the crest of the col and started on the long descent under the leaden sky. To either side of the pass, the rock rose sheer and far. "In a channel like this," said Aksel, he and Durgan now afoot, "the wind sometimes roars. If it carries rain, the drops will strike like sling bullets."

"Then let us hope it doesn't come to that," said Durgan, and they mounted up and rode onward.

As if Aksel's words were prophetic, a chill wind began to blow at their backs, and the dark clouds roiled above. Within a candlemark or two, a raging storm came shrieking across the range and howling through the pass.

Night was upon them by the time the last of the brigades had struggled to the foothills below. The hurling rain hammered upon them as into a woodland they fared. They eagerly sought the shelter of the trees, though the wall of mountains behind afforded some protection from the worst of the fury. Even so, as Aksel had said, the pass itself acted as a channel, and the blow was merciless, both animals and men suffering under its outflowing wrath.

Westerly they turned, to escape the worst of it, and soon they found some relief. Finally, Röedr called a halt, and the men took care of the horses first and saw to their own needs last.

A time later, the rain stopped, and the clouds above began to break, with a star or two gleaming here and there through the rifts.

It was just after mid of night when Durgan was jolted awake by prolonged and hideous yowling.

"Värgs," said Aksel, sitting up nearby.

"Vulgs, you mean?"

"Aye," said Aksel, gaining his feet and taking up his lance. "Make ready, my friend, for it is this way they run."

Even as Durgan stood and strapped on his saber, the night was split by the squalling blats of hundreds of brazen horns.

Waiting

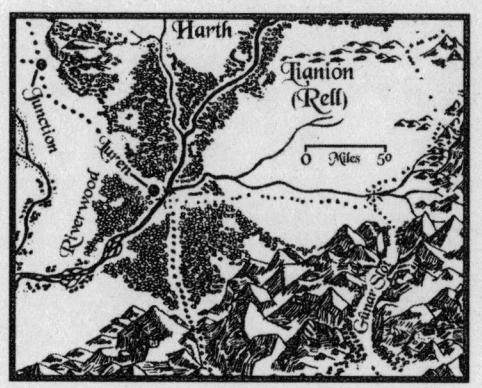

According to the common foot soldier, it seems ever in war that one must "hurry up and wait." But to the commanders who are laying out strategies and tactics, time runs at a different pace, for contingencies must be explored in the event of both success and disaster. What to do for various outcomes of victory or defeat is somewhat easier to plan for in the early stages. It boils down to a minimum of two questions: If we succeed, then what? But what if we fail? The "then whats" continue to mount up the further one tries to plan ahead, for given the first outcome—good or bad—the same two questions then repeat. And given that second outcome, again those two questions arise, the outcomes branching and branching, doubling and redoubling time after time. Quickly, the planners reach a practical limit of tactics to pursue, and they then set specific plans aside and fall back on a general strategy.

Even so, as new thoughts occur, the planning continues. Such was the case at Gûnar Slot, where some nations and commanders and soldiers had been in place for weeks, while others were yet to come as the muster continued to accrue. And with every newcome contingent, the strategy and tactics were reviewed and at times modified. And over the last ten days, ever since King Reyer had ridden into camp, the contingents from Gothon and Jute and Gelen had come, but Thol had not yet appeared. . . .

And so, the intense sessions of review and planning had occurred as the newly arrived leaders as well as the old had gathered before War Commander Raden's tent.

But as far as the common foot soldier was concerned, nothing had changed; hurry up and wait was the rule. . . .

*   *   *

ALRIC GROANED AND SAID, "Ah me, but my head aches from the what-ifs and maybes."

Reyer nodded in agreement. "Still, Alric, as Armsmaster Halon used to say, 'Tis better to have a plan, even a bad one, than to have no plan at all.'"

"Well, I say, just give me a lance and a horse and point me at the enemy."

"Or a pony and a bow," said Perry.

"Not so," said Digby. "King Reyer is right. We need a plan."

Perry shook his head. "Remember what Captain Windlow says."

"What?" asked Alric. "What does your wee captain say?"

"A plan is good up until the first arrow is loosed."

Alric laughed, but Reyer said, "Mayhap so, yet one should keep tactics in mind and—"

Reyer's words were interrupted by the sound of a horn and the sight of a scout galloping toward Lord Raden's tent.

Alric sprang to his feet. "Let's go see."

Moments later, the four arrived even as Raden, a bear of a man, stepped forth from his quarters, and the scout, a slender youth, haled his steed to a halt and dismounted. "What is it, lad?" Raden barked.

The young man looked at Reyer and then at the War Commander, as if in confusion as to whom he should report.

"My lord"—the rider inclined his head at Reyer and then to Raden, and corrected himself—"my lords, Lord Aarnson and the Tholian army are but a half day's march away."

"At last," growled Raden, his red beard all wild and afly. He turned to Reyer and said, "By your leave, my King, I say we give them a day of rest, and then we march."

Even as Alric clenched a fist and echoed Raden's "at last," Reyer's heart suddenly hammered in his chest, and he felt a pang of regret, for men would die at his command. He took a deep breath and glanced down at Digby and Perry and then up at Gûnar Slot, and he nodded and said, "The day after morrow, then."

Intervention

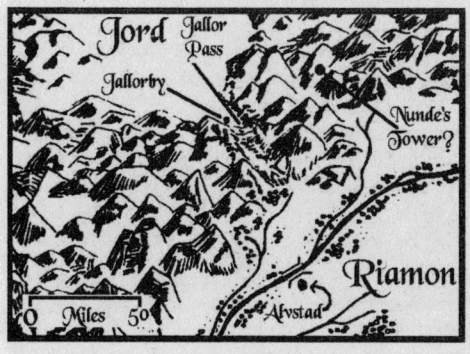

In the land of Jord, riders keep free-running herds well away from the Grimwalls and the Gronfangs, for horse meat is the favorite food of the Spawn. And for those towns nigh the mountains, palisades are the rule, and the horses kept within, while sentries patrol the walls. A nation that lives and dies by the horse makes it a rule to live and die protecting them. Hence, when possible, encamped Jordian warbands stake their horses in the center, with the warriors ringed 'round, for such is the way Jordians live.

As for the Spawn, whenever a chance presents itself, they have been known to abandon a mission, no matter how critical it might be, to capture a horse or a pony and make a meal of it. Only fear of retribution can turn maggot-folk away from gaining such a repast. Nunde wielded such fear, though were the Spawn to devastate the Jordian herd in the woods outside at Jallor Pass, well, that, too, would accomplish Nunde's end.

VULGS HOWLED AND BRAZEN horns blatted and the hard-running treads of massed Spawn bore down upon the Jordian army. And all the horses in the middle of the camp skittered and shied and stirred in alarm.

"Stand behind me, boy," shouted Aksel.

"*Chun Ifreann leis sin!*" spat Durgan, refusing. "I am a Kellian, and you have none better in your ranks than me."

"What did you say?" demanded Aksel.

"I said to Hèl with that," replied Durgan. "I am Kellian trained, Dylvana trained, and I am as good a warrior as any in this band."

Aksel growled and said, "You'd better be right, else Röedr will have my head."

* * *

High above and in the night, Nunde in astral form gloated at the scene unfolding below. To his sight, light was dark and dark was light and all colors reversed, the trees bright red, the ground pale red-violet and other such inversions. And he watched as his stark white Vulpen with their poisoned bite raced ahead of the Chun—Drik and Ghok and massive Oghi and Gok on Hèlsteeds driving them forth.

The jordian army kicked up their hard-won, wet-wood campfires, the better to see by, though dim was the light among the enshadowing trees.

Again the howls sounded, closer and ever closer.

"Vulgs," said Aksel. "And I hear the roar of Ogrus. Ah, me, but we will be hard-pressed if there are many of those monsters, for we've not a great deal of fire at hand."

"The horns?" asked Durgan, fitting an arrow to string, even though the light was muted.

"Maggot-folk, as you would say in Common. Most likely Hlôks driving the Rûcks."

On the far side of the camp to the north, Jordians shouted and Foul Folk yawled, and there sounded the clang and skirl of steel on steel, as well as the screams of the dying—men and Spawn both.

"Let's go," cried Durgan.

"No!" shouted Aksel. "For they come this way, too." And he lowered his lance to horizontal. "Stand ready; they are nigh upon us."

But then deeper howls split the air.

Aksel frowned. "What th—?"

Up above, nunde also heard the deep roars. His gaze swept the bright red forest. And then he saw black shapes, charging at his white Vulpen. "Draega?" he screamed. "Silver Wolves?"

And then a vast and blinding blackness bloomed among the trees.

Glaring light blasted throughout the forest. Durgan staggered back, his forearm reflexively shielding his eyes.

And yet he could see as silver shapes flashed past him, charging toward the oncoming Spawn.

A great wail rose up among the Foul Folk, for it seemed as if day had come upon them, and they reeled hindward and shrieked, for, were it the sun, the Withering Death would follow.

Turning, they fled toward darkness, even as the Draega leapt upon the escaping Vulgs, and with savage teeth the Silver Wolves shredded their ancient foe.

Durgan squinted toward the source of light and cried, "Dalavar!"

For there midst frightened horses stood Dalavar Wolfmage, a terrible aspect of effort distorting his face and form.

And in the distance flames sprang up among the fleeing Spawn. Trolls screamed and batted ineffectually at the spectral fire upon them, and even as they ran they tore off their greasy hide garments and flung them away.

"DALAVAR WOLFMAGE!" shrieked Nunde far above, his plans fallen to ruin. He watched in frustration as illusory dark green flames wreathed the Oghi and they cast off their clothes in fear.

And in his aethyrial form, Nunde could do naught to turn the tide.

And he fled away ere the Wolfmage might espy him, for Dalavar was a foe Nunde dared not meet.

AND STILL THE LIGHT flared among the trees, but of a sudden it vanished, as of a blown-out candle, and Dalavar swooned and fell to the ground unconscious.

50

Long-march

When trekking overland, unlike the Vanadurin, most armies do not have the luxury of a horse for every man. Hence, in the main, the common soldier marches afoot to reach the battle site. Most often their supplies are hauled by mule- or horse-drawn waggons, and at times heavy armor is hauled by waggon as well, along with spare weaponry.

Any riding horses within a given army are used by scouts and messengers and officers and, if there are enough, by a cavalry.

But, for the most part, the men of the main body march.

Thus it has been and thus it will be and thus it was at Gûnar Slot....

EVEN AS, FAR TO the north, the Harlingar at Jallor Pass laid their slain upon pyres and sang their souls unto the sky, to the south, at Gûnar Slot, Reyer strode before the massed commanders, Alric and Lord Raden at his side, Digby and Perry trailed after, along with Silverleaf and Conal and Driu. The sun was not yet risen, but dawn was faring toward day. The full of the army had broken their fast in darkness, and then the officers assembled to hear their King.

Reyer leapt to the back of a waggon so that all could see him in the beginning light, and his gaze swept across the lords and marshals and lieutenants and such, as well as wee Captain Windlow in front. And he smiled down at the Warrow, then he raised his face and called out for all to hear: "This I ask you to say to your men: those who wish to do so can turn about at this time and leave for their homes, for I would not have the unwilling marching with me. Yet this I also say: those who begin the march are henceforth my liegemen, and should anyone then turn away, it will be a breach of fealty, and he will be outcast from my lands to never return. This, too, I declare: once we are engaged in battle, those who turn tail and run, they will suffer the well-deserved fate of cowards. But those who are brave and stand with me, those I shall remember forever, and I shall serve them the best I can, and that is my sworn promise as well as my sworn allegiance to you."

A murmur swept over those watching, and officers looked at one another and nodded in general agreement, for this youth, as young as he was, well, by his heritage and by his words he was a rightful King.

Reyer raised his voice to quell the rustle and murmur. "On this day, let it be said, that brave men walked at my side." Even as Reyer stepped forward to leap down, in that very same moment, as if it were an omen, the sun lipped the horizon and illuminated his face and frame, and his golden hair formed a halo about his head, and in that instant he seemed to be more than a king, more than a man, some-how . . . more.

A mighty cheer rose up and calls of "King Reyer, King Reyer" delayed his descent. But finally Reyer signaled Alric, and the lad raised his black-oxen horn to his lips and sounded the call for the march.

And thus began the long walk toward an unknown destiny.

THEY FARED INTO THE morning shadows of the vast cleft known as Gûnar Slot, a wide pass slashing through the Grimwall Mountains to connect the land of Rell to the realm of Gûnar. Here it was that the Grimwall Mountains changed course: running away westerly on one side of the Slot, curving to the north on the other. And as the march made its way southward, clouds began to gather above, and a wind sprang up to blow in their faces.

"Rain," said Alric, glumly. "It's coming."

"Aye," said Reyer.

Trailing behind, Perry looked up at the glum sky and said, "So much for your omen, Diggs."

"Oh, I wouldn't say that," said Digby. "I mean, after all,

Reyer was luminous when this day began. Besides, what better omen to have since we march toward a gathering storm?"

"I can see that, Diggs."

"I meant the battle to come," said Digby. "Not the weather."

"Oh."

Their ponies plodded along in relative quiet, but for the sough of the wind and the clop of hooves, and the treading of the men afoot.

And still the wind grew, and finally the rain came, funneled into the slot by the ever-growing bluster. And the rest of that day into the teeth of the storm they rode and marched through the great rift.

The Slot before them ranged in breadth from seven miles at its narrowest to seventeen at its widest. And the walls of the mountains to either side rose sheer, as if the pass had been cloven by a single blow from a great and monstrous axe. Trees lined the floor for many miles, though now and again long stretches of barren stone frowned at the army from one side or the other or both. The road they followed, the Slot Road, would run for nearly seventy-five miles through the Gûnar Slot ere debouching into Gûnar.

A third of the way through, Reyer called a halt, and that night the army camped well off the road and within a lengthy, strung-out stand of woods, the forest growing out from great set-back fissures to extend along the eastern side.

And still the rain fell and the wind blew, all of it channeled up the passage by the high sheer stone to either side.

The scant shelter of the trees and clefts did little to ward away the swirling showers from the blowing rain.

IT RAINED THE NEXT day as well, though not steadily, but rather in spates. Hence, at times water poured from the skies, while at other times only a glum overcast greeted the eye.

"Adon, but I wish the sun would shine," said Perry.

"Me, too, bucco. Me, too."

"If I were a certain ninny-head," said Perry, "I would say this is an omen of worse things to come."

"Worse things *will* come," said Digby.

"Oh?"

"We are going to war, Perry. Not a picnic. And if I had to choose, I'd take rain and glum skies over combat any time."

THAT EVE THE RAIN stopped and the skies above began to clear, and again they camped among thickset trees well off the road.

"Another day should see us out of this slot," said Conal, as he shared out jerky and crue.

"We should reach Stede morrow eve," said Driu.

"Stede?" asked Alric.

"Aye. A small village: it was burnt to the ground during the War of the Ban, yet it has recovered, though but a small hamlet still."

Silverleaf nodded. "Back in the day it was a sizable town of import, when trade flowed into and out of Rell."

"What day was that?" asked Reyer.

Silverleaf frowned, then said, "Not long before Awain became the first High King."

"That would be—what?—something like nine thousand years ago," said Reyer.

"Longer," said Driu. "More like ten thousand."

"More like ten thousand?"

"Aye."

"But Awain is only nine thousand years back."

"True, but when Silverleaf says 'not long,' he might mean a thousand years or more."

"Back in the day, eh?" said Digby, then he broke into laughter.

Silverleaf simply smiled and shrugged, for he had done much trading in Stede when it had been a full-grown city ere falling to ruin following several plague years when the city was abandoned. Rain and wind and snow and storms and erosion and decay as well as lightning strikes and fires slowly erased the town, the char and other remains to gradually disappear into the soil until it had vanished altogether.

"Well, it might no longer be a large town," said Perry, "but will it have an inn?"

"I think not," said Driu.

"Barn rats, I was hoping for a soft bed to sleep in."

Digby looked at Perry and made a sweeping gesture toward the full of the encamped army and said, "You and sixty thousand others."

Perry burst into laughter, as did the rest 'round their small fire.

THE FOLLOWING MORN, the day rose to bright sunshine with a scatter of billowy white clouds serenely sailing across the blue sea of the sky. The scouts reported that the pass ahead was clear, and a warm wind began to waft, and once again the marchers got under way.

A mile or two along the Slot Road, someone among the ranks began to sing, and many of his comrades joined him, and though the words were in a language the Warrows and others did not understand, it lifted their hearts toward joy. After that, the various contingents sang in their own native tongues, and the march continued in good spirits.

In the eve of the third day, as Driu had said, the army reached Stede. It consisted of seventeen houses, none of which was an inn. Even so, the villagers did offer King Reyer hot tea and a meal. Reyer tried to repay their kindness with a small gold coin or two. Yet they would have none of it, and instead, led by a village elder, they all swore fealty to the one they called their true and rightful High King.

THE NEXT MORNING, Silverleaf and Driu stood out on the plain and gazed long at the wide land before them. It was a prairie, relatively flat and featureless, but for occasional stands of thickets and a low rolling hill in the distance.

"What of Dalavar?" asked Silverleaf.

Driu frowned. "There was a great disturbance in the aethyr three nights back. I believe he was responsible."

"Does he yet live?"

Driu nodded. "Aye, but if it were he alone, then he was dreadfully weakened."

"And the Jordians?"

"I believe they are on the long-ride, I hope under Dalavar's guidance, for he knows ways they do not. Yet they have far to come and little time to do so, and whether they will arrive ere combat begins, that I cannot say."

Wolfmage

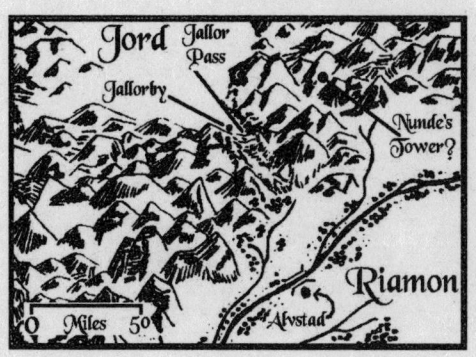

Dalavar Wolfmage has a strange lineage: his mother a Seer, his father a shape-shifting Fiend—one who is said to be a mix of Demon and Spawn and Human. It is this lineage that sets Dalavar apart from others of Magekind, for Dalavar seems immune to the loss of youth when casting spells; is that due to the portion of Demon blood said to flow in his veins? Regardless, he has always seemed to be as he is now, neither aging nor growing younger, and were he a Human, in spite of his silver-grey hair he would seem to be in his late twenties or early thirties. Yet he has been on Mithgar for millennia.

Some know Dalavar as a recluse, dwelling in the Wolfwood, where it is said legendary creatures also dwell. Yet, recluse or no, there are times Dalavar takes up a cause—the destruction of his own sire one of these. Yet there are other missions he has undertaken as well: he was active during the Great War of the Ban, and he single-handedly brought about the destruction of one of Modru's Hordes. Too, he aided Elyn and Thork in their quest for the Rage Hammer. It is a mystery as to why and how he takes up a stand; perhaps it is because he is a Seer, and he perceives things he must help to prevent or to enable.

Yet whether a Seer or an Illusionist, at times it seems the extent of his powers go well beyond. . . .

. . . As was the case at Jallorby Pass. . . .

"DALAVAR!" CRIED DURGAN, taking off at a run for the fallen Mage.

The hue and cry of fleeing Spawn faded in the dark distance, though wails of the Vulgs being savaged by the Draega seemed closer now that battle between the Jordians and the Foul Folk had ceased.

Aksel snatched up a burning brand from the nearby campfire, and, holding it high, followed Durgan into the milling herd, the warrior shoving agitated horses aside to reach the lad and the Wolfmage.

As to the horses themselves, they gave wide berth to the fallen spell-caster and the lad, more or less forming an irregular and stirring circle about the two.

In the wavering light of Aksel's torch, Durgan knelt by Dalavar and put an ear to the Mage's lips. Moments later Durgan looked up at Aksel and said, "He yet breathes." He took up Dalavar's wrist, and after a while: "His pulse is steady. I think he must have swooned."

"Who is he?" asked Aksel.

Durgan said, "The one responsible for causing the bright light and casting fire on the Trolls, or so I do believe, for he is the Wizard Dalavar."

Aksel sucked in a breath through clenched teeth. "A *Heksemester*?"

Durgan smiled. "Fear not, brave warrior. He is on our side."

Aksel breathed a sigh of relief. "Living as we do so close to Gron, well . . ."

"I understand," said Durgan. He gestured at Dalavar and said, "Yet no Modru is this Wolfmage, but a—"

"Ah, the Wolfmage," blurted Aksel. "From the Wolfwood. We have legends of him. He is always cast in a good light."

Durgan grinned and said, "And cast a good light he did."

Aksel smiled at Durgan's allusion, and then he glanced at Dalavar and said, "Let us get him to our fire."

"All right," said Durgan. "Shall we—"

"I can walk," said Dalavar, opening his eyes, grey as a storm-laden sky.

"You're awake!" said Durgan. "—Er, of course you're awake. Silly me."

Aksel dropped to one knee and inclined his head and said, "My lord, Dalavar Wolfmage."

Durgan gaped, for it had never occurred to him that Dalavar was to be considered a lord.

The Mage waved a hand of dismissal and said, "Might

you have some tea and mayhap a bit of crue or such? The casting took much from me."

In that moment, six Silver Wolves came trotting among the herd, and the horses seemed to calm down at the sight of them, vicious fangs, Wolf shapes, or no. The Draega named Shimmer, if Durgan rightly recognized her, came and nuzzled Dalavar. With wonder in his eyes, Aksel looked upon these pony-sized Draega even as Durgan said, "Quite a sight, aren't they?"

"IT WAS A POWERFUL CASTING," said Dalavar. He took a gulp of strongly brewed tea, followed by a bite of crue. Then he added, "Much like the <fire> I burned upon a time in Gron, during the Great War of the Ban."

Durgan and Aksel and King Ulrik and Prince Valder waited, but the Wolfmage said no more.

The Iron Duke strode into the firelight. "Two hundred and six dead," he said. "Another two hundred disabled."

Ulrik sighed and shook his head. "So be it. Assign as many as needed to care for the wounded. When we get to Alvstad, we can ask the citizens there to take on that task."

"What of the slain?" asked Durgan.

Röedr turned to Ulrik. "My lord, I think we have not the time to bury our dead 'neath green turves; besides, these woods seem to be lacking such. Hence, I have ordered pyres to be set, though the wood is wet."

Ulrik nodded and said, "As we must."

Röedr said, "I repeat, the wood is wet. We had enough of a problem starting even these small blazes in camp. As to the pyres, we must of needs leave someone behind to—"

"Fear not," said Dalavar. "I will aid."

Durgan said, "He set the Trolls afire."

Dalavar shook his head. "A mere illusion, lad. Just to terrorize the Ogrus. But as to the pyres for the fallen, I will set real flames, damp wood, wet wood, or no."

Röedr sighed in relief, and Ulrik said, "Well and good, Lord Dalavar."

Valder nodded his agreement and said, "Then we will sing them into the sky."

A long silence fell upon them all, but finally Valder said, "Tell me, Dalavar Wolfmage, what brings you to this place?"

"Why, to guide you and the army of Jord to King Reyer's side, Prince Valder."

"Guide us?"

"By a way unknown to you," replied Dalavar. "I have negotiated your safe passage through Darda Galion and down the Great Escarpment."

IN MIDMORN, with the sun well into the sky, great pyres sat ready, with slain warriors in repose atop the wooden mounds. As to the slaughtered Foul Folk, they had withered to dust in the light of day, yet their weaponry lay at the feet of the dead Vanadurin. King Ulrik stood upon a boulder before the living. He signaled to his bugler, who raised his black-oxen horn to his lips and blew three long mournful notes. And all the Harlingar raised their own horns and replied in kind, with somber echoes ringing from the stone of far mountain sides. And then Ulrik led his legion in an ageless invocation in the warrior tongue of Valur:

> *"Hagl, Krigers av de Spyd og Ryttersable! . . ."*
> *[Hál, Warriors of the Spear and Saber!*
> *Hál, Warriors of the Knife and Arrow!*
> *Hál, Warriors of the Horn and Horse!*
> *Ride forth, Harlingar, ride forth!*
> *Into the clouds on sky-running horses,*
> *Carry your spears in pride,*
> *Into the clouds on sky-running horses,*
> *Ride forth, Harlingar, ride.]*

Stalwart men wept, and Durgan, who had not understood a word of the incantation but who nevertheless knew the meaning, found his own cheeks wet with tears.

Ulrik then nodded to Dalavar standing among a solemn group of warriors who held unlit torches in their grips. Dalavar looked at the men, and of a sudden their brands burst forth in flames. And Dalavar followed the procession to each and every mound, and as the grim-faced warriors thrust the fire upon the wet wood, lo! it, too, blazed up and fiercely.

And when all were aflame, Ulrik signaled his army, and he along with the others knelt upon one knee, heads bowed. And then they stood and stepped to their horses and mounted up and rode away, not looking back as they went.

LATE IN THE DAY they camped, and midmorn the next the army reached Alvstad, and they turned the care of the wounded—some who had ridden, some who had been hauled on travois—over to the citizenry there.

And then they rested the remainder of that day.

GUIDED BY A PACK of Silver Wolves, the following morning Ulrik's army rode away from Alvstad just after dawn.

Riding near the head of the legion, Aksel turned to Durgan and asked, "Where is Dalavar?"

Durgan looked left, then right, and he leaned closer to Aksel and in a low voice said, "That 'Wolf in the lead, the darker one, that be him."

Aksel's eyes flew wide, and he hissed, *"Skifteskape,"* and with a finger he circled his heart in a plea for Elwydd's protection.

THREE DAYS LATER OVER gentle terrain, late in the evening Ulrik called a halt at Landover Road Ford, there where it crossed the River Argon.

It was two days after Reyer and his army had marched out of Gûnar Slot and into the hamlet of Stede.

52

Redholt

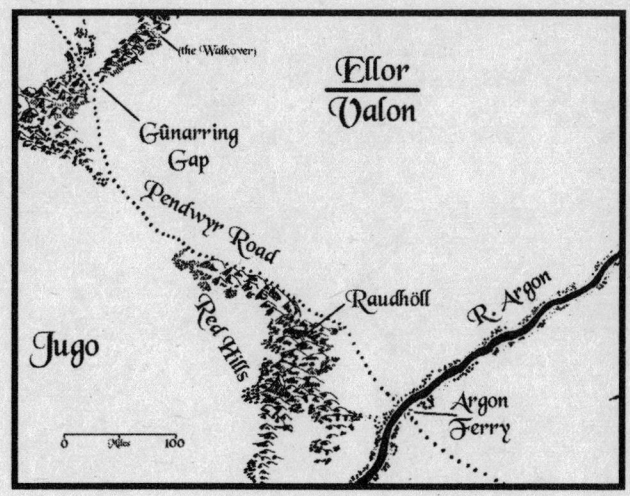

The iron-rich Red Hills lie along the border between Jugo and the abandoned land of Ellor—called Valon by some. 'Neath this chain of tors and crags and low mounts is delved the Châkkaholt of Raudhöll—a Dwarven word that properly translates as Redhall, though most men know it as Redholt. Millennia agone, First Durek journeyed among these hills and claimed them for the Châkka, and the Dwarven ownership of them has never been challenged.

From the rich ores mined under this ancient range the Châkka forge arms and armor, much sought after by kings and nations. The finished metal of its making is dark and is named black-iron by the Dwarves; mayhap it is a form of steel, but only the Châkka smiths know the secret of its creation, and—warriors all—it is a secret they guard jealously.

Raudhöll is made wealthy by its trade in this weaponry, and oft do heavily laden wains fare out from the holt along the Pendwyr Road, a trade route skirting the northern flanks of the range and beyond: northwesterly toward Gûnarring Gap and the nations afar; southeasterly toward the docks along the River Argon, and from thence to Pellar and elsewhere.

And it was along this road one day . . .

"MY LORD, MY LORD."

DelfLord Regga looked up from the ore-map he studied. One of the high scouts rushed toward him.

"Delek?"

"My lord, a large army comes."

"Whence?"

"East."

As Regga took up his axe and clapped a helm to his

head, he called out to a standing warder, "Sound the alarm; close the gates." Then he turned to Delek and said, "This I will see for myself."

Aiming for the spiral stair to the heights, together they headed out from the chamber and along the lantern-lit corridors, the blue-green phosphorescent glow lambent.

Reaching the flight, up they went—one hundred, two hundred, three hundred steps, and perhaps a few more—and they came to a bronze door standing open, with guards just beyond and to either side.

Regga stepped through and onto a shadowed stone balcony nearly invisible 'neath a dark craggy overhang. He moved to the balustrade, and spread out below and before him sat hills and foothills of the chain, and beyond their fringe and extending far into the northern distance lay the green grassy plains of Ellor. Yet his gaze did not seek those verdant waves swashing in the gentle wind, but instead he looked down Pendwyr Road to the southeast.

A vast army came marching northwesterly along the route: first the scouts, spread wide, rode far in the lead; well behind rode the vanguard; they were followed by the main body.

Long did Regga look, and he was joined by several warrior captains come late.

After a while, Regga said, "How many do you estimate, Balor?"

To the DelfLord's right stood a grizzle-haired Châk, Regga's warlord.

"Ninety, a hundred thousand," said Balor.

"I concur," said Regga, even as other captains nodded in agreement.

Behind Regga, Delek breathed, "No wonder refugees fled past."

"Aye," growled Balor. "Mostly from West Bank I would say."

Long they watched as the main body drew on, and finally Delek said, "I see the flags of the Fists of Rakka."

"The flags of Chabba, too," said Varak, another of the eagle-eyed scouts.

"And Alban and Garia," said Delek.

"I see in the lead ..." said Varak, but his voice fell to silence.

"What?" asked Regga.

"My lord, it is the High King's standard," replied Varak.

"Kruk!" snarled Balor. "Arkov!"

Regga took a deep breath. "The rumors are true, then. Arkov leads an army of Gyphon worshippers."

"Where do they go, Lord Regga?" asked Delek.

"To meet King Reyer and the Northern Alliance," said Regga.

"And their coming together will not be gentle," said Warlord Balor.

They continued to watch as the army drew near, none saying aught.

Finally, without turning his gaze away from the force below, Warlord Balor asked, "Do we march, my lord?"

Regga nodded and said, "We do."

Gûnar

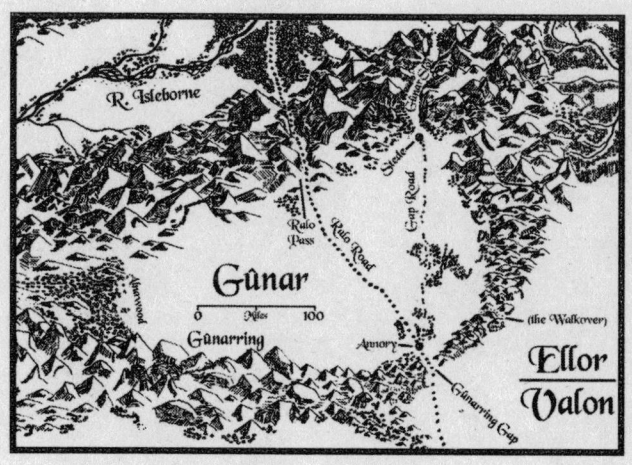

Where the north–south run of the Grimwall Mountains turns southwesterly, a breakaway spur of that chain continues on southerly for some sixty-odd leagues before also curving southwesterly to come to a gap, beyond which the run continues to bend until it heads due west to rejoin the mother range. That long-curving arc is called the Gûnarring, and, combined with the Grimwalls, the land of Gûnar is surrounded by mountains, with the Grimwall lying along one bound, and the full two-hundred-league curve of the Gûnarring forming the opposite marge.

A large forest, called the Alnawood, flourishes in the angle where the Gûnarring rejoins the Grimwall, and in that forest lies the baronial estate of a long line of King's Thieves—the most famous of which was Fallon the Fox, son of Delon the Bard and Ferai the Thief, two of the companions of Arin Flameseer and Egil One-Eye in the perilous quest of the Dragonstone. Other than that forest, Gûnar is mainly a prairie, with scatters of thickets here and there nestled against rare runs of rolling hills, but for the most part the land is a rather flat and featureless 'scape.

There are two primary roads through Gûnar, each some two hundred miles long: the Ralo Road, angling down slantwise across Gûnar from Ralo Pass in the Grimwalls to the gap in the Gûnarring; and there is the north–south Gap Road, running away from the south end of Gûnar Slot in the north to join the Ralo Road just ere it enters Gûnarring Gap. In past days, the Red Coach as well as traders' wains, waggons, drays and carts, and a few carriages traveled along these routes, but the only waggons that had of recent journeyed through this realm were the supply wains of the Northern Alliance, all of which had been stationed for weeks along the route the army would march, the waggons standing by to reprovision the forces on their way to Gûnar-ring Gap. Yet that dearth of rolling traffic in Gûnar had now changed....

...For, as southerly along the Gap Road the legion of the Northern Alliance tramped, the provisioning wains the army had passed had fallen in behind....

SINCE LEAVING GÛNAR SLOT, the Alliance forces had marched for nigh upon a sevenday altogether—the weather fair, but for one morning of foul—and they were perhaps but a day or so from the ruins of Annory, there where the Gap Road joined the route known as Ralo. Yet on this day an Alliance scout came riding at speed from the south. He sounded a horn and Reyer called a halt, and the army slowly ground to a stop.

The scout, a lithe youth, haled his blowing steed to a standstill, but for its sidling steps. "My lord, there are people along the road. From West Bank they say, and they flee ahead of Arkov's horde."

Reyer frowned. "Horde?"

"Thousands upon thousands."

"Gave you a count?" asked War Commander Raden.

"No, my lord, they only said 'twas a horde, and the West Bankers say there be Chabbains among the mass."

"Then the rumors are true," said Silverleaf.

"So 'twould seem," said Conal.

"And they are starving, my lord," said the scout. "The people from West Bank, I mean."

Alric turned to Conal. "What is this West Bank, Da?"

"At the Argon Ferry along Pendwyr Road there are two towns: West Bank on this side of the river, and East Bank on the opposite."

"How many West Bankers?" asked Reyer.

"I tallied nigh three hundred," replied the scout

"Where lies the nearest supply train?" asked Reyer.

"A half day south, my lord. Though another is camped just outside Annory."

"And which way do they fare? —The refugees, I mean."

"West along Ralo Road, my lord."

"Then tell the quartermaster of that train to feed the hungry."

"My lord," protested Baron Fein, "should we not—?"

"Baron," interrupted Commander Raden, "we have sixty thousand to feed, so another three hundred means little."

"Ah, yes," said Fein. "I withdraw my opposition, though if several thousand follow, then we must needs ration their take."

"We *must needs* ration it regardless," said Raden.

Reyer nodded, then said, "Tell the quartermaster to give them enough to reach Luren."

"I will, my lord."

Reyer turned to Ewan. "Captain, would you see that this man gets a fresh horse?"

"Aye, my lord."

Then Reyer looked at the scout. "How many are you? Scouts, I mean."

"Nine, my lord."

"Who is your captain?"

"Sergeant Deyer, my lord."

"And you are . . . ?"

"Scout Alden, my lord."

"Well, Alden, after you've a drink and a bite to eat, return and tell your sergeant to go with caution; he and you and your comrades are to fare along Pendwyr Road. He is to give me a count of Arkov's force, and to remain at a distance and shadow Arkov till he makes camp. He is to send whatever information will benefit us back to me."

"As you will, my lord."

"And take care."

"I shall, my lord."

Moments later, the march got under way again, and not long after, Alden galloped away upon a fast-running fresh piebald mount.

ONE DAY LATER IN the early afternoon, the army reached the ruins of Annory, a village destroyed by a large force of

Hlôks and Rûcks during the Great War of the Ban. Only a few yet-standing but vine-laden stone walls remained of the once-thriving town, and it was there that the army rested.

"Ninety thousand?"

"Aye, my Lord King Reyer," reported Alden. "They camp mayhap a day's march away from Gûnarring Gap."

Reyer glanced at his war commander.

"As are we," said Raden.

"They are half again our strength," said dark-haired Lord Aarnson of Thol.

"Aye," growled Raden.

"How many horse?" asked Viscount Axton of Wellen.

"Six thousand, my lord."

"Then we are evenly matched there," said the Wellener, grinning, his sharp features reminding Digby of those of a hawk.

"Don't forget my ponies," said Captain Windlow.

"Never," said Axton.

"I say we can help even the odds if we make our stand in the Gap," said Conal, stabbing a finger to the map.

"If we start just inside Ellor," said Raden, "and, if needs dictate, we slowly fall back, I deem that will give us the best chance to defeat them."

"We can get the jump on them if we march this eve," said Alric. "Choose the best battleground for our advantage."

Reyer shook his head. "Nay, Alric. We will leave in the yet-dark early morn. Recall what Armsmaster Halon taught us: warriors fight better when not exhausted."

"Good advice," said Rader.

Axton studied the map and then looked at Reyer and Raden and said, "There is this: should we overmatch their cavalry, then we can circle behind and split their forces fore and aft, and perhaps gain an upper hand."

Captain Windlow grinned and said, "How about my riders target theirs? Seems a good strategy to me."

Axton laughed and clapped the Warrow upon a shoulder.

They talked into the dusk, and before full dark fell, their strategy and tactics were well set.

That eve as they bunked down, Digby turned to Perry and said, "As Windlow says, bucco, a plan is perfect till the first arrow is loosed."

54

Long-ride

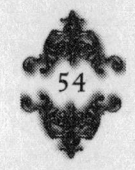

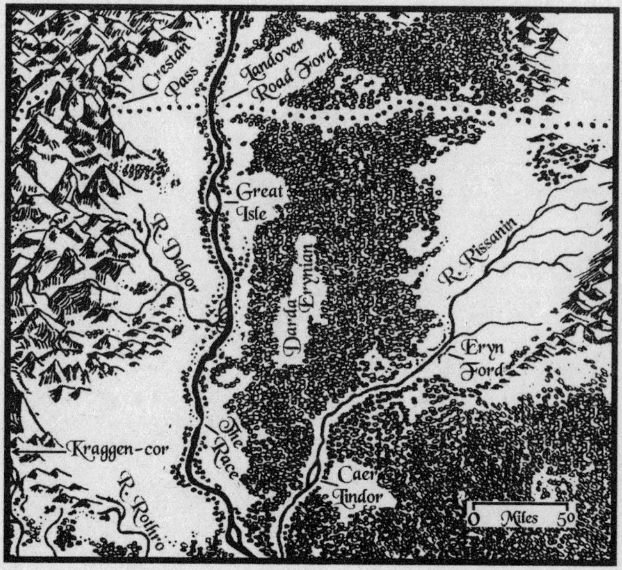
Crestan Pass
Landover Road Ford
Great Isle
R. Dalgor
Darda Erynian
R. Rissanin
Eryn Ford
Kraggen-cor
The Race
R. Rothro
Caer Lindor
0 Miles 50

The secret, if one can call it a secret, to the Jordians' ability to cover long distances in relatively short times is to have well-conditioned horses, lightly loaded, and to vary the gait often during the ride. In addition, the riders themselves must be fit, well trained, and matched to their steeds. Both man and horse must be watered and fed often while traveling, for long-rides require vigor to be maintained, else stamina suffers. And at times when the gait is a walk, the riders, too, should be afoot to relieve the horse of its burden and let it recover. Except for emergencies, one should not ride at speed in the darkness, else the animal might be maimed by burrowers' holes, unseen rocks, sudden sharp dips or rises, and the like. In stopping for the night, the needs of the horse take precedence over that of the rider—water, food, and grooming, especially currying to keep saddle-knotted hair from galling. So, too, in the mornings the horses are watered and fed, and as they eat, the men take their own breakfasts and then break camp ere saddling up and otherwise preparing for the ride. And the first mile or so, the horses are walked, and not ridden, to warm them up for the ride ahead. In camp at night and in the morn, as well as throughout the journey, riders must care for the horses' hooves, to remove any pebbles and prevent lameness or loose shoes and loss. If possible, when stopping to camp, the riders must select a good place to rest—a site protected from predators and sheltered from the elements.

There are more things to be considered when engaged on a long-ride—for example a longer route over level ground is preferable to a shorter one over rugged and steep terrain. Oft one or more of these needs cannot be met, in which case both riders and horses must simply endure ... such as not getting enough rest overnight, as was the case at

Jallorby Pass. Even so, the riders and horses had remained the rest of that day in Alvstad, recovering, and the following morn King Ulrik's Legion had pressed on, and they now found themselves at Landover Road Ford....

... IN THE TWILIGHT ULRIK looked toward the Grimwall Mountains to the west and turned to Dalavar and asked again, "Are you certain, Lord Dalavar, that we will go swifter by the route you advise rather than over Crestan Pass?"

Even as Commander Röedr lit a candle and unrolled a map, Dalavar said, "I am. The route I would have you take is more or less in a straight line to Ellor, and if the High King's force is anywhere in that land, we will have a direct route to it. However, should we use Crestan Pass, the way to the Gap will be at least one day farther, and should the High King be deep in Ellor, it will be another several days ere we reach him."

"But what if he is in Gûnar instead?" asked Prince Valder, peering at Röedr's chart.

"That is the gamble we must take," said Dalavar. "Yet, heed, it is less risk to assume he is in Ellor. E'en if we find him at the Gap, still we will be a day or so swifter by the route I propose."

"How far, then?" asked Valder.

Dalavar's finger traced a line. "As the raven flies, 'tis some hundred eighty-four or -five leagues to Gûnarring Gap."

"Just over five hundred fifty miles," said Durgan.

Dalavar nodded, but Valder said, "We are not ravens, Lord Mage."

"True," said Dalavar. Again he traced a route. "As the Wolf runs, it falls short of two hundred leagues by eight or nine."

"I make that about five hundred seventy-five miles, or nigh," said Durgan. "That's but twenty-five miles more than the raven's straight line."

Ulrik nodded and said, "Indeed, lad. And we know that the route using Crestan Pass is nigh two hundred twenty leagues." As he spoke, his finger went across the map and down.

"Then Lord Dalavar's way is some thirty or so leagues shorter," said Valder, "yet is it as swift?"

Ulrik looked at Dalavar and said, "Horses are not Wolves, Lord Mage, and by Crestan we ride along roads, all quick but for the twenty leagues up and over the pass. How lays the land by the way you suggest?"

Dalavar pointed here and there along his proposed way and said, " 'Tis mainly wold 'tween here and Darda Galion; forest within that wood, but gentle and easily rideable; a short stretch of narrow passes through the Grimwall to fare 'round one end of the Great Escarpment, and then the plains of Ellor beyond."

"Grimwall? What of the Wrg?" asked Ulrik.

"Since the Felling of the Nine, they dare not the wrath of the Lian in Darda Galion," said Dalavar, smiling.

Ulrik cocked an eye, but said naught.

"What of these rivers?" asked Valder, pointing at the map.

"Easily fordable," said Dalavar. "The pack and I had no trouble."

"If it rains . . . ?" asked Durgan.

"I see no major storms coming," said Dalavar.

Durgan smiled and nodded, for after all, Dalavar was a Seer.

"So the route is swift, then," said Valder.

Dalavar said, "Only when faring down through the narrow passes of the Grimwall will we go at a slower pace, yet no slower than if we were faring across Crestan Pass."

Durgan frowned and said, "Then, by Dalavar's route, it is—what?—some eleven, twelve days to Gûnarring Gap, assuming, that is, we ride fifty miles a day. But were we to go over Crestan Pass, it would be some thirteen days."

"And rockslides in Crestan are an issue," said Valder.

"They are in all the Grimwalls," said Ulrik. He smiled at Durgan and said, "Yet, by this lad's reckoning, Dalavar's route will save us a day or two."

Speaking up for the first time, Commander Röedr said,

"But how shall we know where the army of the Northern Alliance is?"

"I will send two of the 'Wolves to find them, and then they will come back and lead us," said Dalavar.

"You can do that?" said Durgan. "Send two of your Draega, that is?"

"They are not *my* Draega," said Dalavar, "for they answer only to Greylight. Yet, I deem they will take on the mission."

"Well and good, then," said Ulrik. "Lord Dalavar, as you will, when morn comes, lead on."

FOLLOWING SEVEN SILVER WOLVES, west the legion fared, crossing the mighty River Argon to come into the wide wold 'tween river and mountain, where they turned south for Darda Galion, the Grimwalls on their right, the Argon to their left.

Two days they rode down the wold o'er rolling green hills and flat, and only occasionally did they have to veer 'round rocky upjuts or ledges or drop-offs; thick runs of gorse blocked the way at times, yet the legion circled these to left or right. On early morn of the third day, they came into sight of the Dalgor Marches, where they would have to cross a reed-filled place of muck and mire. In that bog during the Great War of the Ban, Galarun had been slain and a great token of power, the Silver Sword, had been lost. But those were days long past, and the Draega led the legion to a point higher upslope from where that disaster had occurred. They guided the Legion to the place where the Dalgor River first began to divide into many streams to form the swampy delta, but even here the waterway was filled with sludge and reeds. Spreading the force wide, into the marsh they plunged, the bog sucking at hooves, the shallows slow and arduous but fordable, unlike the swift deep waters of the Dalgor River upstream flowing down from the high Grimwalls to the west. The crossing was wide where the 'Wolves had chosen to ford, and the cavalcade slowed to a walk. The horses who came late found the way even more grueling, caused by the churning hooves of those who went before them. At times the riders dismounted to slosh alongside their mounts, giving the horses respite. At other times, men gathered together to aid a steed that had become bogged. But the brigades endured and slogged onward.

Yet, even though any individual rider was not long in the crossing, with ten thousand riders, each towing two pack animals, the total time involved to get the entire force through was considerable.

As for the Silver Wolves, they splashed across without hindrance, and waited afar for the riders to come.

The first of the legion came upon the wold again, and rode onward as others made the crossing. Finally all were beyond the mire and south the cavalcade fared for the rest of that day.

ALL THE NEXT DAY THEY RODE, and off to their right in the Grimwalls they could see four great peaks, tinted grey, black, azure, and red. And they knew that under these peaks was delved the Dwarvenholt of Kraggen-cor, though the Vanadurin called this place the Black Hole. In there Dwarves dwelled, and ever since the days of Prince Elgo, hostilities between the Harlingar and the Châkka lay ever under the surface.

When they camped that eve, Prince Valder turned to Dalavar and asked, "What think you the Dwarves imagine, now that an army camps nigh their doorstone."

"They were expecting you," said Dalavar.

"They were?" blurted Durgan.

"Aye, for I negotiated with them for passage across their realm."

"We are on their land?" asked Ulrik, surprised.

"Nay. It lies somewhat west of here. But I thought it prudent to tell them you were coming."

"You call that 'negotiating'?" said Ulrik, laughing.

"I was very diplomatic when I visited their holt," said Dalavar, smiling.

"Are they sending a contingent to aid Reyer?" asked Durgan.

"Sadly, not," replied Dalavar.

"Pussyfooting Dwerg," said Commander Röedr.

"Now, now," said Ulrik. "We are at peace with them. DelfLord Thork and King Aranor made it so."

The Iron Duke growled but said no more.

"Even so," said Durgan, "why do not the Dwarves support Reyer?"

Röedr snorted in disgust, but Dalavar said, "Tell me this, Durgan: were the command of the Châkkaholt in dispute, would you counsel that we champion one Dwarf over the other?"

"Nay, I would not, but this concerns the High King, and not some Dwarf fiefdom."

"Nevertheless, 'twould be a Dwarven matter to resolve, would it not?"

Durgan nodded. "It would."

Dalavar smiled. "The Dwarves think the matter of the High King is a Human affair."

"Even though they might be affected?"

"I believe they think no matter the King, they will endure without change."

"I see," said Durgan. "Still it is shortsighted, in my opinion."

Ulrik laughed. "Shortsighted? My boy, Dwarves live for two, three hundred years. Any king they do or do not support will be gone well before their lifetime is over."

"Shortsighted, long-sighted: I believe that was at the heart of the dispute between the Jordians and the Dwarves of Kachar," said Dalavar.

Ulrik nodded and said, "It was. In that case, we were the shortsighted ones."

"Argh," said Röedr. "Enough of this jabber. I'm turning in, for we have another long day before us."

"A very shortsighted view, Duke," said Valder, laughing. "Even so, it's to my bedroll for me as well."

THE FOLLOWING DAY THEY continued southward yet on the open wold. And in the distance before them, they could see the tops of tall trees of a forest.

Durgan said, "Dalavar said we'll espy Darda Galion soon after we begin today's ride, so that must be it."

"Well," replied Aksel, "we'll be there soon, then."

"I don't think so," said Durgan. "He also said we wouldn't reach to the fringes till nightfall."

"Nightfall?" replied Aksel, gesturing at the trees in the distance. "Surely we must be closer than that."

"No, according to Dalavar, it's still a day's ride away."

"Are you certain?"

"That's what he said."

"Then that must not be Darda Galion," declared Aksel.

On they rode throughout the day, the trees slowly coming into view, yet they seemed no closer.

A low chain of hills appeared on the right, and the cavalcade fared straight onward, staying on the open wold.

And still the forest lay before them.

"Elwydd!" exclaimed Aksel. "How tall are those trees?"

Finally, in early eve, and following the 'Wolves, they splashed across a river—the Rothro, according to the map—and Ulrik called a halt, for a squad of Elven warders stood before them in the fringes of Darda Galion. The Draega pack loped forward to greet them, and Shifter trotted behind a tree and Dalavar stepped forth.

And the trees, the great-girthed Eld Trees, towered above all a thousand feet or more. And the leaves themselves were not like those of pine, but broad and dusky green, for Elvenkind dwelled within the forest, otherwise the leaves would not take on that shade.

Ulrik dismounted and stepped to the fore, and the Lian who bore a black spear stepped forward and inclined his head in recognition of the Jordian king.

"Lord Ulrik," said Dalavar Wolfmage, "I present Alor Tuon, the Chief Warder of the Northern Bound and bearer of Black Galgor."

Now Ulrik inclined his head in recognition of Lord Tuon.

And Tuon said, "I welcome you to the Larkenwald, Lord Ulrik. And even though some herein intend to go with you, know this: the mission you pursue is not of our concern. We will render safe passage, yet I would have you remind your warriors that they are now in our domain and to act accordingly."

"A rather chill greeting," murmured Aksel.

Durgan nodded his agreement.

"As you will, Alor Tuon," said King Ulrik. Then he stepped forward and held out his hand, and Tuon took it unto his own.

And Ulrik said, "Quite a spear you have there, Alor Tuon. We of Jord are familiar with lances. Might I heft the one you name Black Galgor?"

Even as Tuon and Ulrik compared weapons, Prince Valder signaled the bugler, who then blew the call to dismount and make camp, even as riders in the long Jordian train continued to splash across the Rothro and arrive.

55

Darda Galion

There are many magnificent forests in Mithgar: the Skög is perhaps the most ancient, there next to the Wolfwood. Perhaps the largest of the Mithgarian forests is the Greatwood in which the Baeren dwell. Lying just north of the Greatwood is Darda Erynian, where Hidden Ones and Dylvana share the tree land. But perhaps the most magnificent of all is Darda Galion, for the trees therein had been transplanted as seedlings from the Hohgarda—the High Plane—many millennia apast. And over the ages they have soared upward, hence this forest is also known as the Eldwood. Too, it is also known as the Larkenwald, for therein the Silverlarks used to sing, but no more, no more, for the sundering of the planes during the Ban War stranded them on the Hohgarda, and they have flown not among this forest on Mithgar since then.

And at the northern edge of this great woodland the Jordian Legion rested. . . .

THE EVE THEY ARRIVED, they made a cold camp, for the orders were to take no wood from the trees of the Larkenwald, for it was too precious to burn. Besides, there was something about the forest that made the whole of it seem almost awake and aware.

And as Dalavar said that night, "These giants sense when Elves are among them, and they gather twilight unto themselves. It is said absent Elvenkind the forest will grow drab, as if lonely or in mourning."

THE NEXT DAWN, A number of Lian Elves rode into the campsite, and among them was Coron Eiron, a simple golden circlet upon his forehead announcing his rank as the equal of a king.

"We have come to guide you, King Ulrik," said Eiron.

"I thank you for letting us this passage, Coron Eiron," said Ulrik, "even though you do not take up the cause."

"Some five hundred Lian do," said Eiron, "and they will ride with you to High King Reyer's aid."

"Hola! Five hundred? Five hundred Guardians? I welcome them, and gladly."

THE NEXT TWO DAYS the legion rode among the wondrous trees of the Larkenwald, faring south, ever south, and a bit eastward. They crossed the River Quadrill on the first day, and then the Cellener the next. And the five hundred Lian had now joined them. That eve they made camp in the foothills of the Grimwall.

Now free of the Larkenwald, there was wood to be had, and the Jordians sat about campfires that night. During the evening meal, Lian spoke of the Felling of the Nine, when *Spaunen* had slaughtered nine Eld Trees, and the terrible vengeance wreaked upon the Foul Folk in return.

War Commander Röedr and Prince Valder and King Ulrik, along with several brigade commanders, pored over a sketch and listened as Dalavar said, "This is the route we will take." His finger traced across the drawing.

One of those at hand was a Guardian who had lived long in Darda Galion: Alor Loric, leader of the five hundred Lian.

After Dalavar had completed his description, Ulrik said, "No Wrg along the way?"

Dalavar looked at Loric, and the Lian said, "Mayhap, yet ever since we took our vengeance for the Felling, they flee in fear at the sight of us."

"That's good," said Valder, "for this is a twisty way and quite suitable for ambush."

"Who in the world might ever find this route?" said Captain Hann.

Loric looked at the tall Jordian and said, "Other than the Lian, I know of only one who did so: First Durek, on his way to discovering Drimmen-deeve."

"Do you discount me and the pack I run with," said Dalavar.

Loric grinned. "Who?"
Dalavar broke into laughter.

THE NEXT MORNING, there were but five Silver Wolves leading, for Dalavar had asked Seeker and Longshank to go far ahead and down into Ellor to find the whereabouts of Reyer's Host, Gûnarring Gap their first stop, for surely there they would pick up the trail.

The legion itself wended among hills and crags and tors, passing by slots and gaping Troll holes and dark Rucha passages and dead-end canyons and such, faring ever on a southerly course though the way was full of twists and turns. Finally in the eve they stopped. Darkness fell, and after they had cared for the horses and then had seen to themselves, the legion bedded down. Somewhat after, a distant rumble sounded. Shifter and Greylight left camp at a run, and a time later returned.

And the news they bore was appalling.

Guarantee

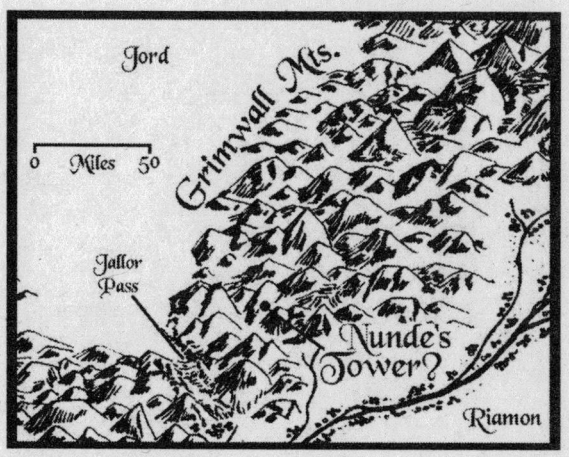

<Magic> is powered by <fire>. Among most of Mage-kind, youth is spent to cause a shift in the aethyr, and, much like a landslip, a cascade in the aethyr follows. By knowing exactly how to trip and shape that cascade, a given effect follows. But unlike the Mages who spend their own <essence>, Black Magekind steals <fire> from victims, and they use torture and terror to increase the level of available <lifeforce> in the ones they sacrifice, hence they rarely spend any of their own youth to achieve the desired end. But even if one of Dark Magekind at times spends his own <essence>, he can always rend <fire> from others to regain what he might have lost. . . .

FOR SEVERAL DAYS AFTER the debacle at Jallor Pass, Nunde brooded.

And he made a number of aethyrial flights following.

He tracked the course of the Jordians, and finally deduced their intended route. It was then he struck upon a perfect plan to guarantee the outcomes he desired.

And thus the torture and slaughter began.

"More, Radok, bring me more, for I will need much <fire> to cause what I wish."

And so Drik after Drik died screaming under Radok's hand, while Nunde soaked up the largesse.

NOW NUNDE FLEW THROUGH the night, and, swinging wide of Darda Galion, he sailed above the Grimwalls. He kept his distance out away from the path of the Jordians, for, even in aethyrial form, he dared not be espied by Dalavar Wolfmage. Nunde oft paused in his flight and carefully scanned among the slots and passes and crags and hills. Finally: *There! There are the troublemakers, the would-be res-*

cuers, Ulrik's legion and Dalavar. And I was right! Fool Dalavar plans to lead them along that narrow way and no other passage will do.

Now Nunde headed for the place he had scouted two nights earlier, with its unstable rocks above.

He settled down upon the crest, and, gathering his will, he spoke a <word> and loosed a great deal of <fire>, for casting an effect while in aethyrial form takes an incredible amount of <essence>—not his, of course, but the great store Radok had loosed for Nunde's consumption. What matter that hundreds of Drik had died? There were always more.

And a rock tumbled and then another, and of a sudden it seemed the entire mountainside had given way.

Gûnarring Gap

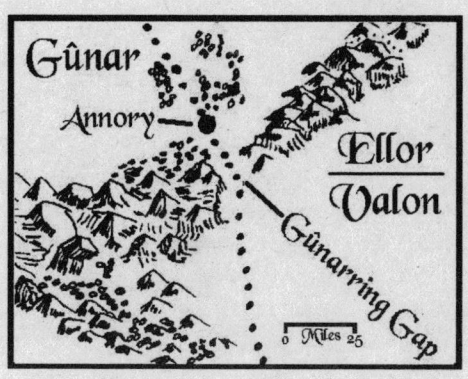

Gûnarring Gap is a slot in the Gûnarring, and through it runs a trade road called the Ralo Road in Gûnar, and Pendwyr Road in Ellor. The Gap itself shoulders up into the Gûnarring on either side, and it varies in width from five to ten miles, though it is only level where the road runs through. If one has a legion of several tens of thousands, the gap can effectively be a choke point for battle. . . .

AFTER LEAVING ANNORY IN the dark before dawn the Alliance Army reached Gûnarring Gap in early afternoon. And when they had marched through and stood in Ellor, naught whatsoever greeted them but wafting waves of tall grass stretching to the horizon and beyond.

And the scouts brought word that Arkov's army remained in camp, as if they were waiting for something.

THE FOLLOWING DAY, the outriders reported that Arkov's army was now on the march, and somewhere nigh the noontide, out in the distance before them on the very rim of the horizon, the vanguard of Arkov's Army hove into view, and not long after came the full of his force.

For much of the day, they seemed to pour over the brim of the world, the multitude dark and vast.

And even as the Alliance scouts rode inward to report, one came galloping from the south.

Reining his horse up short, the scout leapt to the ground and knelt before King Reyer. "My lord," he panted, glancing at the army marching toward them, "to the south, mayhap a day distant, mayhap less, for most surely they will be here on the morrow, another thirty thousand Chabbains tramp this way."

58

Fruition

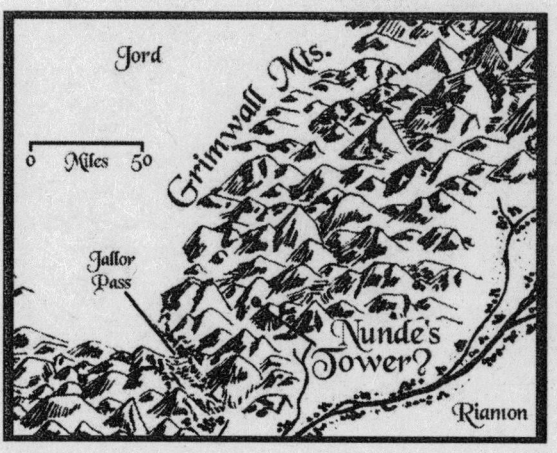

Far to the north and concealed in the Grimwalls there sits a dark tower under the harsh command of a dreadful master of necromancy. This monster is well accomplished in the art of aethyrial travel, and upon returning from a night flight ...

CHORTLING IN GLEE, Nunde called for his apprentice to attend him. And as Radok entered the inner bed quarters, Nunde, unclothed, said, "It is coming to fruition, my splendid plan."

"Master?"

"Little do they know victory is in my grasp."

"Neither Arkov nor Reyer?"

"Neither!" snapped Nunde, irritated that Radok didn't seem to grasp the full of all the subtle nuances of his master's brilliant scheme. But then, what can one expect of a mere apprentice? Little more than a lackey, that is. "Neither they nor their allies nor that stupid King Fadal in Chabba, nor the numb-brained Fists of Rakka, nor any of my idiot fellow Mages." He whirled around, his waist-length black hair flying outward as of a twirling woman's skirt.

"What of the Jordians?"

Stopping his whirling gyre, "Oh, I have guaranteed they will be late to the dance," cried Nunde in joyous merriment. "And when and if they ever arrive, by then I will be master of this world, for when the High King falls, so does all of Mithgar."

"What of Driu?"

"That fool," sneered Nunde. "I remained at a remove and she saw me not. And even had she espied my aethyrial form, there is little she can do."

"But she's a Seer, my master."

Nunde ground his teeth at these unspoken inferences Radok was making. "My plan will surprise all, even Seers," he snarled.

Then he glanced at his bed, where a mutilated corpse lay. "Rid me of her"—Nunde took up a thin-bladed knife—"and send a fresh female. I would take my pleasure."

Radok sighed and spoke a <word> of command, and the corpse groaned upward and, trailing entrails, heaved itself from the bed. With the corpse shuffling after, Radok, a sour look upon his features, took his leave. Someday, yes, someday he would be giving the orders and taking his long-overdue pleasure as well, or so he surmised.

Behind him, Nunde thumbed the keen knife and looked at his retreating apprentice. He had been surprised at the ease with which Radok had animated the corpse. He would have to keep a sharp eye upon his lackey, else Radok might take it in his head to overthrow his master, just as Nunde had overthrown his own.

Troll Hole

grus are dreadful creatures: massive; ten to twelve feet tall; with bones like stone that not even the Ban affects, for, though Adon's light rends a Troll's flesh to dust, the bones lie undisturbed. An Ogru's hide is also like stone, and it turns ordinary missiles and blades aside. Yet Trolls are vulnerable in their eyes and mouth, can one pierce them when they are open or agape. Among other things, Ogrus fear fire and Magekind and drowning, this latter because the weight of their bones render swimming impossible, and they sink like rocks. They live in large Troll holes in the Gronfangs and the Riggas and other mountain ranges ... such as the Grimwalls, where the Jordian Legion now found itself. ...

DALAVAR CALLED THE COMMANDERS TOGETHER. When all had assembled, he said, "The way ahead is blocked by a massive rockslide. It was not natural, nor *Rûptish* set, but fell by an act of Magekind."

"Landslide?" said Röedr.

"Mage-set?" asked Valder.

But Ulrik said, "The question is: what do we do now?"

"Can we not ride over?" asked Captain Hann.

"The 'Wolves can pass," said Dalavar, "but not any horse. All would be lamed, or worse, in any attempt."

"What!" shouted Valder. "But we must! Else all is lost! And my son might be slain. Dalavar, tell me it is not so."

Dalavar simply shook his head and remained silent, and Valder slammed fist into palm, as tears of frustration and rage welled in his eyes.

"We've ten thousand men and thirty thousand horses," said Durgan. "Surely we can move enough rocks out of the way to press on."

Dalavar shook his head and said, "Mayhap in a sevenday or so, but by then we'd be too late."

"What of an alternate route?" asked Ulrik.

"I know of none," said Dalavar. "And to ride back to Darda Galion and take the Olorin ferry across to Darda Erynian and thence ride down to Pellar and cross the Argon back to Ellor, well, that, too, will take too long, as would a return to Crestan Pass."

"Then we are stymied," said Ulrik.

"Had we but first chosen to take the pass—" began Captain Hann, yet a soft voice cut him short. . . .

. . . And all eyes turned to that speaker. "There is another way," said Loric, "though perilous it might be."

"Say on," said Ulrik.

Loric nodded and said, "During the Retribution—"

"This 'Retribution,'" said Ulrik, "you speak of the time when the Lian went after the Spawn?"

"Aye," said Loric. "'Twas for the Felling of the Nine."

"Let the Alor speak unhindered," said Valder in agitation, desperation in his voice.

Ulrik inclined his head, and Loric said, "During the Retribution, I led a warband into this area. We raided Ruch lairs and Troll holes and other such foul places. And not far back from here, there is a Troll hole with two entrances"— Loric gestured at the steeps to the west—"one on this side of that sheer ridge, the other on the opposite. Should we pass through this Troll hole, we come out here." Loric stabbed a finger to Dalavar's sketch. "And thence we can fare along this way and finally reach the plains below."

"How long is the journey underground?" asked Valder, somewhat calmer, now that there might be a way forward.

"Mayhap a league," said Loric.

"A league in the dark?" asked Durgan.

"For the most," said Loric.

"And horses can pass?" asked Ulrik.

"Aye, 'tis a broad, water-cut cavern and I ween most of the way three or even more can go abreast."

A murmur whispered among the commanders, for though the Jordians interred their dead 'neath green turves, to go deep underground was like unto journeying into Hèl itself. Nay, open space and green grass was their domain, and faring far down in the earth was akin to a dreadful damnation.

"And the peril?" asked Ulrik.

"I know not whether the Troll hole is occupied," said Loric.

All eyes turned to Dalavar and he gestured toward the Draega and said, "We can determine that."

"If there is a Troll," said Durgan, "then it alone could lay waste to this army."

Loric shrugged. "When last we met a Troll in that hole, Black Galgor did it in."

Durgan frowned. "Black Galgor?"

"Tuon's spear," said Ulrik. "I handled it. A fine weapon with fine balance."

"We have spears," said Röedr.

"I ween not like Galgor," said Dalavar.

"Well," said Captain Hann, "if there is a Troll, won't the smell of our horses attract him? And if it does, then as the lad says, it alone can lay waste to the legion."

Durgan nodded and asked, "Should one be there, what will we do?"

"The best we can," said Valder in the ensuing silence.

Durgan turned to Dalavar. "What about fire? I mean, like you did last time."

"Illusory fire is no guarantee," said Dalavar.

"Even so," said Valder, "the High King needs us, as does the child of my loins."

A quietness fell among them, but finally Ulrik said, "It seems we have no choice."

AT ULRIK'S COMMAND, men fared up the eastern slopes where grew stands of scrub pine, and they hacked branches to act as torches for the ride through.

Dalavar and the Draega returned from their scouting trip to the passage and reported that Spawn dwelt therein. Partway through, a deep side-corridor seemed to be the Troll lair, perhaps recently occupied, but whether from an Ogru or from Rûcks and such, they could not say.

And it was yet dark when the Jordian legion stood ready, each man with two pack animals tethered behind.

But it was Dalavar and the 'Wolves who went first, while the riders waited. Moments passed and long moments more, and of a sudden there came a savage snarling and rending, and a shrill shrieking. Long it lasted, and then all grew quiet, and more long moments passed.

And then there sounded a distant bellowing, but it grew no closer nor faded away.

Just at dawn Shimmer appeared, and she turned to face the Troll hole once more, and she took a few steps and then glanced back over her shoulder.

"I think we must follow," said Loric.

"What of the roaring?" asked Ulrik.

"Dalavar would not have sent one of his Draega back but to lead us inward," said Loric.

"I'll go first," said Valder. "Follow me."

And into the Troll hole the legion fared, some men gritting their teeth in fear, for they remembered the old legends concerning the domain of Death into which heroes had gone and had never returned.

Elves rode among the men, in the hope that any Foul Folk within would remember the Retribution and flee upon the sight of the Lian.

Durgan lit his pine torch from the bonfire at the entry, and, following the battalion that rode before him, inward he went.

As promised by Loric, the cavern was wide, and Aksel rode with his charge, though it seemed that Durgan had the better courage in this instance.

Water yet dripped from overhead only to disappear through cracks in the floor, and the walls glistened with wet running down. Crevices yawned to either side, and things scuttled away from the torchlight to vanish in the dark, yet whether it was Spawn or something else, Durgan could not say.

But there was this: Rûcks and Hlôks lay slain along the route, rent apart by the savage fangs of the Draega, and this, too, gave the men pause.

And the horses were skittish as well, even Steel, for they smelled or sensed unseen danger. Yet the Elven horses stayed calm, and that seemed to aid those of the men.

And the way twisted and turned, and small passages wrenched away into the dark at either side. They plashed through puddles and streamlets, and clattered over dry rock beyond, only to come again to water along the way.

And from far ahead there came the dreadful roaring, and mounts shied and would have bolted but for tightly tied tethers and firm hands on the reins.

The farther they rode, the louder the bellowing roar, and as Durgan and Aksel rounded a turn, in the distance beyond riders before them they could see reflected upon one wall the light of a large fire burning.

And horses balked, and Men dismounted and led their steeds onward, the animals somewhat reassured by the sight of their trusted riders pulling them ahead, and by the sight of the spirited Elven horses walking in calm.

Durgan and Aksel, too, went afoot and tugged their mounts after, their tethered packhorses following.

At last they came to where the fire reflected, and there in a side passage stood Dalavar and four of the Draega, and a large blaze of greenish flames crackled and whooshed and burned just beyond. And far back in the deep passage whence came the bellows and well away from the fire, two reddish eyes gleamed some ten feet off the floor.

And then Durgan and Aksel were past, and the animals they towed picked up speed, just as did those before them. And so they mounted up once more and rode onward apace.

And still to one side or the other, *things* scuttled away, and words in a foul language slithered out from the dark.

Finally they spilled out into daylight, and Durgan said, "Illusory fire," and Aksel drew a circle about his heart and said, "Thank Elwydd for Dalavar."

Following Loric, the Legion rode southerly among the soaring peaks and crevices, and the land sloped gently down. And toward sunset, they came to the green grassy plains of Ellor.

It was well after dark when the final battalion arrived, and with it came King Ulrik and a pack of Silver Wolves.

AFTER CARING FOR THE HORSES, and then setting up camp and tending to his own needs, just before going to sleep, Durgan overheard Röedr say, "War? Why, war is simple."

"Oh?" said Loric, his voice, like that of the Iron Duke, carrying through the still night.

"Aye, Guardian," said Röedr. "In war you need only to find your enemy. Get at him as soon as you can. Strike at him as hard as you can and as often as you can and keep at him till he either surrenders or is dead."

"Such is belike to lose many warriors along the way," said Loric, "when there are other means to get the enemy to retire from the field."

"Oh, Guardian, and just what would those be?"

Durgan fell asleep ere hearing Loric's answer.

IN EARLY DAWN TIME, even as the horses were fed and watered and camp was breaking, Seeker and Longshank loped in among the Legion. The two found Dalavar and there ensued a conversation in Draega, and with postures and turns and growls and yips and whines they told Dalavar what they had seen.

"Reyer's army is at Gûnarring Gap," said Dalavar, "and as of yester Arkov's force faced them."

More Draega conversation ensued.

"Dark men make up most of Arkov's army," said Dalavar.

"Chabbains," growled Valder.

After another round of posturing, Dalavar said, "Arkov's army is a good deal larger than Reyer's."

"Do either have horses?" asked Röedr.

Moments later: "Aye, but not as many as the horses here."

Ulrik groaned and said, "They already face one another and we are—what?—fifty-five, sixty leagues away?"

"One hundred seventy-five miles from them," reckoned Durgan, glancing at Ulrik's map.

"Thereabout," said Valder.

"Do they fight yet?" asked Durgan, the pit of his stomach churning.

"They had not yet done so when Seeker and Longshank left," said Dalavar.

"That was yester," said Ulrik. "What of today?"

Dalavar closed his eyes and said a <word>. Moments later he said another. Then his eyes snapped open and he said, "We must ride, for today they battle."

"Today?" cried Valder.

"Aye."

"But we cannot ride one hundred seventy-five miles in an instant."

"But we can in a day," gritted Ulrik.

"How?" said Durgan. "—I mean, even Steel cannot do that."

"By using the packhorses as remounts," said Ulrik, "and riding through the night."

"Even doing that," said Röedr, " 'tis most likely we will arrive too late to save my grandson as well as the King."

Ulrik nodded but said, "Just as with the Troll hole, Duke Röedr, we have no other choice."

So it was that just as the risen sun shone through slots in the peaks, black-oxen horns and silver Elven trumps rang echoes off the nearby Gûnarring.

"Ride, Harlingar, ride!" cried Dalavar. "Warriors of the Larkenwald, ride! For e'en now the King engages in combat." Then, in a dark flash Mage Dalavar vanished and formidable Shifter appeared.

And, stringing unladen packhorses after, the Jordian legion and the Lian Guardians rode away at haste and out into the green grasslands of Ellor, Silver Wolves running ahead.

60

War

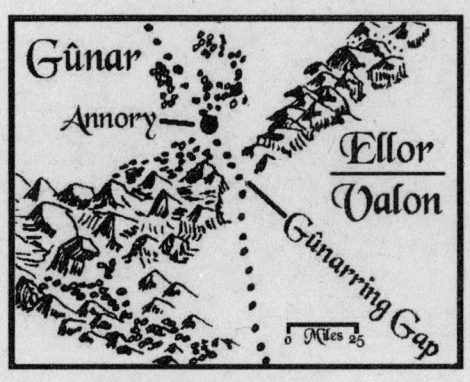

Glory you not in the slaughter of War, for, in victory or defeat, e'en should you survive, Death and Blood and the screams of the dying will surely follow you home. . . .

"Driu, what do you glimpse?" asked Conal.

The Seer looked up from the rune stones cast before her. "Bloodshed, disaster, and defeat, yet all is confusion. Some Dark Mage is blocking, even so I <see> ruin and devastation."

"Ruin and devastation?" asked Captain Windlow.

"Aye, but for whom, I cannot say. Were Dalavar here, he is powerful enough to break through the dark one's veil."

"And the Jordians?" asked Silverleaf.

"Those I cannot . . . cannot <see>," groaned Driu.

"My liege, forget these vague mumblings," said War Commander Raden. "This I do know: we must attack before the Chabbain reinforcements arrive."

"Attack?" Reyer looked at the Rian warrior.

"Aye, draw them into the Gap, where they cannot bring all of their force to bear, a place where we can rend them."

"I agree," said Aarnson, his gaze fixed upon Arkov's unmoving army. "Draw them in ere any more Chabbains can come."

"Can we lure them into the choke point?" asked Baron Fein. "Were it me standing yon, I would refuse the gauntlet."

"I deem they will follow if my Welleners ahorse assail their cavalry," said Viscount Axton. "We will strike and flee, and pull them after."

"Then we will close in upon their flanks and target their riders," said Windlow, the wee Warrow grinning.

"And their foot soldiers will follow?" asked Digby.

"If they would protect their cavalry, they will," said Axton.

"Their own archers are likely to assail thee, Lord Axton," said Silverleaf.

"Aye, Alor Vanidar, I expect they will," said the viscount, "yet if the Alliance sends a hail of arrows their way, mayhap we can strike and flee during the distraction."

"Let us not dilly-dally," said Raden. "Thirty thousand Chabbains are on their way, and will be here anon. Again I say, we must attack now before those reinforcements arrive."

"They will arrive regardless," said Reyer. "Yet can we slaughter enough of their countrymen, well, mayhap that will give them pause." He turned to Rader: "Have the men ready a barrage. Dara Riessa, Captain Windlow, get your archers into position to flank Arkov's cavalry, and, Captain Windlow, take Digby, Perry, Jame, and Jace with you, for every shaft must count."

"My liege, what about our charge to ward you?" said Digby. "I mean, if you get killed, then all is lost."

"For the nonce, Driu will remain back, and I will have a King's guard about me."

Digby looked at Driu, and she nodded her agreement.

"At last," said Perry, and Jame and Jace each clenched a fist in agreement.

Raden looked at the other commanders and said, "Ready the men, for things are like to become brutal." Then he turned to Reyer and said, "My lord, I would have you walk among them, for they need see the one they might die for."

At these words, Reyer's heart pounded and it seemed he could not get enough to breathe. And using Reyer's old name when he was but a lad, Conal said, "Rígán, they do need to see their King."

With that, Reyer's spine straightened and he nodded and said, "I would have you and Alric at my side."

"My lord," said Alric, "I would ride with the Welleners."

"Oh, but yes," said Reyer. "You must go with them."

"I will walk with thee in Alric's stead, King Reyer," said Dara Riessa, the Dylvana stepping forward.

"Will not your bow be with the Dylvana?" asked Reyer.

"Indeed it will be, yet there is enough time for me to walk with thee ere then, my lord," said Riessa.

And so, a High King and a Dylvana Dara walked among the men, the Dylvana smiling, and her beauty brought sighs into the breasts of fierce warriors. And as for the High King, by now all the men had heard of his pledge to them, and their own hearts lightened as he went among the army, bidding all that now was not the time to kneel, but to instead ask the gods and their own strong arms not only to protect them, but to lay their weapons upon the enemy in force. Men cheered at these words, and then returned their attention to their commanders who set forth the battle plan.

BY MIDMORN ALL WAS READY, and each man knew his role, and the Wellener cavalry eased along the ranks and to the side of the gap opposite Arkov's own horsemen.

And upon command, the Alliance released flight after flight of arrows, and they fell upon Arkov's army as would hail rain down upon wheat.

Foemen screamed as missiles struck home, and Reyer's forces moved forward, as even then came the return, enemy shafts falling upon the Alliance.

With Alric the Jordian in the lead with his sharp lance lowered, the Welleners charged, their horses thundering out at the enemy. And they hammered into the opposite cavalry ere the foe was ready, and lances slew. Horses fell screaming, taking men down with them, and a mighty clanging arose as sabers met tulwars. Blades struck flesh, and blood flew. Welleners died, as did Chabbains, and now the arrows were turned upon the riders of the Alliance, and more fell to the shafts.

With Arkov's men leaping toward them, the surviving Welleners turned and fled, dark horses in pursuit, and a roar went up from the Chabbains, and Arkov's army surged after.

Back fell the Alliance, into the Gap, and the Wellener horses raced into the slot after, Alric riding last. The Alliance parted to let them through and then closed behind. Then came the cavalry of Arkov's army, enraged at the sudden strike, and as they, too, sped into the Gap, Warrows and Dylvana leapt up from concealment and loosed arrows upon them. And Warrows and Elves were deadly, each shaft felling a man. And in the slaughter Arkov's cavalry turned to flee, but their own army pushed them inward, to fall to spears and swords and flying shafts, and few if any survived the onslaught.

And then the two armies raged into one another, and swords and hand axes hacked and slew. Daggers stabbed and maces smashed and Men fell screaming, wounded and dying.

To left and right and to the fore and behind Reyer his kingsguards fought. Yet still the numberless foe bore down upon them, and many broke through the ring. Reyer's sword licked out like a steel tongue upon the foe, and left naught but slain men after. At his right, Conal kicked a Garian in the groin as he pulled his blade free of a Chabbain, and then his own edge sliced and reaved and hacked, meting out destruction in its wake. On Reyer's left Aarnson bashed down a Fist of Rakka and stomped on his neck, breaking it, and then he wove steel upon other foe, fending strikes at Reyer, while at the same time dealing death. Blood flew wide in this brutal craft; guts spilled, releasing their loads; screaming throats chopped short their shrieks as blades slashed through; bones broke, shattered by morning stars and maces; and all was accompanied by the shouts and curses and cries of men fighting for their very lives.

And the Alliance was driven back and back, taking a dreadful toll on the enemy for every foot yielded. Yet for every foe slain, two stepped into the gap, and the Alliance gave way, leaving their own dead and dying behind.

"They are too many," cried Conal. "Reyer, you must flee, while the rest of us fight a rear guard for you."

"No!" cried Reyer, fending a tulwar blow and counter striking to bring down a Fist of Rakka, and then he backhanded the pommel of his sword to smash into the face of an Albaner. "I promised the men I would live or die with them, and I'll not break that oath." And with blood flying,

Reyer and Conal and Aarnson fought on, kicking, bashing, stabbing, hammering, cutting, and falling back and back and ever back.

And upon the slopes above, running and stopping and loosing arrows, only to run again, across the hillsides Warrows and Elves fell back with the Alliance, Vanidar with his silver-handled white-bone bow singing a deadly tune, as did sing those of the other archers.

Though the Alliance gave as good as it got, and perhaps even better, still Arkov's men pressed inward, their numbers clearly yielding them the dominant hand, as deeper into the choke point they drove and slew and were slain.

And the battle raged for a seeming eternity, though it was but a candlemark or less; yet then, of a sudden, horns sounded. And the Southers hearkened to the call. As if it were a signal they had been expecting, the Chabbains and the Fists of Rakka and the men of Thyra and Hurn withdrew, leaving naught but the men of Garia and Alban behind to fall by the numbers, ere they turned and fled after.

Wounded and bloody and somewhat stunned, the men of Reyer's army gaped after Arkov's retreating forces. The Alliance had been thoroughly beaten, yet somehow they had been given a reprieve.

And still the horns sounded, and marching into view came the thirty thousand Chabbains.

"What th—?" Digby began.

"Come back, you bloody scuts!" shouted Perry, winging a futile arrow after.

"Waste not thy shafts, Wee One," said Aliser. "I fear on the morrow thou wilt need even more than thou didst spend today."

Perry shook his head and gritted, "There's plenty more out there." He pointed at the fallen, many with arrows jutting. "We only need to retrieve them and trim them to size."

"It APPEARS ARKOV IS RAGING," said Silverleaf, his sharp Elven gaze locked upon the enemy camp.

Reyer, Vanidar Silverleaf, Conal, Perry, and Digby stood upon the southern slopes of the Gap. Down below, men, some of them weeping, others retching, and yet still others silent and grim, hauled away their dead. As well, Alliance warriors dragged slain enemy off to the sides, making a barrier of them up on the flanks. At the rear of the army, the wounded were being cared for, Riessa and the bulk of the Dylvana aiding in that chore.

Reyer looked at Silverleaf. "Arkov, you say?"

"I am certain he is the one raging," said Vanidar. "He wears a crown and has the High King's standard at hand: Golden Griffin upon scarlet."

"Thieving dastard!" snarled Perry. "That's your sigil, King Reyer."

"Remember, Perry," said Digby. "Arkov is a usurper, so naturally he would—"

"I said," snarled Perry, "that's Reyer's sigil."

Digby fell silent.

"I suspect Arkov is raging at the Chabbains' withdrawal when we were all but conquered," said Conal.

War Commander Rader came trudging up to the hill where Reyer and his comrades stood.

"Twenty thousand, about," said Raden.

"Ours or theirs?" asked Conal.

"Ours: dead and wounded."

"And theirs?"

"Some thirty thousand, now all dead, though, no doubt, some of their wounded made it back to their lines."

"Three to two, eh?" said Digby.

Reyer nodded. "Three to two. Still that still leaves us outnumbered: with their reinforcements replacing their slain, they are again at ninety thousand, whereas we now have but forty."

"Oh," said Digby, his face falling. Then he brightened and said, "But, if as the commander says, some of them who retreated were wounded, that cuts the odds down a bit."

"That would still leave us woefully outnumbered," said Conal.

Raden sighed and said, "Much as I hate to say it, my lord, we should withdraw in the night. Live to fight another day."

"Even should we withdraw," said Reyer, "Arkov will pursue, and we will yet be outnumbered."

"But not outmanned," said Raden.

"Ahem," said Digby, adding, "nor out-Warrowed or out-Elved, either."

Conal smiled, then said, "King Reyer is correct. No matter our decision—stand or withdraw—Arkov will come at us again."

"Then let us fight here and now," said Rader, "where we have a choke point. If we are to die, we'll take many down with us."

"What if I meet Arkov in single combat?" asked Reyer.

"I think he will not take up the gauntlet," said Conal.

"Then I and I alone can surrender, gaining the men of the Alliance their freedom."

Following a chorus of protests, Conal said, "Again, I think Arkov will refuse. He clearly has the upper hand."

"Besides," said Raden, "he would not have the rest of us set free to plot his overthrow."

"You may be right, Commander, still I can but try," said Reyer.

Warrow and elven scouts slipped through the dark, ready to warn the Alliance should aught occur in the night, whether Reyer decided to offer single combat or to surrender or to stand and fight.

But at the mid of night, there came a great stirring among the enemy.

In moments the screaming began.

"What th—?" hissed Digby, out on the southern flank of the foe.

"Let's move closer," said Perry, and he and Digby crept through the tall grass until they were all but in the enemy camp.

Steel skirled on steel, and shouts rang through the night.

"They are fighting among themselves," said Digby.

Horses hammered away in the dark, running easterly.

"Look," hissed Perry, and by the firelight they saw a

Chabbain throw down the griffin standard, and raise the one of Chabba in its stead.

Now the buccan could see dark men dragging corpses toward the fringes, and Digby and Perry slipped hindward as foe came their way.

In a candlemark or two, dead bodies lay everywhere, and in the camp the Askars of Chabba and the Saranian Fists of Rakka and their allies from Thyra and Hurn celebrated.

"THEY KILLED ALL OF ARKOV'S MEN," said Digby.

"Aye," agreed Riessa. "The men of Alban and Garia: all murdered."

"Some of the Southers were killed as well," said Jem.

"How many, think you?" asked Conal. "Total dead, I mean."

"By our count, at least fifteen thousand Garian and Albaners," said Captain Windlow. "Nearly all of their throats were cut."

"Slain in their sleep," said Conal.

"Then this was planned," said Reyer.

"Aye," said Silverleaf.

"Yet, why?" asked Raden.

"Perhaps they covet the High King's throne for themselves," said Riessa.

"Souther treachery," said Windlow.

"I add," said Aliser, "some five thousand others of theirs also lie dead. Mayhap from the fights during the treachery, mayhap from wounds taken in the battle today."

"Then that leaves, um, something like seventy thousand enemy on the field, should we meet them tomorrow in battle," said Alric.

"What of Arkov?" asked Reyer.

"We know not," said Riessa.

"Mayhap he escaped the slaughter," said Digby.

Frowning, Perry looked at Digby.

"Remember, Perry, we heard horses gallop away to the east."

"If he is gone, I cannot challenge him to single combat," said Reyer.

"Bah," growled Raden. "With this skulking overthrow, it would have been meaningless regardless."

"I think, then, we must meet them in battle," said Alric.

"I say, let's do it," urged Perry.

"Forty thousand of us against seventy thousand of them," said Reyer.

"We yet hold the Gap," said Riessa.

"And we still have a cavalry," said Axton, "whereas they do not."

"Four thousand horse," said Reyer.

"There is this," said Silverleaf. "In past wars, when the Chabbains lost most or all their jemedars, they also lost heart. Can we slay them—the jemedars—the Askars might throw down their arms."

"Jemedars?" asked Perry.

"Their commanders," said Conal.

" 'Tis a gamble," said Aliser.

"How will we know which are the jemedars?" asked Digby.

"We need to know where to aim," added Perry. "Which ones to kill."

"I ken their ilk," said Silverleaf.

"And I will also point them out," said Driu. "I might be blocked from <seeing> what is to come, yet I ween I will not be hampered in <seeing> those who lead the foe."

All eyes turned to Reyer, and Conal said, " 'Tis yours to choose, my King."

Reyer stared at the ground and pondered long moments, while none said aught. Finally, he looked up and said, "As Sir Perry says, let's do it."

"Art thou certain?" asked Riessa.

Reyer glanced at Alric and said, "As my blood-sworn brother would remind us, there is an old Jordian saying: Lady Fortune favors the bold."

"Yes!" said Alric, clenching a fist.

And so it was that the High King's army did not withdraw that eve. Instead, facing daunting odds and chancing all in a desperate gamble, they remained at Gûnarring Gap.

*   *   *

DAWN CAME.

The sun rose.

In Gûnarring Gap, the Alliance stood ready, the ranks arrayed in battle order, with Raden to the fore on this day. Concealed behind, Viscount Axton and the cavalry cinched saddles and checked lances, Alric among them.

King Reyer and Dara Riessa strode among the men, bucking up their spirits, while at the same time assuring them that come what may, they had been noble in their cause. Conal, trailing in their wake, said, "This day will be remembered through all time, and to your children and grandchildren you will say of this day, 'I was there.'"

Up on the hillsides, archers waited to target the jemedars, Driu on the southern slopes with a number of the Dylvana and Perry and Digby and Squad-leader Jem's half of Captain Windlow's Warrow band. On the opposite slopes stood Billy's half of the Warrows along with the remaining Dylvana, with Silverleaf to direct their arrows; he, too, could tell them which of the foe were the commanders to target, for in the past he had battled their like.

Out before them and in their own camp the Chabbains, Saranians, Thyrans, and Hurnians stood, their numbers far in excess of those of the Alliance. And they jeered and capered, for they knew they would take the day.

"Come on, you slime," gritted Perry, glancing their way as he reset an arrow point. "Come taste death."

As did most of the Warrows, both Perry and Digby sat with their backs to a boulder and trimmed the recovered arrows to length and refitted the heads and fletched as needed.

And they, along with the rest of the Alliance, waited for the battle to begin.

Finally, one of the Chabbains rode to the fore. He raised a scimitar, and one of their twisted animal horns sounded a long drawn-out note. With that signal his troops stopped capering, and they all faced forward and stood ready.

"There's my first target," said Perry.

"The one in the lead?" asked Digby.

"Right, bucco."

"Well, I'll wager I feather him before you do," said Digby.

"You're on, Diggs," said Perry, grinning.

Yet both continued trimming and fitting and fletching.

And the Chabbain sidled his horse 'round and looked at his ranks, then he turned once more to face the Alliance. And he slashed his curved blade down.

Horns yawled, and men shouted, and the enemy charged. . . .

And the Alliance ranks parted, and Axton's cavalry thundered through, Alric in the fore.

"Which are the jemedars?" called Captain Windlow, as the enemy came on.

Driu said a <word>, and it seemed her very eyes became all white. And she pointed, and cried, "There, and there, and there." And Warrows and Dylvana, now on their feet, strung arrows and stood ready, waiting for their targets to come within range.

"Barn rats!" shouted Perry. "Barn rats!"

"What?" cried Digby.

"Look!" Perry pointed. . . .

. . . And Digby's gaze followed Perry's outstretched arm just in time to see . . .

. . . Alric's lance pierce into and through the Chabbain on the horse.

"He took my target," growled Perry.

"Mine, too," said Digby, even as Viscount Axton's cavalry plowed into the lead ranks, "but I don't begrudge it."

They were quickly surrounded, but they hacked their way free and out to the side, even as the bulk of the enemy flowed onward like a rushing tide.

The front ranks of the Alliance threw up their shields, and yet, with a mighty crash, the Askars and Fists and Thyrans and Hurnians slammed into the front line and drove them hindward.

The main body of the foemen pushed forward, and arrows sissed from the hillsides, and jemedars fell. Yet shafts flew in return, and both the Dylvana and the Waerlinga took dreadful wounds, and Jem and Captain Windlow fell slain.

Of a sudden, Digby cried, "Perry! Perry! Alric is down!" and he took off at a run.

Out in the grass just beyond the edge of the Gap, Alric's horse lay slain, and Alric, an arrow jutting up from his chest, struggled to regain his feet but fell back, floundering, even as several of the Fists of Rakka took note of the fallen lad.

Perry and Digby were in a flat run toward Alric, and, even though dashing, they loosed arrows, some finding their mark, and they drove the Fists back.

Yet Hurnians and Thyrans rallied, and started for Alric as well, just as Digby and Perry reached his side.

"Barn rats, but I think we're in trouble," shouted Perry, loosing shafts at the oncoming foe.

Digby knelt beside the youth. "He has swooned," said Digby. "But he yet breathes."

Digby then leapt to his feet and joined Perry in loosing deadly arrows. Yet even more turned their way and, shouting oaths, charged.

"Come on!" shouted Perry. "You Gyphon-sucking stinking piles of—"

Of a sudden, the onrushers shrieked and bolted hindward.

"What th—?" said Digby, just as . . .

. . . *"Châkka shok! Châkka cor!"* Four thousand armed and armored Dwarves thundered past and, axes dealing death, charged into the foe, even as . . .

. . . Rounding the shoulder of a hill, from the north ten thousand black-oxen horns called upon weary steeds to give their uttermost in a noble charge, and proud horses responded, for they were Jordians all. Silver horns rang, too, Elven horses answering the call. Thus did they arrive in the nick: King Ulrik and ten thousand Vanadurin and five hundred Lian, and Durgan on Steel, spears leveled, sabers clutched, thundering death . . .

. . . With seven Silver Wolves leading the charge.

Caught between the hammer of the Harlingar on one flank, and the anvil of the Châkka on the other, and 'twixt the surge of the remnants of the Northern Alliance to the fore and the Lian Guardians of Darda Galion to the rear along with the survivors of Viscount Axton's Wellener cavalry, and with seven snarling, slashing Silver Wolves midst all, the Chabbains knew not which way to turn. And horses ripped through, trampling dark warriors underfoot, spearlances impaling and sabers cleaving, while Châkka double-bitted axes hewed, and Warrow and Dylvana shafts pierced, even as Elven swords rived and savage 'Wolves rent flesh, and Alliance men afoot shouted "King Reyer! King Reyer!" their own blades hacking and maces bashing as they charged among the panicked Chabbains, stabbing, felling, slaying.

And assailed from all sides and with nearly all their jemedars slain, the Askars and Thyrans and Hurnians threw down their arms and surrendered, but the fanatical Saranian Fists of Rakka did not and were slain to the very last man.

61

Wrath

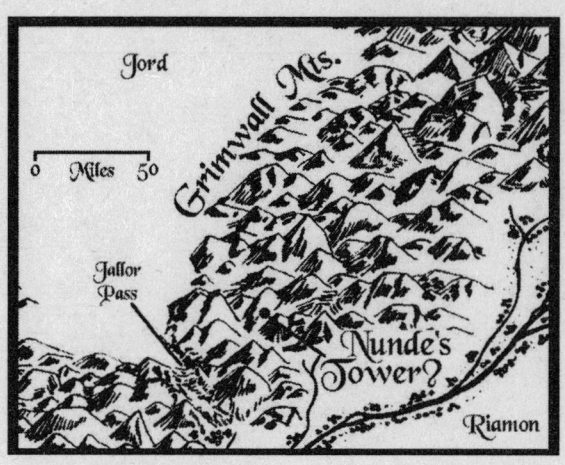

In a concealed tower high in the Grimwalls nigh Jallor Pass ...

... RADOK TREMBLED IN HIS dark hiding place, not chancing even a visit to the pits to relieve his bladder and bowels. Instead he voided them in the small chamber where he cowered ... and he waited; how long it might be he knew not. His master slew and slew, and had done so ever since his aethyrial visit of the night. Just ere the flight, his mood had been one of gaiety, and he chortled in glee, for his splendid plan, no doubt, had come to completion that very day. But upon his return his wrath seemed unbound, and Radok had taken to his heels and had hidden away. What had happened, he did not know, but whatever it was Radok did not wish to be accidentally caught in the rage. His master tended to kill messengers of ill news, and even though Radok had no ill message to convey, still some dreadful event must have occurred. Nay, Radok would not be caught in his master's blind fury, as hapless Chun most certainly were. And so Radok trembled and hid in the tiny closet and squirmed in his own urine and feces ...

... while Nunde slew and slew.

Reckoning

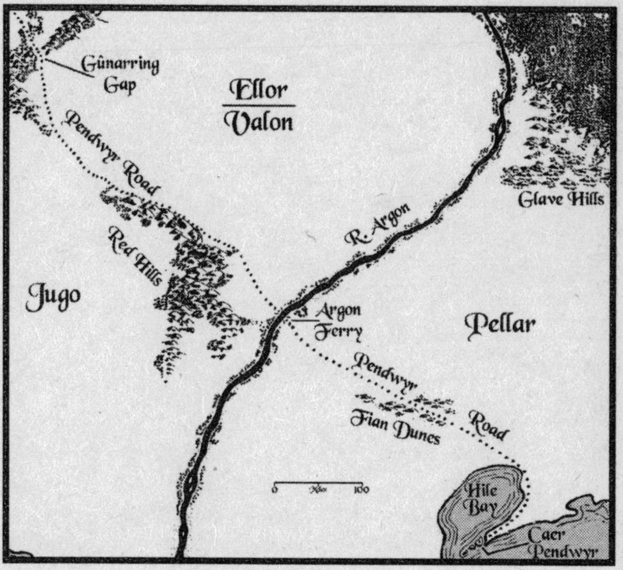

The consequences of war are quite dreadful: treasure spent; property destroyed; lives lost; warriors forever maimed in body, mind, spirit, heart—one or more or all. But perhaps the most profound damage occurs to those not directly involved in combat, for wars produce widows and orphans and bereaved sweethearts and lovers and kindred, and for every warrior slain there are many left behind who must grapple with inconsolable grief and with living a life bereft. And given the total number killed in a war, the entirety of those with grieving hearts is enormous.

And in the battle fought at Gûnarring Gap . . .

". . . SEVENTEEN WARROWS, five Dylvana, thirty thousand Alliance men, two Lian, and ninety-seven Jordians are fallen.

"Among the enemy, thirty thousand Garians and Albaners are dead—fifteen thousand in battle, fifteen thousand murdered—along with just under fifty thousand Southers.

"No Châkka were slain, though some took minor wounds. I take that as proof of the merit of the black-iron armor as well as to the proof of the excellence of the Châkka in combat.

"And of Arkov, there is no sign."

"What of the wounded?" asked Reyer, his head bandaged where he had taken a cut.

Aarnson, now War Commander, replacing Lord Raden, who had been slain in the second battle, looked at his list and said, "Eight thousand Alliance warriors took damage— light to severe—while nine hundred Jordians—including Alric—took harm. As to the Southers—"

"I am not concerned with the Southers," said Reyer.

"My King," said Conal, "you might not be concerned with how many are wounded or slain, but you need to decide what to do with those who survived, those who are now our prisoners."

"And there are some forty thousand in all," said Aarnson.

"Have them bury the dead—Alliance first—in the plains of Ellor," said Reyer. "Make certain that any surviving jemedars and other commanders of theirs work beside their soldiers. After which, I will pronounce verdict upon them all."

"My lord," said Silverleaf, "the Waerlinga and the Dylvana will wish for pyres."

"As you will, Alor Silverleaf," said Reyer. Then he turned to King Ulrik.

"My slain Vanadurin," said King Ulrik, "must of needs be buried 'neath green turves in a common mound, for they fought together and died together and shall be buried together, wearing their arms and armor as well as having the arms and armor of the foe they slew lying at their feet. — My own men and I will see to that."

Reyer nodded.

"And I would have the slain enemy buried far away from the Harlingar mound," added Ulrik.

"Were it mine to do, King Ulrik, they would not e'en lie in the soil of Mithgar," said Reyer. Then he sighed and added, "But we must clean up these grounds."

He looked off to where the battles had occurred, where gorcrows and ravens and kites and other carrion-eaters gorged upon the fallen, rising up scrawking in dark milling clouds when disturbed, only to settle down once more to the feast, where they tossed torn-away dangling gobbets of meat down ravenous, bottomless craws.

Then Reyer stood and said, "And now, my lords, if you will forgive me, I will see to my brother, Alric."

"I would go with you as well," said Ulrik.

Together, they strode toward the hospital grounds.

North and a goodly distance upwind and away from the smell of blood and gore and slaughter on the battlefield, horses, weary and hungry, grazed upon the lush green grass of Ellor. Mounts and remounts, Jordian and Elven, they had run long and hard, and had covered just under sixty leagues—or as Durgan would have it, one hundred seventy-five miles—from one morn to the following. An incredible ride, all told ... improbable, many would say; impossible, would say others. But now these noble steeds fared on rich and grain-headed grass and drank of the cool waters of nearby streams running down from the tors of the Gûnarring.

"Elwydd!" exclaimed Ulrik, upon approaching Röedr and Valder and Alric, "but he is the spitting image."

Valder grinned but Röedr said, "All but his eyes. They belong to my Gretta."

Alric, wincing, sat up and said, "King Reyer, I present my sire, Prince Valder, and my grandsire, Duke Röedr."

And although they had already met in the field, Reyer inclined his head as both men stood and bowed.

Then Alric turned and gestured for Conal to come, and when he arrived, he added, "And I also present my Da, Captain Conal of King Valen's court."

And both Jordians clasped Conal's hand and Duke Röedr said, "Thank you, Captain Conal, for raising such a splendid young man."

"All of my lads, all of my sons, whether sired by me or not, are splendid men—Reyer, Alric, and Durgan, as well as Cuán, who is not here." Then he turned to Alric and said, "How is that hard noggin of yours?"

"My headache is almost gone, Da. I don't know what I hit it upon when Runner fell, but hit it I did. Knocked me into next sevenday."

"And your chest?"

"The leather and chain took most of the hurt, but enough was left over."

"And here come the two who saved your ratty hide," said Reyer, gesturing for Perry and Digby to approach.

After they were introduced, Perry said, " 'Twasn't us who saved Alric, but—"

"Ahem, Perry," said Digby, "but it's Lord Alric, I understand."

"Prince, lord, or just a giddy youth," snapped Perry, "no matter—"

"Giddy youth?" sputtered Alric.

But Reyer roared, and Valder joined him, as well as did Ulrik and Conal, and Ulrik said, "Giddy youth: that seems to fit his sire, too."

"Like sire, like son," said Valder, and his face split with a wide grin.

"Ahem, if I might have your attention," said Perry, "it was the Dwarves who saved Alric, and me and Diggs, too."

FUNERALS WERE HELD, and Men and Elves and Warrows wept, yet all understood that death was a dreadful cost of war. Riessa sang them into the sky, including the slain Southers.

In all it took a tenday to deal with the dead and the burials. During this time, feeding upon rich grasses and drinking pure water, the horses of the Jordians and of Elvenkind rested and recovered.

As to the foe, Reyer sentenced all the jemedars and other commanders to hang by the neck until dead. And the common foot soldiers among them were exiled from Reyer's realms forever.

He sent the wounded of the Alliance on their way home, escorted by hale and fit countrymen. As to the remainder of his Alliance army, he ordered them to march the prisoners down through Jugo and to Arbalin Isle, where they were to commandeer ships and sail them to the shores of Chabba. There the prisoners were to be offladed upon the beaches to fend for themselves. In this task, the Raudhöll Châkka asked to accompany the march. "It will be good to see them gone from this land," growled Regga. "Delek has asked to go with them, as have others, in the hopes that the prisoners take it in their heads to rebel. I am of a mind to send them. They seem to fear us."

"Imagine that," said Digby, and he broke into laughter.

Reyer and the Jordians and the Elves and Warrows and a number of other Men, along with Driu and Dalavar and Draega and a smattering of Châkka, then set out for Caer Pendwyr in the hopes they would find Usurper Arkov there.

* * *

IT TOOK BUT FIFTEEN days for this army to reach West Bank on the River Argon, where another four days were spent in ferrying horses and riders across to East Bank. They rode onward, and some twelve days after, the outriders reported that distant scouts were tracking their progress.

"Make no move against them," said Reyer. "I would have Arkov know I am coming."

And onward they rode, shadowed by others, for a two-day more.

Thus it was that a fortnight after leaving the Argon, they came into sight of the city of Caer Pendwyr, where outside the first and easternmost defensive wall, a heavily timbered palisade, stood an army across the way.

Röedr threw up a hand, and the legion came to a stand-still.

Somewhat back in the ranks, Digby groaned. "I thought we had beaten them all."

"Ready your bow, bucco," said Perry, pulling his own from its saddle scabbard.

Yet as the buccen strung their weapons, a rider broke away from the distant army, even as a wide central gate in the palisades swung open and driven waggons and carts and people afoot came streaming out, each pausing only long enough for the army to pass them through.

The rider, though, continued galloping toward Reyer's army.

Durgan, bearing the High King's standard, broke away and rode forward to meet the oncoming rider.

Out some distance, they met. And after but a moment, Durgan turned Steel about, and he and the rider both galloped toward the legion.

Digby and Perry, bows strung, arrows nocked, moved to flank Reyer, for they yet were charged with his protection.

"Mayhap they send a messenger to ask for parley," said Alric, at hand.

But Driu smiled and said, "See the tabard the messenger wears?"

Alric frowned and said, "A silver circle on a field of

blue? Wait, I remember my mother's lessons in heraldry. Riamon, right?"

"Aye," said Driu. "It represents the ring of the Rimmen Mountains, the singular feature of Riamon."

"Why would they be siding with Arkov?" said Alric.

"Wait, my boy," said Valder, now also grinning widely.

The messenger haled his steed up short before Reyer, and leapt to the ground and knelt. "My King."

"Rise," said Reyer.

"The lords of Riamon and Aven bid you welcome. We have conquered the Garians occupying our lands, and would join you in the overthrow of Arkov the Usurper."

"What?" said Perry.

"Shh!" hissed Digby, relaxing his draw.

"We have been waiting, my King," said the messenger. "Our scouts reported your progress."

"That's who they were," said Alric.

"And the city?" asked Reyer.

"Even now we allow the citizens to evacuate," said the messenger, "for neither King Ian nor King Galar would wreak destruction upon the innocent."

Röedr growled and said, "I would not have the Usurper in disguise sneak away among them."

"We inspect each and every one," said the messenger.

"You examine the carts and waggons for false bottoms?" asked Röedr.

"Aye, my lord. And we make certain none are hidden among bales and—"

There came a shouting from among the distant army.

"See to that," said Reyer, glancing at Alric.

"Gladly!" said Alric, and he spurred his horse forward, with Valder and a group of Jordians galloping after to catch up.

"I AM NO ONE, my King," quavered the man on his knees, cowering, bowing and scraping, mumbling to the ground.

"No one? Hiding in a waggon among carpets?" said Alric.

"Let me see his face," demanded Galar, King of Aven.

A soldier grabbed a handful of stringy pale hair and jerked the man's head upright.

"As I thought," spat Galar. "I recognize this rat from days bygone: 'tis Baloff, Arkov's prime counselor."

"No, I am just a poor—"

"Deny it not!" shouted Galar. Then he turned to Reyer. "My liege, I say we put him to the sword."

Reyer held up a hand of abeyance, and, without taking his gaze from the coward, he said, "Lie to me not: you are Baloff?"

The man's "Yes" came out as a squeal, and weeping, the man blubbered, "I counseled him against war, truly I did, yet he was determined to take the crown."

"Where then is Arkov?" demanded Reyer.

"Where he has been ever since he returned," wailed Baloff. "Sitting on the throne. I said we should flee, but he would not, and now it is too late."

"Right," said Perry.

"Hush," said Digby.

Reyer turned to Captain Hann and said, "Manacle him. I will deal with his ilk later."

"My lord, we have no manacles," said Hann, smiling grimly, "yet we will truss him up tightly until we come upon some."

Reyer nodded, then turned to Galar and Ian and Duke Röedr and said, "As soon as the city is emptied, we will enter. Until then, have all of our men examine those leaving. As you said, Lord Röedr, I, too, would not have Arkov slip away."

TWO DAYS LATER, into the city rode Reyer's legion, and now with the Avenians and the Riamonians added to their ranks they were some twenty-eight thousand strong.

As planned, several hundred warriors stopped inside the gate and closed it and stood ward to make certain that none else from within could leave.

The streets were empty of all but the wind blowing swirls of dust before it. Now and again, a face would peer out from behind a curtain or doorway and look on in silence, and men would stop and make certain whoever it might be was of no immediate interest to the legion.

And on they rode, through the subsequent gates set within the defensive walls of the town—four walls altogether—counting the easternmost wooden palisade with its wooden gate—followed by three more of heavy stone with iron gates set therein.

At last they reached the tip of the headland, and, level with the eye, just beyond stood three broad and tall stone spires towering up from the Avagon Sea far below; perhaps they were once part of the headland, but no more. A swing bridge gave access from the headland to the first spire, and one would have to cross a rope-and-board span to go from the first to the second, and again from the second to the third.

And upon the first spire loomed castellated stone walls surrounding the High King's palace.

"My liege," said Röedr, "I suspect treachery, for the swing bridge to the spire is deployed, and the gates beyond are open. Mayhap the bridge is rigged to fall once we set foot upon it. I will send some to see."

"I will go myself," said Reyer.

"Nay, my lord," said Captain Hann, leaping down.

But before Reyer could say otherwise, Conal said, "Rígán, you must let us do our duty to you."

Then Conal dismounted and followed Hann, even as Reyer said, "Da, don't—"

"Let him," said Driu, and Reyer fell silent.

FINALLY, BOTH CONAL AND HANN signaled that all seemed right, and Röedr himself and a warband of Jordians rode across and through the gate and onto the palace grounds while Reyer waited. Long moments passed and long moments more ere the Iron Duke returned and declared it safe enough for Reyer and the others to enter.

UP THE STEPS AND into the palace they strode, past the great bronze portal to come to the outer chamber, there where Valen had fallen. With Reyer in the lead, and Digby and Perry at his side, through halls they pressed until they came to the high-vaulted Chamber of State. And at the far end and upon a stone dais Arkov sat upon the throne, the crown of the High King of Mithgar gracing his brow.

Reyer stopped and held up a hand and said, "Stay."

The warband with him hesitated, and Silverleaf said, "Art thou certain, King Reyer?"

"I am," said Reyer, then he started forward, and both Digby and Perry started with him. And Reyer paused and said, "Not this time, my friends. This I must do alone."

Perry ground his teeth in frustration, and tears filled Digby's eyes.

Driu said, "It is his right, Wee Ones."

DelfLord Regga nodded his agreement.

"But I can spit him from here," said Perry.

"Nevertheless," said Dalavar.

And as Alric clenched his jaw and shifted his lance from hand to hand, Conal said, "Go, Rígán."

And Reyer smiled at his "Da," then turned and strode toward the dais.

At the foot of the steps leading up to the throne, Reyer paused and said, "You have something of mine, Usurper."

Arkov sneered and said, "And what might that be, Pretender?"

"My father's crown, and now mine."

"It was never his by right," said Arkov.

"You lie, Usurper."

"Do not call me that, *boy*."

Reyer drew his sword and said, "Since you will not yield to me that which is mine—"

"You?" sneered Arkov. "A mere child? You would dare combat with me?"

Reyer circled the tip of his blade and said, "Dying by my hand is better than being gutted, quartered, and hanged in chains."

Arkov stood and smiled and said, "We will see which of us dies at the other's hand, *boy*."

And Arkov drew his own blade while at the same time he reached up to remove the crown, which he threw at Reyer even as he leapt toward the youth.

Reyer ducked the throw, and but barely got his own blade up to fend Arkov's strike.

Heavier and stronger than Reyer, Arkov battered the youth back and back, Reyer fighting a defensive battle, Arkov charging.

And as Arkov hammered against Reyer's guard, Perry raised his bow, but Silverleaf pressed a hand down upon the buccan's arm.

Both Regga and Riessa looked on in silence, but a darkness came upon Dalavar, and Shifter stood where he had been. And the 'Wolf snarled, its savage gaze locked upon the two in the duel, but Shifter did not advance. Even so, his intention was clear, should Reyer be defeated.

And Arkov continued to batter at Reyer, yet the Garian's blade could not penetrate the lad's defense, Reyer's parries too quick, and so Arkov stepped back and, sneering, invited Reyer to engage. Stepping forward, Reyer took up the challenge, and steel skirled against steel as the two circled in a deadly dance, striking, lunging, parrying, deflecting, and youth was on Reyer's side.

Of a sudden, Arkov leapt forward and grappled with Reyer. Using his bulk, Arkov drove Reyer hindward and hindward, across the wide floor hindward.

Gripping his spear, Alric took a step forward, but Valder laid a hand on his shoulder and Alric stopped.

And just ere Arkov smashed the youth against a wall, Reyer seemed to stiffen, to rally, and he slowed and then stopped Arkov's charge. Gasping for air, the Usurper freed his right hand and hammered a hilt-gripping fist into the lad, aiming for his face, but Reyer deflected the blow, catching it on his left shoulder instead. Reyer countered with a knee to the groin, yet Arkov twisted, his thigh taking the strike.

Reyer shoved Arkov away and riposted a cut, Reyer's blade stabbing into Arkov's free arm, even as Arkov's own blade sheared across Reyer's chest, but it drew no blood, striking naught but Reyer's leather and chain.

Arkov began to flag, and Reyer's youth and quickness and Armsmaster Halon's Dylvana training began to show, as Reyer fended and struck and riposted and drew blood with cut after cut as he dodged Arkov's increasingly desperate and futile strikes. Now it was Arkov who was driven back and back, until he finally stumbled hindward against the steps to the throne.

And then with a flourish, Reyer engaged Arkov's sword, Reyer's blade sliding down Arkov's own steel, and with a stab in the Usurper's wrist, Arkov's blade clanged to the floor.

Reyer stepped back and away and said, "Here is my judgment, Usurper: I shall not slay you out of hand, but instead in the city square you will be drawn, quartered, and hanged in chains."

Panting, sweat running down his face, Arkov snarled, "Never!" And, screaming, he lunged for his weapon and snatched it up, and reversed it and fell upon his own sword, the blade stabbing through, cleaving his spine in twain, and he fell stone dead to the floor.

Crying, weeping, Perry and Digby rushed forward, as did they all, and even as Reyer turned away from the body, Conal embraced him and, tears running down his face, said, "Rígán," even as Reyer wept and said, "Da."

Aftermath

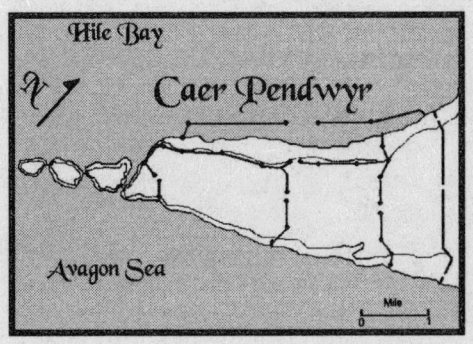

Stories might seem to end but in truth never do, for any given event simply leads to the next in an endless string. And the world turns and disasters occur and people come and go. This seems especially true in the World of Mithgar, where ...

AMID GREAT CELEBRATIONS among the returned citizens of Caer Pendwyr, in pomp and circumstance, and with representatives from most of the nations in his realms, Reyer publicly ascended to the throne. And the representatives knelt before their newly crowned King and swore their nations' fealty to him.

He was now officially recognized by all as the true and rightful heir who had finally taken lawful command.

And his justice was swift—deadly for some—especially for those who surrounded Arkov and urged his overthrow of Valen. One of these was Chief Counselor Baloff. Others were banished back to their own lands after swearing fealty to Reyer and to all rightful High Kings who were to come after.

And Reyer abrogated all agreements and levies and seizures made by Arkov, returning to those of High King Valen.

As rewards to those who supported him, Reyer bestowed much, notably he offered the abandoned land of Ellor to King Ulrik, but the Jordian asked that it be awarded to Valder instead. And Reyer deferred to Ulrik's wishes.

When Silverleaf said to Valder that his new-given land had been known by two names—Ellor and Valon—Valder declared, "Henceforth it shall be Valon."

Valder took Alric to be his heir.

And so it was that many of the Harlingar came with Valder and Alric to live in that green grassy land.

One of the people who for a while dwelt in Valon was Durgan, and Steel stood at stud during that time and sired many a champion. One of Steel's foals was given to Reyer, and thereafter all the mounts of the High Kings down through the ages could trace their lineage back to Steel, Durgan's Iron Horse.

Gretta returned to Kell with Conal, for she had come to cherish the farm as well as her husband.

Dalavar and Driu went to the Wolfwood together. That they were lovers was without question.

Reyer declared, with his ascension to the throne, the end of the Third Era and the beginning of the Fourth.

Some years passed—no more than six or seven—and across Valon fared a group of Dylvana on their way to see kindred in Darda Erynian. As they came to the new city of Vanar, Prince Alric received a most beautiful lady, one of unsurpassed grace. It was, of course, Caleen, who was traveling with the Dylvana to visit their kindred in Darda Erynian. And though it was a wonder to all who beheld this troop, for seldom were the Dylvana seen outside their shaggy forests, it was Caleen who captured the hearts of bards. They sang of her incredible grace and unsurpassed beauty and gentle manner, and they called her a princess of Elvenkind, though the Dylvana themselves simply named her Dara. Alric had loved her since childhood, and he asked her to be his bride. She confessed she had been in love with Alric from the first, and she consented. It was at this time Reyer discovered what she had whispered in Alric's ear as he and Reyer left the village of Sjøen years past: "You are my prince, Alric," she had said, "and will be my prince always." She lived with Alric in Valon, yet on occasion she did return to Kell and bide awhile with her Dylvana parents, or they came to see her. It was during one of these visits upon Kell that Gretta, the Iron Duke's daughter, weeping, apologized over the cruel things she had said about Caleen. They became fast friends.

Caleen lived a long and fruitful life, and at her death she was mourned by bards and remembered in Elven song.

As to Reyer, he married a daughter of Jord, Arika her

name, her father a Duke, and like Alric and Caleen, Reyer and Arika's palace was filled with the happy laughter of their offspring.

Reyer throughout the years made it a custom to visit each of the nations under his rule. On his rade to Garia and Alban, he was accompanied by a fierce warband consisting of Warrows, Elves, Dwarves, and, of course, Humans. The royalty in those two lands were completely cowed, and no attempts were made on his life. It is interesting to note that among that peerage of Garia, one of the personages absent was a certain Baron Viliev Stoke, one of whose descendants, Marko, would die in a boar hunt. Marko's wife was then to give birth to a son, Béla, putatively Markov's heir. Many thereafter would say that the new Baron Stoke, Béla, was a *Zli*—a Demon....

... But that was yet to come.

As to others in Reyer's time, they, too, were honored by the bards, and oft were songs sung and tales told of them and their fearlessness during the historical events known as the War of the Usurper. And bards sang of the Alliance and of the valor of the Jordians and their incredible ride, and of the Lian Guardians who accompanied them. Dylvana were sung of as well as the Dwarves, known as Châkka in their own tongue.

Oh, yes, and they sang of the Boskydell Warrows, who, in the battles, mayhap were the deadliest warriors of all.

All of them were heroes, and together they restored the rightful heir to his throne, or so they deemed. But one evening abed Dalavar confided to Driu that he believed the child of Jordian King Haldor and his Queen Keth was born first among the three who might lay claim to the High King's throne. Yet King Haldor and Queen Keth immediately renounced all rights to the title, and thus Riamon's King Rand and Queen Lessa's child became High King, much to the displeasure of Garia's King Borik and Queen Trekka, which ultimately led to this tale. Whether or not Dalavar had the right of it, perhaps only Adon could say. One might claim, though, that Dalavar, when he put his mind to it, was perhaps the most powerful Seer since Othran.

Perhaps we'll never understand why Nunde's plan would have had the Chabbains murder all of Arkov's men when victory was within his grasp. Perhaps he thought that if both Arkov and Reyer were dead, the Garians and their ilk as well as the men of the Alliance would lose heart, making it easier for the Southers to conquer all. Then again perhaps it was the Chabbain commander who decided to have it so. No matter the which of it—Black Mage or Chabbain—it seemed a tactical blunder. Yet as to Nunde himself, the day of his reckoning would come, but not yet, no, not yet.

But, as it is with all stories, the one concerning the War of the Usurper did not actually end, for down through the years and making their own marks were Reyer's descendants . . . one of whom some two thousand years later was named Aurion, known as King Redeye, who begat Galen and Igon, and when the Dragonstar came sputtering through the skies and dreadful Modru made his return to his cold iron tower . . . well . . .

Glory you not in the slaughter of War,

for, in victory or defeat,

e'en should you survive,

Death and Blood and the screams of the dying

will surely follow you home.

—WAR'S TRUTH

Afterword

I had said that stories do not end, but most series do. I am considering whether or not to make this the last book I write in the Mithgar sagas.

But you know what? I said that before. But here we are with yet another Mithgar tale.

Perhaps this is the end.

Perhaps not.

I *have* been thinking about the beginning of another Mithgar story. It goes something like this:

A Dwarf and an Elf walk into a bar. . . .

Seriously.

I mean it.

It's not a joke.

It's based upon one of my "Red Slippers," and if you don't know what that means, as I said at the end of chapter sixty-three: well . . .

Regardless as to whether or not I write that story, I do hope you enjoyed this one.

Perhaps you'll see another in the future.

Then again, perhaps not.

—Dennis L. McKiernan
Tucson, 2011